TONY BALLANTINE
DREAM LONDON

First published 2013 by Solaris
an imprint of Rebellion Publishing Ltd,
Riverside House, Osney Mead,
Oxford, OX2 0ES, UK

www.solarisbooks.com

ISBN: 978 1 78108 174 7

A CIP catalogue record for this book is available
from the British Library.

Designed & typeset by Rebellion Publishing

REBELLION

Printed in the US

DREAM LONDON

BY TONY BALLANTYNE

SOLARIS

ONE

CAPTAIN JIM WEDDERBURN

CRUNCH CRUNCH CRUNCH. *Mmmmm, mmmmm. Crunch crunch crunch.*

There was someone in my room, someone crouching at the bottom of the bed eating something. Enjoying it too, by the sound of it.

Mmmmmm, mmmmm. Crunch, crunch.

What time was it?

My mobile had stopped working months ago; I hadn't bothered getting a clock. The threadbare curtains were lit by the yellow gas glow of the street lamps. I held my breath and listened for the knocking of the heating: the prehistoric machine that slumbered in the cellar woke me every morning, no matter how warm the night had been.

Silence. It could be any time between 10pm and dawn.

Mmmmm.

The bedroom door was locked, but things change in Dream London. I scanned the dim room through half closed eyes. The ceiling was a little taller, the room a little narrower than when I went to sleep. Ever so slowly, I

5

slipped my hand under the pillow and found my knife – still the same knife, still in the same place.

The city changed a little every night, the people changed a little everyday. Christine had gone, and not one of the succession of women who crept into my bed had ever stayed more than one night.

Had I brought someone back to my room last night? Some woman drawn to the supposedly dangerous charm of Captain James Wedderburn? I had made some increasingly strange conquests in the past months, some I hadn't always remembered making upon waking. Was one of those women now curled up at the bottom of my bed, crunching and slurping with every sign of enjoyment? I wasn't going to find out by pretending to be asleep.

"Who's that?" I said to the room.

The crunching paused, just for a moment, and then the lazy consumption resumed.

Mmmmmmm...

"Who's there?" I raised my head and looked to the foot of the bed. I saw no one. I crept forward, the springs creaking beneath me, took hold of the brass rail and peeped over.

Two salamanders crouched on the floor, their bodies glowing red and gold with their own internal light. They'd got hold of a green beetle the size of a dinner plate and split it in two to lap at the yellow custard inside. One of them looked up at me with little jewelled eyes, licked its lips with a purple tongue and smiled in evident satisfaction.

Mmmmmm.

Two salamanders were worth a fair sum of money. I was just wondering if I could move fast enough to catch them both when someone spoke up behind me.

"Good evening, Captain Wedderburn."

Startled, I turned to see the fat man lean from the shadows near the wall. He was balanced precariously on a little camping chair, the velvet-clad expanse of his ample backside spilling over the sides. He unfolded a handkerchief and mopped at the sweat on his forehead.

"Luke Pennies," I said. "How did you get in here?"

As I spoke a wave of nausea that had been building almost unnoticed in my stomach rose to overwhelm me. I swallowed hard against the bile that rose in my throat.

Luke Pennies held out a hand. We both looked down to the glass vial in his pudgy palm.

"Two salamanders, one antidote," he said, and he turned to look at the red stain on the bed where I had been lying. I pressed a finger to my left shoulder and felt the sticky wetness of blood.

The fat man smiled. "One thousand sovereigns and it's yours."

"I don't have a thousand sovereigns. I don't even have a thousand dollars."

Luke closed his hand over the vial. He waved a finger at me.

"We both know that isn't true, Captain. They say you've got an interest in every young woman this side of the city." He winked. "Aye, and a straight twenty per cent from every transaction they make."

"Nothing like so much as that."

"You don't deny you have money, though. It's said that you can find a shop that will sell you anything in this city, Captain Wedderburn. I doubt you'll find one in time to sell you the antidote you need. May I suggest that now would be the perfect time to start spending some of your ill-earned?"

7

I felt hot. Hot and sick. My nightshirt stuck to my body with sweat and blood. I had to fight not to throw up.

"Give that to me," I said, reaching for the vial.

"Careful!" he warned. "This glass is thin. Any sudden shocks and I might accidentally break it."

Slowly, I lowered my hand.

"This isn't your style, Luke," I said.

"Maybe not." A spasm of anger on his face. "But you really pissed me off the other night, Jim. You crossed a line there."

"Is there any point me telling you it wasn't me?" I shook my groggy head. "Probably not," I murmured. "Especially seeing as you've poisoned me."

"I can see you understand," said Luke Pennies, coldly. "So, which is it to be? One thousand sovereigns, or a slow death?"

He had a thin smile, a smile weighed out in ounces; it balanced a favour exactly with no warmth to spare. "That fire took half my property, Captain Wedderburn. It took three of my whores."

"What fire?"

The rent on the smile had expired. He leant forward, little eyes hard.

"Don't play dumb with me, Jim. You could see the blaze clear to the docks."

"My name is used a lot in this city," I replied. "Used a lot by a certain sort of person anyway. Everybody knows that I would have chased the whores from the building first. *You* must know that, Luke."

My vision was blurring now. I felt my hands starting to shake; the bite at my shoulder was throbbing.

"People change," said Pennies, but I could hear the edge of uncertainty in his voice.

"People change," I agreed. "This city makes people change. But not that quickly."

Again the bile rose. This time I could not choke it down. I spat something yellow onto the bed.

Luke Pennies stared at the spreading stain. Red blood and yellow bile. His voice was cold.

"Time to pay up, Jim."

"I don't think so," I said, my head spinning. "People don't change that fast. Not even you, Luke. You wouldn't come to my room to murder me. That's not your style. You want me murdered; you'd get one of your men to do it. That way, if the police caught up with you, made you read the Truth Script, you could honestly say it wasn't you."

I retched again, caught the vomit in my mouth, gulped it down.

"No, not your style at all. But if you could get your victim to commit suicide? That would be far more poetic. What if you got them to swallow a vial of poison? What a laugh that would be. And much safer, should the police come calling."

My head pounded, the sweat was cold on my skin. My tongue was thick and coated in bitter bile. Even so, I strove to speak normally.

"I think that the effect of this bite will be wearing off soon. In fact, I'm willing to bet my life on it. So I'm going to give you a choice. You see my jacket hanging on the rack there?"

Through blurred eyes, I saw him turn his head. My jacket hung there in green and gold glory.

"There's a pistol in the pocket." I said. "You want me dead so much, take the pistol and shoot me. Otherwise, I suggest you take your camp chair and your vial of poison and you get out of here, right now. Because if you wait too long, I'll shoot you myself. What do you say?"

Luke Pennies didn't say anything. Or if he did, I didn't hear it. My stomach was rising once more and I dropped to the floor and scrabbled under the bed, looking for the chamber pot. I pulled it out and vomited, all in one movement. Curled up over the china pot, stomach heaving, I was only vaguely aware of his leaving, of him trudging past, camp chair in hand. I didn't care, each spasm brought up more rainbow vomit. I felt as if I was dying.

Eventually there was nothing left in my stomach. Still I retched into the full bowl, until eventually this too ceased. I lay on the floor, waiting for the spinning to stop, lost in the middle of the night.

I forced myself up, looked at the bloodstained bed, looked at the two salamanders now sleeping upon it, curled up around each other for warmth.

I needed to get outside. I needed some fresh air.

THERE USED TO be an underground station opposite my building. Over the past year it had metamorphosed twice: first into a railway station, and then into an inn. I remember the landlord holding court with his customers, telling us about the staircase leading down from his cellar into the tunnels through which trains had once travelled. The tunnels had shrunk, he said, tightened like sphincters. What remained of those narrowed, fat-filled arteries was choked with black and green beetles, walking back and forth in long lines beneath the city, preyed on by silver snakes and cock rats.

"What about the railway lines?" I had asked. "Are they still there?"

That had been a quiet night; the few customers of the Recursive Lion had pressed up to the bar, glasses of gin and porter in hand. One of the other customers, a thin man with a huge red handlebar moustache, had laughed at my question.

"Haven't you heard?" he said, his moustache dipped in white foam. "The railway lines have surfaced three streets south of here. They're sliding sideways, heading towards the river. All the tracks in the city are moving!"

That must have been some time ago, I thought. Back when the changes were first taking effect and I was freshly returned from Afghanistan, a relative unknown. No one in that inn would laugh in the face of Captain Jim Wedderburn today.

Standing in the sallow street, gazing at repeated figures on the sign of the Recursive Lion opposite, I felt the nausea receding in the cold night air. I still had no idea of the time. The life of the inn gave no clue.

What is it that gives a building the feeling of life? There were people in there, I could tell, but that meant nothing. In the morning the place is packed with porters from the flower markets and the beery air is heavy with the scent of pollen. In the evenings the clerks and accountants line the tables in neat black velvet rows. The owners of the workhouse round the corner follow them in at about nine o'clock, propping up the bar as they raise a glass to other people's industry. After midnight the ladies and gentlemen appear, slumming it after the opera or the ballet. Later come the stevedores and the butchers, hooks and cleavers tucked in their jackets, ready for trouble. And at any time there

11

could be matelots, making the most of their time on land and looking for the sort of produce that Captain Wedderburn supplies.

There was a clock in the bar that hadn't stopped working, despite the changes. A big white face with black Roman numerals and the name of its maker written on the front in curly script. I could stick my head around the door and see the time. I began to make my way forwards when a triangle of light swept into being across the road.

The door to the inn opened and Christine stepped out into the street. She saw me right away and gave me a tight little smile.

"Hello, Jim," she said.

"Not you, too, Christine," I said, tiredly. "Please, call me James."

We looked each other up and down, checking out how the other looked. She won that battle. Her tailored suit was well made, her dark silk stocking tops visible just beneath her too-short skirt. Her make-up was immaculate: bright red lips and highlighted eyes stood out against her smooth, almost imperceptible foundation. And there I stood in my frayed grey trousers, my leaking black brogues and my gaudy military jacket.

"Found a husband yet?" I asked.

"Not yet," she said brusquely. "But I keep working my way through the list. Still giving candy away?"

"Do you want some?" I asked. "I have some in my pocket."

I meant the offer kindly, but she gave me a withering stare.

At that point my stomach rumbled, and I realised that I didn't want her to see me like this.

"Do you know what to do about salamanders?" I asked. "There are two on my bed."

"Speak to Fran," she said. "She's got a shop down on Holcomb Street. She's good with pests and vermin." She reached into a pocket and pulled out a velvet purse.

"Here, I got you something," she said. "I was going to leave it with Second Eddie, but as you're here..."

"I don't need any money," I said.

"I wasn't offering you any."

She looked so smart and confident, dressed like that with her little piece of parchment in her pocket, ticking her way through the items on the list of men she had purchased, searching for her ideal husband.

She had bought the thing as a joke, back when the little shops were just beginning to appear here and there around the old city. Back when James Wedderburn was trying to live an honest life and had decided that he needed the love of a good woman to save him. Christine had been that woman, an old flame that had reignited.

Back then it was almost a joke to push your way from the summer streets into the dark, poky interior of one of the quirky little shops that seemed to grow in the glass and concrete façades of the city. I remember the little woman sitting in the armchair by the counter, how overdressed she had seemed, with her petticoats, her grubby skirt, her knitted gloves. The effect was exaggerated when viewed next to Christine in her shorts and crop top, her sliver flip-flops; all tanned flesh and confidence. Christine had handed across the money, all in coins, and the woman had given her a sheet of yellow parchment. We pushed our way back into the sunshine and Christine unrolled her purchase.

I remember the look on her face when she realised that my name wasn't on her list. I was expecting shock, disappointment, annoyance. Instead, she just smiled, rolled up the parchment and slipped it into her shoulder bag. She'd looked at it over the next few weeks, always when she thought I wasn't watching. I didn't realise she was taking it seriously, but, little by little, she had been changing even then. We all were: we just didn't realise it.

Now, one year later, and look at us all.

"What happened to you, Christine?" I said, softly. "You were training to be an actuary. What are you now?" I didn't say what I thought: *more honest than a gold digger, less honest than a whore.*

She paused, one hand in her purse, and looked down at herself, her smart suit, her silk stockings.

"I don't know what I'm doing," she said, and then she shook her head. "But what about you? What's happening to you, Jim?"

"I told you, it's James."

She shook her head. "James, Jim, whatever. I heard what you were doing now. It isn't... nice."

Christine always knew how to push my buttons. If her aim was to lock me up in sullen silence, then she succeeded.

"See?" she said quietly. "Who are you to tell me how to behave?"

"Things have been hard since I left the army," I said. "I have to earn a living somehow."

"You could be better than that, James." She spoke the words softly, and for a moment there was some of the old affection in her gaze.

"I used to feel as if I was, when we were together," I murmured.

We both stood in silence for a moment.

Then she remembered her purse. She pulled out my gift. A tiny roll of parchment.

"Here," she said. "This is for you. Don't dismiss it out of hand. It cost me a lot of money."

"What is it?"

"Your fortune."

Something about this gesture hit me like a blow to the stomach.

"Christine," I said, sadly. "Why did you waste your money on this? You know I don't believe in that nonsense."

"Just take it," she said. She couldn't meet my gaze.

"Is your name on it?" I asked.

"No," she said, looking at the ground.

I took the fortune and unrolled it just enough to read the first line.

You will meet a Stranger…

Just as I suspected. People were still preying on Christine's gullibility.

"It's so vague, Christine. Of course I'll meet strangers. This is a city."

"This Stranger will be special."

"Can't you see, Christine? This is all made up. You've been going downhill ever since you bought that stupid parchment. Why did you bother? We had everything we needed."

She looked at me with real pity then.

"James," she said, sadly. "Don't *you* see? I didn't buy the parchment to confirm that you were going to be my husband. I bought it to confirm that you weren't."

"Oh."

I couldn't meet her eye. I felt sick and lost and detached from everything. She folded her hands over the parchment in my own.

"Promise me you'll read it, Jim. It will help you. I still worry about you."

"The parchment is just stories. It doesn't mean anything!"

She fixed me with a gaze. Memory imposed the blue of her eyes over the dim light.

"Please, James. Promise me you'll read it."

"I promise," I said. Not that a promise from Jim Wedderburn means anything.

She gave me a brittle little smile.

"I have to be off," she said. "I'll see you around."

I watched her walk off up the street, leaving me alone and lost in the middle of the city, uncertain even of the time of night and, now that the poison was sweating from my system, with an empty stomach that was telling me just how hungry it was.

It growled at a changing world, one which was moulding me into someone I didn't want to be.

I took another look at the top line of the parchment.

You will meet a Stranger.

I shook my head sadly at the words, and pushed the parchment into my pocket.

Just then the door of the inn opened once more, and the stranger who was to change my life stepped out into the night.

The man was unmistakably a Molly. Framed by the light of the door I could see his dark red velvet suit, the striped golden shirt and tie. His red top hat was tilted at a rakish angle, but it was the foundation, the hint of eyeliner and lipstick that confirmed it. He was a good looking man, in an effeminate sort of way. And he was gazing right at me.

"Captain Jim Wedderburn, I believe!" he said, holding out a hand for me to shake.

"It's James Wedderburn," I replied, but I took his hand anyway. It was warm and smooth.

"Jim, James, what's a name to a Jolly Japer like you, eh? Jim, I'd like to invite you to dinner. What do you say? A little convivial company and conversation over comestibles?"

"I don't know," I said. "I was thinking of heading for bed."

My stomach rumbled, making its own views known.

"I don't think so," he said. "In fact I *know* that you weren't. I've been watching you, my Jolly Jim. Seven nights now, I've come to this pub, sat in the seat by the door through the lost hours, looking through the glass, just waiting to see if you would step into the night. Six whores have come and gone from your room, but no sign of the gallant captain in the night hours. Then finally, this very evening, I saw Luke Pennies enter your building, half hidden by a glamour, and I knew that this night would be make or break. I had a bet with myself that you would survive his dreadful attempts upon your person, and look if I wasn't right!"

"What do you want with me?"

"I want your help," he said.

"Help with what?"

The Molly waved a hand around the elongated buildings of Dream London, stretched out thin and sharp against the deep purple sky, the moon an over-large crescent that threatened to impale the city itself on its horns.

"Look at this place," he said. "I want you to help me to find out what happened to us."

RED

ALPHONSE/ALAN

"COME ALONG, JOLLY Jim!"

The stranger folded my hand in his arm and walked me down the street, strolling in and out of the pools of light cast by the gas lamps. Everything about him craved attention – his flamboyant dress: the velvet top hat and gloves; the eyeliner and mascara; the richness of his voice. He spoke like a port-soaked old actor, filling the cool night air with warmth and bonhomie.

"We make such a lovely couple, don't we?" he announced, squeezing my hand. "A pretty pair of pals in this pale pedestrian precinct!" He leant closer to me, and I smelt the lavender that soaked his scarf. "Or we would," he whispered in lower tones. "You're not that way inclined, are you? Such a shame." He laughed brightly. "Have I embarrassed you?"

"No," I said, and it was true. Captain Jim Wedderburn asked for nothing more than strong drink, a hearty meal and adventure, with maybe a little whoring thrown in on the side. His biggest concern would be whether he was heading for a late supper, or an early breakfast, and didn't care who his companions were so long as they were entertaining.

James Wedderburn, however, was more cautious…

"What's your name?" I asked.

The Molly gasped.

"Jim, you know the rules! No names." He sighed. "But that's not fair, is it? I know your name, after all. Well, call me Alphonse!"

"Alphonse," I said. "Like that's a real name."

"It's a pretty name though, don't you think?"

He smiled at me and batted his eyelashes, then giggled. I had to smile.

"And where are you taking me, Alphonse?" I asked.

"A private little place I know. A delightful little den where the drink is divine, the food to die for and the company utterly decadent."

"Is it far?"

"Not at all, dear boy. We're here already."

We stopped outside a narrow door squeezed between two shop entrances. A haberdashers to the left, an ironmongers to the right. The ribbons and buttons, the kettles and buckets in the shop windows seemed so definite, so unchanging, and yet I could remember when these two units had housed a mobile phone shop and a coffee bar respectively. The third door hadn't been there at all, but in the past year it had shouldered its way onto the street front, an unassuming blank face with a brass doorknob.

Alphonse rapped twice on the peeling paintwork.

"A really, really big cucumber," he giggled.

"Is that the password?" I asked.

"No," he said. "I just like to make Charles laugh."

The door opened up and a boy of about thirteen stood there, grinning.

"Alright, Alan," he said. "Who's your friend?"

"Oh, Charles, you had to go and spoil it! I'd told Jolly Jim that my name was Alphonse!"

"Call yourself what you like," I said.

Alphonse/Alan waved a hand dismissively.

"Is my table ready, Charles?"

"They'll have it fixed in a jiffy, Alphonse. In you go!"

WE WALKED ALONG a dimly lit corridor at least twice as long as the building's depth. The floor was covered in old carpet, the walls papered in wood chip. As we walked its length, we heard the sounds from behind the shabby doors that lined the corridor. Different rooms, hidden from view, each one a little world in which people laughed or argued or sobbed or played.

"This walk gets longer every time," said Alan. "This city is being stretched and pulled in all directions."

We came to a narrow set of stairs, an old red runner reaching down it like a dry and dusty tongue. We began to climb. Up and up, three flights, four flights...

"Half way there," said Alan.

Doors faced onto the landings, shabby and worn, their paint peeling. I could hear a violin playing a mournful tune somewhere nearby and I felt the floor vibrate beneath my feet.

Higher and higher. The building had only looked three storeys tall from the street. I guessed we would now be high enough to see the river. We passed through a breath of air, exhaled by one of the rooms.

"Is that garlic?" I asked. "Or is it hash?" I sniffed again. "Or are there flowerboys in there?"

"Best not to ask," said Alan.

Finally, we reached the top of the stairs. There was no corridor there, simply a gold panelled door. It opened at our approach and Alan gestured me to enter.

I stepped into a tiny anteroom. One wall was taken by a Welsh dresser lined with wine and brandy bottles. Fur coats, velvet cloaks, caps and hats hung from pegs on the facing wall. Before me stood a matronly woman. She wore a powdered wig and way too much make-up. Her dress was pinched at the waist in a manner that enhanced her décolletage. But then, she had a lot to be décolleté about.

"Mother Clap!" called Alan loudly. "Good welcome to Alphonse and Jim!"

"And which one of you is which?" asked Mother Clap drily, closing the gold panelled door behind us.

My companion laughed. "Oh, Mother Clap! You do tease your little Alphonse! Is our table ready?"

"Of course. I shan't take your hats."

This last was directed at me: I was bareheaded, having pulled on my jacket when I left the room and little else. Alan stood there, top hat and gloves in hand, looking quite crestfallen.

"Shall I put the evening on your account?" asked Mother Clap.

"But of course," said Alan.

Mother Clap led us into a little dining room crammed with tables for two. There were half a dozen couples in there already, all male. My eyes were drawn to a tall black gentleman who sat in the corner. He was incredibly handsome, his face seemingly chiselled from ebony. Obviously royalty, his lapels and cuffs were picked out in leopard skin. Seated opposite him was a flowerboy. The young man's limpid eyes and his lean, shapely frame made him look so pretty. Yet there was slyness to his look, a knowing tilt to his face. There is something about working in the flower market, with its rich, heavy pollens and heady scents that get inside you. All the flowerboys look so pretty and yet so nasty. This one was eating oysters, picking up the shells in his long, delicate fingers and sucking them down whilst his companion watched in silence. Alan leant close to me, his face half covering mine as if he was about to kiss me.

"Show me some consideration," he whispered, his breath sweet. "I have my reputation to consider."

I knew what he meant. I let him take my hand and allowed him to lead me to the table. He pulled out a chair for me and I sat down, then he took his place opposite me.

Mother Clap appeared at our side, her powdered bosom close to my ear.

"Gentlemen?" she said.

"You order, Jim."

There wasn't a menu, I noticed, but I knew the script. I knew what was expected of me.

"Those oysters look good," I said. "A dozen each, I think."

"With champagne!" said Alan, delighted at my response. I warmed to my theme.

"And then steak," I declared. "Rare! And avocados, almonds and asparagus! Raspberries and strawberries, ginger and nutmeg, and chocolate pudding to follow!"

I looked across the room at the black man, but he paid us no attention. The flowerboy, however, had turned to look, oyster in hand. He was smirking. So were some of the other diners. Alan leant close.

"All the aphrodisiacs," he said. "You naughty boy!"

"You wanted to play games," I said. "I played games. Now, I think it's time for you tell me what you want with me."

The surrounding diners resumed their meals. I saw one man looking at his fob watch, and I strained to see the time, but he clipped it shut and resumed speaking to his partner who seemed uncomfortable in his badly fitting dress and wig. Now that I looked, I could see there was something slightly tawdry about the whole place, the flaking golden tables, the worn velvet chairs, the scuffed plush wallpaper. Despite its efforts, there was an air more of seediness than of immorality to Mother Clap's.

Alan was gazing at me.

"You know, you're half way there. That military jacket looks the part. I love the gold frogging. Now, if you grew your hair a little, affected a little moustache, dressed the part, you could look quite Byronesque. You'd have the women swooning at your feet." He winked at me. "And the men."

"I'm not interested in being a poet," I replied.

"You should be. Better than what you are now." He tapped a manicured finger on the table. "Fought in Baghdad and Helmand province. Even been into Burma. Resigned from the army. If only you could have made that a dishonourable discharge you'd be truly irresistible."

"What do you know about my resignation? " I asked, but he ignored me.

"Only twenty-six years old," he said. "Who knows what you might have achieved, if only you could have kept to the straight and narrow. But men like you and me always have trouble keeping it in our trousers, eh Jim?"

I thought of Christine, speaking to me in the street outside my room.

"I was set up," I said. "They didn't have any evidence and they knew it."

"Fraternising with the enemy?"

"We were friendly with the local women."

"And you never made any money out of them..."

Alan gazed at me, and for a moment the foppish air was gone. Then he waved his hand in the air in an affected manner.

"Still, that's all in the past. You're a lucky man, I think, Jim Wedderburn."

"Why do you say that?"

"You've done well out of Dream London. I wonder how you would have fared if the changes hadn't happened?"

He waved a hand around the room. We both saw the occupants of the table in the far corner struggling with the seafood salad. Green tentacles batted their forks away as they tried to spear their dinner.

"I'd have got by," I said.

"Maybe so," said Alan. He tuned to look back at the unsuccessful seafood eaters. "You know, they should squirt that octopus with lemon and chilli. That will calm it down." He turned his attention back to me and beamed.

"I just can't help thinking that in the old city you'd have been just another out of work soldier. Instead, you were lucky enough to return here as a rogue." He winked. "And the ladies love a rogue."

Before I could answer him, Mother Clap appeared with the champagne. A maid shuffled the ice bucket into place.

"Allow me," said Alan, opening the bottle. "Not with a pop," he said, "but with the sigh of a contented lover."

He poured the champagne, golden bubbles in a golden room. I took a sip and felt immediately light headed: champagne on poison and an empty stomach.

"What do you want, Alan?"

Alan wasn't listening, he was too busy enjoying his champagne.

"Lovely," he said, smacking his lips. "You know, you should write your memoirs, Jim. There's good money to be had. After that, set yourself up as a poet. You wouldn't have to be any good at it, you know. It wouldn't matter what you wrote, with an image like yours!"

"I'm not interested in being a poet."

"And why should you be? Jim Wedderburn, a gentleman and rogue, or so they say!"

I opened my mouth to deny it, but Alan was still speaking.

"... but then, this is a romantic age, and people love a villain as much as a hero, don't they? And neither really exists..."

Alan sat back and gazed at me, and once more I saw the shrewdness there. I hadn't doubted he was playing a part when I met him. Now I began to suspect there was something substantial behind the act.

Alan sipped his champagne.

"Have you ever considered leaving Dream London, Jim?"

I laughed.

"Who hasn't? This place is like a lobster pot. Easy to enter, impossible to leave. You get lost on the trains trying to escape, find yourself missing connections or standing on the wrong platform. Before you know it you're riding back into Angel Station once more."

"True. But if there were a way, would you take it?"

"If you know of a way, I'd love to hear of it."

"What? You'd leave all this?"

"Like a shot. Is there a way?"

"Not that I know of."

The oysters arrived, split open and laid out on ice. My stomach was rumbling again, so loudly that I was sure the gentleman on the next table heard it. He was looking across at me now. I flipped him the finger. He poked out his tongue at me in return.

"Try the horseradish," said Alan, pointing to the little tray of accompaniments. "It's delicious."

I was starving. I finished my oysters and ate four of his.

"Lovely," said Alan as the maid cleared the dishes. When the table was clear, he placed something onto the cloth before me. A picture, lights twinkling across it. He looked at me, expectantly.

"That's London," I said.

"Taken from an airship, just before the airport slid below the marshes."

I gazed carefully at the picture. It had been taken using a slow glass camera – a shawscope.

"How long ago?" I asked.

"Five months," he said.

I still felt as if I was in a dream of a dream, lost somewhere between night and morning. I didn't know the time, and Alan had led me to a place without clocks.

I looked at the right hand side of the photograph, looked for the square mile. The towers in the picture cast moonlight shadows into the river. Today the Thames curls around itself like a snake getting ready to strike. Five months ago the river still retained some of its old shape, and I followed it along, finding the Houses of Parliament.

"Look here," said Alan, pointing to a space near to the centre of the map.

"That's Hyde Park," I said.

"Green Park," he said. "Look how the other parks are moving towards it."

I could see, all the other green spaces, distorted as they crept towards the middle of the city.

"Have you ever been to Green Park?" asked Alan.

"Not lately. The river wraps it in bands, and the parks around it are growing wider, and it's virtually impossible to find a way into the parks these days..."

I looked again at the picture. Had all those spaces joined up by now, I wondered?

"Something is happening in the centre of the city," I said, slowly. "That's what I've been hearing, anyway."

"From whom?"

I looked at him.

"Contacts. Business partners. People in the know."

"I think I know the sort of people you mean. What do you hear?"

"Only rumours and tales, Alan. Nothing but rumours and tales. But there are hints. Follow any story back along its course, and sooner or later the parks are mentioned."

We both looked at the map again. I noticed the second river that flowed down from the north to join the Thames in the east. The River Roding, much, much wider than it used to be.

Alan spoke in a low voice.

"We want you to find out what's going on, James."

I looked up at the sound of my real name, and saw that now the mask had slipped away. I was sitting opposite the real Alan.

"Who are you, Alan?" I asked.

"Me? I'm a man who doesn't like the way the world is changing." He tapped a finger on the table. "I'm a man whose way of life is being pushed back into the shadows. I'm a man who doesn't want things to go back to the way they were a hundred years ago when people like me were outcasts. And I'm not alone. This new world is creating winners and losers, and some of the losers still have enough power and influence to try and fight back. We want you to help us."

"Why me?"

"Because of who you are, James."

"Who I am? Captain Jim Wedderburn is a rogue. He drinks and whores, he fights and steals."

"But people listen to you, James. You've got the looks, you've got the voice. There are wiser men, it's true – no offence," he raised a hand at that, "and there are people who may be better placed to give advice. But there's something about you that makes people want to follow you. You're a natural leader, James."

"Maybe so," I admitted. I knew that people listened to me. I'd risen through the ranks in the army because of that.

Alan leant forward.

"Have you heard of the Cartel?"

I said nothing.

"You'll have heard the rumours, I'm sure."

I picked up the champagne bottle, felt the cold weight in my hands.

"I've heard that there are interests who don't like the way Dream London is going," I said, carefully. "Former bankers, some of the underworld, politicians, the minor royals left behind in the city: all the people who have been gradually losing power this past year or so."

I refilled both of our glasses.

"And I have to say," I added. "I'm delighted about that."

Alan pulled a long face.

"Oh James, don't be like that. They talk about you, you know. The Cartel speaks very highly of you."

"I'm delighted to hear it."

"No need to be sarcastic. What if I told you they had a job for you? One that would pay very well."

I gazed at Alan.

"It would depend on the job," I said. "More to the point, it would depend on the money."

"We're not offering cash," he said. "We've got something even better than that. We're offering you land. Freehold. How would you like to be a Lord of Dream London?"

TWO

DADDIO CLARKE AND THE MACON WAILERS

THE MAID ARRIVED at that moment with fresh plates. I heard a sizzling and, at the same time, smelt a deliciously savoury aroma. Mother Clap was approaching, bearing two beautifully thick steaks on a silver platter. She laid the steaks onto our plates, pink blood oozing onto the china. I was torn between hunger and curiosity, impatient as the accompanying dishes – the little glass jars of condiments – were laid before us. I was impatient to eat, impatient to hear more. I watched as Mother Clap ground pepper, first over my meal, then over Alan's, watched as she spooned potatoes, green beans, braised cabbage onto our plates. Then there was a little French mustard, a little salt. A smear of Gentleman's Relish. I was impatient to resume our conversation, but still I had to wait as the Burgundy was poured into my glass to taste. I sipped and nodded and watched as she filled our glasses.

At last, the meal was ready, but still Mother Clap remained at our sides.

"Shall I cut your steaks up for you, gentlemen?"

"No thank you, Mother Clap," said Alan, happily.

"Are you sure? Would you like me to blow on your steak and cool it down?"

"We're both big boys, Mother Clap. We can look after ourselves."

"If you say so."

Finally, we were left on our own. I cut into the meat.

"Freehold?" I said. "Where?"

"Belltower End. That's where your, ahem, *business* is based at the moment, isn't it?"

"You know it is."

"How much do you currently pay in rent?" asked Alan through a mouthful of steak.

"Way too much. And it goes up all the time." I gazed at him suspiciously. "Am I to take it that you're my landlord then? Is that what you're telling me?"

"Me? Hardly." He seemed disappointed. "I can see that you're not as aware of what's going on in Dream London as you maybe thought."

"I know that land in Dream London is at a premium," I said. "The shape of the city changes all the time. A man can go to bed rich with 100 acres and wake up poor with property the area of a postage stamp."

I ate a piece of steak, warm red blood bursting in my mouth. It was delicious.

"Indeed," said Alan. "And the opposite is also true. It would be to anyone's advantage to take freehold of a property that is due to grow." He winked at me. "Take your time to think about it."

"What do I have to do?"

"Two things," said Alan. He laid his fork on his plate, a piece of meat speared on the end. He was obviously not so hungry as I.

"One thing, I suspect that will be rather easier than the other."

"Go on," I said.

"First the easier thing. We want you to find the people behind what's happened to Dream London."

I gulped down a piece of steak.

"Hah!" I said. "Like no one else ever tried!"

"Oh, lots of people have," said Alan. "But I think you could succeed. Join the Cartel. A title and a uniform would look good in the boardrooms up east. Captain Jim Wedderburn would be a valuable addition to our cause."

"And how would you get me into the boardrooms?"

"Come with me. I'll put you up at my place. Give you a veneer of respectability. Set you up with a job in the City, where all this started. You'd be our man on the inside. You know it would work. With your looks and charm, you'd be welcome anywhere."

"And in return you'll give me the freehold of Belltower End. That's a huge price you're willing to pay. I'm not sure the Cartel could afford it."

Alan smiled.

"Ah! That's the interesting thing! You see, if our plans succeed, the Cartel will reacquire large parts of this city. If the Cartel succeed, we'll all be winners, James."

I dipped a piece of meat in the mustard. Cracked brown seeds adhered to the pink flesh.

"I think I'd want more than Belltower End," I said. I popped the meat in my mouth and stared at him as I chewed.

Alan nodded. "That can be negotiated."

"Uh-huh. And the second thing you want?"

"Ah! The second task." Alan placed his fork on the side of his plate once more. He gazed at me with a serious

33

expression. "You must have realised, James, that people are becoming inured to the changes. Dream London is Dream London, they say, and it's not going to change back."

He was right. I thought of Christine and her little piece of parchment, searching for the perfect man.

"Okay," I said.

"Well, that's the second part. When the fight begins, we're going to need a figurehead. A charismatic bad boy willing to become good. We want someone who will stand up and lead the revolution against whoever is doing this to us."

"And that person is me?"

"Who else? Like I said, people follow you, Captain Jim Wedderburn. But you've got more about you than that, though. Do you know what I've heard it said that you could be?"

"What?"

"A hero for Dream London. *The* hero for Dream London."

I laughed at that.

"It's true, Jim."

"I'm sorry Alan," I said. "Me? A hero? I don't think so."

"Well, maybe we could talk about that later on, too. Aren't you a little bit tempted by our offer?"

I shrugged. "I want to know what's going on here. Who doesn't?"

"So what's the problem?"

"The Cartel. They sound like the same people who ran things in the old days."

"Some of them are," said Alan.

"Supposing we do succeed in overthrowing whoever is doing this to Dream London. What will I have gained? We'll still have the same old group of people lining their pockets."

"But you'll be part of them, James. You'll be the Lord of Belltower End."

"It's an interesting offer," I said. "I'll think about it."

"Don't take too long." Alan reached into his pocket and drew forth a silver case. He opened it and pulled out a card.

"My address," he said. He replaced the case in his pocket. "If you do want to join us, you must get to that address before daybreak. Especially, you must get there before you learn what time it is."

I stared at him, wondering if he was winding me up.

"No joke," he said. "You're currently lost in the moment. That's our security. No one can pinpoint this conversation. The Cartel have to protect themselves, you know."

He looked around the room, looked at all the diners who were suddenly paying us no attention.

"I think you've helped me make up my mind," I said. "I hate to be pressurised into making decisions. My answer is no."

I placed my knife and fork on the plate and stood up.

"Thank you for the meal, but I must be going."

"Don't be so hasty," said Alan. "Sit down and finish your dinner."

I looked around the room and its seedy grandeur. I imagined the rest of the Cartel sitting in rooms such as this, full of their own sense of entitlement as they strove for past power. It's not that I didn't want a part of it, I just wasn't sure that they could deliver. I reckoned I'd be better off as I was.

"No, I don't think so. Thank you for your offer, but I don't think I'm cut out to be a hero. I'll bid you good night."

"Good night," said Alan. "I won't pretend I'm not disappointed."

I turned and walked from the room. Mother Clap held the door open for me as I left.

So I RETURNED to the street, still unaware of the time, though now, at least, feeling a little fuller.

… and I stood there, thinking about what Alan had told me, wondering if I'd been too hasty. I was tempted to head back up the stairs to Mother Clap's to find out more. Was I missing the boat? Alan had said I had to act before sunrise, but it's a basic rule of doing business: never let other people impose deadlines on you. Besides, I thought about the sort of people in the Cartel; the sort of people who claimed to be acting for the common good, but all the time were just feathering their own nests. People just like me. They couldn't be trusted. I snorted suddenly. Alan had said I could be the Hero of Dream London. Did they really think I cared about that sort of thing?

I began to walk. Not back to my room, but out, instead, out into Dream London. The stars were so heavy that the purple sky bulged in the middle, sagging down to pierce itself on the city spires. I walked from the seedy tiredness of Belltower End into the more prosperous shadows of Mandolin Vale. The buildings here were shiny with black gloss tiles, the windows reflecting dark shadows of other places.

Captain Jim Wedderburn is afraid of nothing. But James Wedderburn heard a sound that sent a chill through his body. Drifting through the night like an icy wind, weaving its way in and out of the lamp posts, he heard the sound of accordions.

Accordions: the sound of evil.

Accordions are like chameleons. They're just a little bit too unusual even for this world; the mechanism that makes them work is not quite discernible. Have you ever seen the interior of an accordion? It's not as if they contain microchips or anything that would explain the noise that they make. They wheeze out their sounds without any seeming regard for the laws of science. And now, when we inhabit a world where microchips are just so much pretty patterns in sand, accordions seem more sinister than ever. Their shiny cases, like the shells of insects. The way they seem to breathe in and out whilst their keys shine like white teeth in the night.

I should have turned and walked away, but something about their sound drew me in. I turned the corner and I saw them: three accordion players standing under the lamps in the middle of a little square, their music echoing with the tinny reverb of the lost hours. A year ago there had been cars parked all around the railed gardens in the middle of the square, but now the cars had slipped away to the periphery of Dream London, and the houses had crept inwards, huddling the square down to size, looming over the dark locked garden at its heart, blocking off the starlight that sought to illuminate it.

The people who lived in the surrounding houses should have been cursing the musicians who must surely be keeping them awake. Should have, but they wouldn't have been. Musicians are another one of the groups who have done well from the changes. They don't pay taxes. They have the right, if not the duty, to perform where they will. But most of all, they get respect. Even the most tone-deaf sixteen-year-old who manages to coax three chords from a guitar whilst singing songs of whingeing self-justification is accorded a respect, an adulation even, that was once reserved for those who might have discovered penicillin or clothed the poor.

Still the music drew me on. The upper storeys of the houses around the square seemed to lean forward, and I felt as if I had stepped into a bowl of music. That unnatural accordion vibrato swirled in currents around me, streams of melody tangling my head. The three accordionists looked into the distance as I passed them by; they had that blank, half present stare that musicians adopt when they're concentrating. I don't know what it was they were playing: something vaguely Eastern European, something in a strange mode and time signature. It put me in mind of vampires and people dancing under the stars. The accordionists were standing with their boots planted wide, pumping the bellows as they sent a stream of music to fill the garden and to entrance me.

I felt my pace slow, and I realised that I hadn't walked into a space of music, but rather into a web. It was a trap, and one into which I had been successfully lured.

I shook my head in annoyance. Of course it was a trap! Why else would I have walked towards a sound that I hated?

The music softened and I heard footsteps coming towards me. A slow, deliberate pace. Someone was coming closer and closer.

Something metal pricked my back.

"That's a knife, Captain Wedderburn."

"I can feel it."

"The music will stop in a moment. I don't want you making any sudden moves. Really, I don't."

"I won't."

The voice was hesitant. This was a half-hearted threat, if I ever heard of one.

"What do you want?" I said.

"Me? I don't like to say. But this isn't about what I want. I was sent by the Daddio."

"Who?"

The voice sounded a little surprised.

"You haven't heard of Daddio Clarke and the Macon Wailers?" it said.

Now I understood. "Right. The Daddio from the East End. I've heard stories. I'm not sure that I believe most of what I've heard."

"Really? I'm not sure I would admit to that."

At that moment the accordionists' bellows sighed to a halt. The music lingered in the air for a little longer before fading into the night. I heard the clicking of buttons, the snapping of catches as the accordions were placed in their cases and lifted, the receding footsteps of the players. Now my mysterious assailant and I were left alone.

My voice was calm. No sense in panicking a man holding a knife to your kidneys.

"Listen," I said, "I'm not sure why you're here, but you can tell the Daddio that Captain Jim Wedderburn sends his compliments and wishes him well. Beyond that, as far as I'm concerned, we have no other business with each other at present."

"I think you misunderstand me. The Daddio isn't unhappy with you. Quite the opposite!"

"Then why are you holding a knife to me?"

There was a pause whilst my assailant thought of his answer.

"To ensure I have your attention," he said, eventually.

"You have it."

"Good! Then let me tell you that the Daddio also wanted you to know that he admires you, Captain Wedderburn. He wants you to know that a man of your calibre could do well in his organisation. He'd like to offer you a job."

Two jobs in one night. Why had Captain Jim Wedderburn suddenly become so popular? I played for time.

"Why does the Daddio think I'd be interested in a job?" I asked.

"Why do you think you have a choice?" The voice seemed genuinely mystified.

We seemed to be having trouble communicating. One of us had to break the impasse.

"Listen," I said. "I can't think like this. I'm going to step away now."

After a moment's hesitation, the pressure of the knife withdrew. I stepped forward, out of range, and then turned to face my captor.

Any thought of fighting died right there and then.

He was a man, but only just. He was much taller than me, and much, much wider. His arms were as thick as my legs, his legs as thick as my body. He wore what might once have been regular clothes, but if they were the seams had been unpicked and extra panels sewn in so they would fit. There was something slightly grotesque about his body, but that was nothing compared to his head. It was twice as big as it should be. His eyes were narrow and bright, his mouth a wide slit like something cut into pumpkin. But worse than all of that was what lay inside his mouth...

"What's that in your mouth?"

"In my mouth? There's nothing in my mouth."

He sounded so certain I didn't know how to disagree with him. I leant closer to check, but there was no mistaking it. Two eyes were set in his tongue, and they looked down at me with a keen intelligence.

"What are you?" I asked.

"One of the Daddio's Quantifiers," said the man, reluctantly.

"What happened to you?"

"What do you mean, what happened to me?"

The two eyes in the big man's tongue were looking at me. I did my best to ignore them. I looked up into the Quantifier's eyes.

"What sort of a job does the Daddio have for me?"

"The Daddio is getting ready to expand his organisation. Extortion, protection, gambling. He does it all. Vice. Who controls the whores of West London, Captain Wedderburn?"

"Not me! I just keep things ticking along on my own little patch. I look after my girls. Keep them in candy."

"All on your own?"

"Well, Second Eddie helps out."

"But it's mainly you."

"I should say so."

"They trust you, then?"

"That they do."

"The Daddio is expanding. You see all this?" The Quantifier waved his knife around the surrounding buildings. "Someone may own all the property, but

41

there's still money to be made farming the people. That's what the Daddio is good at."

"Farming people?"

"S'right. And I'll tell you what. That's just the beginning. There's whole new worlds going to come crowding in here soon, and the Daddio aims to take control of what he can. He's got plans, and he wants you to be part of them."

"And if I refuse?"

The Quantifier frowned.

"You did feel my knife, didn't you?" He held up the blade for inspection. It looked as if it had been shattered from a ceramic drum: it was black and shiny and wickedly serrated. I know the move: plunge the blade into a stomach, twist it, and watch as the victim's own stomach acid eats into their body.

"Okay," I said. "I'll think about it."

Again the Quantifier looked puzzled.

"I don't understand. You have to answer me. Are you working for the Daddio, or do I have to kill you?"

I looked up at the Quantifier's vast bulk and wondered about fighting him. I had a pistol, after all.

I doubted it would be much use against this creature.

"Very well," I said.

The Quantifier's frown deepened.

"Very well what? Do you mean you'll work for him?"

"Tell the Daddio that Captain Wedderburn has received his message and is delighted to be held in such regard!"

"Okay…" said the Quantifier, nodding slowly. He seemed satisfied, but his tongue leant forward to take a closer look at me.

"Right, can I go home now?" I asked.

"No! There's one more thing. I have to give you a message. The Daddio says you are to have nothing to do with the Cartel."

I paused. Did he know about my meeting with Alan? Or was the timing of this meeting just a coincidence?

"Really? Why not?"

The Quantifier scratched his big pumpkin head with the tip of the knife.

"I don't think it's up to you to ask questions of the Daddio, do you? But, like I told you: the Daddio has big plans for Dream London. He likes the way things are going, and he doesn't want the Cartel hindering this new world."

"What's the Cartel?" I asked, innocently.

There was a moment's pause.

"I think you're pretending."

I changed the subject.

"So what does the Daddio want me to do?"

"The Daddio wants you to do nothing for the moment. Go home, go to bed. The Daddio will be in touch when he is ready. It may be in a few days, maybe a few weeks. Don't you worry about it."

"And if I don't do what the Daddio wants?"

"Why shouldn't you? You're working for him now."

"I forgot. So you said."

Again, the two eyes in that tongue stared at me.

"Okay. Can I go now?"

"Yes."

The Quantifier stood to one side.

Slowly I walked from the square, heading from Mandolin Vale, back towards Belltower End and my flat. Down the long road, framed by the buildings and the purple sky, I could see the tall bulging shape of the belltower from which the area got its name. The moon was hiding at the moment, keeping secret the time of night.

Down the streets, stepping between the pools of light, listening to the call of the blue monkeys, the chitter of the insects, the sound of singing from the half-open pubs.

One of the whores standing outside a shop doorway recognised me.

"On the house, Captain Wedderburn!"

"Not tonight, Suky Sue."

"Come on. We've got the time."

The time. What was the time, anyway? Alan had warned me about checking the time. What if I were to do that now?

Suky Sue fumbled for my hand. "Have you got any candy at least?"

I fumbled in my pocket, passed her a striped piece wrapped in cellophane. She took it and walked off, leaving me lost in thought.

What was I doing?

Going home, obviously.

But by doing so I was obeying the wishes of the Daddio. Or was I? I had planned to go home anyway.

What were my plans? Captain Jim Wedderburn gave the orders, he didn't follow them. Yet whichever choice I made tonight I would be going along with someone, be it the Daddio or the Cartel.

Standing there in the streets of Dream London, I suddenly remembered Christine and her gift from earlier that evening. Caught in indecision, I pulled the fortune scroll from my pocket.

What was going on tonight?

My arrival back in London had coincided with the beginning of the changes. Buildings growing, people changing. It had been almost imperceptible at first, but events had accelerated as time had gone on. It seemed as if tonight things had stepped up a gear.

I didn't believe in fate, in fortunes, in predictions. But there was something about this evening: the air seemed to hang heavy with the promise of... something. The streets were darker; the air had a spicier scent than ever. There was a sense of the world holding its breath waiting... waiting for what? For me to choose?

Curiously, I unrolled the scroll, and began to read the predictions.

You will meet a Stranger
You will be offered a job
You will be offered a second job

I paused at that, unsettled. Hadn't that happened to me tonight? I frowned, thinking. In Dream London, everyone was on the make. People were always trying their hand at things. Would it be so unusual to be offered a new job? I read on.

Go to the inn to meet a friend, one who will betray you
Go to the docks and meet your greatest friend, the one you will betray...

I stopped reading at that point. That was the trouble with fortune tellers. The things they told you were only useful after the event. The parchment had told me I had been offered two jobs, and I had – after a fashion – but it gave no advice on which one to take. What was the point of that?

I rolled the parchment up and tapped it on my lips, thinking.

What was I to do? Before it had been so simple, simply return home to bed. But if I were to do that now, I would be following Daddio Clarke's instructions. I had to make Alan's house by sunrise, that was what he had told me. If I simply stood here, then I was, albeit unwillingly, doing what the Daddio had asked me.

Either way, I was being manipulated, and I hated that. What to do?

In the end, I did what I always did when unsure. I followed the money.

HALF AN HOUR later, I found myself standing outside the door of the Poison Yews, card in my hand.

Alan opened the front door, the look of relief on his face obvious. He stood back and I entered into a wide hallway. A grandfather clock stood at the far end, ticking its way slowly through time.

"Don't look at it!" warned Alan. "This is part of the protection, keeping us unfocused."

I heard footsteps and another man entered the hallway. An incredibly pretty young man, dark and lithe and with eyes like a flowerboy.

"He came, then," he said, a bored note to his voice.

"Of course he did," said Alan. "Come on. Let's get Jim to sleep before dawn breaks."

They took me up stairs to a room with a large brass bedstead. They were holding hands in the doorway as they wished me goodnight.

"We'll talk in the morning," said Alan.

BLUE

THE POISON YEWS

I WOKE TO sunlight and the smell of coffee.

I followed the trail of the aroma downstairs to its end where I found a woman sitting at the table in a large dining room. She smiled at me and lifted the silver coffee pot.

"Black please," I said, and then, "I'm sorry, who are you?"

"I'm Margaret, Alan's wife."

I guessed she was in her late forties. A full-figured, good looking woman with big brown eyes and brown hair neatly cut to just above her shoulders. She was wearing a flowered dress, though she looked as if she would be more at home in a dark suit, on the board of some City firm.

"His wife?" I said, thinking of the Molly house we had visited last night.

"We have an agreement," she said, rising to her feet. "Would you like the full English?"

"Yes, please." My stomach rumbled in agreement, and I realised just how hungry I was. Hungrier than a man who only a few hours ago was eating steak and oysters should be. Last night's meal seemed as ghostly and insubstantial as the other events I had experienced.

"Help yourself to more coffee if you want it."

I looked around at my surroundings, getting a feel for the house.

Alan was obviously well off. This house was large and well furnished, and even if Dream London was altering its topology night by night, the quality of the surroundings spoke for themselves. Polished floors that had gained a deeper shine than was possible by mere beeswax, polished mirrors reflecting worlds glowing in deeper colours than ours, velvet curtains slicked with richness, thickly upholstered furniture festering with paisley and infested with lace. The ornaments that had once decorated this house had transmuted into porcelain jars and vases. And yet the house retained an airiness and sense of light. I paused a moment to breathe in the scent of honey wax and pollen. Perhaps if all went well with the Cartel, I, too, would live in a house like this.

In the kitchen, Margaret was frying bacon at the Raeburn.

"Soon be ready," she said. "I'm making more coffee."

There was a large wooden table in the middle of the room and I sat down at it. Three cookbooks lay on the table, the middle one open at a recipe for a boiled pudding of some description. The photograph of the dish was fading to a woodcut.

"This is all natural food, before you ask," said Margaret above the sound of frying. There was evidence of natural food everywhere stored around the kitchen, from the two hams that hung from the ceiling to the polished green apples laid out on trays on a side counter, ready to be stored away.

"Don't worry about me," I grunted. "I can't afford to be fussy."

"You should be. The Cartel is convinced that street food is speeding on the changes."

She scooped the bacon onto a warming plate, and then cracked two blue eggs into the pan.

"Duck eggs," she said, looking at me over her shoulder with her big brown eyes. "You always get a nice breakfast living near the Egg Market."

The sizzle of eggs, the smell of bacon and coffee, it all conspired to make me feel quite homesick. Homesick for the old days, before the changes.

"Can I have some fried bread?" I asked hopefully.

"Of course you may," she said.

I watched her working, thinking about what she had said.

"Are you part of the Cartel?" I asked.

"Of course not. No women allowed. The changes, don't you see?"

I looked around the kitchen and noticed a brace of pheasants hanging by the hams: the red-gold cock and the brown hen bound together by their necks.

"What does Alan do to afford this place?" I asked.

"When *we* bought it, it wasn't just Alan," she said.

"I'm sorry."

"Now, of course, he struggles to pay the mortgage."

"Things are tough all over," I said, without sympathy. Rents were rising all over the city, families were being forced into the workhouse. It was every man for himself in Dream London, and the women had to hope that some man would look after them.

The eggs joined the bacon on the warming plate. She swiftly cut two slices of white bread and dropped them in the pan.

"It was easier with two salaries," she said, reflectively. "Of course, when the changes began, I saw the way things were going. I took voluntary redundancy before I was pushed out."

She dropped the bread onto the plate and brought it to me. I began to eat. Margaret fetched the coffee pot and two fresh cups then sat down opposite me. Her ample bosom spilled over the top of her dress as she leant forward. She smiled at me, clearly a woman of huge appetites.

"You're a good looking man," she said. "I can see why Alan is attracted to you."

"What does Alan do in the City?" I asked, not wanting to go down that road. She held my gaze for a moment or two. Then her eyes slid away.

"Used to be finance. Still is, I suppose. Now they underwrite the ships that set off sailing to the other places. They place bets on what might be brought back down the river."

"What ships? What other places?"

She sipped her coffee once more.

"Where do you think all the new stuff comes from? You know, it's just the ships at the moment, sailing down the River Roding. It's going to get a lot worse soon. Once they open up other paths here."

"Mmm." I concentrated on eating. The duck eggs tasted unusual in a breakfast.

"You know the changes began in the City?" said Margaret. "The banks sold a stake in the City to someone they shouldn't. They let something gain a toehold…"

"I'd heard that," I said.

"The City keeps it quiet. That shouldn't surprise you.

They were never exactly forthcoming about holding up their hands to mistakes in the past, were they?"

I finished my breakfast, mopped up egg yolk with the last piece of bread. My favourite part of the meal.

Margaret was gazing into the distance now.

"It started in East London. I remember seeing how the buildings there were growing taller as I went to work. Back then I thought it was just my imagination, but no…" She gulped down some more coffee and topped up her mug from the pot. "The houses in Whitechapel began to subside into slums…"

I leant back in my chair and took a deep sigh.

"The first time I became aware was when my flat began to shrink," I said. "No, that wasn't it. I went to buy screws to put up shelves, and the shop wasn't there anymore. I couldn't even find the street. I walked up and down all afternoon looking for it…"

I drained my cup. Margaret refilled it.

"Have you got a cigarette?" I asked.

She brightened up at that. "I thought you'd never ask."

She produced a purple pack and a box of yellow matches. She pulled us out an oval turkish cigarette each and lit them, mine first, and then hers.

She brightened even more as she inhaled.

"That's better," she said, exhaling blue smoke. "One of the benefits of the changes. Cigarettes coming back into fashion."

We smoked in companionable silence for a while, sipping at our coffee.

"Do you have a girlfriend?" asked Margaret, suddenly.

I shook my head.

"She bought one of those lists of men," I said, pausing to take another drag. "She's searching for her ideal partner."

"Your name wasn't on the list, I take it."

I shrugged.

"I often think about buying one of those lists myself," said Margaret. "But then I tell myself things could be a lot worse. The way things are going in Dream London being a housewife is about be the best choice for women, don't you think?"

I didn't answer. I knew what the career choice was for many of the women of Dream London. Captain Jim Wedderburn earned his twenty per cent looking after them.

Somewhere in the hall a clock chimed the hour.

"Midday!" I said. "I didn't realise I'd slept in so late!"

"It'll do you good. You'll not be getting much sleep in the near future."

That brought me up short.

"Why not? What exactly do the Cartel want with me?"

She stood up suddenly.

"I think it's time we had a drink."

IT WAS A gloriously sunny day. The may blossom was burning white on the trees in the garden. The smell of warmth filled the air.

"Anyone who cannot see any good in the changes should be shown the hawthorn trees," said Margaret. "The may blossom was never so white in the past; the leaves were never so green."

She was right, too. The blossom seemed to shine with its own light, and it made the ragged leaves glow greener.

We left the drive of Alan's house and made our way down the sun-dappled street, shaded by the horse chestnuts. Their candlestick blossoms were dying back now, but their leaves seemed freshly minted in green. I saw the golden shapes of tamarind monkeys, making hand signals to each other in the branches.

I felt quite jaunty, wearing a red and white candy striped blazer and a pair of linen trousers that Margaret had supplied. Even accounting for seasonal variation, Dream London gets warmer every month; I felt pleasantly cool in the midday sun. I felt as if I should have on a straw boater; certainly Margaret was wearing a wide-brimmed hat.

"Is it far?" I asked.

"No. We're going to meet Bill Dickenson."

"Who's he?"

"I'll leave it to Bill to explain that."

LONDON HAD ALWAYS mixed its rich and poor close together. In Dream London the effect was exaggerated. Stepping from the moneyed calm of Hayling Street into Egg Market reminded me of how it used to be, stepping off an aeroplane into another country. One moment there is air conditioning, the voices of the other passengers, their familiar clothes and accents; the next there is the heat, the noise, the strange smells, the realisation that you are somewhere else.

It was like that stepping into the High Road, Egg Market. I could hear flutes and drums, the shouts of street vendors, the sizzling of frying. Someone was singing nearby, the sort of self-indulgent introspection that is so valued in Dream London. Someone thrust a yellow and red striped root into my face.

"Fresh in!" he said. "Peel it, slice it, fry it, serve it to your kids. This'll make them behave themselves!"

"No thank you!" said Margaret with a shudder, pulling me on my way.

"I don't remember this place from last night," I said, looking around. The little shops beyond the market stalls had thrown open their doors, the light not penetrating their dim interiors. I saw tin pans and clocks and fur coats, and collections of coloured bottles of alcohol and ether and methanol and much worse things.

"It looks different in the dark," said Margaret. Across the way I recognised the white tiled shape of the Egg Market itself, the building from which the area gets its name.

The Egg Market looks like a cross between an old fashioned cinema and a mosque. Four domes stand at its corners, the walls are covered in clean white tiles from Chinatown. People travel from all over Dream London to the Egg Market. I had visited the place myself, wandered the stalls inside its tiled halls. I had seen the wicker baskets filled with brown and white hens' eggs; goose eggs; speckled plovers' eggs like little stones. I had seen wrens' eggs carefully wrapped in brown paper twists, and ostrich eggs tied around with string, a little loop in the top for carrying. And then there was the chilled hall, where the stalls were filled with ice on which stood bowls of fish roe and caviar. Through them were the more esoteric halls where you could buy leathery crocodile and alligator eggs, mixed bowls of snake eggs, fertilised and unfertilised. And then there was the amphibian room with its pools of frog spawn and then on to the tiny stands selling ant eggs and fly eggs and the eggs of all manner of insects. There was even the hall where only the women went, where jars full of menstrual blood and unfertilised eggs were arranged in lines on tables.

London is very different to how it used to be.

"Here we are."

We were standing outside a pub: the Laughing Dog. A Dalmatian wearing half moon spectacles and a serious expression looked down from the sign.

"Take this," said Margaret, pushing a leather purse into my hand. I could feel the weight of the coins inside. "It looks better if the man buys the drinks."

I followed her into the pub, looked around the dim, grubby interior.

"This place is a dump," I said.

"I'll have a port and lemon," said Margaret. She placed a hand on my arm. "I'll be sitting over there."

She pointed to a set of wooden booths. Most of them were already occupied by women, sitting alone for the most part, and I had an inkling of what sort of place this was. Now that I came to think of it, I'd been here before, on business.

"Pint of lager and a port and lemon," I said to the unshaven barman.

"No lager," he said, looking at me with contempt. "Bitter or mild."

"Bitter, then."

He poured me a flat pint and a glass of sticky port. I carried them across to the booth that Margaret had indicated and slid into the seat.

"Is that for me lover? Cheers!"

The woman sitting opposite was not Margaret. Red headed, she had one of the prettiest faces I had ever seen. She drained the drink and grimaced.

"Strewth!" she said. "That was deadly!"

What was wrong with her accent? It sounded like she had learned cockney from Dick Van Dyke.

"I'm sorry," I said. "I was looking for my friend…"

"I'll be your friend, lover!"

Again, that accent. It sounded so wrong. I rose from my seat, pint in hand.

"I'm sorry, I'll just…"

She took hold of my wrist, jarring it. Thin beer slopped over my hand, onto the table.

"Don't be like that," she said. "Come on, come with me upstairs…"

Even in the confusion I noticed what a lovely hand she had, what clear eyes. Not at all like the whores of my usual acquaintance.

"I'm sorry," I said. "Really, there's been a mistake."

At that she leant close to me, and for a moment I thought she was going to kiss me, but instead she whispered in my ear.

"Don't be a fool. It's me, Bill Dickenson."

What made me pause was not the name, but her accent. It was an accent that used to be so common, but was now rarely heard in Dream London.

"You're an American," I said.

"Shut up!" she hissed

"I'm sorry…"

She straightened up.

Then she called out in that faux cockney accent, "Like them, do you? Want to see more?"

She led me by the hand to the back of the pub and up the stairs, conscious of the amused, resentful and just plain bored stares of the other customers.

I wondered if I should play along, put my hands around her, but something made even Captain Jim Wedderburn pause.

I recognised that Bill Dickenson was not to be trifled with.

(A FEELING OF SETTING OUT ON A JOURNEY)

BILL DICKENSON

WHAT BETTER PLACE to meet with someone in private than a brothel?

Bill Dickenson took me to a small room, the dirty white walls hung with badly executed pornographic paintings. Dusty purple cobwebs decorated the corners of the room like antimacassars.

"Sit on the bed," she said, rather unnecessarily. The only other item of furniture in the room was a chair, and she had already taken that. She hitched up her long skirts, and I caught a glimpse of her shapely, stocking-clad legs.

"Don't even think about it," she said in a clear American accent. All the false cockney charm was gone. I wondered what she was doing, fiddling about in there. All became clear when she removed a leather folder from beneath her skirts. She caught me staring, so I turned on the Captain Wedderburn charm.

"Hey, you can't blame a man for admiring a nice figure."

"I can if he's being a sexist asshole."

I stared at her coolly. Whore or not, nobody spoke to Jim Wedderburn like that.

"You're a long way from home, Missy," I said. "You might do well to remember that fact. Especially if you want my help."

She held my gaze, equally cool.

"Understand this now, James, I'm the one helping you. *You* might do well to remember that fact."

She opened the folder and removed a collection of paper. "Take a look at this," she said, handing me a photograph from the pile. The glossy feel of the paper, that and her accent, sent more waves of homesickness crashing over me. I was remembering the old days.

It was amazing how quickly you adapted to change. Dream London did something to the people here. It brutalised the men, made them both harder and more sentimental. It was softening the women, making them more submissive. Outwardly so, at least.

I looked at the first photograph. All I saw was a collage of scenes. Countryside and city and water, all jumbled together in a pattern of green and grey and blue. Parts of the picture hadn't reproduced at all; they faded away to a pink and orange blur.

"What is it?" I said, turning it around in my hands. "It looks like the printer malfunctioned."

Bill was studying my face intently, judging my reaction to the photograph.

"The printer's fine. The missing sections are from where the satellite couldn't get a focus on the scene. That's London from 22,000 miles up, taken four days ago. At least, it's the parts that intrude into our world."

Now she said it, it began to make a certain sense.

Last night Alan had shown me a picture taken from an airship five months ago. There, the parts of London had been drifting out of true. Here the movement had accelerated, had become a curdling spiral of chaotic interference.

"That's the City," I said, pointing to an area half way between the centre of the picture and the right hand side. "The Square Mile. The towers have grown taller."

"Some of them are almost a mile high now. We're certain that they're the source of the changes."

"That's what Margaret said," I murmured, tracing the path of the Thames with my finger. The blue line twisted its way in a loose double spiral from the top left corner to the bottom right.

"Here's the River Roding," I said. "It used to join the Thames near Barking..."

"I know," said Bill. "Now the confluence has drifted west, and the river has grown wider and deeper. It's the major route for the ships from the other places that have found their way into Dream London. Look at this."

She flicked through the pile and found another photograph, passed it across. I looked down from the satellite at the rectangular blue shapes of London's Docklands. The modern apartment buildings and city blocks had been consumed by the warehouses of old; their glass and steel designs didn't stand a chance against the heavy brick of a century ago. The wharfs had cast loose the lines of the pleasure yachts and the waters had yawned deep and swallowed them up. Now the docks were once more stained with soot, strewn with litter, engrained with dirt, and most of all, busy. The wharfs were lined with working ships. Sailing ships, steam ships, rowing boats. Clippers, barques, cogs, dhows, ketches, snows, fluyts, all the myriad boats of yesteryear. I could just make out the busy throng of people at work loading and unloading the ships, the steam trains crowding into the sidings.

"Look back at the first picture," said Bill. "See how the city and docks are intertwined."

"Logistics," I said, and my eyes widened as I understood the full import of what I had just said. Logistics was half of any battle, getting supplies to the right place at the right time. You couldn't fight a war if you couldn't feed your soldiers. Similarly, you couldn't run a business if you couldn't get your products to the market. Imagine how easy those things would be if you controlled the shape of the land?

"What?" said Bill.

"I just realised," I said, "just how powerful the people behind these changes are." I looked at her, at her pretty face and slim body. "Do you really think we can fight this?"

She scowled. "Don't be fooled by this dress," she said. "I'm not a whore. At least, not yet."

Not yet. I knew what that meant. Dream London has a way of working on your mind. Bill must have known about that. Had there been other Americans here before her? Undoubtedly. What had happened to them? I made a mental note to contact Second Eddie when I left here; perhaps we could track some of them down. Help them out, as it were. You can always charge more for the exotic.

"I know you're not a whore," I said, thoughtfully. "Listen. What do you want from me?"

"How much do you know about the changes?"

"I know they started in the Square Mile. After that, it's all just rumour."

"Then tell me the rumours," she said, impatiently.

"What's the point? Who can tell what the truth is when everything keeps changing? Tell me what you know."

She stared at me. I said nothing.

"Okay," she said, giving in. "Have you heard of a company called Davies-Innocent?"

"No."

"They're a multinational financial house. They have a presence mainly across Europe and the Far East. Virtually nothing in the States. They're responsible for all this."

That was a huge accusation. The Egg Market? The growing spires? The flower market and the railway stations?

"How could a financial house be responsible for all this?" I asked.

She handed me another picture, this one a series of views of London, taken over time. In each view, the streets and buildings were highlighted in different colours.

"The first was taken over a year ago, around the time the changes began. The Davies-Innocent building is the one in the middle. Take a closer look at it. What do you notice?"

I gazed at the picture. It showed a typical London street in the Square Mile as it used to be. A narrow road that dog-legged between tall buildings crowded higgledy-piggledy together. The sight of the white vans and cars crammed up on the pavement, pedestrians squeezing by them, brought a lump to my throat. The buildings themselves were a collection of styles, modern glass and steel, old fashioned red brick. The Davies-

Innocent building was clad in yellow stone, a restrained façade of tall, arched windows.

"What am I supposed to see?" I asked.

"Look at the windows."

Now I saw it. The windows in the middle of the building were taller than those at the sides. They were stretching themselves, beginning to grow. Now I knew what I was looking for, I noticed that the centre of the building seemed to bulge a little.

"Now look at this," said Bill.

She passed me a satellite picture.

"The buildings outlined in red are all owned by Davies-Innocent. Look closely and you can see the changes."

"That's near Liverpool Street station," I said. "Isn't that Spitalfields Market?"

"Yes."

She passed me the next picture. The Gherkin was highlighted in green.

"That building was one of the next to succumb. It was bought by Davies-Innocent just after the changes began. Around that time, Davies-Innocent acquired a large amount of capital from sources unknown. It used that capital to buy up London, piece by piece. As the contracts were signed, the changes accelerated."

"Someone bought up the city? That's what we heard, I suppose." I shook my head. "Couldn't someone have stopped them?"

"It took us a while to spot the pattern. By then it was too late."

I remembered something then, old stories I had read as a child, back when I still read books.

"Fairies," I said. "They sold the city to the fairies."

"Others have had similar theories," said Bill. "This city was sold to someone, or something, that's for sure."

"Just this city?" I said. "You said Davies-Innocent had interests around the world."

Another photograph. This was a satellite picture of southern England, a little of Wales to the left hand side. For the most part it looked so normal, so much as I remembered. And there, to the bottom right, it all went wrong. There was the curdled mess, the spreading area around where London used to be.

"Internationally, the effect is localised around London, for the most part. There's a little in Paris, in Budapest, Prague and Tallinn, but the effect never spread to the same extent."

"Why not?"

"Because when the changes began in those places we had learned from your experience. We knew what to do. People were ordered to stop selling property at the first sign of infection."

"Infection?"

"I've heard it described as infestation. But the effect elsewhere is minor. People have seen what's happened to London. Better yet, they know what will happen to them if they do sell. Twenty years imprisonment, no questions asked. The death penalty in more serious cases..."

"That still won't be enough," I said. "People are greedy."

"We're holding the line. But there's another reason too, we think. A bigger one. And that's why you're here." The briefest of pauses. "And me."

She sagged on the chair, and just for a moment, sitting there in her frilled dress, her red hair on her bare shoulders, her green eyes downcast, she looked so pretty and vulnerable.

"Stop that!" she shouted, and I got the impression the words weren't directed solely at me. "Don't you dare look at me like that! I'm not a piece of merchandise. I'm not a whore, Wedderburn. I'm a trained agent. Do you understand that?"

"Oh yes," I said. "I can assure you our relationship will be purely professional."

She lowered her voice.

"You ever try anything with me, Wedderburn, I will break your arms. Do you understand that? *Do you understand that?*"

"How long have you been in Dream London?" I asked, changing the subject.

She stared at me for a moment or two longer, and then relaxed again.

"Two days. I caught the train here from Manchester. That's where the British Parliament is now located. The real one, I mean."

I knew what she meant. I had been past the Dream London Parliament. It's the same building that used to stand by the Thames, filled with a bunch of liars, incompetents and sociopaths. Feel free to fill in your own joke here, by the way. I've heard them all.

Still, her words gave me pause. All this time in Dream London and I'd thought rarely, if ever, about what had happened to the rest of England. To think it had been doing its best to carry on as normal, struggling to cope with the loss of its capital city.

"There's talk about moving the Royal Family to Manchester from Balmoral," said Bill. "Those who weren't trapped here in Dream London, anyway."

Like I cared about the Royal Family. Another idea had taken hold of me.

"You're not the first agent here, are you?"

"Not by any means. There have been people coming into Dream London to investigate since the changes began. The longest any of my predecessors reported back for is three weeks. After that we can only assume they go native."

"Hmmm. Why not get away after a week?"

She gave me a withering gaze

"Why don't you get away, Jim? Why doesn't anyone here get away? For most people, the trains only run one way."

"For most people?" I said.

She brushed a stray hair from her eyes.

"Have you ever thought about how the rest of the world fits around Dream London?" she asked.

"Not until now."

"There's still a train service running between London and the other cities."

She lowered her voice, remembering. "Two days ago I was in Manchester Piccadilly. You stand there on the platform in the twenty-first century. There are people there using mobile phones, drinking Starbucks coffee, and then you hear a shrieking whine and you see this train gliding into the station, sliding in between the normal trains. Something shaped like a dark green crocodile. All brass and sparks. There are two little round portholes at the front for the driver to look out of. All around you the station descends into silence. Everyone is looking, despite the fact this must happen every hour on the hour. The atmosphere there! Half terror, half fascination."

"Every hour on the hour," I said, a terrible longing creeping over me. Oh, to ride that train, out of this place! A question occurred to me. "But who would want to come here?"

"You'd be surprised," said Bill. "Me for one. But don't forget what I said. Dream London isn't totally isolated. There are traders, ambassadors, people doing business. The city holds loved ones hostage to ensure that traveller's return. They can ride the train because Dream London knows they will be coming back."

"How does it know?"

She didn't answer that question. She was searching through her photographs for another one.

"Come on. You have fifteen more minutes in here with me at most."

"Don't worry about it," I said. "No one will think it odd if Captain Jim Wedderburn spends an extra hour in a brothel."

"You seem proud of the fact."

"It's a different world, Bill."

"Do you want to stay part of it? Now, look at this picture."

Another satellite photograph.

"A park," I said.

"Green Park."

Alan had shown me a picture of Green Park last night. It had been one of the smaller London parks, squeezed in between Hyde Park and St James's. Never quite as busy as the others, it had been a pleasant pool of calm in the midst of the city. Not that I had visited it for some time now as I had been unable to find my way there through the ever changing streets.

What I now saw in the photographs, however, bore no resemblance to the past. It bore little resemblance to Alan's picture. The park had grown enormously in the past five months. Lush green lawns had expanded so they must be at least a mile wide. Trees marched in neat lines either side of wide roads that strapped the place together.

"What's that?" I said, pointing to a glorious gold and white building that looked like a cross between a fairy tale castle and a casino. It had spires, turrets, towers, windows... the lot.

"That was Buckingham Palace," said Bill. "It's grown much larger now, and it's still changing. That shape in front of it was the Victoria Memorial."

I remembered the memorial: a white sculpture of Queen Victoria and various angels, the whole surmounted by a golden sculpture of Victory.

"What is it now?" I asked.

"We don't know. Yet. The figures are changing, growing. Look at the whole picture, James. What can you see?"

I looked, and it all became obvious.

"There are roads leading to the palace. Lots of them. But that's not the biggest concentration of roads..."

The biggest concentration was just to the side of the palace, near the centre of the picture. Many roads, all converging on a point. They made me think of crop circles, of Celtic knots, pale green on green.

She was gazing at me, keenly.

"All those roads, leading to the middle of the park. What do you think it is?"

"It's an entrance," I croaked. "Everyone says that someone is preparing a way into the city. But from where?"

"We don't know. Perhaps you can find out."

Something moved in the corner of the room and Bill was suddenly in motion. The photos she had held fell spinning to the floor as she sprang from the chair, swooping down on the source of the movement, reaching out and snatching at something. She paused, and then slowly began to unwind something from a hole in the floorboards.

"What is it?" I asked. I was impressed by her speed, doubly so given the long skirts she wore.

She straightened up and I saw she was holding a peach and lemon snake, just below the head. The snake's emerald green tongue flickered out, tasting the stale sweat of the room.

"Is this native to England?" she asked, and I laughed out loud. The snake was almost as long as she was tall; its back was decorated in concentric circles of colour.

"No," I said. "I think it safe to say it arrived with Dream London."

"I think it must have a nest beneath the floorboards here. I wonder what it's seen in this room?"

"I can imagine," I said, looking at the excess of pink paint on the pictures that hung on the walls.

"No need to be crude," said Bill, and with a swift movement, she broke its neck. Carefully, she began to feed the snake's body back through the crack in the floorboards.

"You could have got a good price for that, live."

"Don't be an idiot," she said, pushing at the snake. "It could have been spying on us."

"A snake? I don't think so."

And I paused. Why not? How was I to judge what was possible in Dream London?

Something shifted inside me. For over a year now I had looked at the changes with a cynical eye. Even in the middle of my angriest moments over Christine and her leaving me, I had managed to feel a little pity for her,

I had felt a little superiority that Dream London hadn't ensnared me like everyone else.

I had walked through the twisting, changing streets, I had eaten the smoky, spicy new food, I had listened to the overly sentimental music, and I thought how little it had touched me.

Now, seeing myself through an outsider's eyes, I realised how wrong I was. Dream London had been working its insidious way on me all along. Snakes couldn't talk. Was that true? What else was I taking for granted?

Looking at Bill, looking at her pretty face, set hard with determination, I also had my first inkling of her bravery in coming here. I had had no choice. Here she was, acting as a prostitute, in the full knowledge that in three weeks' time that might no longer be an act.

"Who do you work for?" I asked. "CIA?"

"You know I won't answer that," she said, and she straightened up, the snake disposed of.

"Okay," I said, "I guess our time is almost up…" I got up and began to gather the photos she had scattered from the floor. I saw more scenes of Dream London, taken by satellite. A railway station, passengers and porters in uniform swarming across platforms; golden sands by blue waters, holidaymakers in striped bathing costumes eating ice creams by the Thames, the flower markets, scarlet and golden blossoms and the pollen hanging heavy in the air. A street scene…

"Hey," I said. "That's where I live!" I flicked through the pictures. "And here! And here. That's Belltower End! You've been spying on me!"

"Of course we have," said Bill, taking the photographs from me and replacing them in the leather folder. "Now, I've got something for you."

She handed me a thick cream envelope.

"This is for you," she said. "Don't open it."

I took the envelope. I could feel several thick pieces of paper inside.

"Those are your references and letters of recommendation."

"For what?"

"Your new job. Tomorrow morning you begin your new job as junior clerk at Davies-Innocent. You're going up to the Writing Floor of Angel Tower. That's where the answers lie, we think."

"What answers?"

"The contracts that signed the old London over to whoever it is that runs things now. We want you to see if you can find those contracts."

"That's if I decide to go," I said. Nobody orders Captain Jim Wedderburn around.

Bill remained calm.

"Grow up, James," she said. "Do you really think you'll walk out of this situation? How long do you think we'll let you live if you don't follow through? You know too much. You're part of this."

I didn't bother to put up any pretence. I knew she was right. It's what I would have done. I tried another tack.

"But I know nothing about being a clerk!"

"So what? That sort of thing never stopped you in the past. Didn't you once walk through Afghanistan dressed in a burqa?"

I passed the envelope from hand to hand, appreciating the luxurious feel of the paper.

"What about clothes and things? Don't clerks wear suits?"

"That will all be waiting for you at Alan's house tonight."

I nodded. Bill's people had obviously thought of everything.

"How did you arrange all of this?" I asked.

"Through Alan. There are still a few lines of communication left to the outside world, but every month we lose a few more. Oh, something else. You're now Alan's nephew. He'll tell you the details tonight."

"What if I'd said no?" I said. "What if last night, when Alan met me, I'd said no?"

She smiled, sweetly.

"Actually, that wouldn't have been such a problem. There are other people who we could have asked. Identity isn't the problem it once was. That's one thing we have going for us."

That brought me up short. Just when I was starting to feel a little special.

"Now, look the other way," she said, and as I did so I heard the swish of her skirts as she replaced the leather folder in its hiding place.

I gazed at one of the pictures on the wall. A naked woman, holding a yellow snake that bore more than a passing resemblance to the one that Bill had just killed.

"You can turn round now."

I did so. Bill stood before me, no sign of the leather pouch, every inch a working girl.

"Okay. You can go downstairs now. Walk straight out of the pub and go back to the house. Margaret will be waiting for you there."

"Okay," I said. "Will I see you again?"

"Tomorrow night, after work."

"Where do we meet?"

"You come here of, course," said Bill. "Where else would you go to celebrate your first day at work? I'll be waiting for you."

THREE

BELLTOWER END

I LEFT THE room and made my way downstairs to the pub. I could feel the eyes of the other customers upon me as I walked through the dingy taproom, and I wondered if they recognised me. Would they think Captain Wedderburn was sampling the competition?

I pushed my way into the bright June sunshine.

"Buy some spangled asparagus, mister? Put some lead back into your pencil."

The woman on the market stall cackled as she thrust the vegetable into my face.

"No, thank you," I said, pushing my way past her, touching the envelope in my pocket as I went.

I came to the corner of Hayling Street, and looked down into its green dappled depths. I heard parrots squawking down there. Everything seemed so calm and peaceful compared to the chaos of the market.

And I paused. Bill had told me to go back to the Poison Yews and Margaret, and here I was obeying her command...

Not twenty-four hours had passed since I had woken to the sound of salamanders munching a beetle. During that time I seemed to have lost control of my life. Well, maybe not lost control, but rather handed it across to Alan and Bill and some transatlantic conspiracy. A new home, a new job. I had walked out of Belltower End and my old life with barely a complaint.

Was I under some influence or other? There were stories all over Dream London of people losing control of their will. Every brothel had tales of women who had left their home and had been put under the influence, how they had woken up in a bed at the other side of the city as a working girl. Not that I had met any of those women. Every girl who worked for me did so of her own choice, more or less.

How much could I trust Alan and Bill?

More than I could trust Daddio Clarke, I supposed. The Daddio. I'd led his Quantifier to believe I was working for him. What would he think when he found out I'd disobeyed his instructions and had taken up with the Cartel?

I'd deal with that when it was time. For the moment, I wasn't ready to go back to Alan's house, despite Bill's instructions. I had the afternoon to myself, and I had business of my own to attend to. I wanted to check up on how Second Eddie was managing in my absence. I was needed at Belltower End, the heart of my own little empire.

BELLTOWER END LIES just behind the location of a former tube station. The station itself is long gone, having wrenched itself from the ground, raising itself up on stilts to shuffle off and connect itself to the wider railway system.

Before the changes Belltower End had been a shabby place, barely touched by the large commercial chains. The scattering of shops and bars and cafés on the high street were mainly small businesses, just scraping along on the money earned from the locals, mainly people renting the single-roomed flats formed by dividing up the old houses.

Just off the high street itself there had been a gentlemen's club: the Blue Parrot. This was the place where I had found work when I first returned to London. I started there as a bouncer, but a man with my charisma doesn't stay at the bottom for long. Soon I was organising the other bouncers, looking after the girls, making sure that everything was nice and safe. After all, the 'gentlemen' would be more likely to spend their money in a safe, discreet environment.

Then the changes began. The atmosphere in the club became nastier, and the girls looked to me for protection more than ever. They asked me for advice, and I gave them it. I suggested another place they could work, and they took my advice with gratitude.

Don't call Captain Wedderburn a pimp. I keep this area safe, I make sure that people can spend and earn their money in safety. Okay, I don't tolerate competition – Luke Pennies would tell you about that – but then again, who does?

Belltower End was originally a terraced row of town houses, just by the church with the large belltower from which the area gets its name. The houses have grown taller now, like so much else in this city. They've hunched around themselves to form a horseshoe and grown yellow and scarlet ivy across their faces to disguise themselves. There are little balconies on the upper floors where the girls can sit, there are steps leading up to the doorways where they do the same. There's a little garden in the square formed by the arms of the horseshoe, and a man can sit amongst the dark foliage and watch anyone who enters and leaves the area.

There were few people around at this time of day. A young black woman stood in the square, smoking a cigarette.

"Afternoon, Marie. Have you seen Second Eddie?"

"Sorry, Captain. I just got up. Busy night. I haven't been on my feet for hours."

He wouldn't have gone far, I was sure of that. Second Eddie took his duties seriously, particularly where the girls were concerned.

"Tell him I'm looking for him," I said. "I'll try the Heights."

If I was going to be away for some time, helping out Bill and the Americans, I needed someone to keep an eye on things. Second Eddie fancied himself as my deputy: I trusted him enough to not let things go wrong when I was away. I trusted myself enough to wrest back control should he get a little too ambitious.

"Okay, Captain," yawned Marie.

There was a little girl sitting on the pavement, drawing chalk pictures. She tilted her head at me as I approached, blonde curls bouncing delightfully.

"Do you like my picture, mister?" she asked, with just a hint of a lisp.

I looked down at her. She was a pretty little thing; I didn't recall seeing her around her before.

"It's very nice," I replied. She wore a pink silk dress that must have cost her parents quite a few dollars. Her pale arms were pudgy beneath the puffed sleeves.

"Would you give me a penny for it?"

"I shouldn't stay here, little miss," I said. "This is not a place for children."

That's when my mind finally registered what she had drawn. It looked like something Hieronymous Bosch might have drawn, if had he decided to turn his hand to hardcore pornography.

"What the…" I began.

"The Daddio sends his regards," said the little girl. She stared up at me, open mouthed. I felt a shiver of horror as I saw two eyes set in her tongue, looking back at me.

She stood up. I guessed she would be about six years old.

"Did you draw this yourself?" I said, looking down at the picture.

"The Daddio wants to know where you were last night. You didn't return to your flat."

"I… I was with a friend."

"Ah! You were fucking a whore." The little girl nodded wisely. "The Daddio said it would be something like that."

Now, as you can imagine, Captain Jim Wedderburn has heard much worse language in his time. But hearing it from the voice of such a sweet little thing made it seem all the more obscene. I almost blushed.

"I bet your mother wouldn't be pleased to hear you talking like that," I said, weakly.

"My mother can go frig herself." The girl reached up and patted my stomach. "Listen, the Daddio wants you to do something for him."

"Does he now?" I said, rather weakly.

"You're to go to the docks. The Daddio has a shipment coming in. Some new friends for you. You're to bring them back here and set them up in rooms of their own. He'll send further instructions on how you're to pay the Daddio his cut of their earnings later on."

"I don't have time to go right now, sweetheart," I said. "Maybe tomorrow."

The little girl smiled at me.

"You go now, or the Daddio will send someone to cut open your stomach and shit in it."

She stuck her tongue out, and the two malevolent eyes there stared at me.

"That's a pretty turn of phrase," I said, carefully. "What's your name, poppet?"

The little girl spread her pink skirt and performed a curtsey.

"My name is Honey Peppers and I am six and three-quarters years old."

"Well, Honey, you can tell the Daddio that I am going to the docks right away."

And at that I spun on my heel and set off at a great pace. I heard the flip of little footsteps behind me as Honey Peppers ran to keep up.

"Hey! Wait for me! I'm to come with you!"

"Hurry up then," I called over my shoulder. "We can't keep the Daddio waiting!"

"Hey! Slow down!"

"What was that? Go faster, you say?"

I strode as fast I could, pumping my arms like a speed walker. I had left the perfumed shade of Belltower End behind and was already walking down the gentle slope of Crapper Road. The gutters here were filled with the translucent shells of Dream London prawns. Many of the residents of the street earned their money doing piece work for the seafood processors down at the dock.

Honey Peppers squealed at me.

"If you don't wait I'll have your dick sewn inside your ball sack then I'll watch you try and piss!"

This final threat was so extreme it broke my concentration and made me stumble, but I strode on nonetheless.

"I can't hear you!" I called.

I was jogging now, half skipping through the streets. I turned down a street at random and broke into a run. The houses to my right were derelict. Golden trees sprouted through their windows, arching over the road. I heard the chatter of blue monkeys coming from the houses and I stepped up the pace again.

I ducked to the left and the right, plunging down alleys where the rubbish slicked the floor, walking over spongy green moss where I swayed as if drunk, then into a street where three blue monkeys sat torturing a cat. One of them looked at me, considering. I held its gaze as I walked on.

All the time I was heading downwards, heading, whatever my intentions might have been to the contrary, towards the docks. Somewhere up above me, high up in the towers of Dream London, someone was pulling at my strings, and I danced through the streets like a marionette.

I came to a sudden halt at the realisation. Someone was playing games with me. I looked back again. No sign of Honey Peppers. I dodged sideways down an alley and rounded a corner. A pile of broken glass panes lay outside a door, right next to what looked like a brand new gold plush armchair.

Why was there a chair there? I didn't consider this at the time, I simply dropped into the armchair, gasping, and sat there a while, getting my breath back. It was true, I realised: someone was playing with me.

I was sitting on something. Something in my pocket. I shifted a little and remembered Christine's scroll. Someone else trying to control me, I thought.

I pulled out the scroll, unrolled it, and began to read.

You will meet a Stranger
You will be offered a job
You will be offered a second job
Go to the inn to meet a friend, one who will betray you
Go to the docks and meet your greatest friend, the one you will betray...

Go to the docks. Did Honey Peppers know about the piece of paper in my pocket?

I didn't believe in fortunes any more than I did in Christine's list of possible husbands, but...

I lived in a city where the buildings changed every night, where people had eyes in their tongues, where women turned into whores over three weeks. Was a scroll that told my fortune so fantastic?

Everything on the scroll had come true so far, hadn't it? I shook my head. Not necessarily. Meet a friend in an inn? What was so unusual about that? One who will betray you...

Okay. I'd met Bill in the inn. Would she betray me? I had no hesitation in answering that question. Like a shot! She was in the military. My own country would have no hesitation in betraying me, why should another country be any more concerned about my wellbeing?

But it was the next line that gave me pause...

Go to the docks and meet your greatest friend, the one you will betray...

Daddio Clarke had sent me to the docks. Honey Peppers had something about new friends waiting for me there...

Why was everyone taking an interest in Captain Jim Wedderburn all of a sudden? I read the prediction again:

Go to the docks and meet your greatest friend, the one you will betray...

That struck a chord. That sounded like me. Meet my greatest friend and betray him. That was the sort of thing Jim Wedderburn would do. And frankly, I was sick of it. I had had enough of that in my life by now. I wanted to be better than I was. With Christine I thought I was beginning to improve, but she had dropped me and my old life had resumed in earnest. And now I was following the instructions of her prophecy scroll, things were taking another downwards turn.

What was I to do?

Certainly not head for the docks. Maybe it was time to return to the Poison Yews.

Curiosity gripped me and I began to unroll the rest of the scroll, to see the remainder of the predictions, but at that moment I heard a child's voice.

"Captain Wedderburn?"

I looked up and there, beside me, stood Honey Peppers, golden curls tilted.

"I think you were running away from me, Captain Wedderburn."

"Not at all, Honey."

"And yet here I find you in one of the Daddio's traps." She meant the chair.

"I was just eager to do the Daddio's work," I said.

Her pink and white dress remained spotless, I noticed.

"I hope so," said Honey. "If not, I would have to push ground glass into your prick, and that might mean I get my dress dirty. Now, we have to hurry."

"Of course," I said. I stood up from the armchair, pushing the scroll back in my pocket as I did so. "Lead the way!"

She took me by the hand and led me down to the docks.

THE DOCKS HAVE grown and twisted since the changes began. The waterways have crept deep into the city streets, so that you might look out of your window and see a ship sailing by, following a canal that used to be a road.

The cranes have grown taller, like so much else here; their booms are now wide enough that they can lift cargo from the deck of a ship and deposit it half a mile inland. I've stood in the yards of an inn, enjoying a drink in the sunshine, when there's been a flicker of shadow and I've looked up to see the boom of a crane high above, lowering a bundle of crates or barrels down towards an impatient landlord.

The Dockland warehouses bulge like fat sacks, their windows and doors overflowing with the goods that travel here from the strange lands that have plugged themselves into Dream London via the Roding. The streets hop with the oddly coloured rats and toads and lice that have hitched a ride on the boats and barges and now head determinedly up slope, searching for new ecosystems to make their own.

As for the ships themselves: they line the banks in all the colours of the rainbow. Gold and silver, checks, stripes and paisleys. The ships and boats are built to alien designs, their unfamiliar crews lean on the rails and look down at you with dark eyes and half-amused smiles. Sometimes they call out obscene-sounding phrases in exotic languages.

None of this bothered Honey Peppers as she led me by the hand through a maze of tethering ropes.

"Down here," she said.

We were heading parallel to the wide band of the river Thames, walking through the maze of smaller docks that led to larger docks. We threaded a path through the garbage-filled basins of oily water, the backwaters where the less impressive ships gathered.

The ships here were smaller than usual, and a lot less colourful. Most of them were little more than rotting wood and patched black tar. Their decks were dirty and cluttered, the tackle worn. The crews weren't visible, preferring to stay hidden below deck with their mysterious cargoes.

"This is the one," said Honey, looking up at the hull of a ship. A name was written there in fading paint.

"*The Courtesan*," I read with some difficulty.

"What does that mean?" asked Honey.

"Prostitute," I said.

"You mean whore?"

"Yes."

Honey Peppers nodded. I sighed. The ship loomed above us, dark and gloomy, and I had a sense of being far from home.

"Call them!" said Honey. "Let them know you're here!"

"Call who?"

"The crew! Go on, call them!"

I looked down at her for a moment, pink and pretty amidst the gloom and the smell of old fish, then I raised my hands to my mouth.

"Ahoy!" I called. "This is Captain Jim Wedderburn, awaiting the cargo."

"Ahoy?" giggled Honey.

"I'm a soldier, not a sailor. I thought *Ahoy* seemed right."

"Try again," said Honey. "They haven't heard."

"Hello!" I called.

There was no reply. Nothing but the sound of Honey laughing to herself.

"Ahoy," she giggled. "Go on! Grow some balls. Shout loudly!"

I did, and this time a woman appeared on the deck. She was old, dressed in filthy clothes. She looked down at me with utter contempt.

"They sent a *man*?" she said.

"They sent Captain Wedderburn!" I shouted back.

The old woman seemed to notice Honey Peppers.

"Is that your Daddy, little girl?" she called. "Tell him to get back! A *man* won't be able to withstand my girls."

"I'm not her..." I began, but Honey was already calling back.

"He's to take them to their rooms over at Belltower End!"

"No he's not," shouted back the old woman. "These are Moston girls. They'll drain him dry. Send him away. You'll have to do it."

"But..."

"Do you want them to escape? Send him away now!

I'm about to lower the gangplank!"

"You heard what she said, Honey." I smiled down at the little girl. " I don't think the Daddio would like it if I'm sucked dry by the Moston girls. You take the girls, I'll meet you back at Belltower End."

"But…"

Somewhere above a dirty plank of wood was slid forward. I heard the sound of young women singing.

"I'd better go," I said, and I patted her on the head. "See you later."

"You needledicked fucker."

"I know. But what can you do?"

I spun on my heel and quickly marched away.

But not too far.

Just around the edge of a warehouse, just, hopefully, out of range… I leant back around and spied on the Moston girls as they walked down the gangplank.

They didn't seem anything special at this distance. Just sixteen skinny teenagers with lots of bushy blonde hair. Their clothes were ragged, and I got a good view of their pale boyish bodies through the holes. Not my sort at all, I like my women to look like women, with curves. The Moston girls giggled and held hands and pushed each other and took it in turns to pat Honey Peppers on the head and tell her how adorable she was. I couldn't see what the fuss was about. And then – it was as if they sensed me, smelt my male scent – one of them glanced in my direction. She giggled and pointed at me. Then the others were looking at me too, big blue eyes gazing beseechingly in my direction, and I suddenly saw just how attractive they were. Was attractive the right word? No, less than that. It wasn't attraction, but something far more basic: they oozed sex appeal. I found myself moving towards them, and it was with some effort that I pushed myself backwards, back around the warehouse and out of their sight. If I stepped into their full view, I don't know what power they would have over me.

I realised then that the old woman was right. I couldn't handle the Moston girls. Let Honey Peppers take them back to Belltower End. I would deal with them later. For the moment, it was time for a drink.

JUST BEYOND THE Docklands I found an inn standing on the edge of the Thames itself. There I sat down to think as the sun descended towards evening. The inn behind me was crowded, and I could hear the sounds of laughter and drinking.

Three men sat on the bench near mine, and two of them were consoling the third.

"Never mind, Paul," said one. "You'd only have been tied down if you bought this place."

Paul wasn't going to be comforted.

"The gentry are taking over this area," he said bitterly. "I had enough money to buy my pub only last week! I went to the estate agents this morning and the price had doubled. Doubled! How is that fair?"

The other man shook his head in sympathy.

"Yes, but the gentry don't want you to buy properties, do they? Better that you take a loan to buy it and that way they get interest for twenty-five years. Better yet that you have to rent it and that way they get money for life!"

It was a story I was more than familiar with. Hadn't my attempts to buy Belltower End yielded similar results? It was a tough world all round.

I looked out across the water. The river had widened during the past year. The far bank was over a mile away. The buildings over there were not so tall as in the City, and there were things like banana palms growing between them, giving the skyline a tropical air. Large creatures grazed in the water by the far bank, and not for the first time I wondered about crossing over to get a better look at them. There had been no bridges along this stretch of the river before the changes, only the Blackwall tunnel and the Greenwich foot tunnel. Since the changes... well, no one who entered the Blackwall Tunnel had yet walked out the other side. As for the Greenwich Tunnel, it had widened as it had lengthened, the tiles in the walls turning a deep glossy green, crystal chandeliers dropping from the ceiling. Elegant shops had opened in the tunnel walls for those who could afford them.

As I sat there, lost in thought, I noticed that something was moving through the water. Something from another place, from far down one of the alien tributaries that had insinuated their way into the Thames. It looked like an orange man, swimming like a frog. Or maybe it was an oversized frog who moved like a man. Whichever, the creature was naked. It swam confidently through the crystal blue waters of the magically healed river, the dark brown bands that tiger-striped its glistening back rippling in the fading light. As it approached I saw that it carried a bag balanced on its shoulders. Two pale yellow eyes sat high on its head looking forward through the waters. It saw me, and the creature's eyes fixed on my own. I rose to my feet as it turned and headed directly for me.

A set of stone stairs ran down to the river, the base furred in green weed. One wide orange hand reached up and seized the lowermost step, and the creature began to climb out of the river. He was more man than frog and I saw now that he walked upright like a human. But his body was smooth; there was nothing between his legs but smooth orange skin. His face was almost human: his mouth a little too wide, his eyes too large and bulging, his nose two slits, but he looked handsome enough in his odd way. He was smiling at me as he climbed the steps, and now as he approached the top he held out one hand.

"Good evening, kind sir!" he said. "Good evening!"

"Hello," I said, carefully.

"Pardon my ignorance, but whom do I have the pleasure of addressing?"

"Call me James," I said.

"James! James! What a most excellent name! I am Mr Monagan!"

He was jerking his hand at me, eager that I should take it. Slowly, I did so and shook it. His hand was surprisingly warm and already dry, I noticed. The water seemed to have no purchase on his body.

"Pleased to meet you, James," he said, shaking my hand. He looked around himself and then hesitated a moment. "Excuse me for asking, but this is London, isn't it? London, the city of humans?"

"I haven't heard it described that way before, but yes, this is London."

He cut a little jig there and then before me, such was his delight.

"Thank you, kind sir! London! And to think they told me I could not swim that far! To think that they told me I should never make it here! Well, here I am! London. The place where I can finally be accepted as a human being!"

A human being, I thought?
Well, why not? This was Dream London after all.

(A FEELING OF FULFILMENT)

MR MONAGAN

THERE WAS A large, naked frog man standing before me. Despite myself, my eyes kept flickering down to the empty space between his legs. The orange frog man looked horrified when he noticed where I was looking.

"Oh, sir! Of course! I almost forgot! Clothes! They told me, I must wear clothes! They insisted that I bring them with me, and I thought they were joking! It seems that I too was mistaken! Now, just a minute…"

At that he took hold of the black leather bag that he had carried on his back and unlaced the top. A breath of spice puffed into the air, the smell of warmth and other places that waited at the dim ends of sinuous tributaries, lands lost to green moss, pickerel weed and bald cypress. The creature produced a pair of black trousers and quickly pulled them on. That was followed by a white shirt and a red patterned tie that he carefully knotted around his neck.

"I've been practising," he said, with some pride. He reached into his bag once more and pulled out a green waistcoat, a pair of black brogues and, last of all, a bowler hat. This he pulled firmly down on his head so that the brim almost touched his two bulging eyes.

"Now, Mister James. I have money! Allow me to buy you a drink by way of welcome!" He reached once more into his black bag and began to draw out, like it says in the carol, a purse of stretching leather skin. There was something about his trusting enthusiasm that thawed even my cold, suspicious nature.

"Better not to announce your money, Mr Monagan," I said.

He looked crestfallen.

"But why? I earned this myself! Working on the paddleships that made their way into Aquarius."

I glanced around. Mr Monagan's tall orange frame was attracting attention. Already three men dressed in black jackets had nonchalantly leant themselves against the wall of the inn behind us, docker's hooks tucked into their belts. They were eyeing Mr Monagan as if he were a piece of cargo himself. Now, Captain James Wedderburn is not so hard hearted as to leave a stranger to be gulled by others. Not when he may have the opportunity to do so himself.

"How about we go somewhere else?" I suggested. "Come on. There is a place I know that's a little more discreet."

ACCORDING TO ITS landlord, the Spotted Dog had originally been located in Barking. During the changes it had drifted west, passing through the Docklands before ending up in the maze of alleys near Belltower End. It had stretched itself as it travelled, its wooden floors ageing and cracking, its booths becoming deeper and darker. An ideal place to sit unnoticed in the shadows.

"What is this?" asked Mr Monagan, holding up his glass.

"Port," I said, pouring myself a glass from the jug.

"It's very good. And such a pretty colour, too! It's red when you hold it to the light, but dark in the shadows. We never had anything like this in Aquarius!"

"What did you drink there?" I asked, vaguely interested.

"Nothing. Why drink when you live in the water all of the time?"

He sipped at the port and smiled.

"Mmmm. It tastes warm."

"So, why have you come here?"

"To be human," said Mr Monagan in serious tones. I gazed at him in the dim light. His fingers were too thick; they seemed inflated by the fluid that lay inside. His skin shone oddly, and his throat constantly moved like a toad's: *galumph galumph galumph*.

"To be human?" I said. "And what's so great about being human?"

He smiled at that.

"Oh, Mr James! You're teasing me! What's so great about being human? Why! To be human is to be able to live! To be human is to be able to be what you wish to be! A bird will just be a bird, it will live in the air! A frog is just a frog, doomed to remain in the damp, eating dragonflies or mice and snakes. But a human, a human can live where he will! In the air, in the swamp, in the fields! A human can be what he wants to be!"

These words were spoken with such enthusiasm, his eyes were shining so, that I felt quite taken aback.

Behind him, three whores shared a jug of port, resting before the evening's work began, and I wondered how they would feel to hear Mr Monagan's description of the joy of being human.

One of them noticed me and held out a copper coin. I passed her a piece of striped candy. Her hand closed around it and she resumed her conversation.

"Sounds wonderful," I said, turning back to Mr Monagan. "Tell me, what do you expect to live on whilst you're here?"

Mr Monagan's smile wavered a moment.

"Mr James, I don't understand what you mean."

"What I mean is, you'll need to eat, you'll need somewhere to sleep. Both cost money here in Dream London. A lot of money."

Mr Monagan smiled again.

"There is enough food in the river for me," he said, happily. "There are fish and crabs and eels, there are bugs and weeds and crustaceans enough for all! And as for sleeping, who needs to pay to sleep?"

"You need a room to sleep in, or they'll call you a vagrant and call the Dream London police to take you away to the cells. You can't pay your bribe, they'll send you to court. You can't pay your fine, they'll put you in the workhouse."

"Oh! But surely that would be a good thing. I *want* to work, Mr Jim. How else can I earn money to become human?"

"You don't earn money in a workhouse, Mister Monagan," I said. "Not for yourself. You work to pay for your board and lodging, and you're always in arrears. Your debt begins to mount the moment you pass the door, and you're in there for the rest of your life. And then the debt will fall upon your children, and their children, and where will it end? The gates of the workhouse are the door to slavery..."

He stared at me, eyes wide in horror.

"But Mr James! That's not fair!"

I laughed at that.

"Whoever said that humans were fair? There are the predators, and there are the herd. You choose where you stand."

He looked as if he were about to burst into tears. He looked so sad that even I felt a little pity for him.

"Mr James," he said, hesitantly, "do you know of a room where I could sleep?"

I pulled the scroll from my pocket. It unrolled itself just where I expected it to...

Go to the docks and meet your greatest friend, the one you will betray...

I looked across at Mr Monagan, an idea forming. What was waiting for me back at Belltower End? I remembered the Daddio's Quantifier from last night, the big man that had held a knife to my back whilst I was caught in the accordion trap. Honey Peppers might be back at Belltower End now, looking for me. She might have brought reinforcements. What if they were watching my flat, right now? It wouldn't be wise for me to return there...

"Do I know of a room where you could sleep, Mr Monagan?" I said, and the cruel businesslike streak of Jim Wedderburn was now ascendant. "Maybe I do. But I wonder if I should rent it to you?"

He looked crestfallen.

"I would be very grateful," he said in a little voice.

"Would you? Would you really?"

I looked down at the scroll again. Captain Wedderburn had betrayed quite a few people in the past. Why should Mr Monagan be any different? After all, I'd only just met him.

Your greatest friend… said the scroll.

I felt guilty, and as so often happens when people think they are about to do wrong, I took it out on the person I was about to do wrong to.

"So what are you, then?" I asked, unable to keep the question in check any longer. "A frog that got lucky?"

Mr Monagan's mouth dropped open, his eyes widened, and I saw the hurt look of horror that came over his face.

"A frog! Oh, Mr James! How could you be so rude?"

He was so utterly without guile that I felt quite chastened. Something about his innocence ducked under the layers of cynicism I had built up over the years and cut straight to my heart.

"I'm sorry," I said. "I didn't mean to be…"

"No matter," he said. "No offence taken." He looked down at the table as he spoke and it was quite clear just how hurt he was.

"Mr Monagan, I'm sorry!" I was surprised myself at just how sorry I felt. There was something about his innocent trust that touched something inside me.

"Listen," I said. "I can let you have somewhere to live. And something better than that, too. Do you want a job?"

"A job? Oh! Mr James!"

Mr Monagan's eyes were shining with wonder.

I thought about the Moston girls who, even now, Honey Peppers should be settling into their new quarters at Belltower End. Second Eddie and the rest of them would be of no use around their precocious sexual charms. Perhaps Mr Monagan would be just the man to handle them.

Or frog.

TIME WAS GETTING on by the time I got back to the Poison Yews. I'd left Mr Monagan in the capable hands of Gentle Annie, who promised to show him my flat and Belltower End. I walked away smiling as I heard Mr Monagan refusing to speak about a possible Mrs Monagan because:

"... well, Gentle Annie, I wouldn't like to tell a lady of your refined dignity about the behaviour of the women back at the pond. I fear it might distress you..."

The night was warm and indigo, the evening spices skewed towards cinnamon. I passed down the High Road, the Egg Market glowing palely against the purple sky. A man walked by me, his four children trailing behind him. Each of them carried a pale blue robin egg in their hand.

"But Daddy, we're hungry," said a little girl.

"I'm sorry, Nellie. That's all we can afford now the rent has gone up..."

I turned into Hayling Road. The blue monkeys were hooting in the lime trees. I walked up the gravel drive of the Poison Yews and hesitated outside. Should I just walk straight in?

I rang the front door bell. It was opened by a stunningly attractive young woman of about sixteen or seventeen. She wore school uniform: grey pleated skirt, white blouse and tie. Her black hair was pinned up, her large brown eyes weighed me up in an instant.

"You're Captain James Wedderburn," she said. She turned around and called back into the house. "Mother! He's returned!"

Alan bustled up, accompanied by the shockingly attractive black man.

"Where have you been?" he demanded. "I was beginning to think we'd have to send out to look for you."

"I had some other business to attend to."

Alan turned to the young woman.

"Anna, go and tell your mother we'll dine in ten minutes. That should give Captain Wedderburn enough time to get ready for dinner." He looked at me. "If that's okay with you?"

"Fine."

Anna cast me a last glance before turning and walking serenely into the depths of the house. I wondered how old she was. No matter, she'd earn a fortune working in Belltower End. Not that I'd let her work there, of course, a girl like her.

With her undoubted education she'd earn ten times as much up in the West End.

"Is everything okay?" asked Alan.

"No problems," I said. The candy striped jacket I wore was getting grubby now, and it certainly wasn't suitable attire for an evening meal. "I'll go and change for dinner."

I headed up the stairs.

Someone had been into my room to tidy up. The bed was made, two bottles of mineral water laid out on the side table, a little pile of books at their side. I picked up the top one and glanced at the title: *1984: An Erotic Story by George Orwell*. I looked at the back. "Big Brother just loves to watch..."

I replaced the book and went on exploring the room.

The window offered one of those impossible views that only Dream London could provide. Grey buildings ran down a valley, their windows red in the evening sun. Scarlet ivy was rising in a red tide, yellow leaves shivering in the breeze. Jewelled birds fluttered to and fro, nesting amongst the foliage. But my eye was constantly drawn to the bottom of the valley, and the tower that stood there.

It had started out as a glass skyscraper, that was obvious, but over the past year it had grown taller and taller. The top had started to bulge and had turned from glass and steel into something else. It looked like a plant budding. I wondered if those were vines or creepers I could see, spilling down from the top of the tower.

I couldn't guess how tall it was now. Hazy waves undulated half way down the tower's length, and I thought they might be birds. I turned from the view to see that a silver shaving kit had been laid out by the wash basin, and I watched as an orange spider pushed its way into the bristles of the shaving brush. I picked up the brush and tapped it on the side of the basin. Six orange eyes emerged from the bristles and looked at me for a moment before withdrawing slowly into their own home. I replaced the brush on the side and made my way over to the large wooden wardrobe.

There were a number of suits hanging up in there, all newly tailored by the look of them. I saw the strands of white cotton where the pockets had been unpicked. Three dull black suits hung there. Two plum jackets hung beside them, their collars and lapels shiny velvet. A number of grey ties hung on a rack on the door, five white shirts were folded on the shelves. And there, at the end of the rack, freshly laundered, hung my military jacket, the golden frogging gleaming against the emerald green of the jacket.

I quickly stripped down to my underpants and tried on a shirt. It was stiff and uncomfortable, but it fitted. Likewise the suit trousers. The shoes were my size, but the leather cut into the edge of my toes. The leather soles were slippery on the woven mat, even more so on the polished floor. This was what I would be wearing tomorrow, I guessed.

I slipped out of the suit and pulled on some more casual clothes, topping them off with my military jacket. I wanted to look the part for dinner.

There was a knock on the door.

"Come in!"

Anna stood there, looking even more stunning in a grey dress.

"Mother said to tell you that dinner was ready."

She turned and walked away. I followed her downstairs to the dining room, watching the sway of her perfectly rounded bottom through her dress.

The table was spread with a large white cloth. I counted the silver cutlery arrangements to see that it was set for five. Alan and Margaret were already there, along with Alan's 'friend'.

"Thank you Anna," said Margaret. She gave me a brittle smile. "We've had drinks already, James. I hope you don't mind, only we were beginning to wonder if you were coming."

The room smelt of sweetness and gravy.

We sat down. Alan sat at the head of the table. I sat to his left, his lover to his right, facing me. Margaret sat on my left, Anna took her place across the table.

A maid dressed in a blue and white striped dress carried a large tureen into the room.

"Egg soup," said Margaret, and then she added, rather proudly, "Well, we do have the best egg market in the city on our doorstep."

The maid began to ladle clear soup into our bowls.

"We've got the best of everything on our doorstep," said Alan. "Except for a cheese shop of course. That's the only thing that Farringdon does better than us. What do you say, Shaqeel?"

Shaqeel didn't say anything. He gave a louche smile and I guessed from the movement of his arm just where his hand was currently wandering beneath the table. Beside him, Anna kept her eyes fixed deliberately on her bowl.

A bowl of soup was placed before me, eggs floating within, both whole and sliced. Large hens' eggs and tiny wrens' eggs. Cautiously, I dipped my spoon inside. To my surprise, it tasted rather good.

"So," said Alan, breaking the awkward silence that settled upon the table. "How was your day at school, Anna?"

"Very good, thank you, Father."

"Anna is doing five A Levels," said her mother, proudly.

"Really?" I said. "What are you doing."

"English Literature, Music, History and Art."

"That's only four," I said.

"Everyone has to do Sex and Sexuality as part of PSHE now," said Anna.

"PSHE?"

"Personal, Social and Health Education. It's all about sex." She sipped at her soup, making perfectly clear the topic was at an end.

"Still," I said. "All those subjects. You must be quite the artist."

"I wanted to do Maths and Physics, but they are no longer suitable for girls. Even the boys study only Accountancy and Economics now, rather than any real science."

"What did you study at school, James?" asked Margaret, obviously unwilling to listen to a familiar complaint any longer.

To my right, Alan and Shaqeel were playing footsy, oblivious to the conversation.

"I left school at sixteen," I said. "Joined the army."

"Did you kill anyone?" asked Anna, looking at me appraisingly over her spoon.

"Anna! I'm sure that's not a polite question! I'm sorry, James. You were saying." She leant a little closer to me, and I smelt her perfume. She smelt strongly of flowers, the sort my girls used to put themselves and their clients in the mood of a night.

"Well, that's it really," I said. "I left school. I went in the army. I left last year."

"Why did you leave?" asked Anna.

"Anna!"

We finished our soup. The maid took the bowls away and replaced them with white plates decorated in a blue willow pattern. I touched the rim of the plate.

"I see that you've noticed our dinner service," said Margaret. "It's from Chinatown, you know." I felt her hand stroke the outside of my thigh.

"Chinatown," I said. "How nice." I looked directly at Anna.

"I left the army because I slept with the Captain's daughter. He wasn't happy."

Margaret choked on her wine.

"I don't think you should be listening to this, Anna. I think James should change the subject."

"I'm fine, Mother," said Anna. "We hear far worse in PSHE. And English Literature."

"Even so…"

Anna's face remained impassive.

"Besides which, I don't think the Captain is telling the full story…"

She held my gaze. Her eyes were dark, her dark brown hair fell in waves about her face. She truly was beautiful. And very self-composed.

"You're right, of course," I said, easily.

The hand touched my thigh again. To my right, Alan was being touched up by Shaqeel. To my left, Margaret was offering the same service to me. I pushed her hand away.

The maid cleared our places and then re-entered the room carrying a tray. She placed a plate before me. It bore a green egg the colour of a spearmint imperial and the size of my hand, sitting in a pool of brown gravy.

"Cassowary eggs," said Margaret. "When you live this close to the Egg Market, it's silly not to make use of it."

"If only we had a decent cheese shop," said Alan.

"You crack the egg like this," said Margaret, demonstrating. "We've flummoxed it. It's the new cooking process. Have you heard of it? You need boiling water and oodles of salt."

"Which is bigger?" asked Anna. "Lashings or oodles?"

"There are three oodles to the lashing," I said, and I winked at her. She looked away, unimpressed.

I cracked my egg and took a forkful of the grey meat inside. It was spicy, a little like a lamb dhansak.

"So this is a flummoxed egg, is it? Not bad."

"Are you ready for tomorrow?" asked Margaret.

"Oh yes," said Alan. "We'll need to be up at six. I'll get Anna to wake you."

"What am I supposed to be doing?" I said. "I know I'm going to the City, I know that I'm to go to the Writing Floor of Angel Tower. What do I do when I'm in there?"

"Shhh!" said Alan. "The walls have ears, you know."

"But..."

"Shhh..."

We ate our flummoxed eggs. The maid brought us the next course: caviar, and then the next: chocolate mousse.

"Made with egg yolks," said Margaret.

"When you live this close to the Egg Market you may as well make use of it," I replied.

"If only we had a cheese shop," said Anna, dryly.

"Anna! Manners!" said Margaret.

Alan and Shaqeel whispered to each other. Margaret leant a little closer to me so that her breast pressed against my arm.

"Some more wine, Captain?"

"No thank you," I said. "I've got work in the morning."

Margaret filled her own glass to the top. She was beginning to sway a little, I noticed. Alan and Shaqeel were lost in their own private little world, Anna gazed at me without interest, and Margaret leant closer and closer. One of her breasts pushed into my arm.

"I like your jacket, Captain," she said. "It makes you look so dashing."

"It's not real," I said. "I bought this for show. These colours are a Dream London invention."

"Still, it suits you."

The final dish was brought through.

"Lemon sorbet," said Margaret, touching my knee. "Cleanses the palate. Do you like it?"

"Needs more egg," I said.

Her face froze, just for a moment, as she wondered if I was being rude. And then she laughed.

THE MEAL ENDED and Anna said goodnight, heading upstairs to her homework, or so she said. Alan retired to his study with Shaqeel.

"Would you like a brandy, Captain Wedderburn?" A hand laid itself on the top of my thigh. Well, I say top of my thigh, but I'm being polite. To be more accurate, Margaret clasped my balls.

"No thank you, Margaret. I thought I might take a walk before bed. I need the air."

"When you come back, I'll probably still be up. Look for me in the drawing room."

I left the house and spent half an hour or so walking the streets. I couldn't quite relax, though. All the time I wondered if Honey Peppers was out there somewhere looking for me.

To the east, rising up into the purple night, I saw the bulging spires of the City. The place I was going tomorrow. The blue monkeys were whooping loudly. I heard the terrified yowling of cats and I touched my pistol for reassurance. Someday the monkeys would turn their attention from the cats to bigger amusements. When they did, I would be ready for them. I walked through the stillness of the evening, listening to the sounds of the city.

Eventually, I returned to the Poison Yews and slipped upstairs to my room.

I undressed and pulled on the blue and white cotton nightgown that someone had folded neatly on my pillow, then got into bed and picked up the first book from the pile by my side. It was a book of poetry. I turned to the first page.

The Foundation, by T.S.Eliot

April is the happiest month, laughing
Lilacs in the fresh wind, bobbing
Memory and Desire, awakening
Feeding roots with spring rain...

I didn't recognise the poem, but that's no surprise, as I don't read poetry. It was enjoyable though, if rather long. Flicking through the pages I noted the poem was made up of several sections.

I read the first section, *The Welcoming of Children*, wondering at the closing lines where people walked the streets of Dream London.

My eyes became heavy, and from somewhere in the house I heard the sound of someone playing scales on a trumpet.

I laid down the book, turned off the light, and drifted to sleep to the silver sound of arpeggio rain.

YELLOW

THE NUMBERS FLOOR

I WAS WOKEN by the sound of a tap on the door. The maid entered the room carrying a steaming jug of water which she placed by the basin. She nodded at me and left the room. The window was open and I could smell the heavy scent of flowers awakening. Today was going to be hot.

As I was shaving, Anna knocked on my door. I turned to see her looking like jail bait in a grey school uniform.

"I see you're awake," she said.

"Was that you I heard playing the trumpet last night?"

"The cornet. Your breakfast is ready."

There was no sign of Margaret; I guessed she was in bed with a hangover. Anna served us bacon and eggs and mushrooms from the dishes on the sideboard. We ate in silence. I left the house with Alan shortly before seven.

The whores and the costermongers of the night before had faded from the streets, and I found myself part of a growing river of businessmen dressed in identical dark suits and starched white shirts, all heading towards the railway station. The blue monkeys that nested on the window ledges looked down at us, laughing, and I found myself laughing along with them at the absurdity of it all.

"What's so funny?" asked Alan.

"How long before we're all wearing bowler hats?" I asked.

The railway station was set above street level. A green electric train glided towards it between the red tiled roofs, a crocodile swimming between clay river banks.

"Oh, good," said Alan. "I hate the steam trains. They get your clothes so dirty."

We ran up the steps to the station. A ticket inspector waited at the top, dressed in a black wool uniform and peaked cap bearing a polished brass badge with the letters DLR entwined upon it. I showed him the little rectangle of cardboard that Alan had given me that morning. A season ticket.

We boarded the train.

"I usually read the paper on the way in," said Alan, shaking out a pink copy of *The Financial Times* he had picked up outside the station.

"Okay," I said. I looked at the headlines: commercial rents were up by forty-five per cent. Bored, I gazed out of the window, down at the streets below.

London had always been a patchwork, Dream London was even more so.

The train ran on stilts above the streets, and looking down I could see how the disparate elements of the city were stitched together: slums backing onto mansions, little garden squares pushing against crumbling concrete walls. The track split into two and we rolled past factories, squeezed into the V between the railway lines, bright graffiti on their ridged roofs. Then there came a line of narrow gardens, conservatories hard against the factory walls, their light dimmed to nothing by the overgrown greenery, and then more tall factory walls surrounding little courtyards and I realised I was looking down into a workhouse. I saw grey-suited workers carrying boxes across a monotone courtyard. A line of windows, children bent down at machines...

... then with another flick we passed a line of dappled plane trees and we slowed to halt at a station. Lines of black and white passengers waited there. The woman in the purple dress stood out like a plum on a chessboard. Her eyes locked with mine, so it was no surprise when, moments later, she sat down opposite me. She was an attractive woman. A little older than my preferred type in that she was about my age and running to plump, but she had such a pretty face.

"There you are, Captain Wedderburn!" she said. "You've no idea how much trouble I've had tracking you down."

I noticed Alan lowering his newspaper, looking over the top of it at me.

"I'm sorry," I began, "I don't think I've..."

"Of course we've never met, Captain. Or should I call you James? Only I bought your name from a shop. Look, I have it here..."

She opened her purse and pulled out a sheet of parchment. She showed it to me. It took me a moment to make out the words there, written as they were in cursive script.

Your true love is... Captain James Wedderburn.

I read it carefully.

"I thought these things came as a list," I said.

"I paid for the premium service. My name is Miss Elizabeth Baines, and I am your soulmate."

She smiled at me then, a smile of such longing and happiness that, for a moment, I almost felt sorry for her. Almost.

"I'm sorry, Miss Baines," I said. "I think you wasted your money. Someone has conned you. Something like this happened to my old girlfriend. She bought a list too…"

The look that flickered across Miss Baines' face would have melted the heart of one of those cruel statues that have grown in Piccadilly, but she recovered quickly enough.

"They said you would say something like that," she said, in a businesslike way. "They said that it was typical of a man to deny his true feelings where matters of the heart are concerned, and that my best course of action would be to just keep plugging away. Well, Captain Wedderburn, can I assure you of the sincerity of my affections, and that I…"

"How can your affection be sincere?" I interrupted. "We've only just met!"

"… and that I," repeated Miss Baines in a firm voice, "will not be swayed from true love's path."

I wasn't sure what to say to this. Fortunately, Alan folded his paper away and lent a hand. He had turned grey with worry, and it was only now that I realised that Miss Baines had blown my cover.

"Miss Baines. You must be aware that *my nephew* is on his way to work. Could I suggest that a meeting later on may be more appropriate? How about the Tiger Tea House at the corner of Leicester Square, say at five o'clock?"

Miss Baines beamed.

"That would be most appropriate!"

The train was slowing now, coming in to another station.

"And here's my stop already," said Miss Baines, getting to her feet.

Alan watched her go.

"You're not seriously suggesting I meet her again, are you?" I said.

"Of course not," he hissed. "I just wanted her out of here!" He flapped up the pages of his paper and retreated back behind it.

"But..."

He wasn't listening. I thought about Miss Elizabeth Baines. Did I feel a twinge of conscience at that moment? Captain Wedderburn had known lots of women in his time, and rarely given them a second thought. Why should my sentimental thoughts of the plum-coloured women, tearful at being stood up, be anything but evidence of Dream London having its effect on me?

The train was off again, wheezing and sparking and grinding along the warped track. Given the way the railways coiled about the city at night it was a wonder we managed to stay on the lines. I looked out at the passing scenery once more. The train was winding through widely spaced trees, their trunks casting long dark shadows through the golden morning. I thought of the parkland spreading out at the centre of Dream London and all those roads that emerged from the point in the centre and I wondered what was going on there. An eager feeling awoke within me: that was what I was going to find out. That's why I was riding the train to the City.

The train turned a corner and, all of sudden, there were the towers of the Square Mile. Shafts of ebony thrust from the earth towards the heavens, draped with scarlet vine and flocked by birds. They loomed over the city, they loomed over the train, so tall they seemed to lean, falling towards us. A feeling of vertigo spun within me just at the sight of them, and I had another sense of just how futile my task was. Something had bought those towers, there in the Square Mile. The former banks and financial houses had been purchased and through that process something had gained a foothold in London. Gradually its influence had spread, and, as it did so, its hold over the city.

I looked at the towers. The train was running alongside the Thames now, grown to many times its former width and flowing golden in the morning sunshine. The towers were spaced further apart than the skyscrapers of the old city, and they were much, much taller. The base of each tower betrayed the structure's original construction. I saw brick and glass and steel and stone. But as the gaze travelled up the extent of the building the towers started to swell and deform. No two towers were alike. Some of them shone in brilliant colours, some of them trailed with creepers. Though it was difficult to tell at this distance, one of them seemed to be covered in fur. The train jerked to the left and abruptly we entered a tunnel.

All around me passengers were climbing to their feet, folding their newspapers, getting ready to exit.

"This is it," said Alan.

I took a deep breath. It was time.

* * *

WE LEFT THE station and walked down the street towards Angel Tower.

A man in a suit just like mine sat propped against the wall, holding out his hands.

"Please?" he begged. "I lost my job. I can't pay my rent. Don't let them send me to the workhouse..."

Alan ignored him. I did the same. So did all the other men walking past.

"Just along here," said Alan.

I could see the base of our tower up ahead. It looked as if it was made from shiny black marble the colour of a hearse. It made me think of a mausoleum.

"Don't look up," said Alan.

"Why not?"

"Just don't."

I kept my eyes on the ground and followed him along the street. A set of bronze revolving doors rotated at the base of Angel Tower, too small and out of proportion for the vast bulk of the building. They spun around, scooping up the dark stream of suited figures in regular gulps. I felt the gentle pressure of Alan's hand on my back, pushing me inside. Terrified, I was spun into the tower...

... and stepped out into a wide atrium. There was a reverent silence in here, broken only by the gentle pad of footsteps on the dark marble floor. A high marble counter stood to my right, staffed by three older men in dark suits. They looked close to death, with that closeness not being measured from the living side. Tall and grey with cold eyes, they appeared to have accepted zombiehood as part of the terms and conditions of their employment.

Alan took my arm and swept me past them, heading to the lifts at the back of the building: three wide doors set in brass frames, three throats. An arrow was set over each door, turning to point at the floor numbers. So many numbers that the arrow had a magnifying glass set in the end so that the tiny digits it identified could be read. I peered carefully, and saw the digits went up to twelve hundred. Twelve hundred and four, to be precise.

"I can't believe it's so tall!" I said.

"It grows at least a floor every day," said Alan morosely, and at that moment I forgot Alan's warning and made a huge mistake, one I instantly regretted. I looked up.

The ceiling was high above me, five floors up, and in the ceiling there was a hole. And the hole seemed to rise up and up, and I found my eye drawn into its depths, trying to see what was at the end of the hole. And I felt something looking back at me...

"... James! Are you okay?"

Alan slapped me on the cheek once more. I placed my hand there, feeling the sting.

"What happened?" I said. I felt sick to the stomach, as if I had been violated in some way. "What happened?" I repeated.

"I told you not to look up," said Alan. "Now come on."

He took me by the elbow and led me into one of the waiting lifts. I whimpered as the doors slid shut, and then I gasped as the acceleration pushed me down into the floor.

"You never quite get used to it," said Alan morosely.

I looked up at the brass needle of the indicator, ticking off the floors. It passed the 500 mark and I heard the clang of a bell. We began to slow down.

The doors opened and we stepped out, somewhat shakily, onto the 829th floor.

I walked unsteadily into a room that looked as if it had come out of a Dickens novel: a room completely out of place in a skyscraper. The space was subdivided by wooden panels and furnished by wooden desks. Men sat or stood at the desks, sheets of paper in front of them.

A young man hurried up to us, his hair plastered to his head in proper clerkly fashion.

"Good morning Mr. Sinfield," he said.

"This is my nephew, James," said Alan. "Would you be so kind as to show him to his desk?"

"Of course, Mr Sinfield."

Alan turned to me.

"My office is on the next floor. Perhaps you would like to join me for lunch?"

"Of course," I said.

"Collins, when the time comes, would you be so kind as to show my nephew the way to the Executive Dining Room?"

"Of course, Mr Sinfield."

The clerk waited for Alan to leave before fixing me with a look that conveyed exactly what he thought of me and my nepotistic advancement.

"I..." I began, but he didn't give me chance to speak.

"This way," he said, and immediately plunged into the maze of desks and partitions without waiting to see if I was following. I jogged after him, hot and uncomfortable in my thick woollen suit. Collins led me past lines of similarly suited men, all sat at their desks adding up rows of figures by hand.

"What are they doing?" I asked. A man looked up at me and held a finger to his lips.

"Shhh!"

Collins led me deeper and deeper into gloom, further from the large windows in the far wall. We traversed a labyrinth of desks and metal filing cabinets slowly turning to wood. Bentwood hat stands, vacuum tubes that led up the ceiling. All around me there was the suck and pop of cylinders vanishing into the network. The gloom deepened, the desks become more crowded, the stacks of paper taller. Finally, we came to a tall desk crammed into a corner, half drowned in paper. A dull yellow electric bulb hung overhead: it seemed to cast more shadows than light. There was a stack of paper already piled upon the desk, a fountain pen at the side. The office had yet to return to paper and quills.

"Don't I get a chair?" I asked.

The clerk gave a knowing smile.

"Not as a junior. Status is very important here in Angel Tower. *If* you work hard and show due merit, you *may* find yourself promoted to a position where your desk has a chair. Continue to show due diligence and you *might* find that you are awarded a desk closer to the window."

"Oh."

He reached into his pocket and pulled out a silver pencil. He passed it to me with an unctuous smile, as if doing me a great favour.

"Of course, those people with an uncle working upstairs may find themselves progressing faster than others. Let's hope they remember the people who made their life easier when they started."

So that was the game. Life in Angel Tower was the same as life on the street. You eyed up those around you, deciding whether they were worth brown-nosing or shitting upon. Collins seemed to be playing it both ways with me. Well, a partial ally was better than none.

"I can see you're the man to know, Collins," I said.

"As office junior, you may call me *sir*," said Collins. "You'll find everyone else here has the same name. However, if you want to find me in the office you can ask for Collins. And if you want to buy me a port and lemon in the French Horn you may call me Benny. Now, as to your work." At this he pointed to the desk. "You'll be rationalising the numbers."

"Numbers?" I said. "I thought I was supposed to be on the Writing Floor?"

The clerk snorted.

"Don't we all? Who wouldn't want to be on the 839th floor with Miss Merchant as their secretary polishing the balls of their executive toy? However, before you dash up to the 839th, perhaps you could help us out down here on eight two nine? Do a little rationalisation?"

"Of course," I said. "Of course..."

Collins placed a finger on a sheet of paper. Faint lines had been ruled across the sheet, and a random selection of numbers were written in columns.

17,666	23,965	17	1.34
8	14/3	π	15%
9	9	9	1.3×10^{24}
4	5	6,013	6
5	3		

"Let's start with an easy one. See the eight? That factorises to four times two, see?"

He used the fountain pen to write, in blue ink, on the paper next to the eight. Now it read

$8 = 4 \times 2$

"See? Now, the 17,666 is obviously an even number, so that will factorise, so we have..." He scribbled next to the number:

$17,666 = 8833 \times 2$

"Does 8833 divide further?" I asked.

"No point making work for yourself," said the clerk. "You've rationalised the number that you were given. You didn't carry on with the one before, did you? Leave that to someone else. We want to keep ourselves in work, after all. Now, this is the special one... Look at the seventeen."

"It doesn't divide," I said.

He looked at me, and his fat face wore an expression of something like sympathy.

"Think about it," he prompted.

I frowned, and then the answer appeared in my head.

"Of course," I said. "Seventeen is two times green."

I smiled, took the pen from him, and wrote down the answer

$17 = \vartheta \times 2$

I beamed, delighted that I had worked it out. And then I felt a sinking feeling.

"I'm sorry," said the clerk. "It's part of you now."

"But what are we doing?"

"There are no prime numbers in Dream London," said the clerk. "Or there won't be in the future."

I wasn't listening properly. I was too busy counting up to ten in my head.

One, two, three, four, five, six, seven, eight, green, nine, ten.

"But that doesn't make sense," I said to the clerk.

"And this place does?" he said. He patted me on the hand. "Better get on with your work."

He walked off into the labyrinth, leaving me alone with the stack of paper.

I looked at the paper again. All those numbers.

4 was 2x2. That was easy enough. But what about 7? Half seven was 3½, but that wasn't right, it was yellow, because 7 was yellow times 2.

I wrote that down.

$7 = \pi \times 2$

I stared at the black marks on the cream paper. I knew that Dream London was changing the shape of the buildings, and I knew that the books were changing, I was used to that. I was used to the way that Dream London rewrote the words on the page. It even rewrote people's behaviour. I had accepted that. People could be manipulated. Who knew that better than Captain Jim Wedderburn and his lovely girls?

But I didn't realise that Dream London was changing the shape of the numbers as well. That gripped deep inside. It felt so wrong. This all felt *more* wrong.

I didn't want to look at the page again. I didn't want to see the numbers, to feel more of my head being rewritten in the language of Dream London, but I couldn't help it. My eyes were drawn back to the sheet.

3 was red times two. I knew it. I had always known it...

I felt so wrong, as if I were being held upside down by my heels and swung over the abyss, but still I went on. 3.1415... how could such a number be? It couldn't, that was the point. It was something else. Not a colour, but...

I don't know what happened to me that morning. The next thing I remember is Collins shaking my elbow.

"Come on," he said, "It's time for your lunch."

I gazed at him, trying to focus.

"Collins," I said. "Has it been that long? I've been lost in…"

"It takes people like that the first time," he said. "Don't worry. You'll soon get used to it." His fat face showed something almost like sympathy.

"I feel like I've been away somewhere. Travelling for years…"

"Come on. Go and get some food inside you, you'll soon feel better."

I blinked and looked at the sheets of paper. A huge stack of sheets, all covered in my handwriting. Had I done that? I didn't remember any of it.

"But…"

"Come on. You only have three-quarters of an hour."

I blinked at him and felt my eyes fill with tears.

"Don't make me come back," I said. "Don't make me do that again."

He smiled, rather sadly.

"You'll feel better after a glass of port. Come on."

He took me by the elbow and led me from the room, through the labyrinth off towards the lift.

"I don't want to come back," I said.

"Shhh…"

I began to count out loud to ten.

"*One, red, two, blue, a feeling of setting out on a journey, three, a feeling of fulfilment, yellow, four, five, orange, six, cyan, seven, eight, green, nine, purple, ten.*"

"Best not to think about it," said Collins. "Come on. Here's the stairs…"

FOUR

LOVELY CARLOTTA

AT THE END of a narrow corridor lined with stacks of paper, a set of plush red carpeted stairs led upwards. I climbed them in a daze, climbing from the smell of paper, dust and dryness into a savoury scented fairyland. Gold rococo furniture, fabulously patterned wallpaper, dark mirrors barely reflecting the light. And through it all, the smells. The dark smells of roast meat, the golden smells of crisp crackling, the strawberry scent of desert, the rich smell of wine and port and brandy and cigar smoke.

Alan was waiting for me at the entrance. He appeared to have just arrived himself.

"Welcome to the Executive Dining Room," he said. "Don't expect to lunch up here everyday."

"I..." I began. Coming from the dry, dusty atmosphere of the mind downstairs to this sensual barrage was all too much. Another voice spoke up, and it seemed to be the voice of opulence itself.

"Alan, you old dog," it said. "And who's this?"

I turned to face the fattest man I had ever seen. His body was so wide it filled the red and gold corridor, his legs and head tiny in comparison. His face was jowly and shiny with sweat.

"This is my nephew, James. James, meet Oscar Sjöholm."

He reached out a hand to shake mine, somewhere around the orbit of his enormous belly, and I walked around to shake it.

"Don't look at me like that, young man," laughed Oscar. "Dream London amplifies what's already there! I always liked to eat. Now I can do so to a more glorious excess than I ever dreamed possible. Isn't that wonderful?"

I couldn't think what to say in reply, my mind too full of new numbers.

He punched my shoulder in a friendly way.

"What's your vice then, me young buck? You're like your uncle here, I'll bet. A ladies man," at that Oscar cast a sly glance at Alan, "... or so he tells us! What did you get up to last night, you old fox? Rutting like a good one! No woman is ever quite safe from you, I should think!"

Alan laughed a little too heartily.

"Hey, don't you go leading my nephew astray..."

"There'll be no embarrassing him if he's like his uncle, I'll be bound." He elbowed me hard in the ribs. It says something about my state that I didn't elbow him hard in the side in return. Not that he would have noticed. He was rubbing his hands together now in salacious delight. "Have you seen? Carlotta is serving today! You're going to have trouble keeping your hands to yourself!" He punched Alan on the shoulder, laughing again.

I looked up and saw into the dining room proper, and I felt my mouth fall open. The room was obscene.

First there were the waitresses. Fat women, thin women, black women, white women, oriental women, all with their stocking tops showing, the suspenders running from under tiny frilled skirts. Breasts spilled from tight basques and bustieres in glorious plenty, the silky flourishing of their hair was tied back in pony tails, or put up in beehives, or simply left to hang down over their smooth shoulders. Their lips and nails were painted in sinful red or crimson or magenta. They bore trays of succulent meat, plump fruits, sticky sauces; carrying them to the tables where the expensively clothed executives sat.

For the most part the men appeared not to notice the women, accepting food with a courteous nod or wave of a hand whilst they proceeded with their conversations, but I caught the occasional sidelong glance into a deep cleavage that hovered by a sweaty red face as soup was ladled into a bowl, or an appreciative stare at the plump roundness of the derrière opposite as it squeezed past. The only man serving in the room was the wine waiter, a desiccated old gentleman in a dinner jacket who walked amongst the fruitful plenty, pointing out suggestions from the heavily bound wine list or uncorking bottles and pouring out a little to taste.

A Spanish looking woman came towards us, her dark hair pulled back severely, her hips swaying as she walked.

"Come this way, Mr Sinfield!"

As she turned round Alan reached out and pinched her backside, smiling at Oscar as he did so.

"You old dog!" laughed Oscar, elbowing him in the side. He winked at me. "See! You'll have to watch your uncle!"

"Will you join my nephew and me?" asked Alan, but Oscar picked up on his tone.

"No. I can see you two have plenty to talk about! Besides which, the only dumplings I'm interested in are the ones served up in the stew! I shouldn't want to cramp your style, Alan old man."

He raised a hand in acknowledgement to the slender Asian lady who bade him follow, and he walked off in her wake, travelling through the tables like a moon threading an asteroid belt. Diners placed their hands on glasses of wine and water to prevent them being spilled as he jostled past.

Carlotta led us to a table, Alan making a show of gazing at her backside.

"Gentlemen..." she said, indicating that we should sit down.

Alan did so and Carlotta swept a linen napkin in the air, drawing it around his neck and tying it in place with a large knot.

"Thank you, Carlotta."

Now it was my turn. She swayed around the table on her high heels, leant down to pick up my napkin as I pulled my chair in. One of her breasts pressed against my cheek, and I was about to apologise when I realised that this was all part of the service.

Carlotta said nothing, simply swooped the napkin around my neck.

"Now gentlemen, may I recommend the Bearded Oysters followed by Sausage and Mash?"

Alan rubbed his hands together with delight.

"Sounds great to me, Carlotta!"

"I'll have the same," I said.

"Excellent choice, gentlemen!" beamed Carlotta, taking our menus.

Alan waited until she was out of earshot before leaning forward.

"So then, James! How was your morning?"

"I don't know," I said, staring at the table, looking at the cutlery laid out before me. Were there two forks, or *blue* forks or what? "I can't think properly, Alan. They're changing my mind..." Alan reached out and patted my hand.

"You'll soon get used to it!" he said. He made a show of turning to look at a passing waitress. She must have weighed eighteen stone at least, her wide backside like two pillows.

"I'm not sure I will," I said. "I don't think I can do it again, Alan..."

"Of course you can!"

"And I shouldn't be there. I need to be upstairs! I should be on the Writing Floor. That's what I was told..."

"Oh ho! Ambitious, eh? That's what I like to hear! Well, you stick it out for five or six years, and who knows what might happen to a young man with fire in his belly! Eh?"

"Five years? I didn't sign up for five years. I was supposed to be there today! That's what you all told me..."

The wine waiter approached our table.

"Wine, sir? The Pomegranate Burgundy is particularly fine."

Alan looked at me.

"What do you say to the Pomegranate?" he asked. "Reeves knows his stuff!"

I shook my head. I didn't care. Alan rubbed his hands together.

"Then Pomegranate Burgundy it is!"

"Excellent choice, sir," said Reeves. "I can see that your good taste has not deserted you."

He clicked his fingers, and a young oriental woman approached carrying a black bottle with a chequered label. With much ceremony, Reeves uncorked the bottle and poured a little into Alan's glass.

"Mmm, excellent!" said Alan, tasting it.

Reeves filled both our glasses and went to resume his place in the corner of the room. Looking around the room I saw each table had the same black bottle with chequered label as we had.

I shook my head, trying to concentrate.

"Alan, listen to me! I can't stay working on the numbers for five years! One more day like this and I'll be no use to you at all. Dream London will have sucked in my mind and made me into something else. You want Captain Wedderburn in here, not some clerk. I need to be hunting for the contracts. I need to be up on the 839th floor. That's where they are. That's what Bill said, anyway."

"Oh, listen to you," said Alan. "Ambition is a wonderful thing. Look at that!"

He nodded towards a black waitress, bending to retrieve a fork that had fallen from the table.

"Alan, listen to yourself! You're gay! Why are you pretending?"

"I'm not pretending," said Alan, haughtily.

"You're trying too hard," I said. "No one else here is acting as hard as you at ogling the women."

I looked around the room.

"Not that anyone else here is acting normally, either. You're like a bunch of kids, all being fussed over."

Alan smiled at that.

"I don't know," he said. "Up here in the Executive Dining Room, we expect things to be a little better. We're used to this sort of service."

"No," I said. "It's not just that. This tower is affecting you. It's affecting us all! I'm not usually this unsure of myself..."

"First day nerves, that's all," replied Alan, complacently.

The first course arrived. A silver platter filled with crushed ice. On top there lay something that looked like whole oysters with skin-covered shells, fleshy purses that glistened obscenely.

"Excellent!" said Alan, reaching out and wiggling his fingers above the dish, deciding which one to choose.

"I'll bring the accompaniments directly, sir," said Carlotta.

"Oooh," said Alan, disappointedly, and he sat on his hands. "They look so good!"

"Listen, Alan, I need to get upstairs. Is there a back staircase or something?"

"Come on, James. It took me all my clout just to get you a job on the Numbers Floor. You ask too much of your old uncle, you know."

"You're not my uncle!" I hissed. "For fuck's sake! This tower is playing with your mind!"

Carlotta reappeared with a silver tray. She placed it on the table before us.

"Horseradish, Lemon, Chilli, Salt Water and Okinawa Sauce."

"Thank you, Carlotta," said Alan, reaching out to snatch an oyster.

"Manners!" said Carlotta, slapping his hand. "Let your guest go first."

"I'm sorry."

Carlotta nodded in approval.

"Good. Now, if you eat them all up properly, I might bring you something special before your main course."

She turned and walked off, rolling her backside, dusky flesh showing between her stocking tops and knickers. I watched as she took the napkin from the lap of one of the diners and used it to wipe his mouth as she passed.

"Come on," said Alan. "Eat up!"

Hesitantly, I reached out and took the fleshy purse. It felt cold and slippery, not at all pleasant. I lifted it to my mouth.

"Not like that!" said Alan. "Watch me!"

He took one of the oysters in his hand and turned it so the slit faced upwards. He placed a finger from his other hand at one end of the slit and began to rub it, ever so gently.

"See?" he said. "You have to have the touch!"

Slowly, the lips of the oyster began to part, glistening with moisture. Alan rubbed harder and harder, the lips parting all the time, and then, in one fluid movement, he raised the oyster to his lips and sucked down the contents.

"Aaaah!" he said, smacking his lips, his chin glistening. "Now, it's your turn."

Fuddled as I was, I still couldn't quite believe what I was seeing.

"You can't be serious!" I said.

"Mmmph?" said Alan, already working on his second oyster.

I copied his action, and saw the lips of my own oyster parting. Against my better judgement, I sucked down the contents. It tasted exactly as I expected it would.

"This is obscene!" I said.

"Shhh!" said Alan, and he pointed a finger up at the ceiling. There was a hole up there, just as there had been on the ground floor. I quickly looked away, not wanting to lose myself again.

A nearby waitress came up, a smile playing across her lips.

"Come on; eat up your oysters like a good young man."

I picked up another oyster as Alan placed his first on the crushed ice. The fleshy purse was quite drained.

"Alan! Concentrate! We have a job to do!"

Alan just smiled and sucked down more oysters.

One, red, two, blue, journey, three... No! I shook my head. That wasn't how you counted!

"Alan!" I said, "How many oysters have I eaten?"

"Oh, don't worry about that, old boy. The effect doesn't last much outside the building. Come on! Get them eaten. You don't want people thinking you're gay, do you?"

THE FIRST COURSE was quickly finished, and Carlotta cleared the dishes. The dining room was just as full as when we had entered, with new diners arriving at the same rate as the tables emptied.

"Have you noticed?" I said. "There was a table waiting for us as we arrived. Every time someone leaves, someone else comes. They have you completely synchronised. You're all dancing to their tune."

"Mmm?" said Alan. His attention was fixed on an approaching mound of sausage and mash. Nothing obscene this time, just a huge mound of white potato with sausages inserted into it at random angles, like something from an old children's comic.

Alan smiled and picked up his knife and fork. He suddenly remembered something.

"Oh, Carlotta! You said I would get something nice if I ate all my oysters!"

She smiled. "So I did," she said. She produced two little gift-wrapped parcels for us.

"Tie pins," she said. "Set with diamonds and engraved with the Angel Tower crest. An elegant and stylish reminder of your visit here today."

Alan was beaming with delight.

"Alan! Speak to me!"

Alan wasn't really listening, he was too busy unwrapping his gift.

"What is it, James?"

"I can't do this, Alan! You're not taking this seriously!"

Alan was examining his tie pin.

"Isn't this wonderful?" he said. "So classy!" He glanced across the table at me. "Come on, eat your dinner."

I ate my sausages and mash. They tasted surprisingly good, though with that vaguely spicy edge that everything assumed in Dream London. I found myself wishing for something plain and ordinary – a hamburger and fries. Something processed and greasy and salty, but entirely untouched by the changes.

As I ate the thought of the numbers faded a little in my mind.

"You're looking better," said Alan, rubbing a last piece of sausage in the rich ruby gravy.

"You're not."

"Ready to go back this afternoon?"

"It'll do no good," I said. "I need to be upstairs."

"Shhh. Eat your desert."

Carlotta had the dishes ready. Chocolate blancmange, so runny it slopped around in the bowl.

"That doesn't look so nice," I said.

"Watch me," said Alan, and he ran his finger around the top of the bowl. Gradually, the chocolate mass hardened and rose into a mound. It even had a nipple.

"Lovely!" he said.

Carlotta waited by our table as we finished our dessert.

"All of your dinner eaten," she said. "Well done, gentlemen."

"Thank you, Carlotta," said Alan, blushing.

Carlotta signalled to one of the other waitresses, who hurried over carrying a tray loaded with little treats.

Carlotta selected two velvet grey jewellery boxes.

"And now," she said, kneeling down on the floor between us, "for doing so well and finishing your meals, some gifts, before coffee arrives."

She opened one of the boxes and held it out.

"Diamond cufflinks," she said. One blood red nail traced the edge of the jewellery. "Note the arrangement of jewels down the side," she said. "You will both observe the quality of the craftmanship."

"Oh yes," said Alan, knowledgeably.

"Only 550 made," said Carlotta. "A limited edition, to be restricted only to the most discerning of gentlemen. These cufflinks indicate taste and refinement. But subtly. They don't shout it."

"Indeed not," said Alan, taking the box from her.

Carlotta handed the other to me.

"Thank you," I said. "Could I..."

"And that's not all, gentlemen," continued Carlotta. "We have this hand painted, silk-washed and watermarked tie, decorated with a pattern inspired by the music of Francis Poulenc and the dot paintings of Australian Aboriginals. Scented with sandalwood and gingko it affords the wearer a measure of refined calm."

"Oh, that's lovely..."

"And of course, three tailored shirts from Messers Portolboy and Fugues. As you will no doubt be aware, Portolboy and Fugues shirts are triple stitched and double panelled. Their buttons are carved from tortoiseshell, the back panels are topographically shaped and the collars and cuffs are reinforced with thin bark strips of Amazon mahogany."

The shirts were handed across, neatly tied with a ribbon. The ties were placed on top, followed by the cufflinks.

"And now," said Carlotta. "Coffee. I shall fetch the coffee menu directly. In the meantime, would you like to scan the mint and biscuit card in order to choose accompaniments?"

Alan rubbed his hands together.

"Lovely!" he said.

FIVE

THE LAUGHING DOG

WALKING BACK TO my desk that afternoon felt like slipping into delirium. The world reshaped itself in my mind so that a line of desks became green and a pair of chairs were yellow. I began to see other numbers between the colours, too, somewhere between red and blue. And there was something else, dripping down from the ceiling. Words from somewhere else, expressions that were warping out of true: *the alkali test, the rough with the sheer, a license to print music.* If there had ever been any doubt, I now knew for certain that the source of the changes was located in this tower.

But what could I do about it? Nothing whilst I was sat at my desk, correcting the figures. I had to stop, put down my pen and go and take a look around. I would do it right away, once I'd finished the next sheet, but the figures got in my mind once more and the next thing I knew it was 5:30 and it was time to go home...

I RODE THE lift down to the ground floor, feeling as if I was returning to earth in more than one sense. Numbers floated around in my head like butterflies.

"Ah, Mr Sinfield! Your uncle asked me to let you know that he will be working late tonight. He hopes to see you at dinner later on, back at the Poison Yews." The words were spoken by a beribbonned commissionaire in a scarlet peaked cap. He leant closer and elbowed me in the side.

"He also suggested that a young man earning his first wages would probably wish to celebrate." He winked conspiratorially. "A glass of beer, perhaps in the company of a young woman?"

I nodded, understanding. Bill. I was being reminded to visit Bill.

I left Angel Tower and found myself out under a yellow and pink sky once more. It felt so good to see the daylight. I followed the stream of dark men flowing back down the street towards the station, noting the men in suits who sat begging by the side of the road. There seemed to be more than there had been this morning.

I made it to the railway station and climbed to the platform. The silver rails were silent, and my eye was drawn to the posters and adverts by my side. Each bore the same title in a sans serif font.

Explore Dream London.

The posters showed stylised pictures in bright colours, reminiscent of London Underground adverts from the 1920s and 30s. They showed scenes from around the city, each accompanied by a caption.

Bathing in the River: the accompanying picture looked like something Seurat might have painted; men, women and children in long striped bathing costumes splashing in the blue water of the Thames by a yellow beach. On the opposite bank, scarlet vines writhed their way into the water from a yellow spotted factory.

The Flower Market: there was no way of misjudging the look the mother and father were giving each other as they held each other's hands in the middle of the riot of blooms. Their son and daughter innocently plaited daisy chains around each other's necks.

Snakes and Ladders Square: the artist had drawn the ladders in harsh perspective. A red and black serpent was reaching to eat the young lady who stood on the next square, a drink in her hand.

Look into the Unknown: the picture showed the Spiral, and I was peering closer at the detail in the centre when I was distracted by a round of applause.

A young man with a white painted face assumed a declamatory position on the opposite platform, one velvet-sleeved arm held high, a lace cuff drooping from his wrist.

"Oh Gentlemen, I am sad!" he announced.

There was more applause, and a few *awwws*.

"For my love does not know my name! She is the dawn and the sunset to me, she is the sweet and the savoury, the laughter and the melancholy, and yet she looks at me as if I were naught but a stranger!"

More applause.

"I weep, gentlemen, I weep!" He produced a large white handkerchief and gently dabbed his eye.

My train arrived, green as an alligator, humming with electricity. The train was full, so I was surprised to find an empty seat opposite a woman carrying a basket. I slumped into it, suddenly tired. I should have recognised that feeling, I should have realised I had been caught by one of the Daddio's chair traps, but I was too distracted by the singing coming from the woman's basket.

"What on Earth have you got in there, madam?" I asked.

"It's my little Sammy. She gets nervous when she's travelling."

Evil yellow cat eyes stared at me from the basket. I looked away, fumbled in my pocket. My hand touched the fortune scroll that Christine had given me, and I pulled it out.

You will meet a Stranger
You will be offered a job
You will be offered a second job
Go to the inn to meet a friend, one who will betray you
Go to the docks and meet your greatest friend, the one you will betray
Count the colours in the numbers, count the numbers in the words

That was new. A thought occurred to me. Why did I never read the whole of the prophecy? Why did something always distract me from going on? I resolved to do so now.

"Hello, Captain."

I recognised that voice.

"Hello, Honey Peppers."

I rolled up the scroll and replaced it in my pocket. I would read it when I'd finished speaking to the psychotic little girl.

Honey Peppers stared at the man sitting by me.

"I'm sorry," he said, panic-struck, and got up and left. Honey Peppers sat herself down at my side. She was holding a balloon with the words *Dream London Zoo* written on it. A woman in a dove grey uniform sat down in a suddenly vacant seat opposite, next to the lady with the cat.

"I need to speak to Captain Wedderburn, Nanny," said Honey Peppers, shaking her golden curls. "You may read your book."

The nanny nodded and took out a slim volume of poetry and a handkerchief. She dabbed her eyes as she read.

Honey Peppers tilted her head and gazed at me.

"Now, Captain Wedderburn. The Daddio isn't happy with you."

"Not happy with me?" I asked, all innocence. "Why ever not? Aren't I looking after his Moston girls, like he told me to?"

"He told you to have nothing to do with the Cartel."

"What makes you think I have anything to do with the Cartel?"

She frowned at me.

"Don't you know that it's naughty to lie, Captain Wedderburn?"

"I don't think I've ever actually lied to you, Honey Peppers."

I saw the two eyes in her tongue looking out from her mouth at me.

"You realise," said Honey Peppers, "that if I found out that you had deliberately lied to me, I would have you taken to Dream London Zoo to be fucked by the manatees?"

Nanny looked up from her book.

"I think you mean the mandrills, dear. They're monkeys. The manatees are like big seals."

Something dark crossed Honey Peppers' face.

"Don't contradict me, Nanny. I know what I mean. If I say I'll have him fucked by the manatees, then I'll have him fucked by the manatees."

Honey turned back to me.

"Where did you go to last night?"

"Where did I go last night? I went to bed."

"*Where* did you go to bed? I know it wasn't at your flat. The Daddio sent the Greedy Quantifier around there to check up on you. There was some big orange frog sleeping in your bed. It took the Greedy Quantifier forever to wake him up. After he did he couldn't get him to shut up."

"You must mean my friend, Mr Monagan?" I said. "He is chatty, isn't he? Heart in the right place though. He's working for me now. Working for us, I should say, looking after the Daddio's Moston girls. Do you realise what effect they have on normal men?"

Honey Peppers' eyes widened in exasperation. She stamped her foot in annoyance.

"Why do you think the Daddio had them imported? To do the laundry? The Daddio will make a fortune pimping those whores out."

The train was curving around a bend lined with swaying green willows. Long leaves dipped down in the water of a stream.

"Are we passing through a park?" I said, but with a *flick* we plunged into a tunnel and emerged back into a tangle of red brick streets.

"Never mind the parks, Captain Wedderburn. The Daddio isn't planning on moving into them. He's got his eyes on other things. Now, I want to know, where did you go last night?"

"You'll have heard of my reputation, Honey Peppers. Last night I had dinner with a seventeen-year-old girl. Does that answer your question?"

She stared at me with clear blue eyes.

"I can tell when you're lying, Captain Wedderburn."

"Am I lying at the moment, Honey Peppers?" I raised my eyebrows and gave her the hurt little boy look that usually works so well on women. "Well, am I?"

She frowned.

"I suppose not," she said, petulantly. "But there's a cloak around wherever it is you went."

"A lot of the places I frequent like to be discreet," I said, with perfect accuracy.

Honey Peppers clenched her little fists together. She was angry with me, but couldn't actually catch me out. And she knew I knew it. I tried to ease the situation.

"Listen, Honey Peppers, I currently have the Daddio's Moston girls living at Belltower End. I'm following the Daddio's wishes. I don't think that I deserve to be threatened."

"It's not for you to decide what you deserve, Captain Wedderburn. Can I make this perfectly clear? The Daddio is not happy with you. If you return to the City to work tomorrow, then the Daddio will be unhappy. Very unhappy. So unhappy, it will make being fucked in Dream London Zoo by each of the animals in turn a positive pleasure."

"You mean you think it wouldn't be?" I said, brightly.

"You have been warned, Captain." She looked startled. "What was that?"

I didn't know what she meant. The lady opposite, who had been listening to Honey Peppers' language with barely contained disbelief, spoke up.

"Oh, I'm sorry. That was my Sammy. He doesn't like to travel."

Honey Peppers put her hand to her mouth. She had turned white.

"Put your book away, Nanny," she mumbled.

"Oh, but it's so sad! Poor Lavinia will never find love..."

"Put that sentimental bullshit away!" said Honey Peppers, her voice quite shrill. "We're getting off here. It's our stop!"

I RODE THE train back to the Egg Market, staring through the window as I put my thoughts in order.

I had lost control of the situation, that was certain. Two days ago I had been Captain Wedderburn, rogue and entrepreneur, a man who answered to no one. Now I seemed to be working for two sets of people. Three, if you counted Bill and the Americans as separate.

As the train ran into Egg Market Station I found myself wondering who I was. It's always easier to see the faults in other people. It always was. But Dream London played with the mind, it kept you looking away from yourself. Had I changed? Not as much as others, I was sure. Dream London operated best on the weak, the indecisive, the foolish, the pretentious. I was none of those things. But had I changed? What would the Captain Wedderburn of old have done in this situation, I wondered?

I knew the answer right away: Take the money and run.

But there was nowhere to run to in Dream London.

The train halted, and I joined the other businessmen in descending the stairs. They flowed around the plum-coloured obstruction at the base of the stairs without pause, and I felt my spirits sink even further. Was I just paranoid, or was everyone taking an interest in Captain Wedderburn today?

"Captain Wedderburn!"

"Miss Elizabeth Baines," I replied.

"Captain," she began, somewhat hesitantly, "I hope you don't think this forward, but we are supposed to be having a meal together at the Tiger Tea House…"

"I'm sorry Elizabeth, but I don't have time. I'm going to the brothel, you see."

"Good for you, sir," called out a passing gentleman with a red nose.

She fixed me with a steely gaze.

"Captain. I can assure you, there's no need…"

"Oh there is," I said. "The urge is upon me."

She became quite businesslike.

"What I mean to say is… you're my one true love. I know that, the scroll said so. I trust you, Captain. I believe in you. So, well, what I'm saying is, why should we wait…?"

That was enough to stop me in my tracks.

"You're saying you would sleep with me?"

"I wouldn't put it so crudely…"

"As if that was something special."

"I'm offering you my virginity, Captain."

That floored me. Something about the expression that crossed her innocent face touched me, much more than the offer she had just made.

"Elizabeth, listen to me. I don't know who sold you that thing, but you've been rigged. I'm not the sort of person that you want anything to do with, trust me on this! You really don't want to be associated with me. Take my advice, Miss Elizabeth Baines, and take this scroll back to wherever you bought it from and have them exchange it for someone else. Do you understand?"

She blinked rapidly as I spoke, and I could see the little glistening hemispheres forming at the edge of her eyes. Unusually, I felt quite sorry for her. I think it was because, underneath her gaudy outfit and sensible make-up, she really was quite an attractive woman, though, as I have said, a little older than my tastes. Or was I just fooling myself in saying this? When was the last time a woman had liked me just for myself?

She composed herself and spoke in a little voice.

"I understand what you're saying, James, but I don't think *you* understand. I can't simply swap this scroll for another. You are my *one true* love. How can there be another?"

I shook my head.

"I'm sorry, I don't know and I don't care. Now, if you'll excuse me, I'm heading to the brothel. Good day, Madam."

If I'd had a hat, I would have raised it. I pushed my way from the station entrance and through the evening market crowd, making my way to the Laughing Dog.

I couldn't quite submerge the little unfamiliar feeling inside me, though. I felt ashamed.

IT WAS STUFFY and dim inside the Dog, especially after the yellow glow of the Dream London evening outside. I went straight to the bar and bought myself a pint of porter.

"Have you seen Bill?" I asked the barman, and as I did so I felt a hand slide onto my shoulder.

"Hello lover, fancy coming upstairs?"

Bill stood at my side, her red hair curling down to her bare shoulders.

She took my hand in hers and, pausing only for me to lift my glass from the counter, she led me up the stairs to the same room as yesterday.

The room had changed overnight. The wallpaper was now striped in a dusky pink that matched the bed covers.

"Is that bed larger than yesterday?" I said.

"I think so," said Bill. "Never mind that. What did you find out?"

"Nothing! I've been stuck on the 829th floor all day looking at numbers." Suddenly I felt tired and sick. My stomach felt as if it were filling with warm soapy water. My head was tight and hot with the new numbers I'd been looking at.

"What did you stay there for? Why didn't you move up to the correct floor?"

"I can't. You don't know what it's like in there. I gaze at the ledgers and the next thing I know, two hours have passed. I need to get up to the 839th floor. That's where the contracts are."

Bill placed her head in her hands.

"Shit, shit, shit. What the hell is going on here?"

I said nothing. She was a lot less impressive than she had been been when I met her yesterday. She had seemed so much more in control then. She seemed to realise what she was doing.

"Sorry," she said. "I've been out all day trying to find Green Park. You know how impossible it is to locate anything in this city?" She rubbed her temples. "This place is having an effect on me. I just know it."

She looked at the bed, thinking.

"Right. This isn't something for me to handle. We've got no access to the towers. It's got to go through the Cartel. You'll have to tell Alan to get you sorted out."

"I tried telling Alan. He said…"

"Never mind what Alan says! You tell him that Bill is unhappy, and when Bill gets the message out to her friends, they're going to be unhappy too. Shit!" She shouted out the last word. "Ask him if he realises just what we've spent on this, trying to put right the mess that you Brits have made?"

I'd had enough. First Honey Peppers, then Miss Elizabeth Baines, and now Bill Dickenson. Was every female I met that day going to order me around?

"That's enough," I said, raising my hand in warning.

The scorn dripped from her words.

"What are you going to do? Hit me?"

I wasn't, as it happens.

"I don't know what I'm going to do," I said, lowering my hand, "but I'm tired of being told what to do."

She laughed.

"Really? And what makes you think you get to choose what you do? What makes you think that any of us do? You'll do what you're told, Captain Wedderburn, if you know what's good for you. You run along and tell Alan what I told you. Capiche?"

I'd had enough. I made to slap her face with the back of my hand – that's the sort of thing Captain James Wedderburn usually does to keep his women in order…

… but the next thing I knew I was spinning around and landing heavily on my back on the bed.

"I'm sorry," I said. "That wasn't me. That was Dream London."

"I know," said Bill, smiling sweetly down at me. "That's why I didn't break your arm."

"You can let go of me now."

She smiled and stood up in a rustle of material. I rose from the bed, rubbing my arm.

"That was a good throw," I said.

"Mmm. Here's something else for you to think about, James. I'm only Plan B. Me, and all the other agents sent into Dream London."

"Plan B. So what's Plan A?"

"Plan A is the nuclear option. They're aimed at the towers, right now. Missiles, bombs. There are more and more Hawks in the Pentagon saying that Dream London has grown big enough."

"You're saying they'd nuke the city, just to save themselves?"

"Why not? They almost carpet-bombed Algiers when they thought that someone had sold land to the other places. They would have done, too, if it hadn't been for the Arab League blocking it. It turned out to be a good thing too. Someone was trying to set them up..."

"Yes, but nuclear weapons? What is it with you Americans?"

"What about us? I should point out that the French have been pushing to fire nukes for six months now. The only reason that the Germans stopped them was because they were worried about the fallout drifting their way. Don't you get it, Captain Wedderburn? We Americans are the only friends you have."

"I don't have any friends," I said, seriously. Actually, according to the scroll, I had two. One of them was

Bill, and she was due to betray me. Perhaps the nuclear option was more likely than she was saying.

"I know," said Bill, snapping her fingers. "Amit Singh. He might be able to help you."

"Amit Singh," I said. "How could he help?"

"You know him? Of course you do. He's in the same line of business. Asian Babes, he calls his girls, doesn't he? Well, his son was a hacker before the changes: got himself into trouble with the NSA, so they recruited him. Amit Singh was our line into Dream London until very recently, up until the microwave signals cut out."

"Amit Singh was working for you?"

"You'd be surprised." She nodded. "Yes. Go and see Amit Singh. He might be able to get you moved up to the next floor."

She suddenly yawned and stretched, and I saw just how exhausted she looked.

"And now, I think you've had your money's worth. Same time tomorrow night?"

She opened the door to the room at that.

"Same time," I said, without any enthusiasm. I never thought I would say it, but I was becoming heartily sick of brothels.

ORANGE

ACHMED/AMIT

I WASN'T GOING to meet Amit Singh on my own.

I headed to Belltower End to look for Second Eddie. I hadn't heard from him in some time, and that's never a good thing. In my line of work, it's difficult choosing a good number two. He has to be competent, but not so competent he might get ideas about taking over your role. Was Second Eddie off somewhere now, plotting his takeover? I thought of the Daddio, of Luke Pennies, of all the people who might make an offer to an up-and-coming young man...

The evening was warmer than ever, and I wished I wasn't wearing such a dark heavy suit. The orange and pink parrots were building nests in the pollarded tops of the trees. Cloth and twigs, pieces of wire and lengths of lace and braid dripped from the uppermost branches in colourful profusion. Green beetles scuttled in lines along the drains, and I saw one artful salamander standing in the shadows of a shop doorway, watching them, biding its time.

I arrived in Belltower End towards the end of the after-work rush. Men in suits just like mine walked the streets, eyeing the merchandise. Every so often one of them would succumb to a beckoned finger and follow a woman up to her flat.

Gentle Annie sat on the bench by the garden.

"Good evening, Annie," I said.

"Got any candy?"

I fumbled in my pockets. Even going to Angel Tower, I still carried it. You never knew when you might need some.

"I'm looking for Second Eddie," I said, handing it across.

"Good luck with that, Captain. I haven't seen him since last Thursday."

I frowned. That wasn't good news.

"Mind you," continued Gentle Annie, "I shouldn't worry about the old Tallywhacker so much." Gentle Annie and Second Eddie had never got on that well. "Not now we have Mr Monagan. He's a bit of a find! The girls have never met anyone like him! Such a gentleman! And so strict with the customers. We had one man earlier cutting it up rough with Slight Alice. Mr Monagan dealt with him quite firmly."

"Mr Monagan?" I said, rather taken aback.

"Oh yes. He may be mild mannered, but he's very strong and lithe. Comes of living in the water, I suppose. And he's very definite about what he wants."

"Mr Monagan?" I repeated.

"Oh yes. Even those new Moston Girls you brought here. They don't give a damn about anything, they don't listen to anyone. Except for Mr Monagan."

"Mr Monagan?"

"That's the frog." She leaned closer to me and lowered her voice. "If you ask me, Captain, it's because he hasn't got a willy."

"A willy," I said, hoarsely.

"Yes," said Gentle Annie. "A penis. A prick. A willy." She smiled. "A beaver basher, a dong, a flesh flute, a John Thomas, a member, a pink oboe, a schlong, a wiener." She leant in close and whispered. "A yoghurt gun."

"I haven't heard that one."

"Really?" smiled Gentle Annie. "Do you like it?"

"I do," I said. Gentle Annie collected synonyms for penis, one for each customer.

"It's those Moston girls, Captain," she continued. "They have power over a man, power over what you keep in your trousers. All the girls here could say the same, to a lesser degree. But Mr Monagan, they have no handle on him. And he's so nice!"

"Mister James!"

Mr Monagan appeared in the doorway to one of the flats, his orange skin glistening in the late evening sunshine.

"Oh, Mister James! It's good to see you!" He came running up to me in a strange, wide-legged gait, arms and feet flapping.

"Mister James! I can't begin to thank you! Thank you for bringing me here, and introducing me to such lovely people. These ladies who work with you! I've never met such a wonderful, polite, well mannered, pretty and courteous bunch! To think that I've only been here in Dream London for a day and already I have a place to live and a job! And such good friends! Why, I feel like a human already!"

Gentle Annie's face was a picture. She wore the smile of a seventeen-year-old virgin, not the world weary forty-something she really was.

"Well, Mr Monagan," I said. "I think I could make your day even better. Do you fancy a curry?"

AMIT SINGH USED to run a gang out towards the east end of London, but then Daddio Clarke moved in and all rival gangs were destroyed, absorbed, or pushed out to other areas. The last I heard of Amit, his Asian Babes had mostly hooked up with other pimps and he was left running a small time operation from a curry house somewhere in the twisted streets around what used to be Whitechapel.

The evening was fading to inky blue as Mr Monagan and I made our way down a busy street, lined with cafés and restaurants. Mr Monagan was unreasonably excited at being asked out for a meal.

"A curry, Mister James! I've never had such a thing! Will it be too hot for me, do you think? Will there be plates and knives and forks, or will we eat it with our hands?"

"A little dignity please, Mr Monagan!" I said, aware of the looks we were getting from the other would-be diners who walked the street.

"Very well, Mister James." He held his mouth closed for a while, but he couldn't help himself. "Oh look! Curry restaurants! Do you think we will be able to have water if it's too hot? Or should we drink beer? I've heard that's better..."

"Mr Monagan! Act cool!"

The restaurants had sent hucksters to stand in the streets and persuade customers inside. One particularly brash young man with a gold hoop in his ear stepped up to us.

"Best curry in town, sir," he said. "Free drink, ten per cent off the bill, and, to be honest, we need you in there! We have too many women tonight! Too many women in there!"

"Oh! Mister James, did you hear that? The best curry in town! We should go there!"

"I don't think so," I said, smiling.

"But Mister James! You heard what he said! And they will give us a free drink!"

"Mr Monagan, if you're to live in Dream London, you must learn that not everyone tells the truth."

"Hey!" said the huckster with the earring.

"Oh come on," I said. "Are you going to call *me* a liar?

The huckster smiled and shrugged. Truth be told, I think he recognised that a bigger bullshitter than he would ever be was standing before him.

We walked on down the road, ignoring the calls from the other hucksters. Well, I ignored them. Mr Monagan kept tugging at my arm and repeating their claims to me.

Something tingled inside my mind. Danger. Someone placed an arm on my hand and I turned to see a gentleman in a turban. He wore a bright salwar kameez, a sash around his waist. And now other similarly dressed men were stepping out of the crowd, all dressed in brightly coloured clothes. One older gentleman stepped forward, placed his palms together and bowed.

"Sirs, please would you do us the honour of dining with us tonight in our humble restaurant, the Tale of India?"

I looked around the other Indian men. They may have looked like dancers from a Bollywood movie, but they had the faces and bodies of people used to fighting.

"Uh, I should be delighted," I said.

The man beamed, his teeth white between his dark beard.

"Then follow me to a world of oral delight, where the spices of the orient shall excite your tastebuds!"

The Indians surrounded us, forming a path towards a nearby alley.

The man in the turban walked at my side.

"Call me Achmed," he said.

"That's not your name," I said.

"No, but it is the role that Dream London has chosen for me."

We walked by two large bins filled with rancid chicken parts. The smell was enough to make you retch. One of our escorts pointed upwards, and another pulled a bow and arrow from his clothes and fired into the darkening sky.

"Missed!" He swore beneath his breath.

I looked to see what he had fired at, and saw blue monkeys lined along the window ledges like birds.

"They come to steal the meat," said Achmed, and I became aware that my feet were crunching on chicken bones.

The Tale of India was a tarnished confection half way down the alley, one of several Indian restaurants, much poorer and more broken down than those on the street we had just left. A couple of tired pubs stood amongst them, together with something that looked like a church hall or community centre. I heard the sound of music coming from inside, and I tilted my head to listen.

"Isn't that a brass band?" I said. "Funny, I haven't heard one for ages…"

Or had I? I remembered the silver sound of the trumpet as I fell asleep last night. Anna practising her scales. The cornet, I should say. Anna had been keen to correct me.

We walked on, and I listened to the tattoo of the snare drum accompanying the band.

"Hold on, isn't this Brick Lane?" I said. I felt the satisfaction a resident of Dream London does when they manage to stitch back together a little of the geography. "So this is where it got to!"

"It's the bottom end of Brick Lane," said Achmed. "The other end drifted off to Upton Park. Now, welcome to my humble business."

He held open the door and ushered Mr Monagan and me into the restaurant.

I smelt curry, I saw red flock wallpaper, pink table cloths, golden decorated jugs, napkins folded into fans, wine glasses and menus in thick leather binders. It was a proper Indian restaurant, circa 1986.

A waiter dressed in black hurried up.

"Sirs, here is your table."

There were poppadums waiting for us, together with a silver tray of dips: bright orange mango chutney, yoghurt, lime pickle and chopped onions in a bright red sauce.

Mr Monagan broke off the tiniest piece of poppadum and placed it in his mouth. His face was immediately transported to such heights of ecstasy I actually found myself worrying what the effect of the curry would be upon him.

Achmed sat down with us.

"Can I recommend the chicken tikka masala?" he said.

"I never had you down as a restaurant owner, Amit," I said. It was funny that it had taken me that long to recognise him. Dream London seemed to change some people more than others.

"Ah! So you do know who I am! Well, I'm not a restaurateur. Or I wasn't until six months ago. And it's Achmed now, Captain Wedderburn. Dream London has its own roles in mind for all of us."

The door to the restaurant swung open and we all looked towards it. The restaurant was long and thin; in old London style it was the front and back room of a terraced house knocked into one.

Two children stood there, a boy and girl of about ten years old, both dressed in long black coats concealing whatever they wore beneath. They both carried cases. Musical instrument cases.

"Not here," said Amit. "In the hall. Over the road!"

The two of them nodded and turned to go.

"Hold it!" called Amit. "What did you tell your mother, Alison?"

The girl spoke with calm assurance.

"We said that we were going to the free jazz session at the Mill."

"Good. Good girl."

"Thank you, Mr Singh."

The door swung shut.

"This is most excellent, Mr Achmed," said Mr Monagan, taking another mouthful of poppadum. "Truly, you are an inspired restaurateur!"

"Not through choice." said Achmed/Amit. "I used to be in the same line as Captain Wedderburn."

"Then you must have been a generous man indeed! I have never known such a man as Captain Wedderburn! I count myself lucky to have met him."

Amit looked from Mr Monagan to myself.

"Yeeees," he said. "Well, Jim, Dream London likes its Asians to dress like this and run curry houses. How do you think I feel about this?"

"Delighted, I should imagine."

"Hilarious as ever I see, Jim. Well, it's because of these clothes that I'm helping you out. I got a message tonight saying you were on the way. I couldn't believe it at first, but I suppose it makes a certain sort of sense. The outside world seems to have recruited a lot of us."

"Have they, indeed?"

I broke off a piece of poppadum myself and spooned a little red onion over it. It tasted hot and acid, not particularly nice. I swallowed and poured myself a glass of water.

"What happened to you, Amit?"

Amit became serious.

"Have you heard of Daddio Clarke and the Macon Wailers?"

"Who hasn't?" I looked at Mr Monagan, lost in a trance of ecstasy. "What do you know about the Daddio?" I asked, carefully.

"Very little," said Achmed. "It's strange, is it not, that no one had ever heard of him until Dream London began? His men swept all before them, including my humble little operation."

"Have you met the Daddio?"

"No. He works through intermediaries. Have you seen inside the mouth of those people?" He shivered.

"I've seen one of his Quantifiers. And this little girl…"

"We met his Quantifiers. And there used to be an old woman. Evelyn Macaroons. She was evil…"

He broke off a piece of poppadum.

"I don't think the Daddio comes from around here," he said. "I think he came down the river, like so many others. That's what my new employers suggest, anyway."

"Your new employers?" I let the words hang in the air a moment. "And who would they be?"

"You think that the Americans are the only ones who have an interest in what is happening to Dream London? The Indian government has observers here as well, James. The Commonwealth left us with a route into this country, and here we are to exploit it."

"You work for the Indian government?"

"Oh, come on Jim. Don't act so surprised. You work for the Americans. We've all been gathered up, all the rogues and criminals. All of us with more charm than conscience. Dream London loves us, it changes us less than others. The outside world governments are fighting fire with fire."

I suppose that made a certain sort of sense. Other countries would have sent spies into Dream London. But… "What do the Indian government hope to gain?"

"There are long forgotten cities within the subcontinent that lie choked by the jungles. What you westerners now call the rainforests, for it is racist to use the wrong name, is it not? There are those who have visited those long crumbled cities, where the monkeys now walk the streets and nest in the houses, and they have noted the towers that once soared up above the treetops and now lie in ruins on the jungle floor, and they note the similarity with Dream London, and they wonder, has this happened before? More to the point, will it happen again?"

"And that's why you're helping me?"

"Let us say for the moment that the American government's aims are the same as those of the Indian government. And happily, for the moment, their wishes coincide with mine! So, I am here to help! What would you say, James, if I were to tell you I could get you up onto the Writing Floor?"

"What would it cost?" I asked.

"For you, James, no charge! Be grateful that I have someone who is in my debt who can perform that service. He was a useful man, until he went to pieces."

"Who?"

"Rudolf Donati."

"I thought he was dead."

"Not at all. Eat your meal and then we shall go and visit him."

THE CURRY WAS brightly coloured and gut churningly hot and as about authentic as Amit's Indian dress. It popped and sizzled inside as we were led up the stairs at the back of the restaurant. The stairs began to spiral around themselves, the walls became circular.

"We're climbing a tower," said Mr Monagan, delightedly.

"Of course," said Amit. "Rudolf is my prisoner, and where else would one keep a prisoner other than at the top of a tower?"

"I thought he worked for you," I said. "He handled your accounts, didn't he?"

"He still does. He tried to betray me, and so we took steps to ensure he couldn't do that again."

"What did you do?"

"Take a look for yourself," said Amit, pushing open the door.

SIX

RUDOLF DONATI

RUDOLF WAS A man in pieces.

His head lay on the pillow of the great frayed four poster bed at the centre of the room. His legs stood by the side of the bed, ready to go, his heart beat on a white plate on the bedside table; a plate with the same willow pattern as the ones our curry had just been served on downstairs. His body hung in the wardrobe, clearly seen through the open door. His arms were folded in the centre of the bed.

All the parts of his body were connected by long, pulsing, purple cords.

"Hello," said Rudolf, brown eyes turned towards the doorway.

"Rudolf Donati," I said. "What are you doing here?"

"You know him?" said Mr Monagan, in an awestruck voice. "Mister James! I think you know everyone."

"Not quite everyone," I said. "So, Rudolf. I'm guessing that the gambling got out of control again?"

Rudolf raised his eyebrows. I suppose that, just being a head, he had had to learn new ways to express himself.

"Not out of control, just an unlucky streak." He waggled his eyebrows in the direction of Amit. "I got into debt with these gentlemen."

"He tried to run away," said Amit. "Now we have him by the balls."

"He keeps them locked up in the cabinet over there," said Rudolf. I followed the two purple threads that led from the body in the wardrobe to the cabinet in the corner and winced.

"Mr Donati worked in Angel Tower as an actuary," said Amit. "He still has a lot of influence over the place."

"An actuary!" I said. "How could you work there? Didn't the numbers drive you mad?"

"Not if you understand what's really happening up there," said Rudolf. "Dream London isn't a fantasy, Jim, it's science fiction."

"That's enough of that," said Amit. "They want to get Captain Wedderburn here up to the Writing Floor. You're going to help them."

"Sure I will," said Rudolf. "Right after I've finished scratching my nose."

"He thinks he's funny," said Amit.

"Humour is the only weapon I have in this position."

"It's a blunt weapon. Listen, Rudolf. I'm going to let you out for the day. Would you like that?"

"Aren't you afraid he might just run away?" I said.

"Thanks, Jim!" said Rudolf. "Whose side are you on?"

"Don't worry," said Amit. "We'll keep his liver and kidneys. He'll have to come back here to be reattached to them. If he wants to go on living, that is."

I frowned. "How did you learn to do all this?" I asked. "How did you learn to take a man apart?"

"From careful application to the writings in the public libraries and reading rooms," said Amit. "From the scriptoriums and the bibliotechs that are opening all around the city. It's amazing what you can find if you look hard enough amongst all the junk."

"What junk?" said Mr Monagan.

"What junk? Have you read anything in this city, my orange friend?"

"I only arrived here yesterday."

"Ah, then you won't have had a chance to read all that second-rate poetry that people keep writing. Every word ever written in this city is copied down and distributed amongst the libraries and bookshops. Every note played on every instrument is written on manuscript and mixed in amongst the other sheet music. What better way to dilute the culture of our former world than by mixing it with the mediocrity of the masses?"

"No," said Rudolf, in the weary voice of someone who had tried to explain this many times before. "You don't understand, Amit. That's not how it works. There's no need for that, not when the 839th floor is rewriting everything all the time. He'll see that tomorrow if you let me take him there." He nodded at me.

"But why?" I asked. "Why are they doing it?"

"I told you, this is science fiction," said Rudolf. "Dream London is a place where the normal rules of the universe no longer apply. Angel Tower is the place where the rules are rewritten." You could hear the frustration in his voice. "I've told Amit this many times."

"And I think you're wrong, Rudolf," said Amit, in bored tones.

"I'm not. Your governments are all looking at this in the wrong way. You're treating this as a fantasy. You see these towers rising up and you want to seize your swords and cut your way to the top, kill the dragon and free the princess!" His eyes were fixed on me now. "That's the American way, isn't it? Well, I'm telling you now: forget the towers, look at the parks!"

"What's in the parks?" I asked, remembering the paths and roads I had seen from Bill's satellite pictures. I thought of the glorious gold and white fairytale castle that Buckingham Palace had become...

"I don't know what's in the parks," said Rudolf, rather weakly. "But that's where you should be looking."

Amit had had enough.

"Enough talking, Mr Donati. Now, I'm going to ask Mr Monagan and Captain Wedderburn to leave whilst I begin the process of putting you back together. Captain Wedderburn, where would you like to meet Mr Donati tomorrow?"

"How about at Angel Street station, seven thirty?"

"I'll be there," said Mr Donati. "Oh, and don't wear that suit. Wear your your normal clothes. Your Captain Wedderburn clothes."

"Why?"

"Because it will make things easier."

"But then they'll know who I am!"

"Of course they will," said Rudolf, his frustration obvious. "Lying here all the time gives you time to think. You should all try it sometime, instead of simply rushing off to get yourself killed."

"People have gone to some trouble to provide me with a cover story," I said. "All so I could get into Angel Tower. You want me just to abandon that?"

If Rudolf had had a body he'd have thrown his head back whilst he laughed at me. "You don't get it, Jim, do you? You think that they want you because of your leadership abilities? You're a fool. You're nothing more than a good looking thug, and they know it. People only follow you because of your looks. That's the way things work in Dream London."

"Lying in a bed has made you bitter, Rudolf," I said.

"Lying in a bed has given me clarity," said Rudolf.

"Enough chat," said Amit. "Off you go. I need to resurrect him. Oh, and make sure you get him back here by five at the latest tomorrow. He will be feeling quite sick by then, and it will take time to reattach him to his vital organs."

"Very well."

"I have a question," said Mr Monagan, holding up his hand. "Before we go. Do you mind, Mister James?"

"I don't mind," I said. Amit raised his eyes to the ceiling.

"Tell me, Mr Donati," said Mr Monagan. "What did you do to upset Mister Amit so much?"

"I'll answer that," said Amit. "Mr Donati is a man who can make numbers dance. Only when Dream London came, the numbers stopped dancing for him, and then we saw the truth."

"And then I tried to run," said Rudolf.

"And we caught him and brought him here, and he ran away again. That wasn't very wise, was it, Mr Donati?"

"Not when every train that you ride out brings you back in again," said Rudolf. "Dream London is impossible to escape from. Things can come in, but nothing can get out."

"Nothing?"

"Well, perhaps it would be better put that nothing can *escape* from Dream London."

The head on the bed had a way of tilting itself back and forth. Now it tilted to me, and Rudolf Donati was looking at me with big liquid brown eyes and smiling.

"Nothing can escape, James. What does that remind you of?"

"What?" I said.

Rudolf wasn't listening.

"What puzzles me is how time is passing out in the old world. Does everything seem to be moving a little slower in Dream London? Perhaps you could ask the Americans about that."

AMIT LED US from the room and back down the spiral staircase. I was sure it had grown a few steps since we had come in. In the restaurant two boys were looking at something in shiny black cases that had been set out on the restaurant tables. When they saw us, the black salwar kameez-clad waiters hurriedly snapped the cases shut, but not quickly enough. I'd had a good look at the polished brass instruments inside. Trumpets or cornets, I can't tell the difference.

The two boys folded their hands together and smiled at us sweetly as we walked by.

"What are they doing here?" I asked. "What are you planning?"

Amit just smiled.

"Alright, don't tell me. You look ridiculous in that turban, you know."

"I'm just grateful to remain above ground, James. Haven't you noticed there are less of us ethnic types around?"

I was about to ask him what he meant, but Amit held open the door for us.

"I hope that you will return soon to experience the cuisine of the East."

"Oh, thank you!" said Mr Monagan. "Truly, that was the most delightful meal I have ever experienced!"

Amit shook his head in disbelief.

I frowned and followed Mr Monagan into the alley.

WE WALKED IN silence, back towards the main streets. Mr Monagan hesitated. He looked to our right.

"I can feel something," he said. "Something over there..."

I realised where we were.

"That'd be the Spiral," I said. I took his arm. "Come on, it's late. We don't want to get pulled towards that. Not now."

We walked on. High above, in the narrow slit between the two buildings, the stars were out in an inky blue sky.

"What now?" asked Mr Monagan.

"We go home to bed," I said. "You have a busy day tomorrow, looking after Belltower End. And so do I."

"I think I will need a little something to eat first, Mr James."

"Something to eat? You just had a curry!"

"I know, and very nice it was too. But I shall need a little something extra before I go to bed."

I shouldn't have been surprised. He must have had a high metabolism, given how strong he was.

"There's an all night café on the way back," I said.

"No need, Mr James. I can see a trail of ants over there. I'll follow them to their nest. That'll keep me going."

"You eat ants?" I said. "Of course you do."

"I prefer water termites," said Mr Monagan, seriously. "The nests used to grow at the edge of the swamp. My mother taught me where to dig into them so we could take some of the termites without disturbing the others."

"What's so good about water termites?"

"They harvest from both the water and the land. Their meat is a mixture of surf and turf. Utterly delicious!"

The orange man seemed to glow at the declaration. Then he shook his head, sadly. "It's a shame, but they're no more."

"What happened?" I asked.

"Republican ants. Ants which use the power of the river to break free from their caste. They overthrew their hive's queen and caused things to be run to their benefit. They grew stronger and cleverer. They wiped out all the poor water termites."

The power of the river. That was an interesting phrase. Was that how Mr Monagan chose to explain the changes?

THERE HAD BEEN a storm at the Poison Yews in my absence. I returned to find the Sinfield family blown to the extremities of the house.

Anna met me in the hallway, a red circle imprinted on her lips.

"So you came back a second time," she said.

"Where's your father?"

"In the drawing room with Shaqeel. Mother's in the kitchen." Her face remained impassive. "There's been a huge row. I'd stay in your room if I were you."

"I need to see Alan."

I made my way to the drawing room. Alan and Shaqeel sat side by side on a large chaise longue, not touching. Shaqeel wore a deep, self-satisfied grin.

"James," said Alan. "You missed dinner."

"I wasn't hungry. Not after lunch."

Alan glanced at Shaqeel, and then he lowered his head.

"Listen, James. I want to apologise for the way I acted at work today. I did go off the rails a bit. I'm sorry if I wasn't as helpful as I might have been. It's just, well, Angel Tower. You felt it, didn't you? Things are so... different... in there. So much more... intense."

"I understand," I said. I did, too. "Listen, Alan, you need to get a message to Bill."

Shaqeel placed a jet black hand over Alan's. He shook his head.

"It'll wait until morning," said Alan.

I looked at Shaqeel, and I wondered at Alan's choice of partner. Was he part of the Cartel? Or was he something else?

"No," I said. "It won't wait. The message has to go now. Tell Bill I've arranged to get onto the Writing Floor tomorrow."

Alan raised his eyebrows.

"I'm impressed! How did you manage that?"

"Never mind. Get across there and let her know." I thought about her threat to have the towers nuked. Anything that would calm the Pentagon Hawks should be communicated as soon as possible.

"I'm tired," said Alan. "I just got comfortable."

I was tired too. I stepped forward and pressed a finger on his chest.

"I don't care. Do it now."

Silently, Shaqeel rose to his feet. He was a big man, bigger than me. He looked down at me with a broadening smile.

"Do you really want to fight me, Shaqeel?" I asked.

"Leave him, Shaqeel," said Alan, slowly climbing to his feet. "Come on. Let's get some night air. Perhaps we can call around at the club?"

I watched the pair of them leave the room, and then made to head upstairs.

"Jim! Captain Jim! Come in here!" Margaret's drunken voice called out to me from the kitchen.

I pretended I hadn't heard. As I entered my room I heard the silver sound of a trumpet coming from somewhere. I remembered the music from last night.

There was a spider sitting on my bed, about as big as my hand. At my approach, it lifted itself into the air on eight legs and sauntered away, just a little faster than I could move to catch it. It slipped its way into a crack in a wall and was gone.

I undressed and sat down on the bed and picked up one of the books that Anna had left me to read.

Lolita. I read the blurb. *The story of a young girl's awakening passion for an older man. An instructive tale to be read by all teenagers...*

That wasn't right, I thought. At least, that hadn't been right in the past.

CYAN

THE WRITING FLOOR

I AWOKE TO silence the next morning. The rest of the family were still in their rooms nursing hangovers, I guessed. Whether from alcohol or too much time spent arguing, I didn't know.

There was no warm water to shave in. I looked in the mirror, remembering Rudolf Donati's words last night. I was to dress as Captain Wedderburn today.

Very well. A face full of stubble was very Captain Wedderburn. I pulled on a pair of tight black trousers and a loose white shirt. There was a mirror in the wardrobe and I admired myself in it. Captain Wedderburn is tall and good looking, he has messy dark hair, a knowing grin, and a tendency to talk about himself in the third person.

I pulled on my green jacket, noting that the gold braid looked brighter than ever. The jacket had shrunk in length, becoming more of a bumfreezer. I felt the weight of my pistol in the inside pocket.

Somewhere outside was the sound of a door clicking and soft footsteps in the hallway.

I whisked across the room to open my door. Anna glided past in her school uniform.

"Good morning, Captain Wedderburn."

She spoke the words without emotion.

"Do you know where your father is?"

Anna cast a glance in the direction of Shaqeel's room.

"I don't think he's going to work this morning," she said. She walked off. I placed a hand on her shoulder.

"Please don't touch me," she said. She looked thoughtful. "You do know I left you that book as an illustration and not an invitation?"

"Of course," I said, snatching my hand away. "But I wanted to speak to you."

"Very well." She gazed at me, her dark eyes transmitting no information. "Yes, Captain Wedderburn?"

"I heard you playing last night," I said. "You're very good."

"Thank you. May I go now?"

"No. I'm sorry. I just wanted to know..."

My voice trailed away. I wanted to know what was going on, and I was reduced to asking the daughter of my host.

"I mean, well, I don't like to involve you, but..."

Anna spoke. "Captain Wedderburn, I think you must realise that I know everything that goes on in this house. I know all about the Cartel."

"Good. Well. I thought you would."

More silence.

"You had a question, Captain Wedderburn?"

"I was wondering. Did your father mention me before I came here? Did he say why I was chosen?"

Just for a moment I thought I saw Anna smile. But I must have been mistaken. Her voice remained impassive.

"Captain Wedderburn, I have no idea why you were chosen."

"Oh. Well, thank you..."

"... but I will say this. You'd be the last person I'd choose to lead a secret rebellion. You're way too obvious. You walk into a room and everyone knows that you're there."

"You think that they made a mistake?"

"Not at all, Captain. I think that whoever chose you did a really good job."

At that she smiled sweetly and went on her way.

I RODE THE train to the City without incident. Walking from the station towards Angel Tower, I was only half aware of the increased numbers of business men who sat on the pavements, begging, in their grubby, filthy suits. I was thinking back to what Anna had said, and I felt a fool for needing a teenage girl to point this out to me. I was nothing more than a distraction. The real leaders remained in the shadows.

The scarlet and yellow creeper that clung to the grey concrete of the towers crept ever closer to the waiting beggars; it formed little alcoves around them so they sat like religious icons at the fringes of this temple to Mammon. I barely registered their presence. I felt different today, dressed as I was as Captain Wedderburn. The dark-suited crowd parted before me, the women's gazes lingered upon me. The weight of the pistol felt so right in my pocket.

"Captain Wedderburn!"

Rudolf Donati called to me from a pavement café near to Angel Tower entrance. He was enjoying a cup of espresso.

He was a handsome man, now he was no longer in bits, with dark hair fading to grey and dark eyes. He wore a well tailored suit, with silver cufflinks and a silver ring on his right hand. I could just make out the stitch marks about his wrist where it had been reattached.

"Rudolf," I said, sitting down next to him. "Do you really think we should draw attention to ourselves so?"

He laughed.

"Captain, you tried entering Angel Tower in disguise and look where that got you. You really think that whatever controls Angel Tower is not aware of you? You're Captain Wedderburn, famous throughout half of Dream London."

"Half?" I said, rather pleased with his comment, notwithstanding Anna's earlier words.

"The bottom half."

I looked up at Angel Tower, up past the point where glass and concrete turned to stone and wood, up beyond the point where the black dots of the birds circled the tower, up as high as I could to the vanishing peak, lost in a blue of morning so bright it hurt the eyes. The sky seemed deeper in Dream London.

"Do you think that whoever's up there knows I'm coming?" I said.

"Of course they know," laughed Rudolf. He drained the cup of espresso. "Oh, I shouldn't drink this when so far from my kidneys, but a man has to live when he can. I so rarely get out nowadays."

I ignored him.

"If they know, then what's the point of all this?"

"Captain! Where are your manners? You're not listening to me. Indulge me a little on my day out."

Rudolf sipped at his coffee.

"All this subterfuge and running around in disguise," he said, and he took another sip. "That's old world thinking. The Cartel and the Americans, the Indians and the rest of them, they still think that you can conceal the inside. They don't realise that in Dream London, the surface is all that there is! I keep telling them that, but they won't listen. All this messing about in the towers. They should be heading to the parks!"

"You said that before. If that's how you really feel, why don't we go there now?"

"To do what? You wouldn't even find a way in."

Rudolf snapped his fingers, and a waiter in a long white apron approached.

"Three more espressos," he said.

"Three espressos?" I said, but Rudolf simply smiled.

"What are we waiting for?" I asked.

"The right moment," he said. "We won't get on the Writing Floor by subterfuge, but by style."

"What's the point? You just said that the towers aren't important."

"I know that, but maybe this way you get to stick one on the Cartel. Wouldn't that be nice?"

"I hate it when people use levers on me."

He grinned, a brilliant white smile.

"Very good, Captain Wedderburn! That's the thing about the dashing hero! He's so easy to manipulate!"

"I thought I was a rogue."

"Rogue, hero. What's the difference? They both do things the common herd dare not. Ah! The coffee!"

The waiter placed three little cups on the table and Rudolf placed one finger to his lips. With his other hand he pulled something from his pocket. He dropped a little yellow pill into one of the cups.

"You should go to the Writing Floor, Captain Wedderburn," said Rudolf, as if nothing had happened. "That's the place where they are reshaping Dream London. I think that Bill and the rest will find what is happening there interesting."

"Reshaping Dream London through the Writing Room? How?"

"Words, Captain Wedderburn. What is a magic spell but words? And that is the place where they write the words. Not that we are dealing with magic here, of course. I already told you that."

He waved his hand to encompass the entire city.

"What you see here, Captain, is what you get when science is explained by artists! Something which looks beautiful, but doesn't make any sense. Still, that's the world that we chose."

"I didn't choose it," I said.

I heard the sound of a guitar and my mood fell further. A young woman stepped forward, incredibly pretty, with blonde hair and an elfin face. She wore a simple green dress that only just reached her long, shapely legs. She began to sing in a breathless, little girl voice. A song about the past and simpler times.

"Ah, a guitar," said Rudolf. "A street player! That's how *they* defeat us, you know. *We* have been made into individuals, whereas *they* work together. That's what they're doing on the Writing Floor. Rewriting the words to make us value this sort of thing."

"How do you know all this?"

Rudolf Donati rolled his eyes.

"You ask that, Captain Wedderburn, sitting there in that jacket, every inch the dashing military figure, and not at all like a man who barely avoided a dishonourable discharge? Captain, I learned long ago that a good-looking man in the right suit with a winning smile can get what he wants. All it takes is the ability to tell a story. I was an accountant, Captain Wedderburn. I rewrote the world through numbers. The world still had the same number of boats and trees and bottles of wine and loaves of bread after I had finished my calculations, and yet all of a sudden people found themselves broke, or suddenly rich. Dream London is much the same; it's all about surface, and not about substance. Ah, here we go. This is the man that you want. Mr Hellebore! Over here!"

Mr Hellebore was a man dressed in a black suit just like any of the other businessmen who streamed towards Angel Tower. He came to an embarrassed halt before us.

"Excuse me, I don't think that I…"

"Mr Hellebore," said Rudolf. "So glad I caught you! Please, take a seat…"

"I'm sorry, but I'm in rather a hurry…"

"Captain, make him sit down."

He was a lot smaller than I, and easily bullied. I pointed to him, pointed to the seat and gave him a look that showed just how puny I thought he was.

"You were asked to sit down," I said in a low voice.

"Listen," he said. "I don't know what you…"

"Shut up."

He swallowed hard and sat down on the seat. I've used that look before. It's astonishing how easily most people are cowed.

One or two people cast a glance in our direction. When they caught sight of me they simply continued walking.

Rudolf Donati leant forward and gave a charming smile.

"Mr Hellebore. What is the word of the day?"

Mr Hellebore had turned red by now.

"The word of the day?" he said. "I don't know what you're talking about."

Rudolf pushed the third cup of espresso towards Mr Hellebore.

"We bought you a drink," he said.

"I don't want a drink!"

"Don't be so rude!" I said. "Mr Donati has bought you a drink. Say thank you."

"... thank you..."

He looked at me, a flush creeping up his face. I knew his type. Fussy, fully aware of his own importance, more than happy to bully those subordinate to him. If I was working for him, I had no doubt he would make the most of the situation. I felt little shame about picking on him. "Drink up, there's a good boy."

He picked up the cup and touched it to his lips. A monkey helping itself to sugar cubes on a nearby table saw this and began to laugh.

"Lovely," said Mr Hellebore, quickly putting the cup down.

"And the rest!" I snarled.

He drained the rest of the espresso.

Rudolf beamed.

"Now," he said. "I bought you a coffee, you owe me a favour. What's the word of the day?"

"Is there a truth potion in here?"

Rudolf laughed.

"A truth potion? Why would I need a truth potion? I know everything and everyone. That's my power! I know the word of the day. It's lobsters!"

"Lobsters." Mr Hellebore licked his lips. "Then why ask me? Why make me drink this coffee?"

"Because I didn't want you to go to work today."

Mr Hellebore stared at Rudolf. Then he belched. He hiccuped and he belched again.

"Have you poisoned me?" he said.

"No. Just given you a bad tummy. You'll spend the rest of the day on the toilet."

"You..." Mr Hellebore gulped and put a hand to his mouth. He retched.

"In there," said the waiter, reappearing with the bill.

Mr Hellebore stumbled off, one hand to his mouth.

Rudolf Donati was counting out Dream London shillings onto the waiter's tray.

"This should pay for the cleaning costs," he said.

"I wish you wouldn't use my café for this sort of thing," said the waiter.

"Oh, Albert! You can't tell me that no one else has ever thrown up in your bathroom before. Come on, I've tasted your pumpkin ravioli."

"I don't have to listen to this," said Albert, pocketing the shillings and walking away.

Rudolf turned to me and beamed his brilliant white smile.

"Well done, Captain. You make a great bully! Mr Hellebore was quite terrified."

"I'm not a bully," I said. "I was just playing the part Dream London gave me."

Rudolf grinned.

"You sound like Amit. You can't blame Dream London for all your faults, James. You brought them in with you. All the changes did was give them soil in which to grow. You're a bully now and always have been, it's just that you're charming so you get away with it. But a bully you remain, nonetheless. You're nothing but a bully and a pimp."

"Take that back, Donati. I look after my girls."

My voice was low, as it always is when I'm angry.

"Take that back? What does that mean? The words have been said. Okay. I take it back. You still heard what I said."

"I'm not a bully."

"Of course you are. That's what a rogue is. You do things your way and bully other people into accepting it."

"I'm…"

"You are. Don't look at me like that, I was the same myself, only I didn't use my muscles, I used my mind. I know that, because I know everything."

"I'm not really like that…"

"Really? It's on that fortune you carry round in your pocket and don't look at. Like all bullies, you're a coward at heart, aren't you? You can't face the future."

I'd heard enough.

"One more word, Donati, and I'll feel through your pockets and feed you one of your own pills. You know I'll do it."

"Oh, I do," said Rudolf. "But you have more important things to do now. You know the word of the day. Go into Angel Tower and ride the lift up to the Writing Floor. You'll be welcome there."

"How? They'll know I'm not Mr Hellebore."

"So what? I told you, this is Dream London. The substance is unimportant. It's all about the surface. That young woman playing the guitar is no good, but everyone loves her because she's attractive and she's singing from the heart. She's labelled as authentic and that's all that matters. Now, off you go. I have a day to enjoy before I go back to Amit Singh and my kidneys. Off you go to the Writing Floor. I'm heading to Moules' for lunch, and then afterwards I may visit the Race Track. I hear the Giraffe handicap is being run this afternoon."

I clenched my fists as I stared at the man, but I thought better of it. I turned and made my way to Angel Tower.

Walking through the entrance into the grand hall with the eye high above, I caught a glimpse of two people standing outside, watching me. A tall man with a little girl by his side. Honey Peppers had caught up with me again.

I waved to them through the glass front of the tower. They glared back at me.

I guessed the Daddio's power didn't extend into Angel Tower.

I rode the lift up to the 839th floor.

THE SIGN HANGING outside the Writing Floor was written in a particularly curly font. It read:

"   .   ,   ."

I pushed my way through the door and found myself in something like an old fashioned library. Books were laid out on the shelves, piled up on the floor. Posters decorated the walls, travel posters, posters for art galleries.

An old man sat behind a desk by the door.

"Word of the day?" he asked.

"Lobsters," I replied.

"May I ask what business brings you here?"

"My name is Captain Wedderburn. I've been moved up here from the 829th floor."

"Oh, I didn't hear anything about it." He frowned. "Then again, I never do." He looked over my shoulder.

"Miss Merchant! Miss Merchant, I have a Captain Wedderburn here. Says he's been moved up here from the Numbers Floor."

A young woman in a severe suit with an even more severe expression hurried up.

"Captain Wedderburn?" she said. She consulted the clipboard she held in her left arm. "Ah yes, here you are. I have your desk ready. If you'll come this way..."

"Thank you, Miss Merchant," I replied, hiding my surprise.

I followed her into the room, threading between the shelves and stacks of books. She wore a tight skirt, and she rolled her backside as she walked, fully aware, I'm sure, that I was watching it. She took me to a desk covered in scraps of paper. Leaflets, old tickets, ripped pages from notebooks: it looked as if someone had emptied a wastepaper basket onto the desk.

"Take your seat, Captain Wedderburn," she said.

"You were expecting me?"

"Of course," said Miss Merchant. "Your name is on the list."

She showed me the clipboard, and there, sure enough, was my name: Captain James Wedderburn.

I sat down in the big leather chair, so much more comfortable than my workstation yesterday. Miss Merchant perched herself on a stool at the side of my desk. She picked up a notepad and pencil and sat there, poised, waiting for me to begin.

"What do I do?" I said.

"Pick up a piece of paper and start reading."

I picked up one of the scraps of paper on the desk. It was a flyer for a concert.

"The Hot Tramps. Live at the Embassy, Thursday 12th March. Tickets £8 on the door."

I looked at Miss Merchant.

"No changes?" she suggested.

"No changes."

She looked at a waste bin on the floor by the desk, and I dropped the flier into it.

I picked up a piece of pink card, an old underground ticket.

"Travelcard, Zones 1-4," I read. And then, just like yesterday, down on the Numbers Floor, reality changed in my mind. "Dream London Omnibus," I said. "2d."

Miss Merchant scribbled on her pad, and I watched as the letters changed on the ticket.

"What now?" I asked

"Drop it in the bin," she said.

"The same one?"

"Of course."

All around me I saw a similar scene playing out. Men sat at desks reading books and leaflets, all of them with an attractive young secretary at their side.

"What happens to all this?" I asked.

"It gets burned," said Miss Merchant. "It doesn't matter, does it? It's the message, not the medium. Now, come on. Keep reading. We're writing Dream London here."

"Ah," I said, and I began to understand. "Like on the Numbers Floor..."

"No," said Miss Merchant, with a look of faint scorn.

"The people on the Numbers Floor are working at a level below us, both literally and figuratively. They are making reality pliable. It's the people on this floor who are the real creatives, reshaping Dream London into a more suitable form."

"Ah yes," I said. "The real creatives. I know a lot about them." I had seen one only this morning, playing the guitar in the café.

Miss Merchant picked up another piece of paper from my desk, showing me an ample scoop of cleavage as she did so.

"Oh," she said, looking at the lines and tiny writing of a plan of a building. "This is a blueprint. We'll need to take this to Architecture."

She pulled out another scrap of paper and handed it to me.

"Milk, bread, mushrooms, bacon, spaghetti, bolognese sauce..." I read out loud. "Bolognese sauce doesn't sound right, does it?" I said. "Nor does spaghetti." The words tickled in my mind, they shimmered and changed. "Make that potatoes and haddock."

The shopping list changed to reflect the new reality. Was this how it worked, I wondered? Was reality so pliable on the Writing Floor that a man could simply walk up here and announce he worked here and his name was written on a clipboard, a desk was prepared for him? Rudolf Donati had realised that. Of course he had. Rudolf Donati had gone through life reshaping reality with a wave of his pencil.

"Do you know who I am, Miss Merchant?"

"Of course. You're Captain Wedderburn."

"I know that. But I mean, do you know anything else about me?"

"Well, let's take a look, shall we?"

She looked down at her clipboard.

"You're one of the changers," she said. "One of the leaders. You're the opposite of most people in Dream London in that you tell reality how it's going to be, and it reshapes itself around you."

"Well, yes, I suppose I do," I said, pleased to be described as such.

"You're a queen."

"I beg your pardon?"

She smiled.

"I'm sorry, I'm just reading what it says here. What I mean is, people support you. Their life's work revolves around making you more comfortable."

"I don't think so!" I laughed, thinking of Honey Peppers waiting for me downstairs.

"Oh, I think it's true," said Miss Merchant. "Look at Belltower End. All those whores working for you, and you sitting at the top of the heap like Queen Bee."

"They don't work for me, they work for themselves!"

"They pay their cut to you. You're too modest, Captain Wedderburn. You are the master manipulator. You get people to do what you want. Those women don't become whores by accident!"

"No, they do it because they need the money."

Miss Merchant smiled.

"Partly. But you break them down. You don't tell them the other choices, you gradually draw them into the game."

"Hey," I said. "I treat my girls well!"

"Oh yes, I know that you do. You give them candy every day if they behave themselves."

I relaxed back into my chair at that.

"Well, good." I said. "I'm pleased that you know that."

"Of course. They're more profitable if they're happy, aren't they?"

I sat back up again.

"I am not a manipulator!"

"If you say so, Captain."

She crossed her legs, her skirt riding up on her thighs. I changed the subject.

"Look, is this how the contracts are rewritten?

"Which contracts?"

"The ones that says who owns everything in Dream London."

"The contracts? You can't rewrite contracts, Captain Wedderburn. Not the ones that count."

"The ones that count?"

"The ones that anchor Dream London in place. Surely you knew that? That's axiomatic."

"Axiomatic," I repeated. "Of course."

Miss Merchant gave me a knowing look and her skirt rode a little higher. I caught a glance of the bare thigh above her stocking tops. She saw where I was looking.

"Perk of the job," she said.

Looking around the room I saw so many secretaries perched on desks, all good looking, all being eyed up by their bosses. It was worse than the Executive Dining Room.

"Where are the contracts?" I asked.

"On the Contract Floor, of course. You couldn't keep them here. Things are mutable on this floor. On the Contract Floor, what is now shalt forever be."

I got to my feet.

"Where are you going?"

"To have a look around," I said.

"You can't. You have to stay here." She leant forward, giving me another view of her generous cleavage. "Stay here and I'll take care of you…"

"I don't think so," I said, and I rose to my feet. "I'm getting fed up with all of this."

And I was off, Miss Merchant calling to me to come back. No one took any notice of either of us. The rest of the workers were too busy writing or gazing at their secretaries.

I left the main writing room with its leaflets and library atmosphere and found myself in a clean white space filled with rows of drawing tables. Draughtsmen and women sat before clean sheets of paper, tee squares and set squares pressed against the boards, all busy ruling lines and turning compasses. I moved to take a closer look at the nearest.

"What are you drawing?" I asked.

"Redesigns for flats 1-32 on the Mumford Estate, South Wapping," replied the young draughtswoman.

I examined the drawings. The new flats were taller and thinner, like everything else in Dream London. The windows had stretched to look like eyes.

"How do you know to draw them like this?" I asked.

"I don't. I'm just guessing at what looks right. Trying to make them more in the correct style."

The young woman blushed as she spoke, clearly embarrassed by what she was saying.

"More in the style of Dream London," I said. There was a scroll-like pattern around the doors and the window frames. "How can you do this? How do you do it?"

"I just draw the drawings. It's the Numbers Floor that makes the universe more mutable. They pass us the handles to the universe, and we use those handles to change things around."

"I've been to the Numbers Floor," I said.

"Then you'll know what I'm talking about. Everything is different down there, and nothing makes sense."

Miss Merchant bustled into the room at that point. She was flanked by two large men in dark uniforms that reminded me more than a little of the Quantifiers.

"Captain Wedderburn! You are to return to your desk at once!"

"Certainly not," I said, and, without further hesitation, I ran. The two men were too big for pursuit in such a place and I quickly lost them by dodging down another corridor. I emerged into a room that looked like a large lounge. It was filled with grey-haired ladies and dark young men, all busy writing on scrolls with quill pens. I knew where I was as soon as saw the place.

"This is where you write the fortunes, isn't it?" I said.

The old lady nearest me looked up. She had a cup of tea on a little table by her side.

"I write fortunes, yes," she said. "What do you want to know? When you'll meet the girl?"

"I've already met plenty of girls."

"Ah, but I'm talking about the one who will save you."

"But how do you know?" I asked. "How do you know what's going to happen? You just make it all up, don't you?"

"Make it up?" said the old lady, indignantly. "This is the way things should be!"

"Says who?"

The old woman fixed me with a stare.

"Young man, are you saying that I should write that you will *not* meet the girl? Is that what you want?"

"Well, maybe, yes, that is what I want."

"Then all I can say is, it's a good job that you're not writing the fortunes, isn't it?"

She nodded her head and turned back to her work. I wasn't finished.

"What happens to them?" I asked, waving a hand at a pile of scrolls.

She sighed and looked back up at me. "You're an inquisitive young man, aren't you? Once they're completed they're sent up to the Contract Floor so that they can't be changed."

"Which way is the Contract Floor?"

"I don't know. Now, if you don't mind, I'd like to get on with my work. There's a young lady out there who's going to meet the man of her dreams in just three weeks time..."

"Captain Wedderburn!"

Miss Merchant shouted at me from the end of the room and I set off again. Why did she shout? Why do people do that? Why not creep up on me and catch hold of my arm before I ran off?

The next section looked like the original room I had been taken to, but rather than resembling a modern library containing leaflets and games and magazines, this place was more like a traditional library in that it actually contained some books.

People sat at typewriters whilst the librarians brought them books from the shelves. They patiently worked typing manuscripts onto yellow paper.

A typist near me fed a sheet of yellow paper into a machine and began to tap at the keys.

It was a bright cold day in April, and the clocks were striking twelve.

187

"That makes more sense!" said the worker with some satisfaction.

A hand dropped on my shoulder.

"Captain Wedderburn, I do believe! I think you need to come this way."

For a big man, the security guard was awfully quiet. I looked up at him. I could have taken him bare-handed, I suppose, but why waste energy? I reached into my inside pocket.

"Look at this," I said, pulling out the pistol.

"It's a pistol," said the guard, unnecessarily.

"Very good," I replied. "Now, I've had enough of this place. I'm leaving. Don't try and stop me."

The man stepped back.

"I can't help thinking you're taking this a bit too far," he said.

"Step back."

He did as he was told.

"And now, which way to the lifts?"

"Down there," he said.

"Don't try and follow me," I said.

He didn't.

I walked from the typing room and into another that was a pornographic dream. Centrefolds lay spread on every surface. Pictures of women and men were stuck to the walls, the whole room was pink and chocolate and yellow with flesh. The men who worked in this room all wore little round glasses through which they peered short-sightedly at the pictures.

I didn't stop to look, I'd seen it all before. I headed on to the reception. The old man at the desk looked up at me.

"Leaving so soon, Captain Wedderburn?"

I pressed the button. The lift door opened straight away and I stepped inside. I didn't know for sure where I was going, but I had had enough of Angel Tower for the moment.

I hated the Writing Floor. I hated what it represented. All this time living in Dream London and I had wondered what was happening, but now I had my worst suspicions confirmed. Dream London was being made by people who were too frightened, or more often, too lazy to figure out how the universe works. All they did was write down what they wanted and it came true.

You know what the trouble with that is? All you ever get is what's in your own imagination, and I'm telling you, until it's been stretched by the Universe, the human imagination isn't very big.

SEVEN

THE BOYS IN TAUPE

I EMERGED INTO the great cathedral of the entrance hall. The hole in the ceiling, high above me, seemed to be calling for my attention. I ignored it. What was at the top of Angel Tower? Was it watching me now?

"There he is!"

I recognised the piping voice of Honey Peppers. At the same time I saw the large shape of a Quantifier pushing through the crowd towards me. I guessed I was wrong when I assumed that the Daddio had no power here in Angel Tower. Men in dark suits tumbled across the floor, scattered like skittles, bowled over by the huge mass of the Quantifier. For the umpteenth time that day I didn't bother to argue, I simply turned and ran for the huge revolving door. I spun through it and found my way out into the daylight.

"Captain Wedderburn!"

Miss Elizabeth Baines was waiting outside in a blue gingham dress. She waved a hand at me.

"Later!" I called, and I ran off up the street, heading towards the railway station. Never let it be said the Captain James Wedderburn couldn't outrun a six-year-old girl, a love-lorn woman and a thirty-five-stone man.

Another Quantifier was waiting by the steps of the railway station. He began to lumber towards me and I turned and made to run on up the street, only to find still more people blocking my way.

"Everything all right here, sir?"

I found myself face to face with Dream London's finest: the Boys in Taupe.

"Excuse me, officers!" I said. Behind them, the first Quantifier paused and stepped back into the crowd. The Daddio's men obviously didn't feel quite so confident on this territory.

"Why, it's Captain James Wedderburn!" said one of the browncoats. His long tunic was decorated in silver and contained many, many pockets for accepting the numerous bribes and gifts that enable Dream London justice to function.

"Hello there, er... Officer Morrison, isn't it?"

"That's right, sir!" He turned to his companion. "Captain Wedderburn here runs a little business over on my old beat. You might remember me talking about it?"

"Captain Wedderburn of Belltower End!" said the other officer, grinning the grin of one who shortly expects to be on the receiving end of someone's largesse. "Who doesn't know Captain Wedderburn?"

Who didn't, I wondered? I was beginning to think all of Dream London knew who I was better than I did. The serifs on Rudolf Donati's words seemed to have broken off underneath my skin... Nonetheless, I affected a careless bonhomie, all the harder given the look Honey Peppers was giving me in the distance.

"I was just heading back there now as it happens, officers. Perhaps you'd like to accompany me? The girls at Belltower End always appreciate the attention of the Boys in Taupe. It makes them feel *so* much more secure."

The two police officers looked at each other.

"Not on our beat, sir," said Officer Morrison, pulling a sad face.

"... but perhaps," suggested the other, "perhaps if we were to walk with you part of the way there? We could maybe come and see you another time?"

"Of course," I said.

We set off down the street together. It was the end of the morning, and the sun was high in the sky, and it seemed that it too was following the path of Captain James Wedderburn.

THE OLD BILL accompanied me to the railway station by the Aviaries. Golden orioles and scarlet tanagers fought in cages, cheered on by the excited spectators who pushed forward through the clouds of dusty red and yellow feathers.

"They always get excited when there's a big match coming," said Officer Grove. "Who do you support, Jim? The Hammers or the Armoury?"

"I support the winning team," I said, and the pair of them laughed. I plunged my hand into my pocket and pulled out two pieces of candy.

"Here you go, boys," I said. "A little present."

"Thank you," said Officer Grove.

"And I was just wondering. Do officers always carry the Truth Script with them whilst on duty?"

"We do."

"Do they ever get lost?"

They looked at each other.

"Occasionally, sir," said Officer Morrison.

"And do the officers get into trouble when they get lost?"

"Oh yes," said Officer Grove. He looked at his partner. "Though there are ways that can be mitigated. With the right... understanding."

"I see." I smiled.

"Do we have an understanding, officers?"

The looked at each other again. The briefest of nods were exchanged.

"And here we are," said Officer Morrison. "We'll see you on your train, sir,"

He reached out and shook my hand. I felt a scrap of paper there.

"And I'll see you soon," I replied with a wink.

I climbed the steps to the station and rode the train back to the Egg Market, where I made my way to the Laughing Dog.

"Where's Bill?" I demanded.

The barman gave me a look of bored contempt.

"She's upstairs with a client."

"Which room?"

"None of your business. You wait down here until she's ready."

I reached across the bar and grabbed him by his greasy leather lapels.

"I said, which room?"

He looked at me, blinking rapidly. "Room 5."

"Thank you." I let go of him, then wiped my hands across the front of his jacket before running up the stairs and slamming open the door.

A man lay naked on the bed, face down, crying. Bill sat, fully clothed in a chair, reading a book.

"Wedderburn!" she said, without looking up. "Wait your turn..."

"You." I pointed to the man on the bed. "Get out."

The man had turned to look at me, his face a picture of misery.

"But I..."

"I said, get out."

I took hold of his arm and manhandled him from the room, then I returned and scooped up his clothes, grimacing at the filthy state of his underpants, and threw them out after him.

"I never realised you were that attracted to me," said Bill, closing her book. "Well, get undressed and start crying."

"Don't make jokes," I said. "You've set me up. You, the Cartel, everyone!"

"Why do you say that?" Bill's face was unreadable. Whatever emotions she was feeling at the moment, she wasn't letting on to me.

"You let me think that I was walking into that tower undercover. It turns out that everyone in there knows who I am!"

"Nonsense," she said.

I'd had enough of this. I pulled the piece of paper that Officer Morrison had given me from my pocket and handed it to her.

"What's this?" she said, reading it. Too late. She obviously hadn't recognised what it was. She did now.

"You bastard," she said.

"Ain't it the truth?" I smiled. "Now, tell me. You set me up, didn't you? Everyone knows who I am."

"Wouldn't you be disappointed if it was any other way? You love the cult of Captain James Wedderburn! You even talk about yourself in the third person!"

She made it sound like a fault. But Captain Wedderburn doesn't like to be distracted. I leant forward and lowered my own voice.

"Okay. Why did you send me in there?"

"To find out what was going on."

The look she gave me made it clear that she didn't think much of my question.

"But they know who I am!"

She rolled her eyes.

"Of course they know who you are! Angel Tower was going to invite you in there anyway. We just got to you first, put you to work for the good guys."

That silenced me. Bill was still showing no emotion. She was a cold woman. A competent woman.

"They were going to invite me in anyway?" I said, softly.

"Of course. They've been working their way down the hierarchy. First the big fish, then the middle rankers. This past month they've invited in all the small time criminals. All the little Napoleons. Hollis, the Devenport Twins, Howling Woolfe, Sweet Sweetlove. All of them have been asked up the tower. It was inevitable that you would be asked, too."

"Sweetlove?" I said. "Wasn't he found dead inside an egg in Dream London Zoo?"

"He was."

"Hollis and Howling Woolfe are doing all right for themselves, though," I said thoughtfully. "But the Devenports have gone missing…"

Bill smiled.

"There's a turf war being fought in this city between the gangs and the Daddio. I'd guess that Angel Tower is helping things along."

I thought about Saturday night, how Luke Pennies had accused me of burning down his buildings, how I'd met both the Cartel and the Daddio's Quantifier.

"You don't think I'm special at all," I said. "You're just using me."

Bill's mouth creased. Finally, the emotion was breaking through. She began to laugh. And laugh and laugh. She seemed to almost lose control of herself.

"You thought… You didn't…"

She wiped the tears that formed at the corners of her eyes. I waited patiently for her to regain control of herself.

"Of course we're using you!" she said. "And you didn't guess? Are you upset? You're an arch manipulator yourself!"

"Me? How dare you!"

"Oh come on, Jim. You call yourself Captain to try and dignify what you do, but what are you really?"

"I look after my girls!"

She said nothing. I'd heard her implied accusation before, of course, but for some reason this time it struck home. What was it that Miss Merchant, my secretary on the Writing Floor, had said to me? That I was a Queen. A master manipulator. And I was. But now it didn't seem such a compliment. It seemed grubby. Shoddy.

"I'm not just a pimp," I said. I lowered my voice, looked at the floor. I spoke in serious tones. "You've only been here a few days. You don't know what it's been like here. Women lost their jobs. Some had no one to support them. I looked after them, gave them a place to live, let them earn a livelihood."

I gazed at her, one professional to another. And I realised just how outclassed I was by the professional in front of me. Bill had read the Truth Script and turned it to her advantage. She was using the truth as a weapon.

"You put them on the game," she said.

"Sorry, Bill. I don't accept that. All my girls are adults. They made their choice. You have to take responsibility for your own actions."

"I agree with you there, Jim."

I smiled at that, more confident. She tilted her head.

"Tell me, what's MTPH?"

My eyes narrowed.

"What do you want to know that for?"

"I was interested. The girls here talk about it."

"It's a drug," I said. "A Dream London drug. Like Blue Glass, or Speckle. Or Cherry Pie. Have you ever tried Cherry Pie? Everything you eat tastes wonderful afterwards."

"I don't want to talk about Cherry Pie," said Bill. "I want to talk about MTPH. Do you give it your girls?"

Who was interrogating who here?

"Some of them take it, yes."

"Do you give it to them?"

"Hey, they'd only buy it from someone else! At least from me they get the real thing, uncut."

"And at a reasonable price?"

"I don't make a profit on it. It comes out of their takings."

"You're a saint in human form."

"Hey, if it makes things easier..."

"What does MTPH do?"

"I've got some here," I said, pulling out one of my little striped candies. "Try some for yourself."

"I don't need to. I know what it does." She curled her lip. "Maybe you should read the Truth Script, Jim. Can you really be that unaware about yourself?"

Bill's voice was steely cold again. I felt uneasy.

"I've got nothing to hide. MTPH helps the girls," I said. "It helps them to get on with the job. Not all their clients are Adonises, you know."

"Go on, Captain Wedderburn. How does it help them?"

She leant forward on her toes at this, gazing up at me with green eyes.

"It helps them to enjoy themselves," I mumbled.

"Enjoy themselves? How?"

"It gives them empathy with their client."

She was silent now, just staring at me. Leaving a conversational hole for me to fill.

"It helps them to feel what their client feels," I added. "Their client's pleasure becomes their pleasure."

"And if their client despises them?

"Why should they do that? Why pay to go with a girl they despise?"

"That's part of the attraction, isn't it?"

"Only if you're of a certain sort of mind."

"So you admit that some men are of that sort of mind? And some of them will use the services of your women?"

"Well, perhaps..."

"So if the women have taken MTPH, and they feel that loathing directed against themselves, what then?"

I saw there was no use in lying.

"Then they will feel that loathing, and they will enjoy it. They will come to loathe themselves."

She said nothing else, just stared at me.

"But that hardly ever happens," I said. It sounded weak, even to me.

"Are all the women who work for you happy?"

"Who's really happy in this city?" I countered.

"Answer the question!"

"They're happy enough."

But I thought of Sweet Sue who had walked into the Thames, and Lovely Annabel and Karen and Amelia who had just lain in bed and refused to get up.

Bill was gazing at me as if she could read my thoughts.

"And you complain when you say that you've been manipulated, Captain Wedderburn?"

There's nothing like attacking someone else's weaknesses when you know that you're in the wrong.

"Yes, I do say that I've been manipulated," I countered. "What exactly do you think that you're playing at, sending me into Angel Tower like that?"

Bill Dickenson smiled.

"Well, as you were going to be summoned anyway, we thought we might as well give you the opportunity to help someone else for once in your selfish, worthless life."

"Help someone else? What are you talking about!"

"I'm just saying that Angel Tower have got you sewn up. You're an arch manipulator, and Dream London has a use for selfish people like you. Dream London is the place where the individual takes precedence over the group, after all."

"Hey!" I said. "Hey. And since when did the group care about Captain Jim Wedderburn? Everything I've done in my life, I did it on my own."

Bill laughed at that.

"Well fucking good for you!"

Without thinking, I raised my hand to her.

"Do you really want to try that?" asked Bill, and she gazed at me, sweetly. "I'm telling the truth, remember? You do that and I'll really hurt you."

Slowly, I lowered my hand.

"Now, Captain James, here's something to think about. You're going to go back to Angel Tower. That's inevitable. Trust me on that. So, why don't you ask yourself this? Are you going to go back there on your own, or are you going to do something to help us?"

I stared at her, almost shaking with anger.

"What's in it for me?" I asked.

She snorted.

"I thought the Cartel had already offered you the freehold of Belltower End. Isn't that enough for you? Just think of how much more money you can make when you don't have to pay rent. You'll be able to afford enough MTPH to enslave the female population of West London!"

"I told you, I don't..." I calmed down. She was only baiting me. "Anyway," I said. "What have the Cartel got to do with this? Do you know what it's like in Alan's house at night? If Alan is a representative of the Cartel, I don't hold out much hope for them as a viable force."

"You're not kidding," said Bill. "I told you, Dream London is not a place where groups function, it's just a collection of selfish individuals. The Cartel was pretty effective to begin with, but Dream London has worked upon its members. Now it barely functions. None of the little groups in this place amount to anything. Do you have any idea the difficulty we've had trying to organise any sort of resistance?"

"Who's we?"

"The Americans. The French. The rest of the fucking world. Do you know what it's like out there? Do you think that life is going on as normal now that London has vanished into another place? People out there are terrified. The whole world is scared, and what do people do when they're scared?"

"Go into denial?" I said.

"Yeah, they do that. Or they get angry. They get violent. People want this city destroyed, you asshole."

I was shocked. She was right. I'd never really thought about it that way.

"Okay," I said. "I take your point. But you're wasting your time. There's no point me going back to the Writing Floor in Angel Tower. I need to get to the Contract Floor."

"The Contract Floor?" said Bill. "What's that?"

"It's where the unchanging documents are kept. The Writing Floor is where the changes are happening. There are people there who are writing the future."

"Then surely that's where we need to go," said Bill. She nodded. "Yes. We could get them to change things back to how they were."

I shook my head.

"That won't work. Someone could just write it back again. All of this..."

I waved my arm around the room. "All of this is rooted in the land that was originally sold to... whoever. We need to get those deeds of ownership back."

"Well, duh," said Bill. "How do you suggest we do that?"

"By getting to the Contract Floor," I said. "That's where the deeds are kept."

She stared at me for a moment, thinking.

I waved my hand in front of her face.

"Stop that," she said.

"Hey, I'm surprised you didn't figure that out for yourself," I said.

"I've only been here a few days," said Bill. "But you're right, someone should have figured this out before."

She lapsed into silence again.

I looked around the room, at the obscene pictures. Finally, Bill spoke.

"How long until this Truth Script wears off?" she said.

"About ten minutes," I said. That was a lie. I had no idea how long it lasted for.

"Come on," she said. "We're going out."

"Going out?" I said. "Why?"

"We're going to ask for help. Oh, and James..."

"Yes?"

"You understand that I'm still under the influence of the script?"

"Yes."

She leant closer to me and her eyes were so, so hard.

"If you ever do that to me again, I will kill you."

She smiled as she said the words.

"Do you believe me?"

EIGHT

THE SPIRAL

WE LEFT THE Laughing Dog and hurried towards the railway station.

"Where are we going?" I asked Bill.

"The Spiral," she replied.

"Why there?"

"It's being watched."

"Watched? By who?"

"By my superiors."

"The ones who want to bomb Angel Tower?"

"Yep."

I shook my head as we walked.

"You've not been up there," I said. "I don't think bombs will work. All the old machinery is warped into something else in Dream London." I frowned as I looked at the railway line, soaring above the streets on its green embankment. "You know, the numbers don't work. People get lost when they try to leave. I wonder if it's connected?"

Bill said nothing, moving through the Egg Market with a determined stride.

"Is there a something in science where you don't know where you are?" I wondered aloud. "Where you know where you're moving to, but you can't figure out your position? That's what it's like riding the railways in Dream London."

We were approaching the steps to the station now.

A green alligator train slid into the station. I saw the huge bulk of two men, staring out of the windows.

"On second thoughts, we'll walk," I said.

"No way," said Bill. "We need to get a move on."

"There are two of the Daddio's Quantifiers on there," I said. "Do you feel as if you could fight them?"

"No," she said, perfectly truthfully. "We'll take a taxi, then,"

We turned and began to walk away. Somewhere behind me I could hear the voice of Miss Elizabeth Baines calling after me.

"Captain Wedderburn! Oh, Captain! Stop! It's urgent!"

"Not her too," I said.

"Who is that woman?" asked Bill as I hurried her along.

"That's Miss Elizabeth Baines. She's mad. She thinks I'm going to marry her."

"She sounds pretty upset."

"Of course she's upset," I replied. "She thinks I'd make a suitable husband. Wouldn't the thought of marrying me upset you? Like I said, she's mad. Just like everyone else in this city."

There were two pedalcabs and one hansom cab waiting outside the station.

"Not the horse," said Bill.

"Okay."

We climbed into the first pedal cab. The driver was a young woman barely five feet tall. She stood on the pedals above a mountain of silver cogs and gears, her legs like young trees.

"The Spiral, please!" called Bill.

"Twenty minutes," replied our driver and she let out a huge grunt and began to pedal. Slowly the cab began to move. A scatter of filigree-patterned starlings erupted around the cab as we glided down a side street, and then we were rolling down the ramp onto the Kingsway. A flight of bright green parakeets arrowed alongside the road, heading for the docks and passage to other lands.

"You talked about the Numbers Floor," said Bill, suddenly. "Did you hear about the mathematicians, James?"

"No? What about them?"

"They committed suicide. All the ones remaining in Dream London. At least, it looked like suicide."

"It'll have been suicide," I said, thinking of the Numbers Floor. "Trust me."

THE SPIRAL HAD begun in Piccadilly Circus, back when Piccadilly Circus still lay at the end of Regent Street, back before it had spun off to its current stamping ground.

Now the electric displays had crackled and died, and the buildings had pulled back into the distance, a grey horizon of broken teeth, a broken Stonehenge. The ground had crumbled and turned over itself and slipped downwards in a wide concrete spiral. The spiral formed a path lined with two queues of Dream Londoners. One queue of eager observers descended to look through the hole at the bottom of the Spiral, the second ascended in stunned silence.

Barrows and stalls had been set up all around the perimeter, selling ice creams and coffee, flowers and jewelled beetles.

"Look at the statues," said Bill, pointing beyond the stalls. "What are they supposed to be?"

"I don't know," I said, squinting. "They don't quite make sense... Why are we here, Bill?"

"To send a signal. Stop asking me questions. Don't make me tell you anything else. Now, take my arm. Let's look as if we're enjoying ourselves."

I did as I was told. I was past arguing. The brightly dressed people walked amongst the broken forest of stone that rose from the concrete ground, and I peered closer.

"They're people," I said, and I suddenly smiled, despite myself. "They're hugging!" I said.

"They're not just hugging," said Bill.

Now I knew what I was looking at the statues resolved themselves into figures of men and women in various erotic positions. Sometimes alone, more often in pairs or threes or fours.

"And parents bring their children to this place?" said Bill in amazement, watching as a young girl skipped by, her hair in curls. I shuddered. The girl reminded me of Honey Peppers.

"Look at that one," said Bill.

We walked around the edge of the stalls to see the statue that stood at the top of the Spiral. Women in white crinoline, men in striped blazers, children in sailor suits: no one could pass it by without stopping a moment to stare.

The figures on this statue were still uncompleted, still half focused, but the meaning of the tableaux was obvious. Two women, five men and some shorter figures, all engaged in group sex. The two women in particular were enjoying themselves immensely, the half formed expressions on their faces caught between joy and ecstasy.

"Why?" said Bill. "What does it mean?"

"It means there's more sex than love in Dream London," I said. "Or hadn't you picked up on that?"

"There's diminishing amounts of sex, according to what the other girls tell me," said Bill. "More and more of the men seem to just want to tell the girls about their problems then burst into tears."

She flashed a look at me. "Is that what's happening to the girls at Belltower End?"

"Not my girls," I said. "You wouldn't waste what they had to offer by crying into their bosom."

"You're loathsome," said Bill.

I was rather hurt. I wasn't being serious, but Bill was. She was speaking the truth.

"Tell me now, what are we doing here?" I demanded.

"Sending a signal." She jabbed me in the side with her fingers. I don't know what she hit, but I doubled up in incredible pain. She bent over and hissed in my ear. "I told you, don't demand answers from me when I'm like this."

We joined the thinning evening queue and began the slow descent. The crowd shuffled forward bit by bit as those at the front took their turn looking through the hole.

"Have you been here before?" asked Bill.

I said nothing. Two could play at her game.

"Stop acting like a child. Have you been here before?"

"A couple of times," I said, grudgingly. "The Spiral gets deeper all the time. The hole gets wider."

"What do you think is down there?"

"Another world," I replied.

"Do you really think that it could be Pandemonium?"

"I don't believe in Pandemonium."

Bill looked up into the violet sky. "Which reminds me…" she said.

She pulled a mirror from somewhere within her dress and pointed it to the sky. She began to flick it this way and that.

"Heliography?" I said. "You're flashing messages?"

"The spy satellites can still pick up the reflections," she said. "Dream London hasn't managed to reach up high enough to affect them yet."

"Give it time," I said.

"What're you doing, darling?" asked the man behind us in the queue.

"She's trying to do her make-up," I said.

"There's no need," said the man. "Pretty girl like you." His girlfriend elbowed him in the ribs.

We shuffled forward down the Spiral. From where we stood we could look over the heads of three spiral turns of people, all waiting their turn to look down the hole. It was like queuing for the rides at an old theme park. There was the same air of expectation, the same sense of carnival. Still we shuffled on until, just as evening was falling, we reached the front of the queue.

The hole lay at the dead centre of the Spiral. It was the size of a manhole, just big enough for someone to climb through. A woman in a peaked cap stood nearby, keeping order.

"No more than two at once," she said to us. "Take your time. You don't want to fall in, do you?"

Bill and I got down on our hands and knees and crept forward to the edge of the hole. I looked down and saw a patchwork of green fields, far, far below.

"It *is* another world," I said.

You could make out cities in the middle of the fields, irregular grey blobs.

"There's a city directly below us," said Bill, in awe.

"Is it directly below?" I wondered aloud, looking down. "I'm sure it used to be more off centre..."

"It's below," she said. "And look. Look at the shadow."

"Where?"

"Look to the centre of the city. A shadow. Cast by that tower in the middle. The tower is foreshortened at this angle, the shadow gives it away."

I looked again. I couldn't see anything.

"Are those cranes down there?" said Bill. "They must be building the tower..."

"Time's up, sir and madam. Let someone else have a look."

We crawled back from the hole and got to our feet, brushing off our knees as we did so.

"It's incredible," I said.

"I know," said the attendant. "And it gets a little closer every day."

"Do you know there is a tower in the middle?" said Bill. "I think it's growing towards this hole."

The attendant agreed. "Professor Humphrey brings his telescope here in the early morning to take measurements."

"I think the tower will join to this hole," said Bill.

"And when it does, I think something will climb up it and come through."

The attendant laughed.

"Madam! Let's not frighten the other customers."

WE WALKED BACK up the ramp away from the hole and crossed the wide space around the Spiral.

"I have to get back to the Laughing Dog," said Bill.

"I'm not sure where I'm going," I said.

"You need to get back to the Poison Yews."

"Why? The place is a madhouse. Margaret keeps making passes at me. Alan is under the spell of Shaqeel..."

"Shaqeel," said Bill. "I wish we could do something about him... I'm sure he's working alone, just another guy out for himself..."

"The only sensible one there is Anna," I said, wistfully.

The thing was, I wasn't sure where else to go. Daddio Clarke was sure to have Belltower End staked out. The smartest thing to do would be to get away from the city for a while and lay low, but of course that option no longer applied. You couldn't escape Dream London.

We left the wide open space and headed down an evening-lit street in search of a taxi. Couples out for an evening stroll lined the pavements, and the poets and musicians were emerging. Somewhere nearby I heard the sound of an accordion. Then a harsh voice barked out:

"I spy a soldier!"

It was hard to miss the man who spoke the words. He wore a scarlet jacket covered in silver braid; his tight black trousers were tucked into polished black boots that passed his knees.

"Well?" he said. "Am I right, sir?"

"I was a soldier," I admitted, looking down at my bright green military jacket. "Not any more."

"Once a soldier, always a soldier, sir! I knew it! You can't fool me!"

Now I saw the desk, tucked back in a shop doorway. A man and a woman dressed in similarly old fashioned costumes. Both were good looking, though my eye was naturally drawn towards the woman, the way her long curly blonde hair spilled down, the way she filled her jacket, the way the stripes on her white trousers curved over her hips.

"I see you've noticed Gloria, sir!" He nudged me in the ribs. "What soldier wouldn't?" Gloria was standing to attention; her brown eyes slid to meet mine and she gave me a saucy wink before resuming eyes-front. "Plenty more like her in the Dream Londoners!"

"The Dream Londoners?"

"Prospect Tower First Infantry, ma'am!" The soldier gave Bill a second look: she was dressed like a whore, after all. "Ladies like yourself are always welcome there, too."

"What's that supposed to mean?" demanded Bill.

"Prospect Tower First Infantry?" I said. "Why does a tower need an army? Is there a war?"

The soldier laughed. "Not that I know of, sir. But there are other places. Sail up the river and you're in other lands. They're always in need of people to keep the peace. Old soldier like you would be welcome in the regiment, sir."

"I don't fight anymore."

The man held out a hand, fingers spread wide, and waggled it back and forth.

"Not much fighting, really. Most of the time we keep the peace. There're a lot of primitive people down the river. We do our bit to bring a bit of civilisation to them."

"What people?" asked Bill. "You mean humans, like us?"

"Weeeeelll," said the soldier, shaking his hand. "It's debatable as to whether they're like us, isn't it? I mean, look what we've achieved. Cities and books and things like that. The people down the river, well, they just live in little huts. It's not like they're like us, is it?"

"I meant, do they have two arms and legs. Are they humanoid?"

I thought about Mr Monagan, the orange frog who insisted he was a man.

"Oh yes. They're humanoid. Quite good workers some of them, when you can get them to understand what you want. Can be really quite on the ball, when they want to be. That's what I mean sir..." He turned back to me, effectively dismissing Bill. "Sign up today and you could get yourself dressed up in a smart uniform like this! Girls like a man in uniform..." He winked again.

I was tempted, there was no denying it. Sign up, sail up the river and live the life of Reilly, lording it over the savages. The uniform, the women, the chance to make a little on the side. It would be just like the old days... But what would I really be letting myself in for? I'd be astonished if this man was telling me the full truth.

"I'm sorry," I said, regretfully. "I'm not interested."

"Come on, sir. Tell me that you're busy, tell me that you are earning more at the moment, tell me that you've got commitments, but don't tell me that you're not interested! Old soldier like you. Admit it, you miss it, don't you?"

"No..."

"Come on, you miss the camaraderie. Just think about it, sir, sailing up the river with your mates, new lands to explore. And that's not all..."

He stopped, clapped his hand over his mouth.

"Sorry sir, said too much. Only, well, listen sir. I shouldn't tell you this, but I can trust you, can't I? Old soldier and everything?"

Bill rolled her eyes, the soldier ignored her.

"Only, well, there are rumours, you know how it is, the word is, that well," he came closer, lowered his voice, "face it sir, it's obvious. This is just the beginning. The Spiral is only part of it. You've heard what's happening in the parks, haven't you?"

"Tell me," said Bill, suddenly alert. "What's happening in the parks?"

"Not for your ears, ma'am!" He leant closer to me again. "But you know something's up, sir. No one can get near them! Something big is happening there, sir. Something that will make the river redundant. A new way to the other lands, sir! And I tell you what, when that happens, they're going to need a lot more soldiers! I tell you what, sir, sign up now and get yourself established. Get yourself promoted and dug in. Get yourself behind the counter in the quartermaster's stores where you can get your hands in the honey, a little for you, a little for the troops. Things fall off the back of the lorry, and into a smart man's bag. You know how it works, sir. You know how it works..."

I looked at Bill; her eyes were alive with interest.

"I'm convinced!" she said. "Where do I sign?"

"Are you sure, Bill?" I said. Was that the truth? Was she still under the effect of the Script?

The soldier laughed.

"She's got some balls, sir! I'll say that! How about you? You wouldn't let the lady join on her own, would you?"

He took Bill's hand and led her to the desk by which the other two soldiers stood. Gloria smiled at me as I approached. She more than smiled at me; she made it perfectly clear how she was interested in me.

The recruiting sergeant sat at the desk and opened a leather folder. He pulled out two sheets of yellow paper and laid them on the desk. Bill took one and examined it.

"I can't read the writing at the bottom," she said.

"Don't worry about that," said the recruiting sergeant.

"And I've never heard of some of these names. *Cleronic Bovaclus, Valvius Methostophile.* Some of these words aren't even written in any script I recognise."

I picked up the other one of the sheets, and looked at some of the strange letters inscribed upon it. Not in black ink, but of a colour that seemed to shimmer like a beetle shell, and all of a sudden strange numbers were swimming before my eyes. Reds and greens and the other numbers from the tower. At the same time I felt someone gently stroke my bottom. I smelt perfume, and Gloria leant closer to me, her long blonde hair tickling my face.

"Pen, sir? Pen, madam?" said the recruiting sergeant, smiling as he held out one in each hand.

Despite myself, I was reaching out to take one. As I did, it seemed to me that a fresh wind blew from the sealed shop doorway behind him. I smelt grass and the sea.

I would have signed there and then if Bill hadn't suddenly laughed loudly.

"Oh yes," she said. "It doesn't affect me so much. I am new here after all."

"Excuse me, miss?"

"The flowers you have in your pocket, Sergeant. And you too, Gloria. Look at Jim here. He's quite bewitched!"

I shook my head. She was right.

"And I feel so much better," she said. "Completely back to normal." She glared at me.

"Oh, that's good," I said. With some effort, I placed the paper back down on the desk. "I think I need to go and think about this."

"Not to worry, sir, I'll be here all week." The Sergeant winked at me. "And so will Gloria!" he added.

THE SKY WAS darkening, blue ink seeping down from above. The air was filling with the smell of flowers, and the birds chirruped and squawked their evening messages.

"You wanted to go," said Bill.

"It was the flowers."

"Do you always run away when things get tough?"

"Why do you say that?"

"You left the army. You're thinking of abandoning Alan and the Cartel."

"I told you, you don't know what it's like in that house."

There was a beef stand up ahead.

"Two please," I said, holding up two fingers. "And two teas."

"I hate the way you Brits drink tea, strong and milky."

"There's a coffee stand further along."

We watched as the vendor sliced beef from a joint onto two slices of bread.

"Onionsmustardhorseradish?" he asked.

"Yes please," I said.

"And me."

The vendor wrapped the sandwiches in paper and handed them across. Two cups of tea were placed on the edge of his barrow.

"Polystyrene cups," said Bill. "How appropriate."

I took a bite of the sandwich, hot greasy paper on my fingers. It tasted so good...

A hand snatched the sandwich from me. I spun around, ready to throw a punch at whoever had stolen my meal, and came face to face with a wide-eyed Mr Monagan.

"Oh, Mr James! I looked all over for you! Come now! Come now, Mr James! It's urgent!"

"Calm down, Mr Monagan. Just calm down! What's the matter?"

"It's Belltower End, Mr James! The Daddio is there! He's set it on fire!"

GREEN

DREAM LONDON ZOO

Mr Monagan led me through the darkening streets towards Belltower End. Ahead I caught glimpses of flames licking at the purple sky. Soft white ash rained down upon me.

"What happened?" I gasped as I jogged along.

"Three big men and a little girl, Mister James. They came along and stood in the square. The little girl was laughing."

"Honey Peppers," I said.

"They'd brought your friend along. He'd been badly beaten."

"My friend?" I said, already guessing the answer. "Who?"

"Second Eddie."

Second Eddie. So he hadn't betrayed me after all.

"Is he okay?"

"No, Mister James." Mr Monagan was silent for a moment. "He's dead."

"Dead," I said. I staggered as I ran, unbalanced by the shock. "How?"

219

"It's a horrible story, Mister James. Horrible! You see, when the little girl came, no one paid her any attention. One of the girls went to help your friend, but no one else seemed to care. They were too busy enjoying themselves. The little girl didn't like that. She shouted out for everyone to listen, but no one did. She stamped her foot and one of the clients laughed and then one of the big men hit him."

"The Quantifiers. They're called Quantifiers."

Mr Monagan seemed unphased by the running. He loped along at my side with his strange frog-like gait.

"The little girl told everyone they had three minutes to get out of the buildings. She said that the Moston girls were her property and they should come to her, and that everyone else could just..."

He was embarrassed.

"I can imagine what she said," I panted. The street here was the consistency of tar. It clung to my feet as I ran. "She's not a nice little girl."

"She's not, Mister James. She's not. Still everyone ignored her, despite her appalling language. No-one did anything. Some of the girls looked out of the windows. A lot of the men just drifted away, or headed back up to the rooms. The little girl lost her temper."

"I can imagine."

"She stamped her foot again. She told the Quantifiers to stop just standing there and to start burning."

We turned a corner, ran into a haze of ash. I wiped my face and went on running.

"The Quantifiers picked up big barrels. They must have brought them there with them. Oh, Mr James! The barrels contained yellow liquid. They splashed it over the buildings. Where it touched stone, it burned! The stone burned away like wood! They took Second Eddie, and oh, Mr James! They pushed him into the fire. A spark jumped on his hand. Just one spark, and he burnt away, just like that. Like a spark jumping from a fire. He was there and then he was gone!"

I was gasping for air now. I slowed to a walk. It would do little good to arrive there exhausted.

"The little girl said it was to send a message to you, Mister James. She said it was to show that you couldn't protect your property."

"I can't," I said.

"Everyone began to panic then. They screamed, they pushed each other out of the way. The men, the way they mistreated the girls, just to get away, Mister James! They were no gentlemen. The little girl stood in the square and just laughed as the girls began to run from the buildings. The flames, Mister James! The flames! They jumped so high!"

"The girls! My girls! Are they alright?"

"The girls? No, Mr James! They aren't. Catherine and Gemma and Caroline and Julie and Margaret! All of them caught in the flames! I heard them screaming, Mr James. Screaming! And the men in there with them! They screamed too! And the little girl just laughed!"

Anger gave me energy. I began to run once more.

"The Quantifiers made sure the Moston girls were all safe, though. But then they just stood in the middle of the square, giggling, getting in the way. They tried to hug the Quantifiers, but the Quantifiers slapped them. I don't think the Quantifiers are very friendly."

We turned a corner. I could smell the smoke now, smoke overlaid with a strong scent of flowers. Perfumed smoke from a Dream London fire.

"They just stood and watched as the rest of Belltower End burned. Honey Peppers turned and spoke to us all: 'Tell Captain Wedderburn, the Daddio is looking for him.' And then I ran. Ran to warn you."

I slowed to a walk again. I was running into a trap, I knew it. Twice Honey Peppers had warned me about going to Angel Tower, and twice I had ignored her. I knew that the Daddio would exact retribution. I would too, in his shoes. That's how you got respect. I think, in my heart of hearts, I had thought to talk my way out of the situation. Use the old Captain Wedderburn charm. I had obviously misjudged the situation badly. The Daddio's retribution was swift and fierce.

I slowed to a halt.

"Hold on, Mr Monagan. I need to think."

We stopped in the deep shadow of an alley. Salamanders stirred in the darkness, crunching on the beetles that scavenged the bins.

"Mr Monagan, is there anything I can achieve by going to Belltower End, apart from getting myself captured by the Quantifiers?"

"But Mister James! The girls! They need you!"

A voice spoke from the shadows.

"Captain Wedderburn. I owe you an apology."

The night suddenly seemed very deep. The rest of Dream London seemed to recede into the distance. Mr Monagan and I turned towards the alley as a familiar figure stepped forward.

"Luke Pennies," I said.

Except it wasn't quite Luke Pennies. Somehow, in the past three days, he had lost weight. He was still fat, he was no longer obese. Something about his manner had changed, too. He was quieter, more confident.

"Were you waiting for me, Luke?" I gasped.

"I saw your orange man go running by to find you. I guessed you'd come back this way."

I was still trying to regain my breath, I had little to spare for talking.

"What do you want to apologise for?" I asked.

"I accused you of burning down my brothel. I realise now it was nothing to do with you. I'm sorry for trying to kill you."

"Apology accepted," I said. "Perhaps you can make amends. Take a walk back to Belltower End. Scout the area. Tell me who's waiting there."

In the dim light of the alley, I saw Luke Pennies give a mournful smile.

"I don't think you understand, Captain. I apologised for the other night. That doesn't mean I'm on your side."

His mouth fell open, and two eyes looked out at me from his tongue. Mr Monagan stepped between us, pushing me gently backwards.

"Oh no, Mister James! Be careful, now!"

"Take my advice, Jim," said Luke. "Angel Tower has established Dream London, but it's the Daddio who will exploit it. The Cartel will never defeat the ants."

"Ants?"

"It's not too late to join the winning team."

The eyes in Luke's tongue gazed at me.

Mr Monagan tugged at my arm.

"What should we do, Mister James?"

What should we do? Belltower End was in flames, Honey Peppers and the Quantifiers were waiting for us there. There was no point heading back to my flat. They'd have that covered too. The only place of safety I knew of was the Poison Yews.

"I think we should go now, Mr Monagan," I said.

"Hold on," said Luke Pennies. "Take my advice Jim. The Daddio's already annoyed with you. Go to him now, apologise, he'll be reasonable. I'm sure of it. Run away again and you'll just make things worse."

"I'm not running away, Luke. I just need to attend to things. As soon as I'm done, I'll be happy to speak to the Daddio."

Luke laughed.

"Oh, Captain! That sort of thing might work with a child like Honey Peppers. I feel quite insulted that you'd try it on me."

"What might work on a child like Honey Peppers?"

The little voice piped up from somewhere behind me. A child's voice, for sure, but full of the malice and bitterness of someone who had festered in the backrooms of places far worse than Belltower End. All the old whores in the attics and cellars, selling themselves at cut price, full of resentment at the world: they had nothing on that voice.

Honey Peppers stood at the entrance to the alley, holding hands with her Nanny. One of the Quantifiers stood behind them. The big man was greedily eating a large sandwich: a loaf of French bread cut lengthwise and filled with meat and cheese and slices of blue egg.

"Honey Peppers!" I said. "I was just coming to see you."

"Yeah, of course you fucking were."

"Language, Honey, please!" said her Nanny. "You know how cross you get when you stay up late. Half an hour more, and then it's bed time. Okay?"

Honey looked up.

"Nanny, will you please hold your tongue? You know that I'll be staying up late tonight. I'm going to take Captain Wedderburn to the zoo to be fucked by the manatees."

"But…"

"Don't argue with me, Nanny!"

Honey Peppers took a deep breath and shuddered. She turned back to me and smiled.

"Now, Captain Wedderburn, I think it's time for your punishment. Come along."

I reached into my pockets and pulled out both my knife and pistol.

"Run!" I called to Mr Monagan, who was gazing at me stupidly. The orange man immediately erupted into a flapping run that carried him away with surprising speed. Luke Pennies grabbed at me; I slashed at his arm with the knife and followed Mr Monagan. The pair of us plunged down the alleyway. The far end opened out into the inferno of Belltower End. Two black shadows eclipsed the flames, and the remaining two Quantifiers stepped into view, blocking our escape.

"Mister James! This way!"

Mr Monagan was kicking off his black shoes, going nowhere. The two Quantifiers advanced towards us.

I watched in amazement as Mr Monagan leant forward and pressed his hands, then his feet onto the dirty surface of the brick wall and began to climb, slowly at first, and then faster and faster until he was running up the side like a salamander. He paused thirty feet up, turning to see why I wasn't following.

"Mr James! Come on!"

A hand took hold of my shoulder and I slashed at it with my knife, to no avail. Someone gripped my hand and squeezed hard.

"Don't damage him!" called Honey Peppers.

The grip eased and the knife fell from my numb hand. Someone took the pistol.

"Mister James!" called Mr Monagan from somewhere above.

"Don't come back!" I called. "Run!"

I WAS DRAGGED through the warm evening streets of Dream London. One Quantifier held my wrist, and I found myself pulled away from the excitement of the heat and the flames and out into the twilight peace of the better class areas of the city. I smelt the green of the trees above me, their feeling of evening calm completely at odds with the knot of fear in my stomach. In the distance I could hear the whoop and growl and roar of animals.

"We're going to the zoo, are we?" I said.

"I don't think I should tell you that," said the reluctant Quantifier.

"Please yourself." His grip on my arm was like a manacle. I'd given up trying to shake it off. We walked at a brisk pace, the streets widening and becoming cleaner. I saw a grey-suited nanny in the distance, and I looked for Honey Peppers, but this was another woman, taking two little boys dressed in checked coats home to bed.

We turned a corner, and there, ahead of us, was the entrance: a large metal arch set in the middle of the tall pointed bars that enclosed the zoo. The metal railings had grown so tall, twice the size of the Dream London plane trees that stood before them, their bark dappled in yellow and gold. The words *Dream London Zoo* were written on the arch in curly script. I gazed up at them as we passed beneath and the sounds and smell of the zoo enfolded me. The excited chatter of apes, the shriek of birds, the howl of wolves, the trumpeting of elephants, the buzzing of insects. And the smells: the tang of salt water, the green of jungles, the sweet smell of excrement, the spice of musk. So much musk. There were flowers and animals in here, and I could smell the excitement.

"Honey Peppers wasn't serious, was she?" I said, the first stirrings of real fear inside me.

"I wouldn't like to say anything about that," said the reluctant Quantifier.

The animals in Dream London Zoo had changed just like the rest of the city. We passed three bears that walked on their hind legs, paws clasped behind their backs. Two dolphins perched on a wall, looking down at us with a hard expression. Blue monkeys walked the zoo, taunting their caged brethren. Ahead of me I heard the gabble of voices, and I realised we were heading towards some sort of arena, a place for patrons to sit and watch the animals perform. The banked seats of the arena were filled with people, men and women, dressed in their Sunday best, all come to see the show. A group of drummers were playing nearby, banging on the bongos and the tom toms in mismatched wild rhythms that overlapped each other in typical Dream London fashion.

The crowd let off a huge cheer as they saw me being dragged into the arena. It was a sound to make you empty your bowels, to make you want to burst into desperate tears. A hateful, catcalling, jeering cheer. As the noise rose, the scent of flowers thickened, the sickly perfume cloying in the air.

The arena was set out like a theatre: a semicircle of seats facing onto a large pool, half covered in boards. There were two people waiting for me there, standing on the boards over the water. A woman dressed in grey and a small girl with golden curls. Honey Peppers.

"Captain Wedderburn," she said.

"Ms Peppers."

"The Daddio isn't pleased with you," said Honey Peppers.

"Really? Why ever not?"

She stamped her foot.

"Don't you dare try and play your games with me, Captain Wedderburn! You were told not to disappear again last night, and you did!"

"What do you mean, disappear? I knew where I was…"

"BE QUIET!"

She was shaking with anger, her voice becoming shrill.

"YOU WERE TOLD TO HAVE NOTHING TO DO WITH THE CARTEL, AND YET TODAY THIS QUANTIFIER SAW YOU COMING OUT OF ANGEL TOWER!"

"Well…" I began.

"If you speak again out of turn, I'll have to hurt you," said the Quantifier. "Don't think that I won't enjoy it."

I looked up into his piggy eyes and I knew he meant it. I held my tongue. The Quantifier's tongue popped out just to see if I'd got the message.

Honey Peppers seemed to regain control of herself.

"Well, Captain Wedderburn, I warned you! I told you, if you disobeyed again, I'd have you brought here to be fucked by the manatees, and that's what's about to happen… what is it, Nanny?"

The child looked up impatiently at the grey-suited woman who had leant forward to whisper in her ear.

"Yes, yes, I know!" said Honey Peppers. "I know that it's the mandrills that are actually going to fuck him, but the manatee tank is just underneath us, isn't it? Well, isn't it?"

"Well, yes," said the Nanny, hesitantly.

"So he'll be fucked right by the manatees? Honestly! Don't embarrass me, Nanny!"

"Actually dear, he's going to be more *on* the tank than *beside* it..."

Honey Peppers inhaled deeply. She was shaking as she spoke.

"Nanny, I swear, if you don't shut up, I'll have you seen to by the manatees even if it means getting one of the Quantifiers to hold you under the water whilst they do it."

"Sorry, dear."

Honey Peppers took another deep breath, and calmed herself.

"Very well, Captain. Let's begin."

She signalled across the arena. The drummers took up their random, unsynchronised beating once more. Something was wheeled towards us. A cage, covered in a white sheet. Inside it I could hear the shrieks and whoops of the cage's occupants. The cage halted before me and, as the sound of drumming intensified, the cover was pulled away. Three faces pushed their way through the bars, white snouts, striped in red, little eyes looking down from above. Mandrills. You'll know what mandrills look like; they're the largest species of monkey, the ones with the big purple bottoms. These ones were even bigger than normal, almost my height.

They gazed through the bars with a sly, knowing sort of intelligence. I felt like throwing up. I think Honey Peppers saw it in my eyes, because she grinned at that point.

"Okay, Quantifier. Throw him in the cage."

"Hold it!" I said. "Just a moment."

"What is it?" asked Honey Peppers. Behind her, I saw the crowd, standing up on the benches, their tongues sticking out to get a better view.

"Okay," I said. "The Daddio is upset. He thinks a punishment is due. Okay. But not this. Not here. You realise this will ruin my reputation? What use will I be to the Daddio then?"

Honey Peppers smiled so sweetly.

"Ruin your reputation? But what do you mean, Captain Wedderburn?" To the side of me, I heard the impatient whoops of the mandrills. A hand reached out to grab at me, and I slapped it away.

"Whip me," I said. "Make it physical punishment. But not this!"

"But that's exactly the point," said Honey Peppers. "Don't you think the Daddio realises that? If you were to be beaten, that would only add to your mystique. I'm sure you could take the punishment in silence, and the myth would grow, about how Captain Wedderburn can take whatever is thrown at him. The Daddio knows that, Captain. That's why he has brought all these people here to watch you being fucked by the mandrills. Because after that, people won't speak in awe of you behind your back. They'll pity you. They'll laugh at you. They won't fear you so much."

She held her hands beneath her armpits in imitation of a monkey. "Ook ook eek" she said.

I was terrified, I don't mind admitting it. She was right. I could take pain. What I couldn't take was the humiliation.

"Okay, Honey Peppers. I understand. The Daddio has made his point. I won't do it again."

"Oh, Captain. Can't you take your punishment like a man?"

The crowd laughed at that.

"Honey..."

"Honestly Captain, what's the problem? This is what happens to your whores every day, and you make money off them as a result. Well, you'll be just doing the same as them!"

"There's a difference," I said. My mind went back to Miss Merchant on the Writing Floor. Why was everyone suddenly having a go at the honest businessman? "They made the choice to work that way. This isn't my choice."

"They made the choice? Really, Captain? I don't know. I've noticed that when people talk about choices, it's usually the people who are in charge who are setting the alternatives. Do you think your women would have chosen to be whores if they had another alternative?"

"I didn't make the world the way it is," I said.

"Enough talk," said Honey Peppers. "Throw him in the cage."

NINE

THE SEWERS OF DREAM LONDON

DON'T BELIEVE THE lies you might have heard about me ending up in that cage. I know there are people who will say that I was in there for an hour, but, trust me, that's not true. As you might expect, I managed to talk my way out of trouble. Captain Wedderburn has still got a honey tongue when he needs it.

I'll skip how I did it though. You'll want to get on with the action.

"Okay, Honey," I said. "We're even now. I guess I'll be on my way."

Honey Peppers shook her head, those delightful blonde curls bouncing.

"Not yet. You see, Captain, despite everything, the Daddio still believes in you."

"He does?"

"He really does. The Daddio still believes you're a valuable man. You know what he says about you?"

"No. Tell me."

"The Daddio says 'He's not to be trusted, but he's

competent enough. Not as good a leader as he thinks, but it's amazing what you can get away with when you're as good looking as he is. We could have chosen someone more suitable, but they wouldn't have his charm. The looks won't last, but people will rally around him for long enough to achieve our objectives."

"Oh."

"The Daddio believes in you, and those the Daddio believes in become valuable in the eyes of others. Even after this."

I looked away from the laughing, pointing crowd. Standing there, naked and scratched, sore and bleeding, I have never felt less valuable in the eyes of anyone.

"I'm pleased to hear it," I said.

"Here," said Honey Peppers. "Put these clothes on."

The reluctant Quantifier brought me a green uniform jacket with gold braid across the front, a white shirt and breeches, and pair of long leather boots. The outfit was just like the clothes I usually wore, but of better quality. I pulled them on, covering my shame.

"See?" said Honey Peppers. "Every inch the dashing hero. The Daddio looks after his own." The crowd didn't think so; they still pointed and spoke about me behind their hands. "And now, something to eat, I think."

She nodded to the side of the stage, and a man in black came forward. He was holding something in his hand. Something red and round and shiny. An apple.

Honey Peppers took it from him, polished it on the front of her cream dress, and then handed it across to me.

"There you go," she said. "Eat it all up, Captain. Nice and healthy."

I took the apple. It looked so nice and shiny, banded in red with russet lines of longitude focused on the green stalk. I felt my mouth begin to water, and I raised the apple to my lips. And stopped. I looked again at the apple, wondering at the flicker of movement. Had the apple really just opened its eyes to look at me?

"What's the matter, Captain? Come on. Eat up."

"I..."

The two eyes in Honey Peppers' tongue were watching me. So were the eyes in the reluctant Quantifier's. I looked back down at the apple.

"I... I'm not hungry."

Honey Peppers' expression hardened. "Eat it!" she said.

"I don't want to."

"Eat it, now."

I drew back my arm and made to throw the apple as far away as I could. The Quantifier caught my hand in his manacle grip and slowly bent it around.

"You have to eat the apple," said Honey Peppers, "to show that the Daddio can trust you."

The apple opened its eyes, now that there was no need to hide. It stared at me with the same cold, dead stare as the eyes in the tongues of all those present.

"Let go," I said.

Honey Peppers nodded and the Quantifier released me.

"Captain Wedderburn," said Honey Peppers. "I get the impression that you aren't entirely on our side! If that's so, you only have to say so. You can always go back in the mandrill cage. For good, this time."

"No," I said. "I'll try to see the Daddio's point of view."

I polished the apple on the front of my new green jacket, all the while looking around. There was nowhere to run to. I was surrounded by ill-wishers, all gazing at me with eyes in their tongues. And now I had to eat the apple and join them. Either that, or face death in the mandrills' cage.

"Oh, I've had enough," said Honey Peppers. "Make him eat it."

The Quantifier seized hold of my neck and my hand. He began to force the apple towards my mouth. I tried and failed to struggle against the inexorable force.

"Leave me alone." I spat the words against the cold silky flesh of the fruit. "I'll eat it!"

"Too late, Captain," said Honey.

The apple was forced between my lips. Another Quantifier stepped forward and forced my teeth together. The apple didn't so much crunch as ooze like toffee down my throat, and stop there. I began to gag, to choke on it. I couldn't breathe. I tried to struggle, but I was only held tighter. I tried to gasp out words – which words, I don't know – but I couldn't.

And then, all of sudden, the blockage in my throat vanished. The Quantifiers released me and I fell to the ground, gasping for breath.

"Well done, Captain Wedderburn. The Daddio will be pleased with you."

At that the crowd in the bleachers stood up and applauded.

I felt my throat, I smacked my lips, I rolled my tongue. What had happened to the piece of apple? Everything felt so normal.

"The first bite is always the hardest," said Honey Peppers. "Perhaps you can finish up now?"

She held the apple in front of me, a white flash in its side where I had taken a bite.

I looked at the apple. It didn't look back at me. Had I eaten the eyes?

"Come on," said Honey Peppers. "There's a good Captain."

She pushed the apple closer, and I looked at it, unable to take it.

What was I to do?

And then I heard a voice, the last voice I expected to hear.

"Mr James! Over here! Run!"

I didn't have to think, I just had to run. Run straight to Mr Monagan, who had surfaced from the pool and was now looking at us from the edge of the stage that half covered the water. How long had he been there, watching?

I felt the big hands of the Quantifier fumble at my jacket as I ran. I let go of the apple, skidded and dropped into the water by Mr Monagan, pale orange skin naked in the pond.

"Take a deep breath, Mr James," he called. "Take the deepest breath that you can!"

The water was cold, and it was difficult to move in my sodden clothes. Mr Monagan took my arm as I gasped for air and then I felt myself being pulled down. I half felt, half heard a splash behind me, but I didn't look back. Mr Monagan was pulling me towards the dark space that lay at the side of the pool, some sort of drainage vent. I made to pull away, but he was surprisingly strong and far more agile than I in the water. I relaxed, allowing him to guide me down into the hatch, and then pull me along a narrow passage to a much larger pond next door. We surfaced, me gasping for air.

"Mr Monagan! What are…"

"Save your breath, Mister James! You'll need it for the tunnel!"

"What tunnel?" I asked, but I saw the answer already. The pool into which we emerged was home to seals and sea lions. Most of them sat on the edge of the pool, watching us with black eyes like sunglasses. Some of them, however, had swum to the bottom to investigate the dark hole where Mr Monagan had pushed aside a manhole cover.

"Oh no," I said. "I can't swim down there. Not in this condition. I'm… I'm not well, Mr Monagan."

"I estimate it will take only forty seconds, Mr James. That is, if you don't struggle. Can you hold your breath for that long?"

"I don't know…"

"There he is!"

The voice was followed by a bubbling eruption from the crowd from next door. They rushed to the edge of the pool, some of the more adventurous jumping in. Their eyes were full of angry amusement, full of the joy of the chase.

"Now, Mr James!"

And so I allowed Mr Monagan to pull me down into the tunnel. We travelled through blackness, I don't know for how long. My arms and legs ached: I was sore and bruised inside.

My lungs were starting to ache. I was losing the energy to kick. I felt Mr Monagan grip me tighter and begin to pull with more urgency…

… then, suddenly we burst out into open space and I was gasping for air.

"Mister James! Mister James! Are you okay?"

Weakly, I managed to raise a thumb. I was still gasping, coughing, spluttering.

"Let me pull you to the side, Mister James. There is a ledge where you can get your breath back before we go on again!"

Go on again? I was too weak at the moment to care. Now, however, my eyes were growing accustomed to the strange green illumination of the space into which we had emerged.

"Wh... where are we?" I gasped.

"Beneath Dream London, Mr James!"

"I know that, but where?"

"I don't know. Somewhere not too far from the zoo."

"What is this place?"

"I don't understand, Mr James. Surely you have seen the underworld before?"

"No," I said. "Never!"

It made sense, though. As above, so below. Just as Dream London was changing above ground, so it was down here. Someone had been blowing great bubbles in the earth and lining them with green tiles. Stone statues of naked men and women stood waist deep in the water, green lanterns hung from the ceiling to illuminate the black reflective surfaces beneath.

"This wasn't here in the past," I explained. "Everything is changing. We didn't build this place. We humans, I mean."

"Oh," said Mr Monagan. "Oh ...good. I wouldn't like to think that we humans are responsible for some of the things I saw on the way here."

"Things? What things?"

"Oh, perhaps I shouldn't speak of them, Mr James.

Now, I see you have your breath back. Perhaps we should get moving. There may be other things following us through the waters now."

"Other things? Like what?"

"Only thirty seconds this time. Now, take a deep breath…"

AND SO WE made our way through the dark waters beneath Dream London. I was aching and short of breath, but Mr Monagan was patient and gradually we made our way back home. Well, not home. We climbed back above ground near Belltower End.

"But I don't think we should go there, Mr James. It might still be burning! Perhaps we should go to my – to your place."

"No," I said. "That'll be the first place they look. There's only one place they can't find us."

"Where's that?"

And that's why, half an hour later, Mr Monagan half carried me through the door of The Poison Yews. The sound of a cornet playing ceased as I approached the house, and Anna appeared in the doorway.

"I thought you'd run out on us," she said coolly. "Perhaps you hadn't heard that Father has lost his job? Something is happening at Angel Tower. The bank has frozen Father's account. Mother says there was even an assessor from the workhouse at the door earlier on…"

Her voice trailed away as she took in my appearance.

"What happened to you?" she asked, peering closer. It was the first time I had seen her lose her composure.

"I want a bath," I said.

"You're bleeding! Your trousers are covered in blood…"

"Just get me to a bath."

Anna nodded and ran upstairs.

A door opened and Alan shuffled into the room. There was no sign of Shaqeel.

"You're back," he said, despondently. "Have you heard?"

"Can you tell me later, Alan?" I said. "I'm soaking wet. I've been swimming through shit to get here."

"It's all going wrong," said Alan. "They know. They know about us."

"They've always known about us," I said. "I'm going for a bath."

I could hear the sound of running water coming from upstairs. I headed up there, supported by Mister Monagan.

I STAYED IN the bath for what seemed like hours. Mister Monagan kept knocking at the door to check that I was alright. From downstairs I could hear the sound of the door, of people entering and leaving the house. I thought I heard Bill's voice. I didn't care. I didn't really care what was happening in Dream London any more. It all seemed to be completely beyond my control.

As I lay in the bath I felt the weight of my tongue in my mouth. What was in the apple that Honey Peppers had forced upon me? Had I eaten enough to grow a set of eyes in my tongue? Would I end up like Luke Pennies: one of Daddio Clarke's Wailers?

I finished my bath and went to my room where I dressed in a plain white shirt and dark trousers.

Hesitantly, I stuck my tongue out at the shaving mirror and I examined it closely. My tongue was darker than before. I looked carefully – there seemed to be two slits at the end. Nascent eyes.

I turned away from the mirror and something lying on my bed caught my eye. A scroll. The fortune that Christine had bought for me. How on Earth had that got here? I was sure it had been left behind with my old clothes in the zoo. My new clothes, the ones that Honey Pepper had given me, had been taken outside by Mr Monagan to be burned. Who knew what power the Daddio might have over them?

That fortune. They wrote them on the Writing Floor of Angel Tower.

I had a sudden inkling that my future was held in that scroll, not because the scroll saw the future, but rather because the future was being written by the same people who had written on its yellow parchment: a group of well-mannered men and women who sat on the 839th floor of a building that had grown up in the middle of the Square Mile and was casting its shadow over this world. A group of people who thought they knew the way the world should be run.

I carefully unrolled the scroll across the bed, and for the first time I read its full length.

You will meet a Stranger
You will be offered a job
You will be offered a second job
Go to the inn to meet a friend, one who will betray you
Go to the docks and meet your greatest friend, the one you will betray

Count the colours in the numbers, count the numbers in the words
Avoid the Monkeys in the cage
Attend the meeting at the tipping point of the world
You're everywhere and nowhere, baby.
Be reminded of the fact that the answer is always love...

Love. The answer is always love. I let go of the scroll in disgust and watched as it rolled back up.

The answer is always love. That's what you get when you write a fortune. If you don't look beyond your own experience then all you ever get is what you are and this is what you end up with. Clichés and homilies.

I sat down on the bed feeling something close to despair. The room around me was taller and thinner than ever, stretching its way up to some future where people screwed and drank and recited poetry and sang songs in crowds, and then returned to sit alone in places like this.

A future where people just looked on the surface and disregarded the fact that underneath it all we were just stinking, damaged people who traded each others' lives whilst reeking of monkey semen.

I hated myself.

There was a knock on the door. I didn't answer.

Anna pushed it open.

"They're all downstairs," she said.

"Who are?" I asked.

She gave me a cool stare.

"Go and see. It's beginning to move at last. We're approaching the tipping point."

"I don't care," I said.

243

"I think you do," said Anna. "The meeting starts in five minutes in the dining room."

She walked off, leaving the door open.

The scroll creaked a little on the bed as it rolled itself a little tighter. A line of text sat in plain view.

Attend the meeting at the tipping point of the world

PURPLE

THE MEETING AT THE TIPPING POINT OF THE WORLD

IT WAS AFTER midnight in the dining room of the Poison Yews.

The spies and plotters and criminals and outcasts of Dream London were seated around the Sinfields' dining table.

Alan sat at the head of the table, a dazed expression on his face. Margaret sat by him, holding his hand. Bill was at the opposite end of the table, Amit Singh by her side, incongruous in a bright green turban. Two of Amit's men sat on the other side of Bill.

Mister Monagan sat in the middle of the table, a bowl of freshly peeled eggs before him. As I watched he placed two eggs in his mouth at once and chewed them with a rapturous look on his face. Anna stood by the door, as inscrutable as ever.

"Captain Wedderburn," she announced, as I entered the room.

I took a seat by Mister Monagan.

"Captain," said Bill. "Mister Monagan has told us

where you've been."

I couldn't meet Bill's gaze. "It wasn't how it looked," I muttered. "She was putting on a show." I shuddered. "She still forced me to eat an apple though."

Amit Singh rose from his chair and came to my side.

"Let me see your mouth."

I look at the ceiling, closed my eyes and opened my mouth. I felt warm fingers touch my jaw.

"Hmmm."

"Well?" asked Bill.

"It's taken," said Amit.

"What's taken?" I asked.

"The worm," said Amit. "One bite was all it took."

"Oh." I didn't feel as concerned as I thought I might have done.

"How do you feel?" asked Amit.

I smacked my lips. "Can I have some water? I'm thirsty."

"Sorry," said Amit. "No food or drink for you. It will only feed the thing that's taking the place of your tongue."

"How long has he got?" asked Bill from the far end of the table. She sounded as if she were asking about the warranty on her car.

"About six hours if he eats or drinks. Until he dies of thirst, otherwise. I can't remove it," Amit said to me, apologetically. "I have no power over it."

"I feel the same as I did yesterday," I said.

"Perhaps Honey Peppers and the rest do as well," said Bill. "Maybe you can't tell the difference in yourself. Remember that."

She paused to allow that to sink in. The bitch.

"For what it's worth, you seem the same to me at the moment."

I was gripped by a raging thirst.

"I need to drink," I said. "I have to eat and drink sometime."

"Try and hold out for as long as you can," said Amit. "I've got some people scouring the new libraries. They might come up with something."

"But they probably won't," I said. I rubbed my chin and looked down at Bill.

"I might as well go out in a blaze of glory then. Get me a gun. I'm going after the Daddio."

"A gun!" said Alan suddenly. "Where will we get the money to buy a gun from? I'm ruined. Shaqeel betrayed me!"

Margaret stared at him dispassionately. There was no sympathy to be found there. "Sit down," Bill snapped at me. "You're not going after the Daddio. And Alan, we'll sort something out about money."

"Oh no," said Alan, shaking his head. "You don't know what it's like here. I used to work on repossessions. They don't *want* you to have money, you know. They want you in the workhouse..."

"You selfish bastard," said Margaret. "You never gave a toss about signing off someone else's bankruptcy, but now it's going to happen to you, it's all different."

"Why did I trust Shaqeel?" asked Alan of the room in general.

"Be quiet!" said Bill.

Silence descended. Bill turned to me.

"Never mind the Daddio," she said. "We've got a better use for you."

"Uh huh," I said. "Captain Wedderburn has had enough of acting for other people. Captain Wedderburn is back to looking after number one."

"Oh, stop being so pompous," said Bill.

"Pompous?" I said. "Do you have any better suggestions as to what I do?"

"Do the job you were supposed to do. Get up to the Contract Floor."

"And what good would that do?" I waved a hand at Alan, tearful at the other end of the room. "This plan was doomed from the outset. The Cartel is a joke. We're never going to achieve anything."

"Of course the Cartel was never going to achieve anything," said Amit, smoothly. "They were simply playing another role in Dream London. But they were our route into Angel Tower."

"How?"

Amit smiled.

"Angel Tower has been summoning the rogues and gangsters to itself since the very beginning." He laughed. "The biggest crooks were the first to be assimilated! All those money men in the City! See how quickly they worked for their new bosses, acquiring land and property throughout London!"

"But..." I paused. It made sense.

"All those lawyers and accountants, selling their services to the highest bidder. But Dream London didn't stop there. After it had them it went after the estate agents, the landlords, all those people who earn a living off the sweat of someone else's brow. Dream London bought and sold them all."

"The bastards," I said.

Amit smiled at that.

"Ah, but we are all bastards to varying degrees, aren't we? Because what about the black economy? Dream London hadn't forgotten that. All those business leaders who would turn a blind eye to a shady deal, and then those who turn both eyes full upon it. The out-and-out criminals. One by one we were summoned to Angel Tower and offered a new deal. And so the corruption reached lower and lower through the strata of Dream London society." He laughed. "The trickle down effect, I believe it's called."

And at that point Bill interrupted.

"All the high ranking criminals," she said with a nasty smile. "Then those in the middle. And then the little Napoleons. All those nasty little people who feed on the misery of others, who bring others down to make themselves seem better in their own eyes."

She was talking about me. She leant across the table, eyes blazing.

"One by one they were summoned to the tower. That was our opening, we realised. We just had to stake out some of the bottom feeders. We had someone working in Angel Tower to tell us who was next to be summoned."

She looked at Alan, slumped at the other end of the table. He turned away from me, he couldn't meet my eye.

"Standard procedure. Move in on some poor unsuspecting schmuck who's about to be offered work there anyway, and convince him that he was working for the good guys. Get him to go into the tower to collect information for us. Clever, eh?"

I'd heard all this before. But I wasn't going to let them tar me with the same brush.

"Very neat," I said. "Apart from one thing. I'm not some low level criminal. I just do what I do to get by."

"You pimp a stable of whores, Captain Wedderburn.

You're scum."

"Hey! I will not sit here whilst you insult Mister James like that!"

Mr Monagan had been sitting listening to the conversation in silence. Now he leapt to his feet, the carved chair clattering to the floor behind him.

"Mister James has been the soul of consideration to me from the moment that I arrived here! He has given me a job and somewhere to live!"

"I bet you're paying a pretty penny for it," said Amit.

"Why shouldn't I pay?" said Mr Monagan. "I'm sorry, but I have seen Belltower End. The girls there were happy and looked after! It's not his fault that the Daddio attacked."

Those seated around the table stared at the orange man. Slowly, he sat down again.

"I'm sorry," he said.

"Don't be," I said. "You're a good friend, Mister Monagan."

Bill laughed at that.

"Could you say the same, Captain Wedderburn?"

I scowled at her.

"Can you give one reason why I should stay in here?" I asked.

"The Daddio," said Bill. "He'll be looking for you."

"Don't you threaten Mister James!"

"Thank you, Mister Monagan." I placed my hand on the orange man's arm, then turned back to Bill.

"Who is the Daddio, anyway?" I asked. "What's he got to do with Angel Tower?"

Amit spoke up.

"As far as we know, Captain, nothing. But once you open up a road, all sorts of things come walking down it.

Dream London is open for business, and many creatures are making steps to exploit it."

I thought about the Spiral, and the city at the bottom of the hole that was growing towards us. I thought about the parks, growing in the centre of Dream London.

"Oh hell," I said. "What have we done to ourselves?"

"Never mind that," said Bill. "What are you going to do about it?"

"Me?" I said. "I'm not going to do anything. I'm just a small time crook who likes to use people, remember? What can I possibly do?"

"You can stop acting like a child," said Bill. "Listen to me. You want to do something worthwhile? You get yourself up to the Contract Floor, and then come back here and tell us what you've seen."

"What use would that be?"

"We would know if the Contract Floor was worth anything, for starters. Where should we be concentrating our attention: the park or the towers?"

"How would I decide that?"

"I don't know. I've never been up into the tower. But just imagine what might be there. The original contracts that signed the city over to Angel Tower. What if we could get our hands on them? And even if we couldn't, at least we'd know if they are worth destroying..."

I stared at her, remembering our conversation of the previous evening.

"You'd bomb it," I said. "You'd drop a nuclear bomb on it!"

"If we had to," said Bill.

"What do you think about that?" I said, turning to Amit. He shrugged.

"The Indian government would do the same," he said. "If they thought it would stop Dream London from spreading."

"Why not drop the bomb anyway, by that logic?"

"What if it doesn't work?" said Bill. "Worse, what if it only works once, what if Dream London only needs to see it at work once to find a way to neutralise subsequent bombs?"

"Exactly," said Amit. "For that reason it would be terrible if we were to bomb the wrong place."

I nodded. It made sense.

"So what's in all this for me?" I said. "I risk my life going up to the Contract Floor. If I succeed, I may get killed in a nuclear explosion. If I don't get killed by the bomb, I die of thirst in a week's time."

"Or you could become one of the Daddio's men," pointed out Mr Monagan, helpfully.

He caught my expression.

"Sorry," he said.

"No," I said. "I'm not going to do it. I'm not staying here any longer."

"Then where are you going?" asked Bill. Bill who was going to betray me, I remembered. I was right. I had no loyalty to her.

"Out," I said. "Out of Dream London."

"There is no way out of Dream London."

"I'll find one."

"Really?" Bill curled her lip. "Is that your solution to every problem? To run away?"

"There is no solution to this problem," I said. I rose to my feet. "I'm leaving, now."

Mister Monagan stood up, too.

"Where are we going, Mister James?"

"*We* are going nowhere," I said. "I am going to the station and I am going to find a train out of here, no matter what it takes."

"What about me?"

"I need you to stay here," I said. "Keep an eye on what's left of Belltower End."

And if I keep you away from me, I can't betray you, I thought. I'd heard some bad things about myself that night. Not that I believed them, but I didn't want to add anything else to the debit side of the ledger.

"So long," I said, and I walked to the the door.

"James."

Bill waited until I had my hand on the handle before she spoke.

"What?"

"If you change your mind, I'll be at the Laughing Dog."

"I won't change my mind."

I pushed open the door, and walked into the hall. But I hadn't made it out of the house yet. Anna was waiting for me in the hallway, as cool and inscrutable as ever.

"What do you want?" I asked.

"You're doing exactly what Dream London wants you to do," she said.

I gave her a flat smile.

"No, I'm doing what I want to do," I replied. I shouldered her aside and pulled open the front door. Anna didn't get upset, she didn't scold me. She just spoke in a calm voice.

"Exactly," she said. "Dream London wants us all to be individuals."

I stopped where I was. "What the fuck do you know about it? You're only seventeen."

"I'm old enough to see what's going on. Dream London divides and conquers. It's instinctive. The only thing that Dream London fears is that we might ever join together to fight it."

"You make it sound like it can think."

"It doesn't think any more than a patch of weeds thinks, but like a patch of weeds it affects its environment. Why do you think Dream London messes up the geography? It's keeping us all from staying in contact with each other. It wants to turn us in on ourselves, rather than having us reach out to each other."

"All we need is love?" I said. "Together we are strong? Sentimental bullshit, Anna. You sound like a seventeen-year-old."

"So what do you suggest, Captain Wedderburn? Because I'm really interested in the opinion of a pimp."

I gazed at her.

"Don't think that because you're only seventeen I won't hit you. Move out of my way."

Wordlessly, she stepped to the side.

"Thank you," I said.

She murmured something.

"What was that?" I asked.

"I said you don't have to be like this," she said. "You want to be a better person. I can tell."

"I've got no choice," I said, and I finally accepted something that Christine had understood right at the start. "It's written."

I pushed out into the night.

TEN

NECROPOLIS

I AIMED FOR Euston Station first. A train from there would take me straight to Manchester. That's how it had worked in the old days, anyway.

I slipped through the streets towards Egg Market station, eyes peeled for Honey Peppers and the Quantifiers: they were bound to head back here looking for me. Or were they? I wasn't sure they'd yet made the connection with the Poison Yews.

I was in luck: the streets were empty. Better yet, there was a train waiting in Egg Market station, the yellow destination boards on its side declaring it was bound for Hampstead. Euston Station lay in the direction of Hampstead, or at least it used to. I looked up and down the platform, searching for Macon Wailers. I saw no one suspicious, but the sight of a man eating an orange brought the thirst up inside me. How carelessly he peeled the fruit, juice squirting over his fingers, dropping moist and zesty pieces of peel onto the station platform.

I boarded the train and sat down by a window with a metal frame that was turning to wood. A notice opposite advertised the new Ford Focus, and I wondered why the Writing Floor of Angel Tower hadn't managed to get it rewritten yet.

A figure moved past the window and I felt something grip my heart. Golden curls, a pink dress... but it wasn't Honey Peppers. Just another little girl coming home from a day out with her Daddy.

A whistle blew, there was a bump, and the train began to move. I relaxed a little. I was going somewhere at last. I was heading out of Dream London, leaving all my worries behind me.

We glided from the station and out over the city, heading towards Belltower End, and I slipped down a little in my seat. If the Daddio had any sense, he'd be watching the station.

I saw the broken top of the Belltower in the distance. The top of the tower had collapsed, leaving only a broken chimney that belched dark smoke into the deep purple night sky. My piece of Dream London, now destroyed. Mr Monagan had come to fetch me... Mr Monagan.

At least by running away I'd never have the opportunity to betray him.

Because I would have done so. I knew it deep in my heart. I'd known it from the moment I met him. Captain Wedderburn puts himself first, and everyone else can go to hell. Anna's words in the hallway came back to me: Dream London liked individuals.

No wonder Angel Tower wanted me for a sunbeam.

I sighed and leant against the window. Maybe the best thing I could do was to drink some water, let my tongue wake up, put an end to it all. Surely things wouldn't be so bad as one of the Macon Wailers? Join their ranks, open my mouth and sing along with them, my tongue razzing the world whilst I wailed and wailed.

The train should have been approaching Belltower End station now, but it seemed to be taking a different track. I could see the tower sliding by, but from this angle it looked unusual. I didn't think I'd ever seen it from this side before.

The view from the train looked unfamiliar, too, now that I came to look at it. There was the side of a warehouse, the name of the veneer of the week painted on its side. I had seen that before, but I'd never seen the little pink house surrounded by sunflowers that sat at its side, their petals shining soft sunshine in the night, illuminating the camomile lawn.

The train was slowing now, pulling into a station. Another train was waiting there. Blue as a whale, with silver destination boards on its side that read... Euston Station.

My train juddered to a halt and I rose to my feet, gripped by indecision.

What should I do? My train was heading in the right direction, but the one across the way was going directly to Euston. My course of action should have been obvious, you might think... but this was how Dream London played with you. I knew the game, we all did, all of us who had tried to escape from the clutches of the city.

To catch the other train I had to cross to the far platform. I saw the red bridge that spanned the track. Would I have time to run across there? Through the windows of the other train I could see the press of passengers, even at this time of night. They were still boarding...

I decided to risk it.

I was off the Hampstead train before it stopped moving. Running down the platform, pounding towards the wooden steps of the bridge. I heard a door slam. Up the stairs. A whistle. Over the bridge. Another whistle.

The blue and silver carriages of the Euston train began to glide forward just as I was descending the steps to the platform. I could still make it, I thought...

But no, by the time I reached the platform the train was moving too fast. I swore, and that's when the whistle sounded from the other side of the tracks. My train, my Hampstead train, was leaving. I ran back up the bridge, but too late...

I stood there, above the railway lines, stood beneath the oversized Dream London moon that hung like a golden gong over the city and I twisted back and forth, watching the lights of the two trains, diminishing in both directions. The clickety-clack sound of their wheels died away.

"You were tempted by the easier way," said the old man who passed me by on the bridge, heading for the exit. He must have got off the Euston train.

"I need to get out of here," I said.

"Be patient," said the man. "Accept the train that Dream London sends you."

"What the hell's that supposed to mean?"

But the old man walked on.

"Don't go all mystic on me!" I shouted. "Really, what the hell does that mean?"

Disconsolate, I wandered back down to the platform the Euston train had just departed from.

I saw a porter, dressed in green. His uniform bore the usual linked DLR logo.

"The next train," I said. "The next train to Euston, when is it?"

"Not until tomorrow," said the porter. "Your best bet, catch the next train to Hackney, change at the Angle."

"The Angle?" I said. "You mean the Angel?"

"You pronounce it the way you want to," he said. "Either way, it should be along in five minutes."

He walked off down the platform, leaving me alone. Despite the activity of just a few minutes before, the station was now deserted. All those passengers a moment ago, and now nothing. Dream London was playing with me, I knew it, but I wasn't to be defeated.

The station was called Hayling Road East. Odd that, I'd lived in this area for nearly a year and I didn't remember hearing of a station by that name. I looked down the long stretch of track, seeking out the lights of the next train. I could still see the broken stump of the Belltower, lit up by night, and for a moment I entertained the idea of leaving the station and simply walking towards it.

That would be one way to break the Dream London railway trap. Or would it? You heard stories. Stories of people who had been missing for ages suddenly walking into their homes half starved, of people collapsing in bars telling stories of wanderings through empty streets. Or of people who had come to places where the people didn't speak English, or where they didn't quite look human...

I wasn't quite ready to start walking yet, though. One missed train wasn't reason enough to give up.

There was an old vending machine standing on the platform. Whatever it had once been, it was now something made of cast iron, shell patterns embossed on the corners. There was a place to insert money, and a slot for the product to drop from. I took a closer look at the words embossed on the machine's surface:

TAKE COCAINE

Somewhere in the distance, music started. It drifted up from the darkness and echoed around the walls of the empty railway station. Odd music, music that was different to what you normally heard nowadays. The silver sound of a soprano cornet, the regular beat of a drum. Trombones and euphoniums. Then cornets and horns and baritones. Musical instruments, all playing together, all keeping time. A brass band. When was the last time I had heard a proper band? What was it about that sound that jarred against its surroundings?

I remembered the children carrying the instrument cases, coming to visit Amit Singh. I thought of Anna, practising with her cornet in her room, back at the Poison Yews. The sound of music boomed and echoed from the walls, it threaded its silvery way through the spaces between the yellow lamps. I stood, so lost in a trance that I literally flinched when I saw the lit windows of the electric train that had crept up so silently to the station.

The train came to a halt. I saw the word Hackney on the destination boards, so I climbed on board.

There weren't many people on the train. A group of football supporters at one end of the carriage, brown and cream Armoury scarves tied to their arms. There was a woman with a bag full of cats, their heads emerging from the top and looking patiently outwards in all directions, a young boy reading a chapbook, a man asleep with a large pink badge on his lapel.

"Excuse me," I said to the woman, "does this train go to the Angle?"

The woman looked up at me and replied, "Errgh oll un marv'k."

"Thank you."

The train jerked and began to move. I approached the young boy.

"Excuse me, do you know if this train goes to the Angle?"

"Fuck off," said the boy, without looking up from his book. I noticed now that the cover had a picture of two women locked in an extremely obscene embrace.

I left the boy alone and went to sit near the sleeping man. The badge on his lapel read *Wake me at Victoria Station.*

This was what happened when you tried to escape from Dream London, I knew this from bitter experience. Everyone did. You rode a train and circumstances conspired to stop you reaching your destination. It was happening to me now, I knew it, but I had no choice but to try. What was the alternative? To wake the thing that slept in my tongue? To be captured by the things that controlled Angel Tower?

The train slowed and we glided into another station. A large crowd of people were waiting here, obscuring the signs. Where were we now? The train stopped and the people climbed on board. All of them were dressed in black, men in dark suits, women in black silk dresses, their faces obscured by dark veils. I watched, unsettled, as their dark shapes entered the carriage. Their pale silence unnerved me. I wondered about getting off, but I told myself I was being silly. Captain Wedderburn was frightened of nothing.

It wasn't until the porter let out a whistle and the train began to move that I saw the signs declaring the station name. My unease at the dark-suited passengers increased once more.

DREAM LONDON NECROPOLIS

"Don't worry," said the young man who had sat down at my side. "You turned white when you saw the sign! It's not as bad as it sounds. This is an actual station from before the changes, regenerated by Dream London. The station used to stand next to Waterloo, it was there for the benefit of the people who wanted to visit the large cemeteries to the south of the city."

The young man fumbled in his jacket pocket and produced a pewter cigarette case. He offered it to me.

"Smoke?" he said. "You look like you need one."

"Thanks," I said, selecting an oval Turkish cigarette. The young man lit it for me and I breathed the scented smoke. "Oh, I needed that."

"Where are you going?" asked the young man.

"Euston. Or any of the big stations. I'm trying to escape."

"Good luck with that," said the young man. "I've tried myself a couple of times. I always give up when I get to the mud piles."

"The mud piles?"

The young man's eyes narrowed as he drew on his cigarette. He exhaled lavender smoke with a sigh.

"I don't know where it is," he said. "Somewhere to the west, I should think. The river is so wide and flat, and the muddy banks seem to be miles wide. There are people living there on the flats, they pile the mud into little towers. The railway lines stretch for miles across the mud, and there are little stations set every so often." The young man shivered. "It's awful. So bleak and depressing."

"I've never seen that," I said. "Whenever I've tried to get away I always seem to end up back by the towers in the Square Mile."

"At least you know where you are. It takes me days to find my way back to the centre."

A woman across the way was crying, and the young man leant forward to pat her hand. I looked out of the window. The train glided past a windmill, its shape black against the bright surface of the moon.

"Don't worry about that, either," said the young man. "There used to be windmills in London. This one used to be out near Upminster. You'll see the old tube trains in a moment."

Sure enough, we rode past a wide yard full of abandoned trains, bone white in the moonlight. The lines of carriages were tethered by vines that sought to pull the metal back down into the earth.

The train slowed and the funeral party stirred, gathering their possessions as they prepared to leave.

"I think this is our stop," said the young man. "Good luck with your escape."

"Thank you."

Something stirred inside me.

"I'm sorry about your bereavement," I said.

The young man's eyes widened slightly in surprise.

"I think I owe you an apology," he said. "I had you down as someone who didn't give a damn about the misfortunes of others."

"Oh..."

I didn't know what else to say, apart from that he was right.

"Here," he said, and he pushed a handful of cigarettes into my hand. "Good luck!"

He left the train. The cat woman and the foul-mouthed young man left too.

This station was called East Ham Sandwich. Nothing looked familiar now. I sat alone in the carriage, waiting for the train to move. Opposite me the man with the pink lapel badge slept happily. After ten minutes I realised the train wasn't going anywhere.

I leant out of the door and called across to a nearby guard, stood in a pool of yellow light, drinking from a bottle of Dream London beer.

"I say!" I called. "When are we going to move?"

The guard took his time finishing his drink. He lowered the bottle from his mouth and carefully wiped the top.

"You're not," he said. "That train is out of service."

"Out of service? It said Hackney!"

"This is the Dream London Railway," said the guard. "and things change. Or hadn't you noticed?"

I clenched my fists. No one spoke to Captain Wedderburn like that.

Or maybe they did now. Besides, hitting him wouldn't make the train move. I relaxed, forced myself to speak in calmer tones.

"How do I get to Euston from here?"

The guard screwed the top back on his bottle before answering.

"Cross over to the other platform. Catch the next train to Mud Flats. Change at Coffee Street for the Hackney train. Change at the Angle for Euston."

My heart sank. Two changes this time. My destination was receding all the time. I didn't want to go to the Mud Flats, but what choice did I have?

I lit another of the cigarettes the young man had pressed on me and set off to the other platform to wait.

The silence was the most frightening thing. Nights in Dream London were filled with noise: the singing of drunks, the laughter of whores, the sounds of fighting, of guitars, of accordions. You can hear the shriek of birds, the hiss of lizards, the screaming of cats as they are tortured by the blue monkeys. But here there was nothing, just the darkness of the night that seemed to rise much higher in the deep Dream London sky. I felt a shiver of relief when the rails started to sing. I looked up and down the tracks, but there was no train in sight. Up and down again and then I saw it, closer than I had expected, running without lights, coming closer, racing the wind and then it was upon me: a black engine pulling black carriages. It ran past the platform in a whisper: smoked glass windows revealing nothing, nothing written on the side of the carriages unless it was in black paint. A black train. I had heard of them, the trains that ran the line from no one knew where to no one knew where.

Now I had seen one.

THE MUD FLATS train was a dark electric thing that looked as if it had been built by some distant country at the turn of the nineteenth century. Something about the line of the driver's cabin spoke of distant steppes, and of days spent journeying through bleak landscapes filled with frost and birch trees. The train wheezed its way to a halt and I climbed on board. The interior was old and cracked and torn. The only other passenger was a woman in a white lab coat who slept with a pink badge pinned to her breast that read *Wake me at East Ham Sandwich*. I placed a hand on her shoulder and shook her gently. She mumbled something, but went on sleeping. Outside, the whistle sounded. I shook her harder. She gave a snort and came awake, looked up at me, eyes wide. She slapped me hard on the cheek. I slapped her back.

"What the hell do you think you're doing?" she said, her hand to her face.

"Your badge said to wake you," I said, indignantly. "We're here at East Ham Sandwich!"

"Shit," she said. She jumped to her feet, but she was too late. The train was already moving from the station. She went to the door and I could see her hesitating, wondering whether or not to jump. She thought better of it and softly closed the door. She came back to sit opposite me.

"Sorry," she said. "I was in such a deep sleep, then I woke to see you standing over me. It gave me a fright."

"I understand," I said, and then Captain Wedderburn kicked in, the big man looking after the little lady. That's what the Captain did, it was a way of showing who was in charge, after all. "But don't you think it's a bit dangerous? A woman sleeping on a train like this? Anything could happen to you."

"I can look after myself," said the woman. "Besides, this is the only way to get around if you want to go somewhere that Dream London doesn't want you to go. Haven't you heard about it yet?"

"No…"

She sat up straight in her seat.

"You got a cigarette?" she asked. I handed her one and lit it for her. She took a deep drag.

"Ah! That's better!" She held out a hand. "Cynthia Graham."

"James Wedderburn."

"Ah! The famous Captain. You know, I'd heard you were good looking. I didn't realise just how attractive you would be."

She laughed at my expression.

"Don't look so shocked! I don't fancy you." She gave me a sideways glance and added drily: "I prefer brains to looks any day of the week."

"Hey..."

I realised that she was playing with me then. Just because I was playing the big hero didn't mean she had to play the damsel in distress.

She took another drag of the cigarette and slowly blew blue smoke into the air.

"So, you really don't know about the badges yet?" she said. "I would have thought the idea would be all over Dream London by now."

"I've seen them around," I said. "I thought that only the drunks were wearing them."

"Maybe they are," said Cynthia. "But they won't be the only ones. I used to work for the LSAPM team. Did you ever hear of them?"

"No."

"The London Sub-Atomic Particle Model. We were part of Imperial College, had a lab out in the Square Mile."

"I never heard of you."

"Really? We were in all the papers a year ago, just before all of this started."

"I never really read the papers."

"You surprise me," she said in a voice as dry as the cigarette she was drawing on. "Well, you've heard of the Large Hadron Collider?"

I nodded. She wasn't fooled.

"Mmm. It was a great big physics experiment dug out in a huge tunnel underneath Switzerland. You know how much that thing cost? I doubt it."

She wasn't giving me a chance to speak.

"Well, we at El-spam had a plan to do the same thing, but much cheaper. We were looking for sub-atomic particles, but we were doing it using pen and paper."

"I don't understand."

"We wanted to describe things smaller than atoms," said Cynthia. "Things so small that you can know where they are, or where they're going, but not both at the same time."

"I've heard of that," I said.

"Of course you have," said Cynthia, not quite keeping the sarcasm from her tone. "Well, it worked! We found what we were looking for. We wrote the model for a sub-atomic particle perfectly. We described it in such detail that we captured it so completely that we became part of its system. And now, look at us. We ride the trains and we know where we are, or where we want to go, but never both at the same time."

"So that's why you have a badge," I said. "You're asleep so you don't know where you're going. And of course, I knew where you were." I frowned. "But didn't I know where you were going as well?"

"I'd already arrived there, though. I wasn't going anywhere."

She smiled at me. It all made perfect sense to her, I was sure.

"You're not in the right place now," I said. "Does it ever work?"

"It might take some time, but you get there in the end.

I've been everywhere in Dream London."

"Have you left?" I asked, eagerly.

"Never tried," she said. "This is where my work is."

I couldn't do that, I reflected. I couldn't fall asleep on these trains. Not with Honey Peppers and the Quantifiers looking for me. I needed to keep my wits about me.

We were pulling into another station. The streets outside here looked odd: the houses seemed to be constructed from porcelain, their rounded shapes blending into each other and the street. The station signs declared this to be Chinatown.

"Well, if you'll excuse me," said Cynthia, "I'll get off the train here and cross onto the other platform. Try and catch a train back to East Ham Sandwich."

"Will you be able to fall asleep in time?" I asked.

"Oh yes," said Cynthia. "I travel around by train all the time. We all do. We've developed the skill."

"Who travels by train? How have you developed the skill?"

But the train had stopped, and with a wave of her hand, Cynthia stepped onto the platform. I thought about following her, but decided against it. She obviously didn't think that much of me, certainly not enough to lose any sleep over. Not if it stopped her going where she was going.

I waited as the train pulled out of the station. The streets of Chinatown were neat and rounded and regular. The lights were on in every house.

I'd had enough. I wasn't going to escape Dream London this way, that much was obvious. I would have more luck trying to walk out, or maybe sailing in a boat down the Thames. I'd seen the satellite pictures: the river still connected to the Channel. And Bill had said that France hadn't been touched by the changes.

As I thought this the train plunged into a tunnel and began to twist around, the curve it followed pushing me over in my seat. I felt a tremor of uneasiness. Where were we going now? Dream London was a dangerous place. Where would I end up? I imagined the train plunging down to Pandemonium itself.

But then the train straightened out and with a sudden whoosh it emerged back into the night. I looked at the scenery outside with a mixture of relief and resignation.

Large towers rose up all around me. The streets were lined with men in dark suits and hats. They leant against the walls of the tall buildings, still in shock at the loss of their jobs.

The train was slowing down now, ready to deposit me at Angel Tower station. I stood up.

I was tired, I was hungry, I was thirsty. Worse than that, though, I felt utterly despondent.

Dream London had defeated me again.

ELEVEN

THE CONTRACT FLOOR

THE TRAIN DEPOSITED me on the platform of Angel Tower
Station, then glided off down a tunnel, heading back to
its usual haunts at the edge of reality.

I stood for a moment, dizzy with thirst and lack of
sleep. The night had passed too quickly and now a pale
dawn illuminated the glass roof of the station. Across
on another platform a musician straightened up and
adjusted the straps of his accordion. He looked in my
direction and played a couple of notes, and then just
stood, waiting. Another train slid into the station and
the first businessmen alighted, dressed in their suits.
Not just businessmen. There were other people too,
some with brown and cream scarves tied to their wrists,
others with burgundy and silver scarves around their
necks. Football fans.

The accordion began to play, and the day began.

I walked into the street and was brought to a halt by
the sheer presence of Angel Tower. The building was
oppressive, the height of the place, the way it seemed

to thrust its way down from out of the deep sky, rather than growing upwards like a normal building. I looked up along its length. Somewhere up there, someone was waiting for me. Someone sat at a desk looking at a list of the criminals of Dream London. Somewhere on that list was my name.

I could smell coffee in the air. I saw a stand selling drinks and hot morning rolls. My tongue flexed in my mouth, wanting something to drink, something to bring it to life.

I looked at Angel Tower.

I began to walk purposefully towards it.

THE BUILDING WAS nearly empty. A security man in a purple tunic sat at a desk, watching the line of women who spanned the width of the hall, all on their knees, all scrubbing the floor in unison. The sight of them in their blue checked pinafores brought me up short. This was the other thing women in Dream London did, I realised. On their knees as whores or cleaners. I had chosen to control the whores.

"Yes, sir?"

The security guard was looking at me now. I drew myself up to my full height, straightened out the green material of my military jacket, the better to display the golden frogging.

"Captain James Wedderburn," I said. "I'm expected on the Contract Floor."

"Go right up, sir."

It was that easy.

I crossed the floor, tip-toeing between two women scrubbing at the floor with stiff bristle brushes. The scent of carbolic filled my nose. I left a trail of footprints on the damp marble as I crossed to the lifts.

A set of doors slid open as I approached. I stepped inside and turned to look back at the hall. Ten pairs of buttocks faced me, swaying back and forth as the women scrubbed on. The doors slid shut and I began my ascent.

The lift accelerated, and I braced my knees against the force. Higher and higher...

THE CONTRACT FLOOR was filled with the stillness of a thousand unvisited museums. You felt it as you stepped through the lift doors. The Contract Floor was the absolute reference, it was the harbour for grudges, the bottle for feelings, the pivot of the world.

The Contract Floor was wide and deep. There were no internal walls up here, no light but for that which shone through the distant windows, far away across the empty floor. I saw the pale glow of morning falling on the glass cabinets and cases that filled the room, arranged in regular fashion around the vast space. There were glass-topped tables; wide, thin chests of drawers of the sort used to hold maps; old wooden filing cabinets, many-drawered pharmacy cabinets in dark mahogany...

It looked like a museum, but a museum for children. The cabinets and cases of the Contract Floor were all so low you would bark your shins on them. I leaned forward to examine the parchment laid out in the one closest to me. Pictures of butterflies drawn in cobalt blue and gold had been inked in lines. Each one had a label beneath: *Property of Mr James Geranium; The official butterfly of Florizel Street Station; Property of the rose bushes of the lower East Side.*

"Why would rose bushes wish to own a butterfly?" I wondered aloud.

"I think it's more about what Dream London wishes," said a familiar voice.

I turned to see my blonde secretary from the Writing Floor standing behind me, hair pinned up, a clipboard in her hand.

"Captain Wedderburn. So you made it here at last."

"Miss Merchant."

"I knew you'd get here eventually," she said.

"Where did you sneak up from?" I asked. "Were you hiding?"

"Not at all, Captain Wedderburn. It's the stillness up here. Things have a way of being lost amongst it."

"Do you work on the Contract Floor now?" I asked.

"No one works on the Contract Floor," she said. "There's nothing to do here. Everything on the Contract Floor is constant and unchanging."

"Oh."

"They second people up here from the Writing Floor when a new Contract needs to be written. That's why we're both here, of course."

"Why we're here?"

"To sign your contract with Angel Tower!"

"To sign my contract? But I already work for Angel Tower!"

"No you don't. You were allowed onto the Numbers Floor and the Writing Floor as a guest. You don't work for Angel Tower until you sign a contract."

"But..."

"Come on, James. You should feel honoured. So many people are taking an interest in you. You're a true hero for Dream London. Did you know that?"

"A hero? I don't think so."

"It's true. Come on. Let's go to the desk." She placed a hand on my arm. "Be careful as you walk. The level of permanence in here gets thicker as you get closer to the floor.

She steered me along an aisle between two wide desks. Leather bound illuminated manuscripts lay open upon them, books wider than you could spread your arms. One showed a picture of three silver men dancing around a large letter P. I read the first sentence. *Penrose: Look to the Moon!*

"It feels like I'm wading through water," I said. "Like my feet are caught in mud."

"Take care there," said Miss Merchant, steering me around a silver line pulled like a tripwire before me.

"That's a spiderweb," I said.

"The cleaners have the devil of a job in this place. Once the dust settles it's there for ever."

Every footstep that had ever sounded in the Contract Floor hung in the air. Dip your head down into it and you could hear never ending chords formed of taps and clicks.

"There's no happiness here," I said. "Happiness evaporates, it bubbles away. But misery accretes."

She led me further into the room. The morning light moved slower in this room, it seeped into the place like lemon curd. It settled on the little wooden desk, one like you might see in an old fashioned classroom. A sheet of parchment lay upon it, a long feathered quill stood upright in an inkwell beside it. A grandfather clock stood by the table; too tall for itself, it had to bend down to fit in the room. It didn't tick, it creaked, each note stretched out until it snapped off at its root.

"That clock is three hours slow," I said.

"This room is twenty-eight days slow," said Miss Merchant. "Time passes by slower and slower, the closer you approach the centre."

I looked in the direction that she was pointing, and I saw the stillness that filled the centre of the Contract Floor. I can't describe what it looked like. It looked like ... stillness

"What's in there?" I asked, softly.

"Nothing," breathed Miss Merchant. "You can't pass through the stillness. The closer you get to it, the less you move."

"How can you fight stillness?" I said, half to myself.

"You can't. What you need to do is strike a magnificent pose as the time runs out."

"What makes the stillness?"

"The ants. They spin the motion out of stuff, it's where their power comes from."

"Stuff? What stuff?"

"The stuff that stuff is made from. Once the ants have taken all the motion from it, all there is left is stillness. They use the stillness as the root of their nest. Where you have stillness you have a point of reference. Where you have a point of reference you have an absolute. Where you have an absolute you have certainty. Where you have certainty you have right and wrong. The ants anchor the world and they make it run according to their rules, the rules of the nest."

"Hold on," I said. "What ants? What nest?"

"What nest?" smiled Miss Merchant. "You're in it now. Angel Tower. As for the ants, you mean you didn't know? It's the ants that are responsible for all this."

"The ants?"

"Sign the contract, James. You'll get to see everything then."

I stared at the stillness. I stared at the desk, looked at the parchment laid out upon it. Looked at the quill that stood at its side.

"What am I signing?" I asked.

"Whatever you like," said Miss Merchant. "Angel Tower thinks highly of you, James. You get to write your own contract."

I moved across to the desk.

"Where are the other contracts?" I asked.

"You know where they are, James," said Miss Merchant, waving a hand to indicate the cabinets and cases that surrounded us. "All around you. Sign the contract and your relationship with Angel Tower will become permanent. Your contract will join the other contracts here."

I looked around the room. What if a nuclear bomb was to hit this place? What if all the contracts were to burn away? Would that be enough to free London from all of this?

"I know what you're thinking," said Miss Merchant.

"I doubt it."

"You're wondering about stealing the contracts from the drawers. I wouldn't bother. Do you think that Angel Tower would make it so easy for someone? The ants spent a lot of time opening up this world. They wouldn't relinquish their hold so easily."

"Hmmm." I looked around the room once more.

There was no one there, only me and Miss Merchant. The sense of stillness was unnerving. I felt as if we were being listened to.

I looked at the contract, at the official-looking piece of paper that lay before me.

"What am I signing up to?" I asked.

"To be part of Angel Tower. You will become part of the nest. Don't worry about it, it's perfectly safe. I signed up."

"Good for you. What's in it for me?"

"Whatever you like. I told you, you get to write your own contract."

I looked at the desk and the sheet of parchment, and I shivered.

"I don't think so."

"You don't have the choice."

"There's always a choice." I stared into her eyes for a moment, then reached out and touched the edge of her cheek.

"Don't even think of it, Captain Wedderburn," said Miss Merchant. "We're not on the Writing Floor now. And don't be fooled by my looks. This isn't how I used to be. I got this face and this body when I signed my contract. I know all about your sort, Captain Wedderburn."

"And what sort is that?"

"Face of a fallen angel and no soul. In the past you wouldn't have spared me a glance. Now, sit down and write your contract."

"But I don't want to."

"I don't care. Sit down."

I sat down and gazed at the sheet of parchment.

"There's nothing written here," I said.

"I keep telling you. You get to write your own contract."

"What shall I put?"

"Start with your name."

I picked up the quill and touched it to the paper.

"What will this mean?"

"That you'll be working for Angel Tower."

"I have this thing in my mouth."

"It will have no power over you when you work for us."

I looked at Miss Merchant. She certainly was attractive. If Angel Tower could do that for her, what could it do for me?

I wrote:

I, Captain James Wedderburn...

Text appeared underneath what I had written.

... hereby indenture myself to Angel Tower for the term of seven hundred years or the rest of my life, whichever is the shorter.

"What's in it for me?" I asked. The words appeared immediately before me:

In consideration of the services to be performed by Captain James Wedderburn, Angel Tower will make the following concessions.

> *Angel Tower will grant Captain James Wedderburn the leasehold to Belltower End and associated properties for a term of seven hundred years or the rest of his life, whichever is the shorter.*

"The leasehold?" I said. "The Cartel offered me the freehold!"

"It wasn't theirs to give," said Miss Merchant. "No land in Dream London is owned by humans any more."

"Hmm."

I turned back to the contract.

Angel Tower will grant Captain James Wedderburn exemption from the laws of Dream London applicable to the general public, the semi-skilled tradesmen, tradesmen, the middle classes and the minor aristocracy. In addition, Captain James Wedderburn shall be given license to carry out four (4) murders and six (6) acts of usury per year. Furthermore, he will be granted the license to engage in unlimited sexual activity upon anyone of any class up to and including Dream London Royalty. (Captain James Wedderburn will of course be allowed to carry out any crime upon any person in order to further the aims of Angel Tower.)

Captain James Wedderburn shall have the right to wear the following colours and coats of arms: Purple, silver, purple and silver, Light gold, confectioner's gold and old gold; the mark of the dog, the mark of the goat and the lizards reversed.

In addition to his regular remuneration (stated elsewhere), Captain James Wedderburn shall receive a yearly tribute of three parmesan cheeses, four black forest gateaux, a yard of ale, two furlongs of whisky and a light year of olive oil.

"They're taking the piss now," I said.

"Shhhh," said Miss Merchant. "Keep on reading. I did these for you. They're well worth it."

Captain James Wedderburn shall furthermore be exempt from the laws of grammar. In particular, he shall be allowed to split infinitives, to say 'less' rather than 'fewer' and to begin sentences with 'but' and 'and'. Any persons found correcting his manner of speech shall be imprisoned in a penguin suit in Dream London Zoo.

Finally, Captain James Wedderburn shall be transported in a coach and four at his request.

"Is this some sort of joke?" I said.

"These things are very important in the other worlds," said Miss Merchant.

I looked at the contract again.

"So what are my duties?" I asked.

"These are very straightforward," replied Miss Merchant.

They appeared on the parchment as she spoke.

Captain James Wedderburn shall, in return for these considerations, do whatsoever Angel Tower deems reasonable.

"So, not what *is* reasonable?" I pointed out.

"I wouldn't get too upset about that," said Miss Merchant. "It's a standard clause on human contracts."

I looked down at the parchment once more.

"Is that it?" I said. "Do I just sign this?"

"Not quite," said Miss Merchant. "There's the final part. Who are you?"

I stared at her. Shadows flickered outside. Birds flying by the window.

"Who am I?" I said. "I'm Captain James Wedderburn!"

"Well, yes, but that's just a label. A handle. It's not even true. You're not really a Captain, are you? You never made more than Sergeant in the army."

"I acted as Captain. I've done nothing but since I came to Dream London."

"Precisely," said Miss Merchant. "And isn't that the nice thing about Dream London? You can be who you want to be! Look at me. Plain Jane until Dream London arrived, and look at me now!"

I was looking at her, at all her glorious curves. She was leaning closer to me, her perfumed bosom almost in my face.

"So who do you want to be, Captain Wedderburn? Because that's the wonderful thing about Angel Tower. It tells the common folk who they are. It labels people and categorises them, makes them wear turbans and dress up like Mollies so that they are less like real people and more like cartoon characters."

She leant closer. "But the special ones, the ones like you and me, we get to choose. We become who we want to be. It's up to us. You have the pen, and you have the piece of paper. Simply write down who you want to be."

"Write down who I want to be?"

"Exactly. Do you want to be brave, or a better fighter, or a great womanizer? Just write it down."

"But I'm already all of those things."

"But you're not happy, are you? You have the Cartel on your back, the Daddio in your mouth and monkey semen in your arse. Things could be better, couldn't they?"

"They certainly could."

"Then write down the new Captain Wedderburn. The one you want to be..."

I gripped the pen again, but as I did so, more words appeared on the contract.

The cost of a new personality is an old one. Not your own, but that of your friend. The cost of your contract will be the soul of your best and truest friend.

I only had one true friend. He had chosen me to be so. Mister Monagan.

My one true friend. The one I was going to betray. Just like it said in my fortune.

INDIGO

THE 854TH FLOOR

Miss Merchant had a body built for sex. Her golden hair was pinned up above her head, but strands of it fell to her shoulders, threads of gold that curved in anticipation of those deeper milk white curves below. She wore a plain silk blouse, a tight dark skirt and charcoal stockings and managed to look completely naked beneath her clothes. She had sold her soul for her body. No doubt she was hoping I would do the same.

"I think it's time for you to write your personality, Captain Wedderburn."

"I don't think I want to."

"Think about it. Either Angel Tower or the Daddio is going to own you. Look what we have to offer you. What will the Daddio give you? Nothing but the chance to wail. Sign it."

"I'll tear it up."

"This is the Contract Floor. Nothing changes here."

Of course not. This was the power of Dream London.

I thought about Mister Monagan. I thought about Bill, about all the whores back in Belltower End. I never thought myself a bad person before. But Angel Tower obviously did. It thought I would have no compunctions in signing away another man's soul. And up until yesterday, I think it might have been correct.

"Sign it," said Miss Merchant. "You'll have done worse in the past."

"I don't think so," I said. But she was right. I had done worse. But was that an excuse not to bother any more?

"I'd think about your situation," said Miss Merchant. "You're standing nearly at the top of Angel Tower. There are hundreds of people below you. Do you want to fight them all? Even if by some miracle you did manage to escape this place, you'd be on the streets with a Wailer in your tongue and the Daddio looking for you. You have to betray someone. Do you really want that person to be yourself?"

I stared at her. As I did, the morning sun peeped over the edge of the windows and sheets of lemon light reflected from the glass faces of the cabinets of the Contract Floor. I sat there, waist deep in a kaleidoscope pool. Around me, the dark wood of the cabinets flashed in ruby textures.

And I remembered something.

"Do you have a mirror?" I asked.

"A mirror?"

"To powder your nose. A compact. Something like that."

She produced one from the pocket of her jacket.

"What do you want a mirror for?"

I took the mirror and poked out my tongue. Two slits looked at me.

"Let me take one last look at the dawn," I said. "Let's see what we can see."

We walked across to the windows and looked out.

For the first time, I was able to look across Dream London.

I saw part of the emerald spiral of the Thames, and I noted the way it coiled itself around the tower. I saw the patterns in the city below, fields of red brick and white china, bands of grey concrete. I saw the shadows streaming towards me from the smaller towers further east.

I tilted the mirror into the sun and flashed a message to the sky.

"What did you say?" asked Miss Merchant. She seemed more curious than upset at what I'd done.

"Just saying where I was."

"No you weren't. You said Contracts. I know a little Morse. What did you say?"

"You'll see soon enough..."

Miss Merchant stared at me for a moment, and then shrugged.

"Whatever. Are you going to sign now?" she asked.

"In a moment. Let me take a look around. I might never be up here again."

I walked around the windows, following the loops of the Thames. I saw the wide channel of the River Roding, heading off north to other lands. I saw the plains of windmills to the north-west.

I carried on round the tower, coming to the west, facing out to the centre of Dream London.

There I saw the wide parkland at the centre of the city. It was so green, and so regular compared to the twisted chaos of the streets. The lines of trees, the geometric precision of the footpaths were obvious even at this distance.

"What's it for?" I asked.

"That will be the direct route to the other worlds," said Miss Merchant. "Starting tonight. The workhouses of Dream London are filled with the disenfranchised. They'll be marched through the parks and put to more profitable work elsewhere."

"Oh."

A cross appeared in the distance, where it hung just above the horizon. A handful of crosses, now, bobbing in the blue. I walked around the windows, completing the circuit back to the east. There were crosses all around us, and they were growing bigger.

"Can you see them too?" asked Miss Merchant, frowning.

"I think they're missiles," I said. "Cruise missiles. The Americans must have got my signal. I imagine there are bombs falling towards us, too."

"It won't work," said Miss Merchant.

Sure enough, as we watched the crosses began to diffuse and then fade into yellow petals. Clouds of pale blossom puffed across the sky.

"I told you it wouldn't work," said Miss Merchant.

More blossom, white, this time, fluttering down around the tower. It fell like snow. Below us the streets of Dream London were covered in a blanket of yellow and white.

"Those were the bombs," I said. "They were supposed to destroy everything here."

"And so it ends," said Miss Merchant. "Will you come to the table now?"

"I will," I said.

I sat down and looked at the contract.

"Will you sign?" she said.

"I don't want to," I said. "I've had enough of Captain James Wedderburn."

"Then your luck has run out."

"I'll take all my luck in one last shot," I said, and I began to write.

I hereby resolve to give up my individuality and to work to the best of my ability to better the lot of the people of Dream London. I sacrifice myself for the greater good.

"Why do that?" asked Miss Merchant.

"Because ants fight as teams. Angel Tower is removing that ability from humans. I want to regain it."

"It'll do you no good," said Miss Merchant.

"Maybe," I said. "But I feel much better for putting that on paper. Let me finish writing now..."

I hereby resign my commission as Captain James Wedderburn. I am now James Wedderburn, the repentant man.

Miss Merchant looked at me.

"That seems a poor choice of personality to me," she said. "Just think what you could have instead."

"I don't care."

She bit her lip. Then she placed one hand on my cheek, rubbed the stubble there.

"I don't like to see such a good looking man make a mess of his life. There are so many better things you could be doing."

"Like what? I'm not going to go on using people."

"Hmmm."

She pulled her hand away.

"Before you sign that," she said, "let me show you something..."

She turned and walked to the lift.

"Where are we going?" I asked.

"You're on the 853rd floor. Do you know how many floors there are in Angel Tower?"

I did. I had seen the numbers in the lift

"1204," I said.

"1206 now. The tower grows a floor every day. Don't you wonder what's on the floors above us?"

I didn't answer. Of course I'd wondered.

"It's them," said Miss Merchant. "The ants. The ones who bought their way into this world. Wouldn't you like to come and see them?"

She had pressed the button. Already the lift doors were sliding open.

"Do I have a choice?" I said.

"The choice is yours, James. But would you come all this way without seeing the rulers of Dream London?"

She laughed.

"Oh, and I wouldn't bother about reaching for whatever you've got hidden in that jacket. Weapons will be of absolutely no use to you against them."

Outside of the windows yellow and white blossom blew in the wind.

WE CLIMBED INTO the lift and rode up one level to the 854th floor.

"Here we are," said Miss Merchant as the doors slid open. I looked out in wonder.

There was a city in the top of Angel Tower. A city within the city. A city of convoluted mounds made from paper and mud and jewels. A termite mound grown to impossible size, swarming with millions upon millions of insects. The jewelled motion of them dazzled the mind as they scuttled back and forth.

"Can I go out there?" I said.

"A little way," said Miss Merchant. "They won't really care about you unless you wander too close to an egg bank or a nursery, in which case they'll cut you to pieces."

I stepped from the lift onto the mud and paper floor. It gave a little beneath my feet, and I bent down to touch it.

"Where does the mud come from?"

"I don't know. Not from this city, I should think."

I didn't think so, either. The mud was a pale orange colour that reminded me of Mr Monagan. As for the paper of the mound, it felt like expensive writing paper, the best quality linen finish, thick and substantial. It was woven in thick ropes that spiralled in op-art patterns out from where I stood.

As I stood there an ant came scuttling towards me. Then another, then five more.

"Don't move," said Miss Merchant.

One ant ran across my hand. It ran up my arm. Another joined it, and another. The creatures were quite large, about the length of the last joint of my little finger. And they sparkled in metallic colours, golds and yellows and blues and reds, magentas.

All around me, the top floors of Angel Tower shone like Christmas, the richness of the colours, the sparkle and flash against the velvet darkness.

I felt the brush of antennae on my face, and I did my best not to flinch. Another brush, and then the ants seemed to lose interest. They dropped to the floor and scuttled away.

I watched them go, and then my eye was drawn back and up and I followed the mounds over which the insects swarmed as they rose up higher and higher, up into the heavens of the enclosed space. Waves of vertigo swept over me.

"How tall...?" I asked.

"Nearly four hundred floors," said Miss Merchant. "All the way to the top."

I stared around the space. There were patterns to the movements of the ants. Indigo rivers of movement that splashed down from the highest points like mountain streams. Slow throbbing waves of magenta ants that lapped the base of the mound like waves.

Just above the level of the magenta waves, lines of emeralds and rubies studded the walls, like windows.

"What are the jewels for?" I asked.

"Trade," said Miss Merchant. "There are treasure vaults at the heart of the mound, or so I've heard."

"What do the ants trade for?" I asked, but I knew the answer right away.

"Land," said Miss Merchant. "That's how they bought up London."

"You make them sound intelligent."

"They're not intelligent, James. They just exploit other species. There are slavemaker ants here on Earth that use pheromones to enslave other species of ants. These ants enslave other species, but they don't use pheromones. They use money. They buy other species."

"That's ridiculous!"

"Is it? What would you do for them if they offered you gold? Or property? How about the leasehold to Belltower End?" She smiled at that. "What if they used a third party to broker the contract? You'd have worked for ants and never even known it."

"But they don't understand what they're doing!"

"Do you, James? Do you really know how your actions affect the world? Do you really understand what effect your little business has on the wider world?"

"No, but..."

"I wonder how it happened, James? Somehow or other the ants found themselves in possession of a property in old London. And from that possession revenue began to flow into their nest. Rent. All of a sudden, Angel Tower found itself with a toehold in this world. And with that money, Angel Tower found it had the capability of buying more property. Soon, revenue was flowing in from all over London..."

"And where the ants came, others followed," I said. Of course they did. The ants had opened up a new market.

"Now this world is ripe for exploitation and anyone who is anyone is looking to the opportunities that are opening up in this little corner of England. The City beneath the Spiral is coming. Daddio Clarke is here. Even the flowers are trying to take over. The wind blows their pollen down the river: they're using sex to shape us."

I looked around the vast space once more.

"Ants," I said. "Surely we could take on a load of ants?"

"Of course we could," said Miss Merchant. "If we were to all work together. But that's not happening. You said it yourself. They work as a hive, the humans are all acting as individuals. The ants have shaped us that way."

She was right, of course. Anna had said the same. Dream London messed with geography, it turned everyone into individuals. The ants had their own defence mechanisms. They didn't care about people, or individuality, or sex or truth or anything. All they cared about was the nest. That's why they would defeat us.

"I've seen enough," I said. "Take me back down."

"You can walk around to the other side," said Miss Merchant. "Stay close to the wall and you'll be okay."

"I said I'd seen enough."

I walked back into the lift.

WE RETURNED TO the Contract Floor. I wandered to the windows and looked out to the west, to the green space of the parks.

"What will come through the parks?" I asked.

"More of the same," said Miss Merchant. "More trade. More people seeking to exploit Dream London."

"What about the ants?"

"What will the ants care? As long as the hive thrives, they'll continue as they have done."

She took me by the arm and gently led me back to the middle of the room. We waded through slow time. The ants had built their nest on stillness, she had said. I could feel it in the floor. I could see it in the middle of the room, that column of stillness, that stalk to which the nest was attached.

She led me back to the little desk by the grandfather clock. The parchment still sat on its surface, covered in calligraphic script.

"Now," she said. "Why don't we tear up this contract and write one up anew?"

"Can we do that? I thought things were unchanging here."

"It's not signed yet, is it?" She placed her hand on my arm. "You're too good a man to waste. If you work for Angel Tower you'll thrive. If you don't, you'll be just one of the hoi-polloi, lost in the city."

"Or one of the Daddio's pawns."

"Would that be any better? Do you know what the Daddio is? Nothing more than a pool of water writhing with leeches, somewhere down the river. The leeches attach themselves to animals' tongues and that way the Daddio's influence spreads."

A look of distaste crossed her face as she spoke.

I looked at the desk. I looked at Miss Merchant. Captain Wedderburn would have flung her across the desk and fucked her there and then.

"I'm not Captain Wedderburn anymore," I said. "I don't know why. Dream London has defused me."

I strode to the desk, and before I could change my mind, I signed the piece of paper. "There, contract all done and dusted. I'm a good man now. It says so on this piece of paper."

Miss Merchant seemed to lose interest in me.

"So," I said. "I'm ready for the fight."

Miss Merchant was busy rolling the contract up. She patted the end, straightening it.

"What fight?" she asked.

"Now that I've refused to join Angel Tower," I said, though with less confidence than before. "Bring it on."

"Bring what on?" asked Miss Merchant. "Mr Wedderburn, you are no longer of any interest to Angel Tower. You know where the lift is. Perhaps you could leave the building without a fuss?"

I snatched the roll of parchment from her hands and made to tear it. I couldn't.

"This is the Contract Floor," said Miss Merchant, in a patient voice. "Once a contracts is signed, nothing can change it whilst it remains in here."

"Then I shall carry the contracts outside and burn them."

"You'd never get them out of the room, Mr Wedderburn. Trust me on this. Now, don't let me detain you any longer."

She took the contract back from me.

I looked at her. I didn't know what else to do.

"Still here, Mr Wedderburn?"

Captain Wedderburn would have hit her. James Wedderburn just felt a terrible emptiness.

I turned and walked towards the lift. I pressed the button. The doors slid open and I stepped inside.

"Goodbye," said Miss Merchant as the doors slid shut. And then I was descending, and then I was walking through the large atrium, and then I was standing outside Angel Tower, ankle deep in yellow and white blossom, and the world continued to slowly twist itself in knots, just as it had done before I entered the building.

All I had gained was my dignity.

TWELVE

AROUND ANGEL TOWER

THERE WAS A different feel to the streets outside Angel Tower. The previous feeling of hurriedness and self importance had been replaced by a prickling uncertainty. There was an underlying sense of panic waiting just around the corner.

The towers were emptying. Men were milling in the streets, tears in their eyes.

I walked through the middle of this with no purpose of my own. A man, staggering aimlessly by, noticed me and seized my arm.

"You! I recognise you. You're someone important, aren't you?" He looked at my green jacket and nodded. "You are. You're a man who will recognise talent. Are you looking for a clerk? Hire me!"

His words were enough to ignite the flames in the other men. Pale faces turned in my direction.

"You want to hire a clerk? One moment, let me find my card!"

"Don't listen to these people. My CV speaks for itself..."

"Hire me!"

I found myself in the middle of an expanding crowd of people, all desperately trying to engage my attention, shouting their claim on a job I wasn't offering them. White cuffs emerged from dark suits as hands reached towards me, brandishing business cards.

"The Sheep Tower closed down! Just like that! They're relocating the Head Office, they said. I need work, I need it now."

The man was in his fifties, he had tears in his eyes.

"Inclement Tower has shed fifty per cent of its staff! They say that we're surplus to requirements!"

I wondered, was it the uniform, the old Captain Wedderburn charm, or could they see the new me? The man who had contracted himself to serve his fellow human beings? Whichever way it was, they kept pressing forward. A tall silver-haired gentlemen in an expensive suit shouldered his way through the crowd. The others stood back respectfully.

He reached into his jacket and pulled out a card.

"Sir Hugo Cameron," he said, handing me the rectangular card. "Former MD for Ascension Tower. Shall we retire to your premises to discuss my future employment with you?"

I stepped back. The crowd was pushing closer to me, and I tripped on the shoes of someone behind me.

"Get back!" I said. "What's the matter with you all?"

"Give the man some space," said Sir Hugo Cameron. "We have important business to discuss! This is not a hiring fair!"

"Leave me alone!" I said. In between the legs of the businessmen, faces were emerging. The besuited beggars who had sheltered in the walls of the surrounding streets. "All of you! What's the matter with you?"

"We need work!"

"We want to work!"

"All the towers are laying off! The message went out just after the blossom fell! New premises are opening up in the parks!"

"We'll be sent to the workhouses!"

Those words silenced them. Several of the men choked back sobs, they pulled white handkerchiefs from their pockets and pressed them to their noses. And I felt no pity for any of them. These were the people who had raised the rents and foreclosed the mortgages and cast innocent families onto the streets. It looked as if they were getting a chance to see what it was like on the other side. Let them all rot in the workhouses.

"You want jobs?" I said, and I began to smile. This was so sweet. But then, up the street, I saw the rising bulk of Angel Tower, yellow and white blossom plastered down one side by the wind. And an idea occurred to me...

"You want jobs?" I said, the smile draining from my face. Another expression took its place, and Captain Wedderburn, leader of men, asserted himself for maybe the last time.

"You want jobs? You want something to do? You want to make a difference?"

"Yes!"

The crowd was looking at me expectantly. I had them now. I may have been a new person, but I could still talk, and I'd always been good at persuading people to do things that were bad for them. Well, now it was time to persuade them to do something for their own benefit. I raised my voice.

"Listen," I said. "Listen!"

An expectant hush fell on the crowd.

"I have a job for you all," I said. "I have a task to the benefit of everyone in Dream London!"

"What is it?" asked Sir Hugo Cameron.

"I'm raising..." I paused, building the tension. I saw the crowd lean forward, eager to hear more. I had them now.

"I'm raising... an army!"

You could feel the disappointment. The crowd seemed to diminish.

"An army?" said one nearby man with red hair.

"Yes, an army!" I said. "Gentlemen, listen. Look behind you! Look over there at Angel Tower! That place is the source of all our troubles! That's the place that has made Dream London what it is!"

The crowd was silent.

"Up there," I said. "On the 853rd floor, lie the contracts that have tied our world to the others! If we were to storm Angel Tower, if we were to take those contracts and bring them here and tear them up, then perhaps London would return to normal!"

The crowd was not impressed.

"Perhaps," said the man with the red hair. "But surely fighting is the job of the army?"

"And we could be that army," I said, faltering. I'd never encountered this sort of a response before. In the past, people would have been eating out of Captain Wedderburn's hand by now. But it occurred to me that I was no longer Captain Wedderburn: I'd signed that name away up on the 853rd floor.

"We could be that army," I repeated, a little less confidently. "Surely it's better to try than to just sit here and await our fate?"

"Storm Angel Tower?" said Sir Hugo Cameron. "I'd see myself in more of a leadership position, guiding our forces. Besides, joining an army is hardly likely to help our job prospects, is it?"

"That's a fair point," said red hair.

"Also," said Sir Hugo Cameron, warming to his theme and speaking in a biscuity tone, "Angel Tower is a valuable part of the Square Mile. If we were to attack it, it might relocate elsewhere. That wouldn't be good for business, would it?"

"True, true," said the man with red hair. A few of the other people in the crowd were nodding wisely.

"But Angel Tower is already relocating."

"Only partially," said Hugo Cameron. "There are still jobs here. We've got to allow the people who work there to fuck things up as they choose for everyone living here otherwise they might pull out of the Square Mile entirely. That's just good business sense."

"Good business sense..." muttered a few people.

"But..." I began.

A man in a grey jacket that stood out amongst the dark suits pushed his way forward through the crowd. He wore a ginger moustache and horn-rimmed spectacles and had the air of a freethinker.

"Hold on," he said. "This army. Does it pay?"

"Does it pay?" I said. "No. But it will help to restore..."

Ginger moustache waved me to silence.

"Well, I have a wife and three children to support. I need money. What's the use of a job that doesn't pay? I could find that in the workhouse."

"Yes, but..."

"Although," said Sir Hugo Cameron, thoughtfully, "a private militia is an idea. There is talk of work out along the river. This is an idea we could take to some contacts that I have..."

"No!" I said, "Not a private militia! Listen, people. If we were to attack Angel Tower right now..."

"Not right now," said a man nearby. "Not right now. These things need to be organised properly. We need to tender for contracts to supply the army, form committees to ensure that proper procedure is followed..."

There was a commotion at the back of the crowd. A huge bulk was approaching, pumpkin head visible above the dark-suited men. One of the Quantifiers. I turned and ran without hesitation, pushing my way through the crowd behind me.

The Quantifier ran too. It was gaining on me. I pulled my pistol from my jacket and held it out before me. The dark-suited men who blocked my way scattered. But still they straightened their ties, wiped at their eyes, held out cards.

"Listen, I need to work. I'm offering you the chance to employ..."

"Get out of the fucking way!" I screamed.

I pushed the man aside and dodged through the crowds of people.

Where was I to go, I wondered? Not to the Poison Yews. I'd had it with the Cartel. I needed to get to the Laughing Dog and Bill. Or to Amit. Maybe the Indians or the Americans could make use of my knowledge.

"Apples! Get your apples here!"

The shout rose up above the snuffling and bawling of the crowd.

"Get your apples!"

I stopped, ducked into the café where only yesterday I had breakfasted with Rudolf Donati.

"Coffee, sir?" asked the waiter. "Take your mind off this past half hour? Things have been a bit funny ever since the crash."

"Yes, coffee," I said, not really listening. "That would be good."

I sat down at a table and listened to the hiss of the machine as the waiter fixed me an espresso. Through the golden letters that decorated the window I saw someone tall wheel a barrow down the road, laden with beautiful red apples. One of the Quantifiers.

My tongue was wriggling at the thought of coffee. Out there, soon, hundreds of businessmen would be eating apples. Soon they'd be feeling the same as me. The Daddio couldn't attack the towers directly in the past. Now that all those men had been laid off, he hadn't wasted any time in recruiting his own army.

"Get your lovely apples! Take away those unemployment blues!"

The hiss of the coffee machine, the lovely earthy scent filling the air.

Look at all those people, I thought. *Like children. Dream London has done that to them*. I thought of Alan and the Executive Dining Room, of how Angel Tower took away from the people in there any sense of responsibility for their own lives.

"Your coffee, sir."

My tongue leapt.

"I'm sorry. I can't stay."

I dropped some coins on the table.

"Is there a back way out of here?" I asked.

"Sorry, it's not for customers."

"Do I have to pull out my pistol?"

The waiter was a big man, but a sensible man. He shrugged.

"Through there," he said, pointing.

I WALKED OUT of the café into a little alley out back. A pair of jewelled salamanders crouched there, licking at ants on the pavement. I wondered about capturing a thousand salamanders and letting them loose on the 854th floor. One of the salamanders looked at me and licked its lips.

Mmmmm, it said.

I HEADED BACK to the Laughing Dog. I couldn't think of anywhere else to go. Of all the people I knew in Dream London, Bill was the only one who seemed in control. Second Eddie had gone, Belltower End was off limits, Alan was losing it. I couldn't run, I had to fight. Bill seemed to be the best placed to do that.

The drifts of yellow and white blossom, the fallout from so many nuclear explosions, were piled everywhere in the streets The good citizens of Dream London trailed their feet through the drifts, they wiped their sleeves across their windows to make a space to see out. The children threw handfuls of blossom into the air and ran through it, laughing. It was another hot Dream London day. The big yellow sun squatted in the sky, wobbling in the heat haze. The blossom dazzled the eye.

But for the most part, people were nervous. They were on edge. They felt the change in the air. They felt the sense of something coming. It wasn't just the spreading panic caused by the lay-offs in the City. How many of them had been to the Spiral and seen Pandemonium reaching up towards them? How many of them had heard the stories about the parks?

They pushed down that fear with noise and bravado. The football fans were out, dressed in chocolate and cream and burgundy and silver, ready for tonight's big match. Handclaps and cheers sounded from the the streets.

I walked through the blazing morning, a terrible thirst rising within me. I needed a drink.

It was after midday by the time I came to Hayling Street, hot, tired and footsore, and so, so thirsty. The wind blew thin ribbons of blossom across the smooth white dome of the Egg Market, out across the blue sky.

I walked down the bustling street towards the Laughing Dog, past the market stalls. People were stocking up on food, that much was obvious. They had come from the Egg Market carrying baskets loaded with eggs of all sizes, now they were stocking up on meat and vegetables. I wanted to eat, but my thirst was worse.

There was someone sitting on the pavement outside the Laughing Dog. I didn't recognise her until she spoke to me.

"So, you came back then."

I looked down to see Anna leaning against the wall. She was sitting on a little rectangular case. I remembered the sound of the trumpet that I heard playing at night in the Poison Yews.

"I came back," I said. "What are you doing here?"

"They came for Mother and Father first thing this morning. The workhouse."

"So quickly?"

"They're looking to beef up the labour force," said Anna. "Things are beginning to move..."

"Your father only lost his job last night!"

"The bank came round at five o'clock this morning. They said that now my father didn't have a job, they weren't confident that he could pay the mortgage. He asked them to give him time to get another job. They said he could have one hour. You should have seen him, James. He said he would get one, that Shaqeel would sort it out. That the other members of the Cartel would help. He wanted to run out into the night there and then, still in his pyjamas."

"And did he?"

"Mother wouldn't let him. She said if they were going to do this, they would do it with dignity."

"I hope they did."

"Of course they didn't. Mother opened a bottle and started drinking. Father just stared at the wall. At six o'clock the bank foreclosed on the mortgage. This horrible little rat of a bank manager who had been sitting in our lounge, said thank you, stood up, closed his briefcase, and said he would see himself out. Father and Mother looked at each other as he left the room, and we heard voices in the hall. Father burst into tears."

"Who was in the hall?"

"The people from the workhouse. One man, one woman. Come to take Mother and Father away. They do everything respectfully, you know. No mixing of the sexes. That would be improper."

Anna spoke with a calm detachment. She remained seated on her instrument case, looking at up me with her clear gaze, recounting the morning's events as if they were an ordinary occurrence. Which, come to think of it, they probably were in Dream London.

"They'd brought uniforms for us," she said, in the same matter-of-fact voice. "All our other clothes and possessions belonged to the bank now. Mother and Father changed without a fight. And that was it, they took them away. They didn't even have time to say goodbye properly."

"What about you?" I said. "Why didn't they take you?"

"They wanted to. They had a uniform and everything. I told them no. They didn't know what to do. They're not used to people fighting back. Usually, by the time the bank has finished with people, all the fight has gone from them. It had certainly left Father. He walked away meekly, looking at the ground all the while, lost in shame."

"I'm sorry," I said.

"Why?" asked Anna, rather impatiently. "It's not your fault."

She stared up at me.

"Why are you waiting here?" I asked.

"We can fight them," said Anna, with quiet confidence.

"Fight who?" She hadn't answered my question, I noticed.

"Them," she said. "The people who are doing this to us."

"People?" I said. "Anna, it's just a bunch of ants."

"The ants may be the source of the problem, Captain Wedderburn, but the real resistance know who the real enemy are. We're ready to fight them."

The real resistance, she said. Not the vainglorious selfishness of the Cartel, but the real resistance who waited unnoticed in the shadows. The Poison Yews had been home to the resistance all along. I had just been looking in the wrong direction. Anna was part of it, young and clever and quietly brave. She deserved better than the mess people like her parents had made of her world. She didn't deserve to die to pay for their mistakes.

"Fight who?" I said.

"The people who sold us to the ants. The people who let them go on owning us."

She looked so calm, so clearly unaware of what she was letting herself in for I felt I had to say something.

"Don't sacrifice yourself, Anna. It's every man for themselves in the new world. It's *definitely* every man for himself in Dream London. That's the way they changed us."

Anna rose to her feet. She looked down to check that her cornet case was undisturbed.

"You're different, Captain," she said. "You're different to last night."

"It's not Captain any more. I'm just plain James now."

"You *are* different."

She tilted her head to examine me for other signs of change.

"What are you going to do now?" she asked.

"I don't know. I was going to see Bill. Perhaps she can help me raise an army. I hope she can..."

"An army? To do what?"

"To take on Angel Tower."

I waited for her to say something. She just nodded.

"About time," she said. "We were waiting for something like this."

"Who is we, Anna?" I asked.

She absently patted her cornet case.

"Well done, Mr Wedderburn. I didn't think you had it in you."

"Had what in me?"

"The willingness to stand and fight."

"I'm only fighting because I can't run away," I said, with absolute honesty.

"Even so."

She straightened the skirt of her school uniform and then bent and picked up her case.

"Well, Mr Wedderburn. It's been a pleasure to witness your transformation, but I think that it's time for me to leave."

"Hold on," I said. "Leave? Where are you going?"

Anna checked her reflection in the grubby window of the Laughing Dog.

"I'm going to get the others, Mr Wedderburn. It's time."

"Time? Time for what?"

She raised a hand in goodbye.

"If you do manage to raise an army," she said, "bring it to Snakes and Ladders Square. That's the place to be."

"Snakes and Ladders Square?" I said.

"That's the one. Even if you don't manage to raise an army, be there by sunset. That's when it will all happen, I think."

"All what will happen?"

She smiled at me.

"I might see you before the end," she said. She walked away down the road, through the bustle of the street market, gently swinging the case at her side.

I PUSHED MY way into the Laughing Dog, and I paused, blinking, as my eyes slowly adjusted to the dimness of the interior.

I made out the dirty trails of blossom on the floor, the shadowed shapes of the customers, the sud-stained glasses left on the uncleared tables.

I made my way across to the bar.

"Where's Bill?" I asked the landlord.

"Bill? Who's Bill?"

"Red headed girl," I said. Recognition dawned on his fat face.

"Oh yeah. Bill. You'll have to wait your turn. She's upstairs."

"Right."

"Hey, you can't go up there!"

I stopped, looked him straight in the eye.

"Look, do we have to do this every time I come in here?"

"Do what?"

"Threaten you with physical violence. Oh, here..."

I slapped him, open-palmed on the face. He burst into tears.

I pounded up the stairwell that stank of sweat and semen. The first of the doors to the rooms was closed. I shoulder-charged it open. A man sat on the bed, crying, a young woman holding his hand.

"Sorry," I said.

Bill wasn't in the next room. Or the next.

She was in the fourth room, standing in front of the mirror, lost in thought.

A fat man stood by the bed, neatly folding his trousers.

"Bugger off," he said. "She's taken. You can have her next."

I hit him on the bridge of the nose then stepped in and brought my knee up against his balls. As he doubled over I brought my elbow down on the back of his neck.

"Out," I said.

He slunk out, one hand welling with blood, held to his nose. I kicked his filthy trousers through the door and then turned to Bill.

"James," she said, half in a daze. I suddenly registered that she was topless. "I was…"

Her eyes hardened.

"It hasn't got you yet," I said. "Dream London hasn't got you yet."

"Not yet."

She shook her head.

"Look away whilst I put on a top," she said.

I sat down in the little room with the worn bed and fixed my attention on the pictures on the wall. They seemed more obscene than yesterday.

Bill sat down next to me. She was wearing a pale pink jumper.

"Listen, I got through to the Contract Floor," I said. "That's where everything is. But I don't know what we're going to do about it. Did you see what happened to your government's big bomb attack?"

"I saw it."

"Spectacular failure. All it's succeeded in doing is bringing everything forward." I sighed. "Do you know all of this is because of ants?"

Bill shook her head.

"The ants are just the point of entry."

"Why didn't you tell me?" I said. "Why didn't you tell me who I was fighting?"

"Would it have made any difference? Besides, what sort of hero would fight an ant heap?"

She was right, of course. She seemed so tired. Defeated, almost. I knew how she felt. Still, I pressed on.

"Listen, I saw Anna outside. She says that we should raise an army. Take it to Snakes and Ladders Square."

Bill smiled, weakly.

"Raise an army? Everyone says that sooner or later. No one ever says how, or what they should do. Do you have any idea how to raise an army, Captain Wedderburn?"

Captain Wedderburn did, actually. But I wasn't Captain Wedderburn any more. I thought of the mandrills in the zoo, of the thing in my mouth, of the contract that I signed in Angel Tower. Captain Wedderburn could have raised an army. He was a real Hero for Dream London. What was I, though?

"I have no currency in Dream London any more, Bill."

"Then you'd better gain some quickly. At the moment the only thing that stands between Dream London and whatever is coming through from the parks is the pair of us. Hold it..."

I heard it too. A muffled thumping from downstairs. The edge of violence, quickly quelled.

"Trouble," I said. "Is there another way out?"

Footsteps were hammering up the stairs, coming closer.

"There's a trapdoor at the end of the corridor that leads up into the attic," said Bill. "We might be able to run through the roof spaces."

It was too late for that. The door swung open. A young woman stood out there, giggling.

"He's up here!" she shouted. "Let's pull his clothes off now and lick him."

Big blue eyes and a dirty mop of blonde hair. One of the Moston girls. One breath of her perfume and my body leapt into action. One part of it did, anyway. Bill was unaffected, however. She slammed a fist hard into the Moston girl's chin, and she collapsed onto the floor, held her face and began to cry big tears.

"Why did you do that?" she sobbed. "You big bully!"

"I'm sorry!" I cried, bending down to help her. "She didn't mean it!"

"James!" called Bill. It was what I needed to cut me free of the honeyed web the Moston girl was casting about me. I straightened up, thoughts of easing her tears forgotten.

Bill grabbed my hand.

"Come on!" she said, pulling me into the corridor, but it was too late. The Moston girls filled the shabby space, blonde and alluring, dressed in nothing more than rags. They moved around me, I was caught in soft flesh and scent; it was like drowning in honey...

The Moston girls dragged me back into Bill's room. They laid me down on the bed. They unbuttoned my jacket and my trousers...

"Don't undress him yet... Stand back, now."

The voice was unfamiliar, but the Moston girls responded to it. They withdrew, leaving me lying there on the bed looking up at their leader. I rebuttoned my flies as the stranger stared at me. She was a plump woman, wearing a long dress scooped low to reveal a deep décolletage. Her black hair was pulled back into a severe bun, her lips and fingernails painted the scarlet of sin.

"Hello, Captain Wedderburn. Honey Peppers is looking for you."

"Who are you?" I asked. Where was Bill, I wondered? Had she gone for help? Had she chosen this moment to betray me? I didn't have time to think about it.

"My name is Madame Virtue," said the woman. She sat down on the edge of the bed, and it dipped beneath her weight. She placed a hand on my arm. "You look thirsty, Captain. Let me get you a drink."

"No thank you."

She clapped her hands.

"Someone get down to the bar. Fetch a gin and tonic. Four cubes of ice, three goes of gin and a lemon slice. And let a ten-ounce tonic void in foaming gulps until it smothers everything else up to the edge."

"That sounded like a poem."

"It was."

"Who are you?"

"Someone in the same line of work as you, Captain Wedderburn. Someone who is holding herself together under the changes." She laughed. "I was a bitch before Dream London came and I'm a bitch still today."

"I like you," I said.

"I like you, too," she said. She lay down on the bed, stretched herself out by my side and touched my neck, ran her finger down to my chest.

"It's over, Captain Wedderburn," said Madame Virtue. "The towers tremble and everyone is moving in to take their slice of the pie. The Daddio's got vice and crime."

I looked into her mouth.

"You don't have eyes in your tongue," I observed.

She smiled.

"I joined the Daddio of my own accord. Anyone who has any sense would do the same. Now the entrance is almost open, every interested party in Dream London is making their move. The Daddio's going to do well out of this, and if you have to join the Daddio you might as well do it on your own terms."

"Too late for me," I said.

"That's just your bad luck. Ah! Here's your drink."

The Laughing Dog didn't run to ice, or slices of lemon. It didn't even run to clean glasses. What came was strong gin with a thin dribble of flat tonic.

Still, it made me thirsty just to look at it. My tongue was wriggling. I forced the thirst down.

"Who is the Daddio, anyway?" I said, buying time.

"Few know," said Madame Virtue.

"But you do."

She knelt down at my side, that large bosom pressed close to my cheek.

"I do," she said. "Now, are you going to be a good boy and drink your gin?"

"I want to know first. Who is the Daddio?"

"Not a who," said Madame Virtue. "A what. The Daddio is a great forest down the river. Down past the flower fields and before the swamps. The Daddio is a forest laden heavy with fruit and berries. Animals eat the berries, and the Daddio gains power over them."

"The Daddio is a forest? I heard he was a pool of leeches."

"A pool in a forest. The Daddio is a whole eco-system."

I looked at the gin and tonic. What a cruel way to taunt a man. I forced it from my mind.

"Why all the crime, why all the vice?" I asked. "What interest would a forest have in money?"

"None whatsoever. The Daddio isn't immoral, the Daddio is amoral. That's why he doesn't care what happens to flesh bodies."

I slipped a finger over the top of her dress, pulling it down just a little, exposing a little more of her ample breast.

"Not too much, Captain," she said. "That's what the Moston girls are here for." Her body made a liar of her words. I felt her tense as I touched her. "The Daddio likes it when humans spend their time copulating. It stops them thinking of other things."

I slipped my other hand down her back and cupped the amplitude of her behind.

"Take a drink, Captain," she whispered, red lips so close to mine I felt her breath in my own.

"No," I said, and I flipped her over onto her front, pulling her arm up behind her back, hard. She yelled in pain.

"Tell your girls to back off, or I'll break your arm."

"They don't listen to me," she yelped.

"They'll listen to me, though. Tell them to stay back."

Another voice from the doorway. Another person come to join the fight. But on my side this time.

"Mr Monagan!" I called, and I felt like bursting into tears. To think I'd almost betrayed him... "Mister Monagan!" It was the second time he'd saved me in twenty-four hours. Never had anyone been so pleased to see an orange frog man standing in a doorway holding a large blunderbuss. Who knows where he had found that?

"You think you could kill them all with that gun?" said Madam Virtue. "All my lovely girls? My beautiful, seductive girls?"

"Seduction won't work on Mister Monagan," I said. "He doesn't like human girls."

"Not that way," said Mister Monagan, virtuously. "Now come on, Mister James. It's time to get out of here."

I got to my feet, buttoning my jacket.

"Where will you go?" asked Madam Virtue. "You'll have to drink soon."

"I've got a day or so," I said "Enough time to raise an army."

"Good luck with that," she said. "Even if you manage to get someone to follow you, they'll never fight. Dream London has drained the life out of everyone here."

I knew she was right. I didn't let her see that, though.

"Where's Bill?" I asked.

"Gone," he said. "She said she'll meet you later at Snakes and Ladders Square. If you get out of here in one piece that is."

"At least she's safe." I looked to the doorway, the giggling Moston girls waiting just beyond it.

"Come on then, Mr Monagan," I said. "Let's go."

THIRTEEN

THE STREETS OF DREAM LONDON

WE MOVED DOWN the corridor, the Moston girls writhing around us and dodging out of the way of the wide bell of Mr Monagan's blunderbuss. They reached out and pinched our bottoms, they grabbed us from behind, they crushed flowers in the air, they did everything to slow us down. Eventually, though, we made it out into the market street where we could lose ourselves in the crowd.

"Come back! Come back to us!"

I held onto the back of Mr Monagan's jacket as we pushed our way through the crowds. The smell of the produce – fruit and vegetables; sizzling spiced meats; coffee – all of it was torture to me.

"What are we going to do now, Mister James?" asked Mr Monagan.

"We're going to raise an army."

"An army!" Mister Monagan's eyes were shining. "How will we do that?"

"By acting like Captain Wedderburn."

"But you are Captain Wedderburn."

"Not any more, I'm not. Listen, Mr Monagan, I need you to do something for me."

"Anything, Mister James."

I looked behind me. We had lost the Moston girls in the crowd. For the moment, at least. I slowed to a walking pace, regaining my breath.

"Mister Monagan," I said. "I need you to sneak back to Belltower End. Find Gentle Annie, Miss Take and any other of the girls. Tell them to spread the word that Captain Wedderburn has a big job for them. He needs as many ladies as they can find."

Mister Monagan's eyes were shining.

"That sounds exciting!"

"Tell the girls that they are to be at Snakes and Ladders Square tonight before sundown."

"Snakes and Ladders Square! I will."

"Tell them we're going to fight. Tell them I need an army, and I know they can recruit one. Tell them I'm counting on them."

I looked at the orange man. I owed him my life. But then again, in a backwards sort of way, he owed me his. I reached out a hand. He looked at it, and then shook it.

"Thank you, Mister Monagan."

"For what?"

"For saving me."

"It was nothing, Mister James. Those girls..."

"I didn't mean from the girls."

"I don't understand."

"Never mind."

"Mister James?" He hesitated.

"Yes?"

"Will you be okay?"

"Why shouldn't I be?"

"You can't eat, you can't drink, Daddio Clarke and the Macon Wailers are hunting you and the parks are opening up."

I frowned.

"How do you know about the parks, Mr Monagan?"

"Oh, Mister James! I can read the signs!"

He had a point. Anyone could feel the change coming.

"I just need to make it to sundown," I said. "After that, it doesn't really matter."

I STRUCK OUT at random through the maze of streets surrounding Hayling Street. It didn't really matter where I went, all I had to do was to speak to as many people as possible.

I had the opportunity almost immediately: four men stood outside a pub, drinking a mid-morning glass of porter. Despite the heat, they had burgundy and silver scarves knotted around their necks.

"Gentlemen," I said. "How are the Hammers going to do tonight?"

The men looked me up and down suspiciously.

"You'd be Captain James Wedderburn," said one of them. "How's your arse? Full of monkey spunk, I heard."

"You heard wrong," I said easily, "and I'm willing to fight you if you wish to disagree."

"No need for that," he said, hurriedly. "No sense in listening to rumours on such a lovely day. How about I buy you a drink? The porter here in the Three Crows is rather fine today."

As if on queue three shiny brown barrels descended from the sky, lowered from one of the distant Dockland cranes into the back yard of the ale house. We looked along the length of the line to the distant boom of the crane, high above. Birds swooped and soared around it.

"No thank you," I said. "I haven't got time. I need to prepare for the Snakes and Ladders Square party. What time are you arriving?"

The men looked at each other.

"The Snakes and Ladders Square party?" said one, bluffing wildly. "Wasn't that tomorrow at ten...?"

"No! Tonight at sundown. I changed the date. Don't forget, the girls aren't charging and the first drink is on Captain Wedderburn."

"Sundown, eh? We can call in there after the match. We should be there celebrating, I think. Eh, lads?"

The other men cheered.

"So I'll see you then, okay lads?"

"Maybe you will."

"Which side do you support?" asked one of the men.

"The same side as I always do," I replied. "The winning one." I waved them farewell and walked off down the road.

There were little shops all around here, specialist shops catering to all sorts of people. Shops of all sizes, pushed together, single item shops selling nothing but razors, or caged birds, or walking sticks, or polished stones, or scrolls, or umbrellas, or beetles. One of them caught my eye and another idea occurred to me. Another way to recruit support. I pushed my way into its bright interior. Thousands of Captain Wedderburns looked down at me, turned their backs on me, looked off in other directions.

"Yes sir," said the little man sitting behind the tall desk.

"Good morning," I said. "I'm afraid I need to steal a small mirror off of you."

"I'm sorry to disappoint you, sir," he said, reaching beneath the table, "but I'm armed. You are standing in the focus of all my mirrors. I press this switch and I open a hatch that will allow the ingress of the sun. Happily, my mirrors are arranged to direct its full glare upon you."

I looked around the mirrors, in gilt frames, iron, glass, wood, jewelled, polished, bevelled, plain, decorated.

"You're lying," I decided. "But I have to hand it to you. You've got guts. More than most people in this city."

"Fucking twats, the lot of them," agreed the little man. He pointed to a little mirror by my side. "Take that one over there, and I wish you every bit of bad luck I can."

"If I had money I'd pay you."

"If I had a gun I'd shoot you."

I'm sure he was telling the truth. The man was clearly disturbed, no doubt the effect of sitting in here watching himself all day. A man who knew himself too well was liable to go off the rails. After all, it had almost happened to me earlier that day.

"Listen," I said, stuffing the mirror in my pocket. "I'm raising an army. If you want to do something to help, be in Snakes and Ladders Square at sundown. I could use a man like you."

"Isn't that where the party will be?"

I was surprised to see that my rumour had reached the shop before me, but that's Dream London for you.

"That's the place. All the whores you can handle."

"I can only manage one at a time," he said. "But I can still give a good account of myself."

"I'm pleased to hear it. I'll see you there, then."

Outside, the afternoon sun was bright and yellow and way too big. I pointed the mirror to the sky and flickered it back and forth, signalling the satellite. They had seen my message about the Contract Floor. I hoped they would still pay attention to me.

THE SUN ROLLED up the morning sky and down the afternoon. I walked the streets, passing news of my fictitious party to whoever I met.

The shops thinned, and I made my way through a section of porcelain-faced houses. Squat towers like sail-less windmills peeped over the surrounding houses, gazing at me with blank windows. I was thinking about giving up on this area and seeking out one more populous when I saw a crowd of people ahead of me. I hurried towards it.

"What's going on?" I asked a man in ragged grey overalls.

"I don't know," he said, eyes cast down to the ground. "We were told to come and wait here. We're being transferred to another workhouse."

Now he said it, it was obvious who these people were. The downcast glances, the air of shame, the loss of pride. These were Dream London's outcasts, the dispossessed, the forgotten. Imprisoned these past few months behind the grey walls of the workhouses, they had been stripped of their few remaining possessions, their dignity, their last vestiges of any fight. The men and women stood separately, the children hanging on to the grey skirts of their mothers, pale faces turned away from the sun.

"Who's in charge here?" I asked.

"Master Hodgson," said the man, nodding.

Master Hodgson was dressed in shabby leather breeches and a frilled white shirt. He looked like a cut price copy of the man Captain Wedderburn would have become, had he not given up his former ways.

"Good day," I said, nodding.

"Good day." Master Hodgson eyed me with caution. I recognised his type. He was deciding whether to be bully or sycophant. I helped him to decide.

"What are these people doing here in my street?" I demanded.

"Sorry, sir," he said, touching his forehead. "Master's orders. These are the inmates of Greendock Workhouse. They're being transferred to another world."

"Another world?" I said. "Explain yourself, man!"

"The parks are opening," said the man. "We were told to be ready at sundown."

Now I noticed the railings he stood by. I had thought that we were standing near a stretch of wasteland, brambles tangling at the fence that bordered the street. And perhaps this morning we would have been. But now I came to look, I saw the way the railings seemed to be coming to life. The metal at the top was old and rusted, but down at the ground the railings seemed to burst with green painted newness.

"The parks are coming through," said Master Hodgson. "They're breaking into Dream London."

"And what do you think will be waiting in the parks?" I asked.

"Who can say, sir? New employers, waiting to take these people into their service. That would be something, wouldn't it?"

"And you'd hand these people over to whoever is waiting through there, would you?"

"Just doing my job, sir. Just doing my job."

His expression was one of complacency.

"If you were half a man you'd let them go, rather than force them through there."

"Let them go where?" asked Master Hodgson. A grin formed on his face, the nasty little smile of someone who thought he was about to do something clever. He turned around to his charges. "Hey, Lightfoot!" he called. "You're free. Off you go."

"Go where?" said Lightfoot, eyes downcast with shame. "Where should I live? What would I eat?"

"Go to Snakes and Ladders Square!" I said. "There's going to be a huge party there at sundown. Free beer and women!"

"And after that?" said Lightfoot. "Where shall I go then?"

"Well..."

Hodgson looked back at me in petty delight.

"There's thirty-six of them here, sir. I'd be happy to hand them over to you if you feel you can look after them. You know, feed them, clothe them. Make sure the little kiddies have somewhere to sleep."

"Yes, but..."

He grinned, and a little bit more of the bully reasserted itself.

"Or perhaps you'd prefer to leave this to people who can actually do something? It's all very well to talk about helping the poor, *Sir*. It's only those that have the money that can actually do something though, isn't it?"

I gazed coldly at the man.

"There's no need to look at me like that. I was only speaking the truth. Or do you disagree?"

There was more to it than that, I was sure, but I couldn't think what else to say. In the end I settled for calling out to the crowd.

"Listen, you people. There's going to be a party at sundown in Snakes and Ladders Square. Come there if you can! We could change Dream London!"

A few of them looked at me, most of them looked away.

I took a last look at the fresh green paint that rose further up the railings, and then I was on my way.

I WALKED ON into the evening. In the past few days I had sought privacy and the streets of Dream London had been full. Now I was actively seeking people the streets were nearly empty. The few people I saw were always in the distance, hurrying away on their own business, and I wondered if somehow Angel Tower was seeking to frustrate me. At around six o'clock I emerged into a leaf-blown square.

A square of tall narrow houses. Dried leaves danced in circles; they filled the narrow spaces outside the downstairs flats, leaving the occupants with half-drowned views of the world, they clung fluttering to the iron railings that lined the spaces before the buildings. They lapped the bottom of the wide flight of steps that ascended from the far side of the square to the doorway of a large church. A group of people stood on the steps.

Tramps, waiting for hot soup to be served from a little trolley. The smell of the soup set my stomach rumbling and I was about to turn around and walk away, but someone noted my distress.

"Sit down, mister. Sit down here a moment and take a rest."

The man who spoke wore a long beard and trilby hat. His clothes were old and worn, but they looked to have been of fine quality once upon a time.

I felt so tired I slumped down on the steps next to him.

"Would you like some soup?" he said. He had a lovely voice, one that put me in mind of some old academic.

"No, please. Keep it away from me."

The man looked at me wisely.

"You could always suck on a pebble. It's said to help."

"Thank you," I said drily. "If I see a suitable one I'll be sure to try it."

The man laughed. I sat back and looked up the steps at the building that sat at the top.

"Does it seem familiar to you?" asked the man.

I shook my head. I felt so tired, so exhausted.

"It's St. Paul's Cathedral," said the man. "A lot smaller, it's true, and the dome has almost gone, but that's St Paul's Cathedral."

I stared at building. Now I looked it did seem vaguely familiar, but not like St Paul's. More like the church of my childhood, the one my mother had forced me to attend. It had the same shabby doors, the same noticeboard on the wall by the side of the door with the bright cheap posters pasted one on top of the other.

"It doesn't look like St Paul's," I said.

"Oh, but it is," said the man. "I should know. I've followed it through the city this past year. Watched it as it shrank and shed parts. Watched the dome as it turned to a pyramid, and then into a steeple. I've slept on these steps every night so that it can't slip away from me."

"Slept on the steps? Why?"

"Because Dream London mixes up our heritage and cuts us off from the past. Buildings drift and are shuffled, roads are tangled and unwound, bridges change direction overnight. If I hadn't followed it, this building would be lost by now, just another shabby ex-church lost in the city."

I stared at the man.

"What's the matter?" he asked.

"Nothing. It's just that I haven't met many people in this city who think about more than their balls or their belly."

The man shrugged.

I looked at him, searching his face for signs of understanding.

"I'm raising an army," I said. "I'm trying to overthrow Dream London."

"Good idea. Where do we muster?"

"Snakes and Ladders Square."

"When?"

"At sundown."

The man laughed.

"You're leaving it a bit late, aren't you?"

"Better late than never."

The man laughed again.

"Well, good luck with that. I won't be coming myself, but if I meet anyone in the next couple of hours who I think might be interested, I'll be sure to tell them."

I laughed.

"Thank you."

"Is there anything else I can help you with?"

I looked back up at the shrunken shell of St Paul's.

"I don't think so. It's been good just to take a rest."

"Can I give you some advice?" said the man.

"Please do."

"You're going into battle tonight. You need to prepare yourself."

"What do you suggest?"

"A wash and a change of clothes at the very least."

"That would be nice. How do you suggest I do this?"

"See the street over there? Papillon Street? Half way down there is a blue door. The lady there is most obliging. Tell her that Crispin Welander sent you."

All of a sudden, a bath was just what I needed.

"It's very tempting," I said, "but I can't just knock on someone's door and ask for a bath."

"I think you can," said Crispin. "You see, I've been waiting for you to turn up."

"What do you mean."

Crispin pulled open his jacket. I saw a yellow scroll of parchment tucked into the inside pocket.

"You too?" I said.

"I don't believe in fortunes," said Crispin, apologetically. "Unfortunately, they seem to believe in me."

I LEFT THE square and walked down Papillon Street. The houses here had an air of fading prosperity. The large front doors bore two or three bell pushes, indicating that the interiors had been split into flats. The air felt still, there was no sound, and I felt very much alone. No, not quite alone. A ginger cat sat watching me from a window ledge.

"Hello there," I said.

There was another cat just below the window ledge, a large tabby that sat licking its paws. And another cat, just slinking up from behind me. Now that I looked the street was full of cats, all of them apparently just passing through, and all of them watching me.

I came to the blue door half way down the street and paused. A cat sat inside a window by the door, watching me.

I was about to turn and walk away when the door opened.

Miss Elizabeth Baines stood there, beaming at me.

"Captain James Wedderburn," she said. "Here you are at last!"

FOURTEEN

33 PAPILLON STREET

MISS ELIZABETH BAINES' house was filled with cats. They walked the corridors, they sat on the seats, they ate from little saucers placed on the floor.

"Don't look at me like that, Captain Wedderburn."

"Like what, Miss Baines? And it's not Captain any more, it's just James."

"James. I've always liked the name." She smiled at that and half closed her eyes. "James," she repeated. Then she came out of her reverie and grinned.

"Don't look at me as if I'm some sort of sad old cat lady, James."

I raised an eyebrow.

"Really," she said, "these aren't my cats."

"You allow them in your house..."

"There are many cats around here. So many strays since the changes began. They seem to think that I can look after them."

Miss Elizabeth Baines seemed different on her home turf. That was normal. But what was it about her? She was dressed in the same spinsterish way. Very female, skirt and blouse and make-up, but with every inch of skin covered and nothing left for the imagination.

"Why do they think that you will look after them?" I asked, looking around. The house was exactly as I would have imagined, from the little flowery pictures on the walls to the lace antimacassars on the back of the chairs.

"Why do they think I will look after them?" asked Elizabeth, drily. "Heaven knows. The word seems to have got round the locality. Perhaps the cats talk to each other? Who can tell nowadays?"

"But even so, you still look after the cats." I gazed at her, and something occurred to me that I should have thought before: that Dream London liked to push people into roles, but that some people were better than others at fighting back. Dream London changed the houses, the clothes, the fortunes, but some people resisted. That's what I could see in Miss Elizabeth Baines' eyes – resistance. I should have thought of that before, but of course, Captain Wedderburn would never have thought of anyone but himself.

"I didn't used to be a virgin, you know," said Elizabeth, matter of factly.

"What?"

She smiled at my reaction, and then she changed the subject.

"The cats turn up at my house. What am I to do? I'm lucky enough to have a lot of money. I can afford to look after them."

"Aren't there better ways to spend your money?"

"Perhaps we could compare your charitable acts with mine, Captain? You wish to tell me about them? No?"

She bent down and lifted up a cat that was pushing another aside to get at its food.

"I leave them food and water," said Elizabeth, putting the cat down next to another bowl. "Sometimes the cranes lower boxes of fish heads into the back garden. Someone at the docks seems to like cats and is helping me out." She looked thoughtful. "Sometimes they lower a case of flowers as well. I think perhaps it's not only the cats they are interested in."

"Who sends you flowers?" I asked.

"Are you jealous, James?"

"No!"

That lopsided grin again. There was something about it that I found attractive

"I have no idea who sends me flowers, James. Who knows what's really going on in Dream London?"

I had just been sent by a stranger from the shrunken remnants of St Paul's to the house of the woman who had been stalking me the past few days. I think it fair to say that someone must know what was going on. Someone was orchestrating all of this. I thought of the group of people who sat on the Writing Floor of Angel Tower.

"Doesn't your garden smell?" I asked. To be honest, I was lost for anything else to say.

"The cats are very clean. They can't abide untidiness," said Elizabeth. "Now, would you like a cup of tea? Or perhaps something stronger. A beer perhaps?"

"No thank you," I said.

"Perhaps you want to go straight to bed?"

I was quite floored by her words: she spoke them so directly. I remembered she had made the same offer when I had been going to the brothel to meet Bill.

"I don't think I have the time..." I said, weakly.

"Oh, James! You're not going all shy on me, are you?"

"No, I'm just..."

"You strut around the city acting the big man, but when it comes down to it, you're just a frightened little boy, aren't you? I promise I'll be gentle with you!"

What was going on here?

"Listen, lady..."

"I told you, it's not Lady, it's Elizabeth... hold on."

She tilted her head. I heard it too. A plaintive mewing. Something was in pain.

I followed Elizabeth into a kitchen. A cat flap in the back door led out into a dark green garden stacked with wooden crates. The flap moved, and I heard the mewing. Elizabeth opened the door and went into the garden.

"It's been in a fight," I said. The cat was covered in blood. One of its ears was badly torn.

"Not just a fight," said Elizabeth. "Look, two of its legs are broken. I don't know how it got here. The blue monkeys like to carry them up to the roof tops and torture them. Dream London is a cruel place. Give me your pistol."

"My pistol?"

"I know you have one. I can see the outline in your jacket."

"What do you want my pistol for?"

Miss Elizabeth Baines directed a gaze at me that would have withered a warehouse worth of flowers.

"I was hoping to use both it and my veterinary experience to heal this cat's broken legs."

"You used to be a vet?" I asked.

"Stop asking stupid questions and give me the bloody pistol."

I finally realised what she meant and, somewhat hesitantly, handed the pistol across.

"Thank you," she said.

She pressed the cat down onto the ground and placed the pistol to its head.

"There you are," she said, handing the pistol back to me afterwards. "And I note that, despite the care I took, I have blood on my sleeve. I'll go upstairs now and change." She fixed me with an electric blue gaze. "Why don't you bury this cat for me, and then meet me up there."

"You're not sentimental, are you?" I said.

"I look after the animals, James. Now, are we going to bed or not?"

I finally realised that she was teasing me. She had been teasing me ever since she had met me.

"I only came for a bath and change of clothes. I have to be at Snakes and Ladders Square by sunset."

"I'll show you where the bathroom is. I'm not sure what I have for you to wear."

"Clothes would be nice. A bath would be enough," I said.

I TOOK A bath and... well, that's it. I took a bath. I never really expected Elizabeth to try and take advantage of me. It was nice just to soak and ease the soreness in my legs and backside. But the thirst was building in me, and all that water around me just made me thirstier, so I got out and went downstairs.

"Are you sure you don't want something to eat or drink?" asked Miss Baines.

"I can't," I said, and I stuck my tongue out at her.

"I can see the two slits, but there are no eyes yet," said Elizabeth,

"If I don't die tonight, I don't know what I'll do," I said. "Take a drink of water or kill myself. It will amount to the same thing."

"If you don't die tonight, come back here," said Elizabeth.

"Why should I do that?" I asked.

"Where else would you go?" asked Elizabeth.

I gazed at her, and I felt so tired.

"You know, I'm not Captain Wedderburn anymore," I said. "But it's only been a few hours. I'm not a nice person, Elizabeth. You don't want to waste your time with me. Seriously, there are lots better men out there. I'm not what people say I am, Elizabeth. I'm not a hero."

"Good," said Elizabeth. "I often think that the world needs fewer heroes and more good fathers."

"You just want a husband."

"No, I want a *good* husband."

"I'm not going to marry you, Elizabeth...."

"You misunderstand me, James. That wasn't a proposal. It's just an observation. Dream London wants every man to do nothing. To be weak-willed and selfish. But if it can't break them, it wants them to be heroes, to lead the last desperate charge, to die alone in a glorious last stand. What it doesn't want is people who stick to the daily grind, people who become part of the quiet majority, people who do what's right despite getting paid no notice."

She was right, of course. The ants in Angel Tower worked together, that was the secret of their power. They didn't want others doing the same.

"So which one are you now, James?"

"I don't know what I am any more," I said.

"None of us do," said Elizabeth. "Not really."

She picked an imaginary hair from the lapel of my jacket.

"Come back here afterwards," she said. "Promise me?"

"I'll try," I said.

AND SO I found myself back on Papillon Street.

Dream London was descending towards evening. The sky was on fire as it always was at this time of day, red and yellow bloomed on the streaking clouds, and the air smelled of the usual spices and flowers. I could hear the distant sound of cheering and clapping. The match had started. I heard the roar of the crowd rise and fall as the ball travelled back and forth across the pitch. The buildings echoed to the sound of drums and singing.

A great drama was being played out within the stadium, but a greater one was unfolding outside it.

Tonight, Dream London would be fully joined to the other worlds.

I began to walk the streets towards Snakes and Ladders Square. There was no question of the direction. Everything flowed that way, the other pedestrians, the clouds, the birds. Even the roads themselves seemed to flow downhill towards Snakes and Ladders Square. That was the place to be. I thought it was my plan to raise an army there tonight. If it was, Dream London seemed happy to go along with it.

A sudden roar sounded, the animal howl of the city. It soared over the houses, it echoed from every surface.

Someone had scored a goal. Soon the match would finish and the fans would pour from the ground and head towards the pubs surrounding Snakes and Ladders Square. They would drink and sing and fight in a riot of burgundy and silver, brown and cream. The roar of the crowd died away in a thunder of drums, and I heard other instruments taking up the slack. Guitars and accordions and flutes, all the soloists of Dream London filling the air with white noise.

I was getting closer now. Three teenage girls staggered out of a house in front of me. They wore short dresses and high heels and were obviously drunk already. One of them glanced at me and announced in a loud voice:

"I'm so drunk I'd even fuck him!"

The other two laughed, and they staggered on their way towards the revelries. I stepped up my pace, impatient to be there at the end, but a great silence brought me to a halt.

A long building lay to my right, the sort of grey brick industrial construction that you could find anywhere in the streets of Dream London. Grey walls surrounding the higher buildings beyond. Frosted glass windows peering over the top of the walls. Wide, arched gates in the centre of the wall standing wide open, the emptiness beyond sucking the life from the street.

I read the words written in wrought iron that vaulted the space over the gates.

Snakes and Ladders Street Workhouse.

I walked up to the open gates and looked beyond into the empty yard. I could see the blank walls of the workhouse proper, its doors standing wide open.

"Hello?" I called. I listened to the echo of my own voice.

Standing in the workhouse yard, the sounds of Dream London faded away.

"Hello?"

The workhouse was deserted. Everyone who had inhabited the place was gone. I walked into the main building. There were offices here, furnished with fine walnut desks and leather chairs. I found a cup of tea on one desk, still lukewarm. A half written letter lay beside it, and I read the words *forty strong men and six girls, suitable for service.*

"Hello?" I called again, unnecessarily.

I wandered from the offices, on through the factory floors. I passed lines of looms, strung with ochre wool. Into another room and I saw garments that resembled yellow jumpers hanging from racks. They were too long, the arms longer still, and they had holes stitched into the back of them. I unhooked one of the yellow jumpers and held it to myself and thought, and it occurred to me that if I was a monkey I might wear this garment and stick my tail through the hole at the back.

I passed into the living quarters. Two doors, marked *men* and *women*. I went into the men's quarters. There was nothing there but bunks. Thin mattresses barely thicker than the thin blankets that covered them. Somewhere for the men to sleep in shifts. There was nothing else there. No possessions whatsoever.

I went into the women's quarters, and found them just the same as the men's. I walked down rows and rows of bunks, and something caught my eye. There on the floor, a bloom of dirty pink. I bent down to see a doll's head staring back at me. Some child's makeshift toy, dropped in the sudden evacuation.

Where had they all gone?

I knew the answer. I had seen it earlier. These people had served their purpose in Dream London and now they were to be transferred to where they could be more profitable.

I held the doll's head in my hand, and I squeezed it hard.

OCHRE

SNAKES AND LADDERS

Some people treat life like a game of chess. For most people, life treats them as players in a game of Snakes and Ladders.

Snakes and Ladders Square started out as a tiny space at the back of Dream London Hospital. A tiny cobbled yard, halved by a wooden fence that cut out all the light save for the few shafts of sun that vaulted into the dimness at midday. The caretaker who opened the door leading into that dank space used the yard to dispose of waste cardboard boxes. It was easier than taking them to the incinerator, and besides, he could listen in on the nurses chatting at the other side of the fence, he could eavesdrop as they shared their previous night's conquests whilst smoking their break-time cigarettes.

This was before the changes, back when the rain still fell in a cold drizzle, soaking the boxes and leaving a brown mush on the cobbles stirred only by the rats. Of the former yard, only a little patch of stone was left, ten stones by ten stones.

And then the changes had come, and a story arose.

Back then, the caretaker had looked out the back once every couple of days, and he had watched the little yard grow. He had seen the hundred little cobbles gradually flatten into black marble squares. Over the weeks the yard had grown, and as it did so the former cobbles had grown to the size of flagstones. The sounds of the nurses faded, the wooden fence was overgrown with ivy and light flooded back into the little yard, now not so little. Now the caretaker could walk into the middle of the square and gaze up at the red brick walls of Dream London Hospital. No one ever looked back down at him from those blind windows.

Perhaps the caretaker should have spent more time thinking about the space beyond the walls of the yard. Perhaps he should have thought about what was happening beyond the ivy-covered fence, now turning to metal, but who can blame him if he spent his time looking at the patterns forming on the great flagstones of the floor?

The black marble squares grew bigger than a man. Grooves formed upon them, spaces that wormed their way across the shiny surfaces, hovering on the edge of meaning. And then, from the twisting shapes, symbols formed. The numbers came first, counting from 1 to 100. The pictures that formed behind them were too hazy to make out, or so the caretaker said. Worse, they seemed to rearrange themselves. Every time the door was opened the numbers were in a different position. Or maybe he was just making excuses for his foolishness, because surely any Dream Londoner would know better than to step out of a door onto the square marked *one*?

*   *   *

THAT'S THE STORY anyway, and it's a story told every night in a different pub in Dream London. The door will swing open and a man will stagger in, dressed in rags and with a beard down to his waist. He will ask for a drink, for something to eat, and more often than not he will be given both because everyone likes a good story, particularly if it's accompanied by a good act. The caretaker will tell how he is traversing the board of Snakes and Ladders, how every night he takes another step, and each time he is raised up on a ladder or swallowed down by a snake. The disbelieving crowd will ask the caretaker how he got here, and why he is not still upon the board, but the caretaker will just shake his head and shiver, and go on eating and drinking.

I've never seen him myself. Maybe it's just a story, but nonetheless, Snakes and Ladders Square exists. A vast empty space with Dream London Hospital on one side and the Dream London Footballdrome on the other. There are lines of pubs and cafés at the bottom of Snakes and Ladders Square, and ivy covered railings at the top. There are 98 squares in Snakes and Ladders Square, numbered from 2 to 99.

Squares 1 and 100 are yet to be found.

TRAILS OF BLACK birds filled the skies, streaming in from miles around, heading for a point somewhere beyond Snakes and Ladders Square. The sounds of singing and laughter and drums filled the night, and the perfume of the flowers was enough to make Tower Bridge raise itself in salute.

Snakes and Ladders Square, already vast, had grown larger to accommodate the people who had come there for the party, for the women, for the drink, for the spectacle. The sun was setting in crimson at the far end, bringing a feeling of the end of the world to the red-shadowed people. It felt as if the sun had got it right, and the people who had come for a party raised a glass to the sun as they drank themselves into oblivion.

I was there on square number 3, down at the bottom, waiting for the night to begin.

People were staggering. Streams of football supporters emerged from the Footballdrome, burgundy and silver colours from the one end, brown and cream from the other. Some were heading for the line of shops and pubs along the bottom edge of the square. Those that couldn't be bothered to stagger that far headed for the vendors closer at hand, their carts and barrows dispensing beer and whisky. Across the square, doctors and nurses lined up before the red brick walls of Dream London Hospital, ready for business.

The square was filled with a festival atmosphere. The sounds of laughing and cheering, of people squaring up for a fight...

... but not the sort of fight I was looking for them to take part in. I'd come to raise an army, what I had was a rabble. I had a drunken crowd of hedonists who would fight for their own gain and would run at the first sign of danger. Dream London had done its job well, subduing any rebellion in its own fashion.

Football fans, whores, party goers, sightseers... The musicians were also out in force. Fiddles and guitars, flutes and accordions, each of them providing their own little bubble of contrasting music, adding to the air of cacophony.

This was a party, not an army.

"Jim!"

I didn't recognise the woman at first. She wore a striped dress with a bustle, and a man in a dark scarlet coat stood at her side.

"Jim, it's me."

"Hello, Christine," I said.

"It's Mrs Cadwallader now," she said, holding out her hand to show me the ring.

"Congratulations," I said.

"It's been something of a whirlwind romance, to be honest. Eric is something big in the New Territories. We're heading out there tonight, after the party..."

I looked at Eric. He had a square, honest face, a big moustache. He looked like a man you could trust.

"Good, I am pleased," I said.

"Are you sure, Jim?"

She touched my arm, a look of concern on her face, and as I gazed at her I realised that whatever I had once felt for her had gone. Dream London had eaten up the old Christine.

"Really," I said. "I wish you all the best."

"Thank you," she said.

"You too, Mr Cadwallader," I said, shaking the man's hand.

He smiled at me, and they turned to go. I was distracted by a familiar voice.

"Mister James! Mister James!"

I turned at the sound of my name, Christine already forgotten.

"Hello, Mister Monagan."

The orange man looked as pleased to see me as ever. He had found a camouflage jacket from somewhere, and he wore it over his white shirt and dark trousers with pride.

"I was waiting for you here, just like you asked! I knew you'd make it here!"

"Did you bring the girls?" I asked.

"I did." He pointed over to Gentle Annie and the rest, dressed in their Friday best: stockings and garters and low cut tops. The girls were standing on square 15, flirting with a group of football fans. Lovely Rita was being pulled towards a laughing fan by the maroon scarf he had thrown around her neck.

"Gentle Annie will know what to do," I said, approvingly. "Fire the men up with the promise of something after the fight. Get them drunk enough so they lose their fear, but not so drunk they're not good for anything...."

The fan pulled Lovely Rita close for a kiss. Laughing ,she pushed him away.

"You're all talk," I heard her say. "I like a man who can handle himself."

"I can handle myself," said the fan, over the laughter of his friends.

"Really? Prove it, then."

The fan looked at his friends.

"Come here and kiss me and I'll prove it!" he said.

"No," said Rita, and she slipped out from under the scarf. "I don't think so. You look too delicate for me."

"Delicate?" shouted the man. "I'll show you delicate!"

"Well done, Rita," I murmured.

Gentle Annie saw me. She slipped away from the laughing crowd and crossed to join me on square 3.

The red setting sun highlighted the fine lines around her eyes.

"We're doing our best, Captain, but it's hard. These men would rather watch people fight than fight themselves."

"Who wouldn't, Gentle Annie? Just do your best."

She fumbled in her skirts.

"Here," she said. She passed me something that looked like a wide brass pistol.

"Is that a flare gun?" I asked.

"Sort of," she said. "Dream London has modified it, but it will do the job. It will summon our army to you."

"And then we can march. We can attack Angel Tower." I put the flare gun in my pocket. "Thank you, Annie. You've done well. Now, go out and do your part!"

"Aye aye, Captain!" She gave a mock salute and went to rejoin her girls. I looked at them with pride: they knew their stuff, the way that they constantly danced just beyond the football fans' reach, teasing them, spurring them on. I looked at them with shame. I had done that to them. I pushed the thought from my mind.

"You've done a good job, too, Mister Monagan," I said, turning to the orange man.

"Do you really think so?" He beamed with delight.

"I do. Now, do you know where Bill is?"

Mister Monagan nodded.

"She's gone to Euston Station."

"What for?"

"She didn't say."

"Thanks, Bill," I murmured. I sighed. "Did she have any messages for me?"

"No," said Mr Monagan. "Well…"

He looked a little embarrassed.

"What did she say, Mr Monagan?"

He turned a toe on the black marble floor, traced a stripe on the back of a snake.

"She said that you'd served your purpose. That I should just forget about you now."

Go to the Inn to meet a friend, one who will betray you.

"She was never really a friend to me, anyway," I murmured.

"What was that, Mr James?"

"Never mind," I said. "What about Amit? Where has he got to?"

"Amit says he will meet you on square 73 with fifty men, all armed with swords and chakras."

That was more like it. Although...

"Chakras? What are they?"

"Sharp metal hoops," said Mr Monagan, seriously. "Amit showed me how to throw one. Oh, you need to be so careful with them, Mister James, or you'll cut yourself. Amit's men are well trained."

"I bet they are."

"So what now, Mister James?"

I looked to the east. Angel Tower rose up in the distance, its full extent piercing the darkening sky, dwarfing the floodlights that looked down over the Footballdrome. The tower seemed to be laughing at us. Fifty Sikhs armed with swords and chakras would not cause it much a of a problem, I thought.

"What now, Mister Monagan?" I said, sounding more cheerful than I felt. "We have an army forming, so now we need to look for someone for them to fight. Come on!"

FIFTEEN

SQUARES 95 AND 96

WE PUSHED OUR way into the laughing crowd. On square 14 a man reached around from behind a woman and pulled her back onto himself by her breasts. She laughed and turned to kiss him. A group of men cheered.

"This is your army, Mister James?" said Mister Monagan.

"Not yet, Mister Monagan. At the moment they've got no reason to fight. They're not dissatisfied with what's going on."

And why would they be? They had drink, food and sex on tap. Dream London had tamed them with its bread and circuses.

"How do we make them dissatisfied?" asked Mister Monagan.

"Gentle Annie and the girls are doing their bit to make them dissatisfied one way," I said. "We're going to look for the people who are dissatisfied but just don't realise it yet. I think they'll be at the far side of the square..."

We pushed our way on through the crowds. Men pressed beer on us, women tried to kiss us, everyone asked us to dance, to sing, to sit and look at the sky. We ignored them all.

"Do you know the score, mate?"

The young man stood at the top of a ladder in the middle of square 55, smoking a lilac cigarette. He pushed up close to me now, his pupils vastly expanded.

"I said, do you know the score, mate? The Hammers versus the Armoury?"

"Sorry, no," I said.

"I do," said the young man. He drew deeply on his cigarette. "Hammers won by four goals, two kisses and a logical inconsistency."

"You've no idea how happy that makes me," I said.

"The Hammers will be here soon. The boys in burgundy know how to party."

"Ah, but, do they know how to fight?" I asked.

"Fight? The Hammers? Course they do!"

"Then tell them to meet me at square 93. I'll show them a fight."

"Yeah, right."

I didn't know whether he was being sarcastic or not.

"On second thoughts, forget it. I'll ask the Armoury boys instead. They're the ones to have on your side when it kicks off."

"The Armoury? If you're taking on the Dream London Nursery maybe. For a proper pagga you need the Hammers. Square 93 you say?" He tapped his nose. "I'll have a few of the lads there with me."

"Good man."

We pushed our way on. It was funny the way people stood on the marble stones of Snakes and Ladders

Square. Always avoiding the edges. Step on a crack, break your mother's back. We were approaching the top of the square. Now I could see the green spaces beyond. The parks were rolling up on us like a green avalanche. Sometime during the course of the day the hills and trees that been hidden from us for so long had swollen up like the sea and were now flooding down on us in slow motion. It was like facing the green foothills of a great mountain range, the parks seeming to slope upwards, rising up into the deep sky that seemed to go on forever. And yet it was just some trick of the eye. The deep purple sky hung above us as it always did, filled with the black birds of evening, lording it over us, as they flicked back and forth at tremendous pace.

"Do you see it, Mister Monagan?" I asked.

"Yes."

"You don't sound very impressed."

"Should I be?" He looked around the crowd, uncertain. "No one else seems to be paying particular attention. To be honest, I don't know what's normal in a city as wonderful as Dream London."

Maybe he didn't. He was right when he said that most people didn't seem to notice. They were all too busy partying as the old world ended.

It took us almost ten minutes to make it to the top of Snakes and Ladders Square. Iron railings rose up above the heads of the people there, twisted into glorious patterns.

"Mister James," said Mister Monagan, tugging at my sleeve. "I think I found your army."

"I thought they'd be here," I said.

Squares 95 and 96 lay at the top of the centre of the square. Square 95 had the top of a ladder upon it, square 96 the head of a snake. There was a wide set of gates that stretched the extent of the two squares at their edge, and beyond the gates, the park.

A crowd of grey-clothed people waited hopelessly by the iron gates. More slave labour from the workhouses.

"I've seen people like this waiting all around the city," said Mister Monagan.

"So have I. Come on."

The people from the workhouse stood in neat lines of ten, men on one side, women and children on the other. They gazed at the ground, empty of feeling. I'd tried recruiting them once before without success. This time I was prepared.

I walked up to a nearby fellow and shook him on the shoulder.

"I'm James Wedderburn," I said.

"I know who you are," he replied, his voice as dull as his expression.

"Listen, I'm raising an army. Spread the word."

"An army," he said. He couldn't meet my gaze. "Could you feed us?"

I slapped him on the back, full of the bonhomie that had been Captain Wedderburn's principal coin.

"Feed you?" I said. "Once Angel Tower is defeated there will be steak for everyone!"

"Ah," said the man. "After we fight. But if we go through the gates there will be bread right away."

The other men around him nodded at that.

"Ah, but bread and a life of slavery," I countered.

"Better a life of slavery than death from starvation."

His dour countenance might have disheartened a lesser man, but not Captain Wedderburn. Okay, I wasn't Captain Wedderburn any more, but I could still act the part.

"Listen, man. After the battle, all will be free and well fed."

"Really?" said another man, close by. "I was a soldier once, before the changes. I was laid off by the army after Afghanistan."

"I was in Afghanistan too," I said.

"I know that," said the man. "Did the government treat you well after you left? Has this country ever treated its soldiers well once it had done with them?"

I waved a hand dismissively at this. Captain Wedderburn was a man of dreams, not reality. No wonder Dream London loved him.

"Listen, man! It will be sundown soon. When the sun touches the edge of the park, my army rises! Will you be part of it?"

"Not me, nor anyone else here," said the ex-soldier with finality. "Your army will not rise up, Captain Wedderburn." He turned his back on me.

The sun wobbled lower. The workhouse army refused to rise.

"They aren't listening to you, Mister James!" Mister Monagan wore the expression of one seemingly unable to grasp this concept.

"They will," I said, but with less confidence than before. Even Captain Wedderburn couldn't have roused these people, and I wasn't him any more. I was just another cast-off, another loser.

"Look at the sun!"

I don't know who said that, but we all turned and looked as the sun finally set over the darkening park.

There was a gentle chime, and the crowd went quiet. Just like that.

The end of the old world had arrived.

The red sun was sliding below the horizon. The tail ends of the dark streams of birds fluttered into the night.

Now there was only stillness and the silence of the setting sun.

"What is it?" asked Mister Monagan, speaking in a whisper. "What's happening?"

"I don't know."

Everyone was looking towards the park. Everyone gazing in the same direction, eyes glowing red in the setting sun. My tongue was wriggling in my mouth.

A long, drawn out creaking noise sounded across the square.

"The gates are opening."

The gates to Dream London Park swung inwards, welcoming the city into another world. Somewhere in the distance I heard a crashing sound, a feeble cheer, the sounds of people shushing each other.

Someone blew a whistle, and I thought I heard a collective exhalation of breath. The sound of resignation. The grey-clothed ranks of the workhouse inmates began to shuffle forward.

"They're moving, Mister James! They're moving."

Quickly, and in good order, the dispossessed of Dream London marched in ranks towards their new lives. They marched over the hard shiny surface of squares 95 and 96, *tap tap tap tap*, they stepped onto the gravel path that lay beyond, *crunch crunch crunch crunch*.

And the party crowd stood and watched them go.

Mister Monagan pulled on my arm.

"Shouldn't we stop them, Mister James?"

I shook my head.

"It's sometimes like this in a war, Mister Monagan. It takes people a while to realise what they're fighting for."

And you sometimes had to sacrifice some for the good of others. Of course, I couldn't say that to Mister Monagan.

"But they're leaving Dream London, Mister James! They don't know what it will be like through there!" He turned to appeal to the crowd, stood up hard against the edges of 80s squares. "Everyone! Stop them!"

No one moved. Mister Monagan moved forward, took hold of the arms of one of the marchers.

"Stop!" he said. "Don't go in there! You could be taken anywhere!"

"Wherever it is, it's got to be better than this place," said the grey-clothed man. "At least someone wants us in there."

He shook off Mister Monagan's hand, and then walked on. Mister Monagan stood in front of the next man. The man dodged around him.

"Stop them!" called Mister Monagan.

"Why?" shouted someone from the crowd. "They're quite happy."

Over on the 80s, the sounds of the party gradually resumed. Glasses were clinked, laughter rose. On the 90s, the workers shuffled off to who knew where.

Mister Monagan was almost crying with frustration.

"Don't they care?" he asked.

"They didn't care when they went into workhouses, why should they care now?" I said.

Dispirited, we followed the marching line to the very edge of our world. Standing there on square 95 I looked through the gates into a vast green space. The park was lit by a different sun to ours. A silver sun, it lent the geometric lines of trees that ran through the park a certain coldness of aspect. Everything in the park was ordered. The roads, the trees, the neatly trimmed lawns set amongst the wider green countryside. Vast spaces, divided by lines of trees. Roads that travelled this way and that, converging on one point in the distance marked by the glorious gold and white building that had been Buckingham Palace. The silver sun shone coldly on the towers and minarets of the fairytale castle. It lay like a jewelled egg in the green nest of the park.

The only sign of randomness through there was the dark statues that were scattered across the lawns, statues just like the ones at the Spiral, entwined in sexual poses. Statues of people gagged and bound, or tilted over with their arses in the air. They showed a people defeated, subjugated, humiliated.

Save for the grey lines of workers, heading off to their new lives, the park was still.

Then I noticed movement, and I realised that wasn't true. There were other people in the park too. Several groups, waiting in the distance, scattered across the extent of the green lawns. People waiting for something. People who had come to collect their workers.

Not all of the people in the groups looked quite human: a group to the right of the gates were too tall and thin. The wind shifted their long golden hair, showing how it grew from one point at the top of their heads, and cascaded down over their otherwise bald skulls. A group to their left were dressed in dark clothes and hoods. They moved in an oddly jerky fashion.

What they all had in common, however, was a proprietary air. These were people who dealt in goods and commodities. Even the obviously human group who stood directly before me in frilled shirts and tight trousers had no humanity about them.

As they passed through the gates, the lines of grey workers split along different paths, separated by size and age and health. Now I saw that a man in a bicorn hat stood traffic duty, pointing this way and that, splitting the line of workers, sending them walking in three different directions. The workers seemed resigned to their fate. Why should I get so upset? It wasn't as if Captain Wedderburn would have cared.

But of course, I wasn't Captain Wedderburn anymore. I had signed that life away up on the Contract Floor. I was a different man now, and it was much harder being plain James. I seemed to be the only one here who cared. Not the partygoers, not the grey people. So why should I be so bothered?

And then, off in the distance of that other world, the screaming begin.

"Listen!" I called. "Listen!" I bellowed.

No one did. Still the lines of grey shuffled by. Now women were passing me, dirty faces cast down to the ground. "Listen!" I shouted.

A young man wearing an accordion came closer to me.

"Listen to my voice," he sang, "for I have a song to sing."

The grey women looked up at that and smiled. Here was a good looking young man. Even the months in the workhouse hadn't robbed him of his spell.

"Ignore him," I called. "Listen to me!"

The man played a chord on his accordion and the marching women nodded as they passed by. I broke his nose with the heel of my hand. He fell on his back, the accordion wheezing around his neck.

"Hey..." he began.

"Shut up," I shouted. He cowered as I glared at him. He took his hand from his nose and looked at the blood there.

"Listen!" I demanded.

The screams were louder now. Finally, the shuffling women heard them too.

"That sounds like children," said one.

"Not children," said another. "That's old people. Old people screaming."

Finally, finally, the marchers halted. A grey train, half in this world, half in the next. They began to edge backwards.

"Old people. It is!"

"I can't hear anything."

"Listen. There in the distance."

"She's right."

There was shouting behind us, the other marchers coming up from behind, the grey huddling masses, trying to get through, calling to those who had halted to get a move on.

"Stop pushing me!"

The women by the gates stood their ground, they tilted their heads to listen.

"Listen," I shouted. "Listen to the screams! You don't have to go in! We could fight this!"

The women looked at me. I had their attention. Finally, I had their attention. Caught on the boundary between Dream London and the park, I had my audience. And now I saw a group of men in Hammers scarves, forming back there at square 93, right by the wall of the park. My football fans had come. They were being joined by a group of Armoury fans, dressed in brown and cream. My army was forming...

But in the silence another musician crept in. A young woman with a guitar. She struck a chord.

"Sing, brave women, of the new life that awaits you."

I took hold of the guitar and smashed it against the ground.

"Hey!" Three men disengaged from the party crowd in the 80s and came over to me. They were swaying, brave on alcohol and each other's company. Behind me, I had lost the workhouse women's attention. The heaving crowd forced them on into the park.

"No," I called. "Come back..."

A hand on my shoulder, pulling me back, pulling me over the line from the 90s to the 80s.

"That's no way to treat a young lady..."

"You broke her guitar!"

"Not me, you fools!" I called. "We should be fighting that!"

I pointed over their heads, past the floodlights of the Footballdrome to the looming shape of Angel Tower. The men ignored me. One threw a punch. I dodged it and kicked away his feet. Something hit my back and I was on the floor, struggling to get up. Someone kicked my hands away. I heard a shout and caught a flash of orange. Mister Monagan was there, helping out. He was strong, there was no denying that. Strong and fast. A good frog to have on your side in a fight.

I climbed to my feet, still groggy. The crowd had carried me back into the party section, and I was surrounded once more by drunkenness and fornication.

"Oh, Mister Monagan," I said. "This is hopeless. Really hopeless."

"Never give up, Mister James."

"How could I expect to form an army from this rabble? I thought they would follow me. They're too far out of the habit. They're all individuals. They won't follow anyone!"

"They will, you just need to get their attention."

"How?"

I stared at the ground, and as I did so, I heard it.

Mister Monagan looked at me.

"Can you hear it too, Mister James?" he asked.

I tilted my head. From the distance came a noise completely alien to Dream London.

The crowd heard it. It obviously stirred something within them, the memory of days before the changes. Silence was spreading once more across Snakes and Ladders Square as one of the sounds that Dream London had tried to destroy was heard for the first time in nearly a year.

The sound of a snare drum, and underneath it, the sound of the bass, the sound of steady rhythm, beat by beat. The sound of feet, marching in time. The sound of so many people doing the same thing. Of people united to a common cause, and not expressing themselves freely.

"What is it, Mister James?" asked Mister Monagan.

I stared into his orange eyes. I wondered if, coming as he had from the other worlds, the worlds long conquered by forces such as Angel Tower, he had ever heard people working together like this.

"What is it?" he repeated.

"It's a band," I said. "It's a brass band."

OLIVE

THE DREAM LONDON SILVER BAND

A STILLNESS SETTLED over the square, fighting momentarily forgotten as all faces turned towards the approaching noise. Someone began to clap, and then a ripple of applause spread through the crowd. Something was approaching over the heads of the people. Something large and square that sailed towards us...

"Is it a ship, Mister James?"

Mister Monagan's face was such a picture of confusion that I almost laughed.

"A ship?" I said. "No, Mister Monagan. It's a banner! This is a parade. A good old fashioned parade!"

The parade ploughed through the waves of the crowd, pulled by the sail of the banner. The brass band, led by trombones, followed by tubas and baritones and horns, marched in step through the furrow of people. The street musicians held their guitars and accordions at ease and looked on in scorn at the elderly ladies and gentlemen who marched in the band, their shoes polished, buttons on their black blazers shining, the badges on their breast pockets with the four silver letters curled around each other: DLSB. They blew on their instruments with dry lips, they played with the memory of better days, but they played and marched and their silver music silenced everything and everyone.

"It's not bad, I suppose," said the girl whose guitar I had broken. "But there's no feeling to it. No expression."

"Be quiet," said someone else. "I want to listen."

"What do they want?"

"Where are they going?"

"What does the banner say?"

I read it now in the red light.

London Pride.

London Pride. Not Dream London.

The crowd was muttering now. London Pride? Remember that?

The banner sailed by me and Mister Monagan, and still the band marched, and now a second question occurred to everyone.

Where were they going? I guessed the answer at the same time as everyone else.

"They're heading into the park."

They were. The crowd made way for them, pulled back and pushed forward, looked and shouted words of encouragement and scorn.

"You go for it!"

"You're fools."

"Old fools!"

"You show them boys!"

The crowd pulled back around the entrance to the park. Black marble squares seemed darker in the dying red light. The band moved across the open space. The banner was lowered as it passed through the arch into the park beyond. The trombones followed, their slides pumping back and forth in the motion of a steam engine.

"What are they doing?"

I was level with the centre of the band. A tall man walked there, a bass drum strapped to his front. He hit it to the sound of the footsteps. *Left, left, left-right-left...*

A smaller man strode by him, rattling on a snare drum, and then we were amongst the cornets, their bells singing sweetly in the night.

"Look at that old fart playing that trumpet," laughed someone. "He looks like he's having a heart attack!"

Captain Wedderburn rose up inside me and I turned to smack them across the face, but to my pleasant surprise someone had beaten me to it. A guitarist stood, hand to his burning cheek, looking shocked.

The band was marching into the park now, and I saw that they were followed by more old men and women, all wearing suits or smart dresses, all marching in time, heading into the parks. Emboldened, some of the crowd joined their ranks.

"But why?" asked Mister Monagan. "Mister James, shouldn't they be attacking Angel Tower?"

"Maybe they have some other information, Mister Monagan." I frowned. "It's just good to see that they're doing something together."

More people were joining the parade. What a vision it must have looked from the air, the polished needle sliding into the park, the coloured swirls of the crowd attaching themselves to the rear.

"Should we join them, Mister James?" asked Mister Monagan.

"Maybe we should," I said, thoughtfully.

The parade had shouldered aside the grey masses of the workhouses, and now the dispossessed resumed their march into the park, but with a difference. They no longer shuffled forwards with a defeated air; now they raised their heads and looked around themselves. They were no longer marching as those already sold. Now they were part of a community, part of something bigger than themselves.

"A brass band," I murmured. "I would never have thought of that. It makes some sort of sense, I suppose."

Mister Monagan was excited. He was jumping up and down, his great feet flapping on the floor.

"Mister James! Mister James! We need to find Anna. She could help us to march on Angel Tower..."

His voice tailed away. Because something had changed.

"The band," said Mister Monagan. "What's happening to the band?"

The shouts went up again, in the square and beyond. The band was being killed. You could hear it. It was dying, not like a group of people being killed one by one, but like a single living thing. It shouted out in a cacophony of voices: it spoke in bass and tenor and alto and soprano, it screamed in high notes, it stuttered in low notes, its middle range was cut short.

"What's happening?" I called. "Mister Monagan! Let me climb on your shoulders and see!"

The swirl of the crowd was pushing us sideways as people sought to get away from the entrance to the park. I held onto the orange man as we were carried along with them, pushed along the iron railings at the top edge of the square, pushed away from the park entrance.

"What's happening?" I called.

"The statues!" People were calling. "The statues! They're alive!"

I remembered the statues, those carved shapes that filled the park. I remembered the obscene poses that they had struck.

"Here, Mr Monagan, let me see."

Mr Monagan braced himself against the bars. I climbed up onto his shoulders and peered through the railings. I looked into the park and the band had gone.

Wide green lawns led up to walls of trees. Gravel paths ran from the gates in straight lines. The pedestals on which statues might have stood were now empty. There was no sign of the statues, no sign of the band, nothing but the distant lines of grey workers marching to their new lives, heading off to the yellow and gold mass of the palace.

I jumped back down to the ground, just as the sound of the invisible band died in the last wail of a horn, and silence descended once more. The square was still, unsure what to do next.

People gazed at each other. The guitarists huddled together in a little group.

"See?" said one. "That sort of protest never works."

Mister Monagan was helping an elderly man to his feet.

"I'm okay," said the man. "I'm fine. Let me go."

The man stood up and dusted himself off. And then he began to march once more towards the gates of the park.

"Where are you going? Don't you know you'll be killed?"

The old man would not listen to reason. "I have to show my support," he said.

"Mister Monagan," I said. "Block the gates. We've got to stop more people going through."

"I don't think you'll be able to," said Mister Monagan. "Look!"

I'd seen. Already the grey suited workers were forming up and walking through once more.

"Stop it!" I yelled. "Didn't you see what just happened?"

"Of course they did," said someone close by. "Dream London doesn't like brass bands. You saw that! Everything was fine until the band turned up."

"You mean you were okay!"

"That way of protest always just leads to trouble. It's too aggressive. You need to be thoughtful."

"What do you suggest?" I asked. "An improvised flute solo?"

"It would make a point," said the man.

"What point?"

The man just shrugged and shook his head, pityingly. He was right and I was wrong. This was Dream London. We didn't do things that way any more. When we did, look what happened.

"They've got the right idea, Mister Monagan," I said. "They just need the support."

I pulled the flare gun from my pocket. I had my football fans. Now to see what sort of an army Gentle Annie had raised.

"Not yet, Mister James!" said Mister Monagan, putting his hand on the gun. "We need another brass band! We need to change its direction, head it towards Angel Tower!"

"Not yet? Another brass band? Where are we going to get another brass band from?"

"There's one coming now!" said Mister Monagan. "More than one, by the sound of it. Can't you hear them?"

I listened. The crowd tilted their heads, too. The cynical murmuring began once more.

"More bands! The fools! What are they playing at?"

"Stupid!"

"Cynicism," I said. "Always easier than actually doing something." I took hold of Mister Monagan's orange hand. "Come on! You're right! Let's get to the bottom of the square. We'll change the direction of those bands, send them towards Angel Tower! We'll reinforce them with Gentle Annie's army!"

We pushed our way through the crowds, heading down in tens, heading towards the sound of the music. This sounded different. There was a different tone to the music.

"Kids!" someone shouted. "It's a bunch of bloody kids!"

The next band was coming, and the shouter was right, they were just a bunch of children, dressed in blue military jackets with gold braid at their cuffs and shoulders. These children didn't have a banner before them, they didn't have a group of followers. What they did have was a look of pale-faced determination you could just make out behind the shiny instruments they held to their mouths. The crowd was calling out to them to stop, yet the children ignored them.

"Are they under a spell?" asked Mister Monagan.

"No!" I said. "Look at the way they march to time! They've been trained to do this!"

But by who? And I thought of Amit and the children with instruments who had come into his restaurant.

I thought of Anna, practising all those nights whilst I drifted off to sleep in my room.

The children's band was in the square now, marching grimly down the wide black marble path that had opened in the middle of the crowd, marching towards the entrance to the park. There was a lot of shouting, but I noticed that no one tried to really stop them.

I jumped in front of them, held my arms out wide

"Stop!" I called, to no avail. The marching ranks split neatly in two. The children streamed past around either side of me, still playing. I saw a young girl, blowing on a shiny cornet, and I grabbed her by the arm and pulled her clear. She carried on playing all the while.

"Stop that!" I said, pulling the cornet from her. "Where have you come from?"

"Bow Temperance Hall," said the little girl. "Let me go! I have to play."

"Are you under some sort of spell?"

"Certainly not! We're here to show people what to do. We have to march!"

"But not that way! You'll all be killed! Join me! March on Angel Tower."

"Let go of me!" the little girl squealed, and again I found myself on the wrong side of the crowd's temper.

"Let go of her, you nonce!"

The man who said the words looked like a fighter. Thick muscles, turning to fat, and a shaven head.

"She'll walk into the park!" I screamed. "Is that what you want?"

"I said let go of her, you filthy pervert!"

The man was moving closer to me, fists raised.

"You tell him, Bill," said his girlfriend, straight blonde hair covering her eyes. "Filthy nonce."

"Leave him alone," said an accented voice nearby. "He means no harm, even if he is doing the wrong thing."

"Amit!" I called. I spun around, delighted at last to meet an ally. Amit stood there, dressed in his Hollywood Sikh outfit. Fifty men similarly dressed stood close at hand. The crowd eyed them respectfully. The shaven-headed man lowered his fists and backed away, warily.

"I thought we were meeting on square 73?" said Amit.

"Never mind that, what are you doing to these kids?"

"I'm helping them to have a chance to live in a better world than their parents have chosen for them."

"But they'll be killed."

"Or they'll be taken into the slavery of the workhouse. These children know what they are doing."

"Do they?"

The sound of brass faltered. The children were entering the park.

"You butcher!" I shouted. "Listen to that!"

"The children were warned," said Amit calmly. "They chose to do this. What's the alternative? To walk in there subservient, like their parents, willing slaves for other worlds?"

He pointed to the grey shapes of the workhouse people.

The little girl struggled further in my arms.

"Let her go. Let her join her friends."

"Do you want that?" I asked the girl. "Listen to them!"

She broke free of my grip and stood there, sobbing.

"I want to go home," she said. She sat down and started to cry. No one came to her aid now, I noticed.

369

The shaven-headed man was looking away. Fighting is easier than helping, after all.

"You killed those children," I said to Amit.

"Not me," he said. "That wasn't my band." He looked to the bottom of the square, cupped a hand to his ear. "My band are coming now. Can you hear them?"

I could. I could hear many bands, all of them converging on this spot.

"Listen, Amit," I said. "This is important! Don't send your band into the park."

"Why not? That's what they were trained for."

"No! Send them towards Angel Tower. If we can get in there, get up to the Contract Floor..."

"Taking the Contract Floor is only part of the story," said Amit. "Angel Tower only established a toehold here because we allowed it to. There were always enough people in London to resist its influence, if only they chose to do so."

He smiled complacently and looked around the square.

"Look at them. They're happy to sing a song or hold a peaceful demonstration. That sort of thing never changes anything. That's just playing the game the way the people in charge want it played. They'll give you a pat on the head, tell you that you're a good little soldier for protesting peacefully, and then they'll just continue doing the same thing."

"And getting kids killed makes a difference, does it?"

"It sometimes does," said Amit. "Let's see, shall we? Perhaps by watching their children die these people will rediscover their courage."

"There's got to be a better way," I said.

"I'm open to suggestions," said Amit, drily.

"They'll be killed!"

He fixed me with a black gaze, and I realised that I was looking at a man from the old world, the world that London had been part of, the world that was in fear of what might happen tonight.

"What do I care if English children die?" he said, softly.

Bands were approaching from all directions now. The sound was echoing off the walls.

The crowd began moving again, and I saw that another set of players had come to join the game. There were soldiers entering the square. Soldiers, marching in from the park. Dressed in pale yellow uniforms that glowed orange in the red light of the sun, their rifles held at their sides, the regiment of the Ninth Dream Londoners had arrived. The regiments of men and women who had signed up to the armies of exploration had come back to impose order on their own kind.

Down at the other end of the square the sound of drumming and brass increased, enough to resonate in even the hardest heart. The empty chests of the street musicians reverberated with something else now. The crowd was parting again, allowing a black marble path through the square. The sound of marching feet could be heard.

The Ninth Dream Londoners formed two lines across the gates to the park, barring the entrance to the silver green lands beyond. They stood at the ready, their wooden rifles held crosswise before them, feet slightly apart. Moustaches bristled on the implacable faces of men who knew they were in the right.

"Now hold on," said a woman nearby, slowly. "Now hold on." A great thought was working its way into her mind. "Now, come on. This isn't right."

She shook her head, she looked up at the soldiers. And then, as if in a dream she walked forward to one of the Dream Londoners and tapped him on the chest.

"Yes, ma'am?" he said.

She shook her head again, and then her face cleared. Suddenly, she understood, and at that her expression hardened.

"Don't you Madam me," she said. "Just what do you think you're doing?"

The Dream Londoner was a big man, and he gave a slow smile.

"Keeping the peace, ma'am."

She frowned.

"Keeping the peace?" she said. "Keeping the peace? Have you seen what's happening in there?"

The sound of brass reached a peak, and the third band approached, led by a great square banner, embroidered with all the birds of the world. Orioles and jays, robins and peacocks, emus and parakeets and sparrows. I felt my heart sinking as I saw the birds, I knew which band this would be, even before I read the name embroidered on the banner.

Egg Market Silver Band.

And there, at the back right hand corner, marching to time, dark hair tied up in a bun, was Anna. She wasn't playing her cornet at the moment, merely marching. She saw me, I'm sure, but she ignored me, she looked straight ahead and marched on, down the wide road that had opened up amongst the partying crowd.

"Let her go," said Amit. "She's made up her mind."

The Egg Market band marched towards the gates. Up ahead of them the soldiers of the Ninth Dream Londoners took up positions across the gate to stop the band from entering the park. Still the band marched on. The soldiers held their rifles at their sides as the band drew closer.

"Will they shoot the band?" asked Mister Monagan.

The drummer sounded taps and the band stopped marching. The drummer sounded taps once more, and the music ceased. I hurried forward through the silence, Mister Monagan at my side.

A sergeant in a bright orange tunic walked forward to face the trombones.

"Go home!" he called.

Anna left the ranks and moved to face him.

"Let us through," she said quietly.

The sergeant laughed. "Listen, little miss..."

I was at his ear in an instant.

"Sergeant," I said. "This young woman and her friends are showing more courage than anyone else in this shitty place. I don't think that *Little Miss* is an appropriate form of address. Do you?"

The sergeant looked at Anna and saw something in her eyes.

"Sir, I think you're correct," he said. He lowered his voice.

"Listen, miss. Don't march in there. It's certain death. We came through the park not half an hour ago from the new portal. The things we've seen in there..."

Anna took a deep breath.

"Sergeant," she said. "Please order your men to stand aside please."

The sergeant shook his head.

"I ain't going to do that, miss. There's worse things than death in there. Especially for a pretty young woman such as yourself."

Anna was pale. She was terrified, I could tell. Her face wore the same shiny sheen as the rest of the band. And yet, stronger than her fear, I could see her determination.

"Worse things than death in there, Sergeant?" she said. "But, the thing is you see, if we don't march, then those things, those things that are worse than death will soon be in here with us. Those things will be living here, in Dream London."

The sergeant produced a large white handkerchief from his pocket and used it to wipe his lips.

"That's as may be, miss, but..."

"And surely," continued Anna, ignoring him, "isn't it better to experience certain death now, than to wait for worse than death in a few days' time?"

The sergeant wiped his lips once more.

"Miss," he said. "I don't know what to say. But I can't let you do this."

"Why not?" asked Anna. "You're a soldier, aren't you? You know what it means to sacrifice yourself to a higher cause."

The Sergeant waved his hand around the crowd.

"You call these people a higher cause?"

"They may yet be," said Anna. "Tell your men to stand aside."

The sergeant gazed at her, his lips moving. He made to take hold of her, thought better of it, and then stood back and drew himself to his full height.

"Miss!" he said, saluting. "The best of British to you. What there is left of it, anyway."

A look of terror flickered across Anna's face, but she quickly suppressed it.

"Thank you, Sergeant." she said. She turned to the waiting band.

"Drummer," she called. "Sound taps."

The drummer beat the rhythm to begin. The soldiers pulled back, yellow uniforms clustering at the sides of the park. The surrounding crowd was catching on.

"No!" shouted someone.

"Sergeant! Stop them!"

"Do your job, soldiers! Stop them."

The band began to play, eight bars of some death or glory march, and then they began to march. Left, right, left, right, left. All those children marching to their deaths, and Anna, terrified Anna, bravely marching along with them.

A mother ran forward and began to beat the sergeant on the chest.

"Stop them!" she shouted. She was crying. "What's the matter with you? Are you afraid?"

"Not I," said the sergeant. "Just ashamed. They're doing what you should be doing, madam. What we all should be doing. For Heaven's sake..."

He undid his jacket and walked to the side of the band. He took off the jacket and let it fall as he took up his place, marching alongside the horns.

Someone ran forward from the crowd and seized hold of one of the cornet players. A young boy of around ten years of age.

"Let me go!" he called, hitting at his captor with his free hand.

"Let him go!" called someone in the crowd.

"What?" said his captor, and the boy shook himself loose and was gone, off to rejoin the band.

"Mister Monagan," I said, pulling out the flare gun. "I think it's time."

"I think so too, Mister James."

I fired the gun into the air. A golden light rose and then stopped, hovering above me. An animal roar sounded, the sound of an army rising up.

"I hope it's enough," I said.

The band marched on, and Anna drew level with me, walking towards the entrance to the park.

I heard shouting all around me. I saw men in football scarves pressing forward, I heard the voices of Gentle Annie and my whores spurring people on...

And finally, there and then in the middle of Snakes and Ladders Square, the magic finally ignited. Suppressed for over a year, submerged by the scent of pollen, diluted by sex and food and a hundred other distractions, the old magic that had built London finally gathered itself together for one last glorious fight against the invasion.

Someone began to clap. Then another person, then another. The applause took hold and spread through the crowd, burning like a fire.

I stepped forward.

"Okay! Who's going to let a group of schoolkids show us how to fight?"

"Not us, Captain Jim!" called the football fans.

"Not us, Captain Jim!" called the whores' men.

"Not us Captain Jim!" called the other bystanders who finally got it.

"Company!" called the leader of the Ninth Dream Londoners. "Form up! Escort them!"

"Join in boys!" The last was from a sergeant of the Dream London Constabulary. Even the Boys in Taupe had seen the way the wind was blowing and were daring to show their faces.

The Boys in Taupe. That gave me an idea.

"Come on then, fellow Londoners," I called, gripped by the excitement of the crowd. "Let's go!"

"But Mister James, we need to head towards Angel Tower!"

I wasn't listening to Mister Monagan. We had all seen where the band had gone, we had heard the children screaming.

The applause was growing louder all the time. With it came a guttural roar, the anger of the crowd growing and finding voice at last. A crowd of people, all thinking the same thing. All that rage focused in the same direction.

The front of the band crossed into the park. The sound of the crowd rose and rose, and I began to run, run towards the park entrance...

We plunged forwards into the park, a disorganised rabble that was slowly becoming an army...

SIXTEEN

THE PARK

IT FELT DIFFERENT *inside the park. The air was colder and fresher, there was no smell of human breath upon it, no scent of 14,000 years of human civilisation. Plunging through the gate I was suddenly breathing air untainted by coal smoke or petrol fumes. Air that had never been scented with baking bread or the sweet smell of human shit. At first glance the parks seemed so familiar... but the feeling quickly passed. There was something* other *about everything there, something shifting and impermanent. The silver sun seemed to shine down from many directions at once. What seemed like paths shifted underfoot. They were gravel rivers, flowing from one place to another. What seemed like lines of trees ran along like lampposts seen through the window of a moving car.*

The sound of the brass band seemed alien in that place. Mechanical order was out of place in this wild machine. The grass beneath my feet was soft and neatly clipped, but there was an energy about it, something in its green smell, that suggested that it hadn't been tamed by human gardeners, but had rather spread its way here from some wild steppe in some distant land. The music seemed to empty itself in that air. The players were losing heart, you could hear it in their tone.

Movement.

Statues rose up on the plinths, sliding upwards from beneath the ground. Some of the children stopped playing. I saw a young boy begin to cry, but, and I think this is possibly the bravest thing I have ever seen, he raised his cornet back to his lips.

"Drop your instruments!" I cupped my hands over my mouth to shout. "Drop your instruments! You've made your point! Look at my army! Why carry on playing now?"

The music faded away as the band saw the crowd of people that were pushing their way through the gates. An army of men in scarlet and silver and brown and cream, an army of women in short skirts or petticoats.

The statues were moving towards the band. I saw Anna hold up her hand, I saw her gently place her cornet upon the ground. One by one, the rest of the band did the same.

The crowd held their breath as the statues paused, then turned and climbed back on their plinths.

"What are those statues?" I asked. The cold figures stood on their plinths, watching my army. Seen from this side of the gates they no longer looked as if they were made of stone.

"Those are not statues, Mister James. Those aren't statues at all."

"Then what are they?"

"Workers. They're made of mercury. They are owned by the people out West by the mercury seas. They take on the shape that the job requires. They have no thoughts, Mister James. They are just there to process."

"Process what?"

"Whatever."

"How do we fight them, Mister Monagan?"

"You can't. They are as strong as three men, Mister James."

"Then we will fight them four men at a time."

"If we need to. The statues are standing still. For the moment."

I looked around. He was right. For the moment.

"This place isn't still, Mister Monagan," I said. What looked like a trench dug out from the ground, ready to be planted with a line of roses or tulips, turned out to be a moving stream of mud. It was travelling in the opposite direction to the gravel of the paths.

"Everything moves, Mister James. Everything moves to other worlds."

"Sir!"

The sergeant of the Dream Londoners stood at my side. He pulled off a smart salute.

"We're here now, sir! What would you have us do?"

Something glinted, just beyond the closest line of trees. "Sir! Are you okay?"

"Sorry," I said, putting my hand to my face. "Sorry, I was distracted. Listen, Sergeant, I want you to organise a group of men to hold the entrance to the park. Don't let anyone else through. Specifically, don't let any more people from the workhouses through."

"Very good, sir. And how about you? What will you do?"

"We're going to fetch those that we can back home to safety."

Mister Monagan was hopping from foot to foot at my side.

"But sir, they don't want to come."

"That was then," I said. "I think I know how to change their minds."

WE TROTTED ACROSS the park, over shifting rivers of gravel under a silver sky. The world here was so much bigger, it bent around us, it seemed to go on for ever. We ran past waiting overseers, the people from the other lands, watching and wondering if the stream of grey labour would resume from the gates. We ran past silver statues, waiting on their plinths, still as stone.

Ahead of us we saw the end of a grey crocodile of workers, making its way to the portal by the white and gold towers of the new Buckingham Palace. Dark slits were set in the walls of the castle, and I wondered what could be looking out at this scene.

Mister Monagan flapped along at my left. Someone was running at my right.

"Anna," I said. "You've done your bit. Go back home."

"You go home," she said.

I didn't bother arguing.

We reached the tail end of the crocodile of workers, we raced past grey-suited men and women who looked at us as we went by. On and on, past lines and lines of people, until we came to the head of the line. Two women in leather jerkins walked at the front. I pushed my way before them and halted, staring up at them. They were both at least a foot taller than me, seven feet at least. They had a strong, cold beauty about them that would have scared the hell out of my former clients.

They certainly frightened me.

The pair looked down at me. Behind them, the gold and white towers of Buckingham Palace reached into the air.

"Move out of the way," said one of them.

Mister Monagan and Anna took their places at my side.

"In a moment," I said. Again, something glinted in my eye, a flash that came from beyond one of the lines of trees.

"In a moment," I repeated. "I want to ask you a question first."

"What?" said one of the blonde giants.

I put my hand in my pocket.

"Don't pull out your gun, Mister James," hissed Mister Monagan. "That might annoy them."

"I wasn't going for my gun," I said. I pulled my hand from my pocket and passed something across to one of the giants.

"Read this," I said.

They both looked down at the Truth Script. I crossed my fingers. Surely it would work on these two?

"Where are you taking these people?" I asked.

"The Icefields of Lower Stark," said one of the women.

"And what awaits them there?"

"A slow death. This is a Truth Script. You tricked us."

"How terrible of me. How will these people die a slow death?"

"We will feed them enough to keep them alive for around six months whilst they work on the construction of the Transworld railway."

"Only six months? Why not longer?"

"It has been worked out. The cost of the workers plus food against the labour they can expend in their lifetime. This is the most efficient use of our investment."

The workers heard that. Finally, it was enough to shake them from their torpor. A murmur ran down the lines. It became a roar. The workers broke ranks, they became a crowd, they surged forward and engulfed the two blonde women.

And that was that. The rest of the Dream London army was arriving now. It had followed us here and it was ready to fight.

"You did it, Mister James!" called Mister Monagan, dancing with joy. "You did it!"

I passed Anna the Truth Script.

"You know what to do," I said. "Go after the others."

She took the script and looked at me. She looked as if she was about to say something.

"What?" I said.

"Nothing," she said and turned and ran off down the path. Some of the grey workers ran after her, off to help spread the word.

"You did it!" repeated Mister Monagan. "But what now? Look, the statues are moving."

Sure enough they were, climbing down from their plinths.

"Ignore them, Mister Monagan. My army can take care of them. We've got other things to do..."

There was that glint again, coming from the trees that lined the path.

"But where are we going?"

"Follow me, Mister Monagan."

We worked our way towards the trees, stepping aside for the statues as they ran across the grass, heading towards the army. Mister Monagan was right. The statues were as strong as three people. But I was right too. Four people could defeat them. Four football fans could hold an arm or leg each. A fifth could put the boot in. Brutal, but effective.

"We should help them!" insisted Mister Monagan.

I dived between the line of trees, reached around behind the trunk of one. The man hiding there gave a yelp as I seized him by his coat.

"What are you doing, spying on me?" I said. The man cringed, as if I was about to hit him. The mood I was in at the time, he wasn't far wrong.

"If you touch me you'll regret it," he said. He waggled a finger at me, his face blushing a beetroot shade as he did so.

"No," I said. "No, no, no! That's not how you make a threat. You've got to mean it. All you've done is irritate me further. I'm more likely to hit you now."

The man let out another yelp. He was an odd looking man. Very tall and thin. Stretched out. His skin was pale, as though he spent all of his time indoors. He wore a pair of leather trousers and a jerkin on which were hung all sorts of strange devices. Clockwork and lenses and all sorts of things. The pair of goggles he wore on his head was equally complex. I saw myself in them, reflected in red. I looked mean. I looked more than mean, I looked like a killer.

"Why are you spying on me?" I asked.

"I'm not spying specifically on you," he said. "I'm here to observe this new gateway and then report back to the leaders."

"Which leaders?"

He opened his mouth to reply, but I silenced him with a wave of my hand.

"Never mind," I said. "They're all the same. Give me those."

He flinched as I snatched the goggles from his head. They were made of brass and polished glass. They weighed heavy in my hands. I saw the word Zeiss engraved on the side. I pulled them on and looked through them at the man.

"What are these for?" I asked, gazing at his pale features. "Things look exactly the same."

"Look into the distance," he whimpered.

I turned around and looked across the park, and gasped.

I could see forever.

The green grass of the park rolled away and away. Up and down as it travelled across hundreds of miles – the goggles let me see it all.

"I can see everything," I said.

"Be careful," said the man. "People can get lost. Their minds can't find your way back to their bodies."

There was a black line amongst the never ending grass and I focused on it. A line of coloured ants, just like those at the top of Angel Tower, making their way across the grassy plain. I followed it back to its source. An area of mud and water and abandoned ant mounds. The land there was stripped of all vegetation. The ants were seeking a new home.

There were switches built into the frame of the goggles. I pressed one. I felt the goggles turning my head to see something. My vision swept away from the ants, across hills and fields dotted with great cities filled

with towers, just like Dream London. The goggles drew
my vision on to one city in particular.

"You're looking at my city," said the man. "That's
how I find my way home when my job is done."

The city was brightly coloured and filled with towers.
One of the towers, the one at the centre of the city, was
taller than all the others. It reached up into the sky.
I thought I recognised it. This was the city I looked
down at from the the bottom of the Spiral with Bill.
Had that been only yesterday? I gazed at the city in
awe. Seen from here it must be thousands of miles away,
yet the Spiral must be barely three miles from Snakes
and Ladders Square.

"Mister James, we're wasting time here. This man
cannot help us."

He was right.

"The workers are saved. We need to return to Dream
London. Perhaps now we can defeat Angel Tower."

Angel Tower. The Contract Floor. Of course. I pulled
the goggles from my head.

"I'm keeping these," I said to the man, thrusting them
in his face.

"But how will I get home?" he asked. He began to
cry.

"Oh, for heaven's sake." I thrust the goggles into his
hand, and then turned and ran. Mister Monagan ran
along at my side.

"You gave him back his goggles," he said.

"I know. I'm getting soft."

"You're a good man, Mister James."

I didn't reply. We ran across the grass, back towards
the gates. Two people amongst hundreds, Captain
Wedderburn's army, heading home.

On across the grass, past the scattered instruments of the Egg Market band, on towards the gates of Dream London.

"And then on to Angel Tower!" I called. "On to Angel Tower!"

Through the gates, back into our world, I felt a hand on my shoulder, pulling me to the side, a familiar voice speaking in my ear...

CHOCOLATE

HONEY PEPPERS

"NOT THAT WAY, Captain Wedderburn."

"Bill!" I said. I staggered, disoriented. This world seemed different. Smaller, less wild. More perfumed and sexual. I needed a moment to gather myself. Now I did I took in what I was looking at.

It was Bill, but not as I remembered her. Gone were the skirts and petticoats of a Dream London whore. Now her auburn hair was pinned up beneath a sky blue beret, her slim form decked out in a pale grey uniform. She wasn't alone, either. A group of men and women in similar uniforms stood behind her, looking dangerously real against the kaleidoscope background. It was a sight that seemed so strange in Dream London: soldiers dressed in modern battle fatigues. Dressed in uniforms such as the one I used to wear. Each of them was carrying a long rifle, and I reached out and touched one.

"Will it work?" I asked.

"The weapons will be good for a day or so," said Bill. "That will be long enough." She looked over my shoulder.

There were more of Bill's soldiers moving through the square in good order, easily and without fuss, but there was no hiding the look of wonder on their faces as they scanned their surroundings. These were people only recently arrived in Dream London, and look what they could see: the growing gate to the parks, the warped shape of the surrounding buildings, shot with silver, the moon too big above us.

They had arrived just at the turning point, just as London had awoken from its dream. My army came charging through the gate. Bill's soldiers took charge of them, marshalled them in good order.

"Mister Monagan!" called Bill. "Will you be so good as to direct these men to Angel Tower?"

She waved a hand at the surrounding soldiers. Mister Monagan tore off a smart salute.

"It will be my pleasure, Miss Bill!"

"How did they all get here?" I asked, feeling a little dazed. The square was filling with soldiers of all nations, all of them wearing the same pale blue beret.

"By train, of course," said Bill. "It's easy enough to get into Dream London. All we needed was the reason to attack."

"And I gave it you," I said.

"If you say so, James. This is a last ditch effort since the nuclear strike failed."

Soldiers were still flooding into the square. The contrast between them and my ragtag army was marked.

"What shall I do now?" I asked.

"Whatever you like," said Bill. She raised an arm. "Okay," she called. "We're moving out! Follow Mr Monagan!"

"Mr Monagan?" I said. "But what about me? Don't you want my help?"

Bill shrugged.

"You've played your part," she said, and that was it. I was dismissed from her thoughts.

She turned and moved out.

I watched, stunned as the soldiers formed up in good order and headed off towards Angel Tower. They would succeed, I thought. Dream London feared the organised.

But where did that leave me?

I stood and watched them go, suddenly at a loss. My tongue, forgotten in all the excitement, wriggled in my mouth. Suddenly, I felt very, very thirsty.

"Bill!" I called, but she had gone.

AND THAT WAS how I came to find myself in the middle of an emptying square. All alone in the middle of the changing days of Dream London. Sounds were evaporating from the square. I saw guitars and accordions broken under foot, varnished wood shattered into pieces, bellows torn and wheezing out their last breaths. Even the sounds of the approaching brass bands were muted as they changed direction, heading off towards Angel Tower.

I could hear the sounds of fighting to the east. The sounds of shouting and gunfire. The world had twisted itself around the horizon, the golden moon hung in the purple sky and despite the fact I was in the middle of a crowded city, I felt completely bereft of purpose.

The Hero of Dream London was not required.

He never had been. All the time I had strode to the front of the stage and shouted and postured, I hadn't been doing anything. I was nothing more than a misdirection, a sideshow. I was the magician's assistant, long-legged and lovely, drawing the eye whilst the real work took place elsewhere. Okay, I had saved the workers, but they weren't important. Not to the rest of the world. What did America and Germany and India and the rest care about a few English people marched off to the workhouse? What did the English care, for that matter? As long as Dream London could be destroyed.

I heard the roar of the crowd and the crackle of gunfire, but it all took place elsewhere, in another world, far away.

Nearby a young woman sat, looking at her broken guitar. She looked towards the park, where the band had so recently marched. Then she looked at me.

"I don't know," I said. "I don't have any answers. It turns out that I never did."

All I had was charm and a uniform. Take away the uniform and what were you left with? I was the perfect hero for this city. All gloss and effects, and underneath, there was nothing that was worth having, just sparkle and a heady scent.

I was so hungry and thirsty. There was a line of pubs standing nearby. What would Captain Wedderburn do?

I'd had enough. I needed a drink. A drink would awaken this thing in my mouth, and sort everything out, one way or the other.

I began to walk towards it, but my destiny was wrenched from my hands for one final time. Three figures crossing the square, heading towards me. A small child, two large figures looming behind her. I recognised them right away. I waited for them on square 50, aching and weary and oh so thirsty. They tapped across the stone, they came to a halt before me.

"Honey Peppers," I said.

"You've been a bad man, Captain Wedderburn," said Honey.

"No," I said. "I've just been inefficient." I made to walk around them.

"Stop right there," she said.

"Give him to me," said the possessive Quantifier to her left. "I'll look after him."

"Let me save you the effort," I replied. "I'm going to take a drink, right now."

Honey Peppers laughed.

"It's too late for that, Captain. You've betrayed the Daddio for the last time."

"Does it matter?" I asked. "All this might end tonight."

"It matters to the Daddio."

I felt something give way inside me. This was the end, I knew it. This was finally the end.

"It's time," said Honey Peppers, shaking her pretty gold locks. "The Daddio wants you dead. You're to die slowly. The Quantifiers will pull you apart, joint by joint. And they'll do it now."

I turned and ran. Straight into the arms of the third Quantifier who had moved silently up behind me. He caught me by the wrist, squeezed the two bones there. I felt them rub together and I cried out in pain.

"Hey, he's mine!" said the possessive Quantifier.

"Why don't you take turns?" I gasped, defiant at the end. And then my heart froze with fear...

"Good," said Honey Peppers, seeing my expression. "Terror at last..."

She hadn't seen what I was looking at. A lone woman standing in the middle of the square.

Miss Elizabeth Baines. She wore a little hat and veil, an ivory blouse and pearls. She was carrying a little bag in the crook of her arm. Compared to the Quantifiers, she looked tiny.

"Elizabeth," I said. "No! Get out of here!"

Honey Peppers turned from me to look at Elizabeth. She turned back to me and smiled.

"Would you like me to spare her, Captain Wedderburn?"

"Spare me what?" asked Miss Elizabeth Baines, virginal in her ivory blouse. She pushed her way between the Quantifiers and came to stand between me and Honey Peppers. The little girl's face split in a huge grin.

"The virgin queen!" she said, and she turned to me. "We'll let her watch you die, Captain, and then I'll get the Quantifiers to fuck her to death. How do you like that, Captain? Or, no, no," she began to jump up and down, an excited little girl. "I'll tell you what. How about if I take her to Belltower End? Make her work off the money you've cost the Daddio? What do you say to that?"

"Do what you like to her," I said, deliberately avoiding Elizabeth's eye. "She's nothing to do with me. She's just some mad woman who bought a scroll."

Honey Peppers looked slyly from me to Elizabeth.

"I think you're just saying that," she smiled. "I think that maybe her scroll tells the truth. You care for her, Captain Jim. Don't ask me why, but you do. I can see it in your face."

"What do you know about caring for people?"

"A lot," said Honey Peppers, seriously. "You have to understand what people care for if you want to be truly cruel. How else can you destroy their dreams?"

"You know what," said Elizabeth. "You really are a very unpleasant little girl."

"Fuck you, whore."

"I'm not a whore."

"You will be. You'll be fucked all night by men and all day by the animals in Dream London Zoo."

"You really should watch your language, young lady..."

"Fuck you," said Honey Peppers.

"... if nothing else, it shows a real lack of imagination."

And Miss Elizabeth Baines bent down and slapped Honey Peppers across the face.

Honey Peppers was stunned. She put her hand to her face and gazed open mouthed at Elizabeth.

"That's what happens to bad girls."

Honey Peppers' mouth began to move. She was trying to speak. After some effort, she managed to get the words out.

"You cock sucking cunt!" she gasped.

"Well, that shows more imagination, at least," said Miss Elizabeth Baines. "Not that it's accurate, of course. I never seem to get the opportunity." She said the last with the faintest touch of regret. She fixed her gaze upon the Quantifiers. "Now, are you going to let him go, or do I have to make you?"

"Make us?" said Honey Peppers. "And how will you do that?"

But Miss Elizabeth Baines didn't have to answer that question, because we could all see the answer. It was slinking forward over the ground, in black and white, tortoiseshell and ginger and gold. It was walking from the park striped in orange and gold, it was maned and it was spotted.

Cats. Miss Elizabeth Baines had a rapport with cats, and now she was calling in old favours. Or perhaps the cats were there to look after their protector, to ensure their source of food. Who could tell? From the smallest kitten in the cattery, to the tigers that had escaped from Dream London Zoo, they were all heading this way now. Every cat in London seemed to be pouring into Snakes and Ladders Square.

Honey Peppers put her hand to her mouth. Her eyes were wide with fear.

"Take them away!" called Honey, her voice muffled. "Take them away!"

The cats moved closer, their eyes fixed on Honey Peppers' mouth. I felt the hold upon me slacken, and then the three Quantifiers were backing away, their mouths firmly closed. A cat leapt up at a Quantifier, and was batted away. Another leapt.

Honey Peppers and the three Quantifiers were being overwhelmed by a sea of feline spite.

The cats clawed and scratched, they leapt and yowled and bit. They jumped at the mouths of Honey Peppers and the Quantifiers, and the little girl and the three big men flailed and batted them away, but there were always more cats attacking, seeking their mouths, biting and clawing at what lay there. *What's the matter?* I thought. *Cat got your tongue?*

It was too much for the Quantifiers. They turned and ran, heading for the river, a flowing wave of cats following them.

Miss Elizabeth Baines stood at my side, watching them go. Only a few cats remained now, checking that their work was done, and then they too slunk off into the darkening night.

Honey Pepper lay in the square, a little girl with golden hair, mute, blood dripping from her mouth. She sat up and looked at us, and then she began to scream, a thin keening bubbling scream. She reached out to us for help, and some ancient reflex caused me to bend down.

"Leave her," said Miss Elizabeth Baines.

"She's just a little girl," I said.

"The little girl died months ago." She caught my expression. "What's the matter?"

"Don't you care?"

"Of course I do," she replied, "but like I said, one can care without being sentimental. It's the best way."

She took hold of my arm and turned her back on the broken little girl. I tried to block the whimpering, mewling sounds she made from my mind.

"Come on," said Elizabeth. "I'll take you back to my place."

"But why?" I asked.

She smiled at that.

"Where else are you to go?"

The sound of the fighting, the gunfire, the brass bands, the yelling of the crowd, all of these had become a constant in the night. When it suddenly ceased, the silence seemed to ring out like a bell.

"What's happened?" I asked.

"Look," said Elizabeth.

Off to the east, rising up into the night above the skeletal towers of the floodlights of the Footballdrome, we could see that Angel Tower was burning. Golden flames were licking their way around the building, gradually climbing higher and higher up its length.

"They got it," I said. "They got it. Come on, we should go and help."

"There's nothing you can do," said Elizabeth, taking my hand and pulling me back.

We stood and watched as the flames reached the bulging section near the top. Suddenly, orange light bloomed there. We shielded our eyes, we felt the compression in the air as something exploded. There was a second explosion, and then a third. A circular band of blue flame expanded out over the city.

My skin tingled, my ears rang, I tasted raspberry, I smelled rubber, a spiral turned before my eyes. The ground shook, the air sneezed, the sky flickered. Then there was stillness.

"That was the Contract Floor," I said. "I'm sure of it. Does that mean this is all over?"

"It is for you, you can barely stand up." Miss Elizabeth Baines put her arm into mine. "Come on, let's get you home."

We walked across Snakes and Ladders Square, heading back to her house. Fine black ash began to rain down around us. It settled on our hands, on our faces. We blinked it from our eyes.

Around us, the dark shapes of cats were heading back off on mysterious errands of their own. Above us, blue flames spun across the heavens. From the distance I heard the sound of guns, of fighting, and rather appropriately, I thought, the note of one silver cornet.

SEVENTEEN

JAMES WEDDERBURN

OUTSIDE, THE BIGGEST party that the city formerly known as Dream London had ever seen was taking place. It was played out to the music of brass bands. The sound of music and dancing and general good cheer reached even into the quiet calm of Miss Elizabeth Baines'shouse.

To begin with we had sat in the garden and looked up at the night, wondering if the moon was smaller than it had been. In the end thirst had got the better of me and we had gone inside.

We both climbed up to Elizabeth's bedroom and, fully clothed, we had lain on the bed.

"Hand me the bottle," I said.

She stared at me, and then passed it over. I turned the top and felt the ignition of the bubbles. I raised the bottle to my lips and paused.

"You shouldn't stay here, Liz," I said. "Go away. Leave me for the night. What if the spell isn't broken? What if I become a Wailer?"

"Then the cats will do to you what they did to Honey Peppers," she said, perfectly seriously. Like she had said, you could care without being sentimental.

Then her face softened in a hopeless love. I felt my face do the same. I lowered the bottle and reached out with my other hand to touch hers.

"I don't deserve you, Liz."

"I know that."

I raised the bottle in a toast, and then put it to my lips and drank. Water! It tasted so good. I drank and drank, and as I did so I felt my tongue ripple and drink along with me.

"What's happening?" asked Liz.

"Nothing," I lied. I drained the rest of the bottle, and lay back on the bed. After a moment's hesitation, Liz joined me. I lay on my back, and she cuddled up closer, her head on my shoulder, her leg across mine.

"This feels so right," I said.

"Shhh," said Liz. "Let's go to sleep."

I stared up at the ceiling, so far away above me now. What would it be like in the morning, I wondered?

Somewhere in the room I heard the sound of something eating.

Mmmmm. Crunch crunch crunch. Mmmmmmm.

I closed my eyes and fell asleep.

I AWOKE WITH bright daylight streaming across me. Liz lay beside me, fast asleep. I reached across and gently touched her shoulder.

My tongue felt heavy, so heavy. I closed my eyes again, slowly moving my tongue back and forth. It felt thick and furry, like after a night's drinking. I tapped it against my teeth, feeling the end of it for dead patches, for eyes.

Liz was stirring now. She rolled over and smiled at me, so sweetly.

"James," she said, and then her brow furrowed with concern as she remembered the night before.

"James," she said, rolling up. "Your tongue. How are you?"

She felt it then, felt it at the same time as I did. We looked at each other, held each other's gaze.

"You feel it too?" she said.

I did. The world had lost something, that exciting zing you get when you first breathe anaesthetic gas, that feeling of the exotic, just before it knocks you unconscious.

I smacked my heavy tongue in my mouth. Something broke free from the end. As Liz watched I spat out one, then two little jelly balls into my hand.

Liz looked down at them without shuddering. Two little bloodshot balls, black pupils in the end.

"My tongue is still heavy," I said. I could feel bitter pus oozing from the two holes from which the eyes had disengaged. I didn't tell Liz that.

"You can't speak properly," she said. "That sounded all mushy. Rest your tongue."

We both looked up at the ceiling at the same time. It was lower than it had been last night, much lower.

As one we turned and looked out of the open window. All we could see was the sky.

"It's a paler blue than yesterday," said Liz. "Smell the air."

I sniffed, and knew what she meant.

"The air smells cleaner," I said. "Fresher."

There was still the faint hint of summer on the air, but it was the green of leaves and the white of blossom rather than the gaudy colours of flowers crowding together.

"It's gone," I said. "Whatever it was has gone."

"Stop speaking. You're dripping blood and pus from your mouth," said Liz, and even in the midst of all that, I still found time to be impressed by how unphased she was by my condition. "I'll get you something," she added.

I spat yellow pus into a white enamel bowl.

"It's really gone," repeated Liz.

"I wonder how many people are really pleased about that?" I said, thinking of the Cartel, of the people in the towers.

"What about those who lost their children? Do you think they'll feel guilty?"

I spat into the bowl again.

"We're not all individuals any more," I said. "I'm pleased about that." I looked at Liz. "How do you feel this morning?"

She held my gaze. "You're talking about my scroll, aren't you?" she said. "You're asking how I feel about you, now that the spell has gone."

"Yes."

"What do you want me to say?" Blue eyes held my gaze.

"I want you to say..." My words trailed away.

"That I still love you?"

"Yes," I said. Then I thought about it. "No. That doesn't sound right. That wouldn't be right. What I mean is, I want you to still like me."

I spat more blood into the bowl.

"You want me to like you? Is that all?"

"No. I want more than that. But I want you to decide that for yourself. I don't want it to be because you read it on a piece of paper."

She stared at me. And stared at me, her mouth set in a frown. And then she suddenly smiled.

"That was the right answer, Captain Wedderburn."

"Call me James," I said. "Captain Wedderburn was an invention of Dream London."

"No," said Elizabeth. "Don't blame Dream London for all your faults, James. They were with you at the start. All the changes did was give them soil in which to grow."

I lowered my head. She was right.

"Still, you recognised that in time and tried to change," she said. "I like that."

LATER ON THAT day, we took a walk through the streets. The sky was clouding over, and from all around we could hear the creak and groan of stone as the city shifted position. Perhaps it was shrinking back into shape.

"How's the tongue?" she asked.

"Better all the time," I said.

There was a sucking sound, and we watched as a long section of browning ivy peeled away from the side of a building and tumbled to the ground. A rotting vegetable smell filled the air.

"It feels like it's going to rain," said Liz.

"I can't remember the last time it did."

"I wonder if the underground trains will grow back? I wonder if we'll have to rewire all the electricity?"

"I hope not," I said. "Or maybe I do. It will mean lots of work for people."

"Good point," said Liz. "What are you going to do, James? Go back to your old job?"

I thought of the girls of Belltower End. I wasn't going back to that job. And then I remembered that before that, I used to be soldier.

"I'm not going back in the army if that's what you mean," I said. "I don't know what I'll do yet."

"It's starting to rain," said Liz.

It was a misty sort of drizzle, but we raised our faces to it and gratefully felt it patter over our faces. It was an honest rain, one that left dirty trails, one that dampened down the smell of the rubbish, one that made the crops grow. Just a bit of drizzle on the face.

There was no sweeter feeling.

THE END

BLOOD AND FEATHERS

LOU MORGAN

'A hell of a ride,
but heaven to read:
eerie, compelling
and very funny.'
MICHAEL MARSHALL SMITH

UK ISBN: 978-1-78108-018-4 • US ISBN: 978-1-78108-019-1 • £7.99/$9.99

Alice isn't having the best of days – late for work, missed her bus, and now she's getting rained on – but it's about to get worse. The war between the angels and the Fallen is escalating and innocent civilians are getting caught in the cross-fire. If the balance is to be restored, the angels must act – or risk the Fallen taking control. Forever. That's where Alice comes in. Hunted by the Fallen and guided by Mallory – a disgraced angel with a drinking problem he doesn't want to fix – Alice will learn the truth about her own history... and why the angels want to send her to hell. What do the Fallen want from her? How does Mallory know so much about her past? What is it the angels are hiding – and can she trust either side?

 WWW.SOLARISBOOKS.COM

Follow us on Twitter! www.twitter.com/solarisbooks

'Dark, enticing and so sharp the pages could cut you'
SARAH PINBOROUGH
ON BLOOD AND FEATHERS

BLOOD AND FEATHERS

REBELLION

LOU MORGAN

UK ISBN: 978-1-78108-122-8 • US ISBN: 978-1-78108-123-5 • £7.99/$9.99

Driven out of hell and with nothing to lose, the Fallen wage open warfare against the angels on the streets. And they're winning. As the balance tips towards the darkness, Alice – barely recovered from her own ordeal in hell and struggling to start over – once again finds herself in the eye of the storm. But with the chaos spreading and the Archangel Michael determined to destroy Lucifer whatever the cost, is the price simply too high? And what sacrifices will Alice and the angels have to make in order to pay it? The Fallen will rise. Trust will be betrayed. And all hell breaks loose...

 WWW.SOLARISBOOKS.COM

Follow us on Twitter! www.twitter.com/solarisbooks

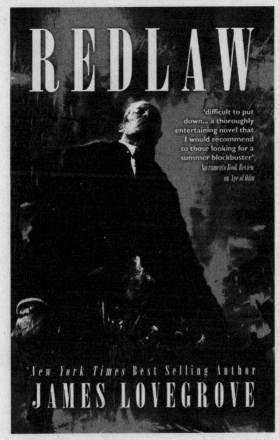

REDLAW

'difficult to put
down... a thoroughly
entertaining novel that
I would recommend
to those looking for a
summer blockbuster'
Sacramento Book Review
on *Age of Odin*

New York Times Best Selling Author
JAMES LOVEGROVE

UK ISBN: 978-1-907992-04-9 • US ISBN: 978-1-907992-05-6 • £7.99/$7.99

They live among us, abhorred, marginalised, despised. They are vampires, known politely as the Sunless. The job of policing their community falls to the men and women of SHADE: the Sunless Housing and Disclosure Executive. Captain John Redlaw is London's most feared and respected SHADE officer, a living legend.

But when the vampires start rioting in their ghettos, and angry humans respond with violence of their own, even Redlaw may not be able to keep the peace. Especially when political forces are aligning to introduce a radical answer to the Sunless problem, one that will resolve the situation once and for all...

 WWW.SOLARISBOOKS.COM

Follow us on Twitter! www.twitter.com/solarisbooks

REDLAW
RED EYE

New York Times Best Selling Author
JAMES LOVEGROVE

UK ISBN: 978-1-78108-048-1 • US ISBN: 978-1-78108-050-4 • £7.99/$8.99

The east coast of the USA is experiencing the worst winter weather in living memory, and John Redlaw is in the cold white thick of it. He's come to America to investigate a series of vicious attacks on vampire immigrants – targeted kills that can't simply be the work of amateur vigilantes. Dogging his footsteps is Tina "Tick" Checkley, a wannabe TV journalist with an eye on the big time.

The conspiracy Redlaw uncovers could give Tina the career break she's been looking for. It could also spell death for Redlaw.

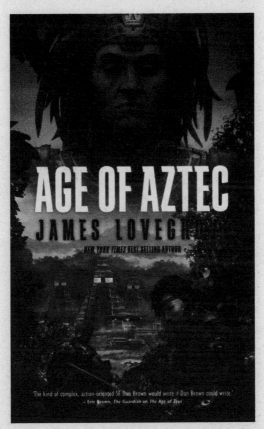

AGE OF AZTEC

JAMES LOVEGROVE

NEW YORK TIMES BEST SELLING AUTHOR

'The kind of complex, action-oriented SF Dan Brown would write if Dan Brown could write.'
– Eric Brown, *The Guardian* on *The Age of Zeus*

UK ISBN: 978 1 78108 048 1 • US ISBN: 978 1 78108 050 4 • £7.99/$7.99

The date is 4 Jaguar 1 Monkey 1 House; November 25th 2012, by the old reckoning. The Aztec Empire rules the world, in the name of Quetzalcoatl – the Feathered Serpent – and his brother gods. The Aztec reign is one of cruel and ruthless oppression, fuelled by regular human sacrifice. In the jungle-infested city of London, one man defies them: the masked vigilante known as the Conquistador. Then the Conquistador is recruited to spearhead an uprising, and discovers the terrible truth about the Aztecs and their gods. The clock is ticking. Apocalypse looms, unless the Conquistador can help assassinate the mysterious, immortal Aztec emperor, the Great Speaker. But his mission is complicated by Mal Vaughn, a police detective who is on his trail, determined to bring him to justice.

![Age of Voodoo — James Lovegrove. NEW YORK TIMES BEST SELLING AUTHOR. 'A full-blown thriller, high on action and violence.' Eric Brown, The Guardian on Age of Aztec]

UK ISBN: 978-1-907519-40-6 • US ISBN: 978-1-78108-086-3 • £7.99/$8.99

Gideon Coxall was a good soldier but bad at everything else, until a roadside explosive device leaves him with one deaf ear and a British Army half-pension. So when he hears about the Valhalla Project, it's like a dream come true. They're recruiting former service personnel for excellent pay, no questions asked, to take part in unspecified combat operations.

The last thing Gid expects is to find himself fighting alongside ancient Viking gods. The world is in the grip of one of the worst winters it has ever known, and Ragnarök – the fabled final conflict of the Sagas – is looming.

 WWW.SOLARISBOOKS.COM

Follow us on Twitter! www.twitter.com/solarisbooks

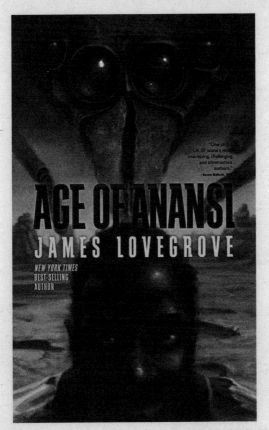

AGE OF ANANSI
JAMES LOVEGROVE
NEW YORK TIMES BEST-SELLING AUTHOR

UK ISBN: 978 1 84997 341 0 • US ISBN: 978 1 84997 342 7 • £2.99/$3.99

Dion Yeboah leads an orderly, disciplined life... until the day the spider appears. What looks like an ordinary arachnid turns out to be Anansi, the trickster god of African legend, and its arrival throws Dion's existence into chaos.

Lawyer Dion's already impressive legal brain is sharpened. He becomes nimbler-witted and more ruthless, able to manipulate and deceive like never before, both in and out of court. Then he discovers the price he has to pay for his newfound skills. He must travel to America and take part in a contest between the avatars of all the trickster gods. It's a life-or-death battle of wits, and at the end, only one person will be left standing.

THE AGE OF ODIN
JAMES LOVEGROVE

"One of the UK SF scene's most interesting, challenging and adventurous authors."
- Saxon Bullock, *SFX*

UK ISBN: 978-1-907519-40-6 • US ISBN: 978-907519-41-3 • £7.99/$7.99

Gideon Coxall was a good soldier but bad at everything else, until a roadside explosive device leaves him with one deaf ear and a British Army half-pension. So when he hears about the Valhalla Project, it's like a dream come true. They're recruiting former service personnel for excellent pay, no questions asked, to take part in unspecified combat operations.

The last thing Gid expects is to find himself fighting alongside ancient Viking gods. The world is in the grip of one of the worst winters it has ever known, and Ragnarök – the fabled final conflict of the Sagas – is looming.

 WWW.SOLARISBOOKS.COM

Follow us on Twitter! www.twitter.com/solarisbooks

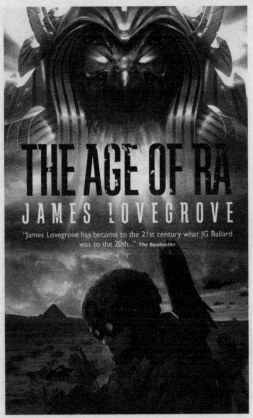

THE AGE OF RA

JAMES LOVEGROVE

"James Lovegrove has become to the 21st century what JG Ballard was to the 20th..." *The Bookseller*

ISBN: 978-1-84416-746-3 • US ISBN 978-1-84416-747-0 • £7.99

The Ancient Egyptian gods have defeated all the other pantheons and claimed dominion over the earth, dividing it into warring factions, each under the aegis of a different deity. Lt. David Westwynter, a British soldier, stumbles into Freegypt, the only place to have remained independent of the gods' influence. There, he encounters the followers of a humanist leader known as the Lightbringer, who has vowed to rid mankind of the shackles of divine oppression. As the world heads towards an apocalyptic battle, there is far more to this freedom fighter than it seems...

 WWW.SOLARISBOOKS.COM

Follow us on Twitter! www.twitter.com/solarisbooks

THE AGE OF ZEUS

JAMES LOVEGROVE

"James Lovegrove has become
to the 21st century what
JG Ballard was to the 20th..."
The Bookseller

UK ISBN: 978-1-906735-68-5 US ISBN: 978-906735-69-2 • £7.99/$7.99

The Olympians appeared a decade ago, living incarnations of the Ancient Greek gods on a mission to bring permanent order and stability to the world. Resistance has proved futile, and now humankind is under the jackboot of divine oppression. Until former London police officer Sam Akehurst receives an invitation too tempting to turn down: the chance to join a small band of guerrilla rebels armed with high-tech weapons and battlesuits. Calling themselves the Titans, they square off against the Olympians and their ferocious mythological monsters in a war of attrition which some will not survive.

 WWW.SOLARISBOOKS.COM

Follow us on Twitter! www.twitter.com/solarisbooks

AGE OF GODPUNK

JAMES LOVEGROVE

NEW YORK TIMES BEST SELLING AUTHOR

AGE OF SATAN // AGE OF ANANSI // AGE OF GAIA

'The kind of complex, action-oriented SF Dan Brown
would write if Dan Brown could write.' *The Guardian*

ISBN: 978-1-78108-128-0 US ISBN -978-1-78108 129-7 • £7.99/$8.99